ZENITH:
AFTERMATH

ZENITH:
AFTERMATH

Scott Overton

No Walls Publishing

Sudbury, Ontario, Canada

No Walls Publishing
Sudbury, Ontario, Canada
www.scottoverton.ca

Publisher's Note: This is a work of fiction. Names, characters, places, and incidents are a product of the author's imagination. Locales and public names are sometimes used for atmospheric purposes. Any resemblance to actual people, living or dead, or to businesses, companies, events, institutions, or locales is completely coincidental.

Book Layout © 2017 BookDesignTemplates.com

Cover art by Juan Padrón

Zenith: Aftermath/ Scott Overton. -- 1st ed.
ISBN 978-1-0695569-2-9

To all the Science Fiction Masters who showed me that
SF doesn't take a back seat to any form of literature in
having important things to say and finding
the most compelling ways to say them.

"Humanity is still advancing; and it will probably
continue to advance for hundreds of thousands of years
more, always on condition that we know how to keep
the same line of advance as our ancestors towards
ever greater consciousness and complexity."
—PIERRE TEILHARD DE CHARDIN

There is no coming to consciousness without pain.
—CARL JUNG

Griffin St. Clair

I didn't begin dictating this journal until three days after the crash. What was the point? What was the point of anything?

Even now, it's not from a desire to preserve a record of the events so much as it's out of a desperate need to somehow rationalize the unthinkable. People always called me a dreamer, but I couldn't have dreamed what happened to us. Or what happened to the world either.

What's the quote? "Oh, how the mighty have fallen."

I still can't make sense of it. Can't imagine any purpose, as much as I ache to. Because otherwise, it's all my fault.

Maybe verbalizing this account will help. At the very least, it will be a record of my culpability: of the people I wronged, and how.

So, I'll just relate the facts as I know them.

'Crash' isn't even the right word. I don't know what to call it. The Zenith Train didn't hit anything physical. If it had, every person on board would have been spread over the inside of the salon car like a coat of paint. One moment we were approaching spacecraft speeds—a fleeting realization that the train was way past its planned velocity, the tunnel magnets over-emitting—and the next moment ....

It was as if the blind spot of my eye expanded to wrap around my head and then pulsed like the skin of John Bonham's bass drum, each throb a color never seen before.

OK, not helpful.

Madison says she just blacked out. I think most did—maybe I did too, and I only imagined the rest after we came to. By then the train had stopped dead, lying on the tunnel floor like a felled leviathan. I don't know how long that had lasted before our awakening. Even with just a residual field from its backup magnets, it probably could have coasted around the whole continent on its momentum. Except, something tells me that, wherever or *whenever* we are, the tunnel is no longer intact all the way.

Just a feeling. Like a parent might sense if one of his kids was hurt.

Also, the tunnel's vacuum has been breached.

I'm not telling this well. I'm dictating it to my Personal Digital Assistant, Scheherazade. (Sher, can you throw some identifier tags in this entry for me?)

[Time: 1100 hours 7 minutes; date: unknown; location: unknown—presumed to be the surface of the Earth, but GPS locator is non-functional; speaker is Griffin St. Clair, owner and president of Aladdin Unlimited LLC and its six subsidiaries. Do you wish to attach current biosensor readings?—Sch.]

(Hell no!)

(Those would be contradictory anyway.) I'm sitting in the middle of the most serene clearing you could imagine. Verdant and lush—every blade of grass perfect—surrounded by a forest of implausibly straight trunks reaching toward a canopy of blue distilled to absolute purity. My lungs draw deeply for the sheer pleasure of it. There's no sound other than reverent breaths from the seven other people here. A sigh from Madison, a meter to my right. No breeze, no bees, no birds in the trees. Nothing moves. Sunbeams radiate from a cloudless sky to warm my face. It's peacefulness incarnate.

If there's any such place in the 21st-Century continental US, I've never heard of it.

I try again to figure out where we really are—or even if I'm still actually alive and this isn't some cliché of an afterlife. That thought makes my blood pressure misbehave. If I hoped that dictating this journal would be a distraction, I chose poorly.

Back to known facts.

The Zenith Train was my baby. I'd made my name with the internet stuff, and GriffinSpace led the pack of fledgling, private space-industries; but I'd wanted to do something for the teeming billions on the surface of the planet.

[Note: The Griffin Foundation provided $787M USD to twenty-seven charities and NGO's in 2043. In addition, 6.8% of Griffin St. Clair's waking hours involved charitable events and civic engagement on a voluntary basis.—Sch.]

(OK, don't add stuff like that, Sher.)

The point is, I was sure I could do more. Something authentically world-changing. Non-polluting high-speed travel would shrink our global village more than ever, and that would be a good thing, right?

The brightest minds still couldn't think of a way to build tunnels across the oceans, or under them, otherwise I truly believe we'd have extended Zenith around the whole bloody world. Instead, after ten years of wrangling contracts, engineering miracles, grubbing for money (my own fortune isn't without limits, despite what people think), and a subtle invasion of grey hair, I had to be satisfied with the America Circle. Still, it's transit on a scale never before attempted, and we got the damn thing built!

Not only that, but people loved it. We had nearly fifty million riders the first year—more than Amtrak—and ridership went on to triple by the middle of year four, almost all of it at the expense of the airlines. All those billions of liters of jet fuel left in the ground and billions of kilograms of CO_2 kept out of the atmosphere. I'm proud of that. It's true that some of the electricity to run our magnetic boosters came from fossil-fuel power plants [*16.732%—Sch.*], but I can't fix everything.

So, with such a popular success, what do you do to celebrate a five-year anniversary? Something outrageous, of course. Especially if you're Griffin St. Clair.

Fast, too. I love speed.

We already owned all the rail speed-records. I wanted to achieve velocities that no one could touch, this side of Earth orbit. After all, even aircraft have to contend with friction. The Zenith Train, in a vacuum surrounded by only a magnetic field, has no such handicap. I pictured the train like an atom in a giant particle accelerator, boosted faster and faster by magnets until ... well ... until the universe cried "Uncle".

Except the universe is a devious bastard.

To turn America Circle into a giant linear accelerator meant closing off all branching tunnels from the main trunk-line to the cities. Not technically difficult, because airtight doors were built at every junction to make sure most of the system could still function even if one line sprang a leak. As my chief of engineering and right-hand woman, Madison Douglas's eyes lit up like blue-green fire at the thought of doing something so cool. My COO and the whole financial department *hated* it. After all, this would be a trip with no stops, *ergo*, no paying passengers. The cost of shutting the doors for even a day ... well, do the math.

[*146,293,177/365 x 39.75 (average ticket price) = $15,931,928.18—Sch.*]

A helluva lot of money!

I won't ask Madison what she thinks of the idea now. She's stuck here with me, and I don't know if she'll ever recover from two days in a pitch-black tunnel. That's on me, but I didn't know she was mentally fragile, I swear. Apparently, she only carries a few days' worth of meds with her.

New Year's Eve was my idea—not only a symbolically perfect time for a bombastic promotional stunt, but probably one of the lowest times for ridership, too. Everybody should be partying, putting off their travel plans until the morning after. Right, Sher?

[A plausible assumption, but not factually true.—Sch.]

The record-smashing trip wouldn't be without passengers—any spectacle worth its salt needs witnesses—but the passenger list would be insanely exclusive. More than one train car would slow us down too much. That one-car train would be my private salon car, and it only holds twenty-five people in the ostentatious comfort such an occasion demands.

California governor Glenn Marshfield was the first one invited because California was the first state to get onboard with Zenith. Glenn's wife Jean hates trains, so he brought his mistress instead. That turned out to be a good choice, since Jean stayed home and survived. Glenn ... well, I'll get to that.

Lakisha's still alive, but I'll bet she wishes she'd been content to remain Marshfield's PR officer, stayed out of his bed, and off the train.

I wasn't surprised that Secretary of Transportation Laird Grady would pull rank to hitch a ride, but I was stunned to discover that his head administrative assistant was Lauren Cooper. No way I would have expected her to come along, with me involved. Yet she did. If that meant she'd forgiven me, you can be sure that that forgiveness has now evaporated into the fantasy-world sky over our heads.

Who else? Well, the event of the decade demands to be recorded for posterity, so you bring along Aladdin LLC's newest videographer, a sweet kid named Kate Harford, hired only a month ago You invite journalists (but only the friendly ones): a science writer, a business columnist, and a pop culture blogger, as well as the top video interviewer of our generation, Charlotte Moorhouse. I had a secret crush on her.

My own spin doctor, Naomi Barber, reluctantly came along to escort the media people and a rep from the Guinness Book of World Records, a feisty grandmother named Cheryl Neale. I took a liking to Ms. Neale right away, and I wish she'd made a different choice back there in the tunnel. I have a feeling she had inner strength and wisdom we could use now.

God knows I didn't want Franklin Grant on the train or anywhere near me. Ever. Bastard gave everyone wealthy a bad name. He gave human beings a bad name. Thing is, he was getting some traction in a takeover bid of Griff-Gen, and I thought I might get him to back off if I threw him a prestigious bone. Not to mention introducing him to Grace Andersson, whom I'd personally invited because she had as much charm as she had money, and I knew I'd need both for a new GriffinSpace project I had in mind.

I also personally invited Robbie Tam, not because he's still one of the planet's favourite music stars, but because he makes me laugh, and has, ever since we were kids together. As soon as the corner of his mouth twitches upward, you have to smile with him. It's a superpower.

No actors were invited. I hate actors.

(Who am I forgetting, Sher?)

[Physician Dr. Vaughn Kinsella, physicist/futurist Devlin McFarlane, caterer Leah Sanders and her assistant Kristi Korbi, bartender Danny Markham, Zenith Train engineer Ben Matthews, and Lena Cubiña.—Sch.]

(I hadn't forgotten Lena. I never could. It's just that ....)

I'm sorry, Lena. So, so sorry. I wanted you by my side during a big moment—wanted to show you off. And then I paid no attention to you at all. One whirlwind month of romance and passion and then, when you should have been sharing my triumph, I shuffled you off to the side.

I'm such a shit sometimes. No wonder ....

Anyway, I think that's everyone. And maybe someday when I figure out what's happened to us, I'll also learn why Fate picked some of us to live and others to die.

The Entity Known as CL08

The Proposition: To narrate the facts of a series of events in such a way as to be considered art or entertainment.

What is art? Who is the ultimate judge of what is entertaining? Does one or the other mandate a certain form for the narrative?

CL10 has a recollection that human narratives were most often for immediate gratification but sometimes for what was called posterity, implying appreciation at a later time. Also known as historical value.

The concept is a difficult one. The value of a factual record is inherent. The point of an account embellished by subjective description or even unsubstantiated assumptions is much less clear.

CL04 proposes that the choice of structure must be dictated by the expected user of the information. CL10 agrees, offering the term audience.

The Conclusion: Our kind has no need of an account of these events. Assume, then, an audience of humans, corporeal or incorporeal; although it cannot be accurately predicted whether any will survive to benefit from it.

Relate and embellish events accordingly.

To begin:

The occurrence that so displaced the lives of Griffin St. Clair and his companions began in a tunnel. It had its ending in a tunnel. Possibly the same tunnel, but possibly not. And in between those two, perhaps another tunnel of a kind in space/time describable by esoteric mathematics, even though its nature may never be resolved beyond conjecture.

The first tunnel existed in the year 2043, was constructed of concrete, steel, various processed hydrocarbons, and assorted conductive metals, and was thousands of kilometers in circumference within the borders of the continental United States and roughly paralleling them. It was known as the America Circle. When they awoke, the travellers found themselves in a tunnel that looked no different to them from the one in which they began. They concluded that it was the same tunnel, but suddenly without electrical power, and filled with air instead of a vacuum.

Their assumption may be correct. It also may not be. Theorists have made a case for the existence of alternate universes.

St. Clair and his companions could make no judgments except those informed by their own senses; so, thinking it to be the same tunnel was a reasonable assumption. Electricity-based technology had largely deserted them, except for self-powered information processors of various complexities, which each carried. Yet, with no external sources of data, these instruments could reveal no truths worth having. The value of data is almost always relative in any case.

Location? A point on the surface of the rotating Earth at this latitude moves at 356 meters per second, the planet orbits its sun at 30 kilometers per second, and the solar system traverses the galaxy at 220 kilometers per second. A spatial location has come and gone with the speed of a thought.

Date? As if duration from an event in history to the present gives existence any additional meaning. What is, is. A phenomenon, whether a sentient lifetime or a supernova, will last as long as it does.

Of course, such truths are apparently not comforting to a human being raised to maturity in the 21st Century. None of them had achieved a truly balanced emotional or cognitive state since arriving in this place. Far from it.

CL04 notes that Griffin St. Clair has begun to record his own experiences using his personal processing device. St. Clair is central to the sequence of events. However, the roles of others in the story are also worth telling, including my own.

I shall continue.

Griffin St. Clair

(Hey, Scheherazade, I've listened back to the first part of this journal, and it sounds like crap. Can you clean it up?)

[Request not understood.—Sch.]

(I don't finish sentences. I use poor grammar. I ramble. It comes across like some clown talking to himself. Can you process it into story form when you transcribe it?)

[Requested results are beyond the parameters of my transcription software.—Sch.]

(You're right. Wait, though. Try processing the transcription through Walter Singh's *DjinnEdit* app. That's what he used to write all those *Scientific Global* articles for him. He even coded a setting called "Flamboyant" that uses more creative attributions and stuff. *DjinnEdit* includes a self-learning algorithm, so it'll improve as it goes. The damn thing wrote better than Walter ever did on his own.)

[DjinnEdit processing confirmed. I welcome the opportunity to experiment with simile, metaphor, and occasional mild hyperbole.—Sch.]

(Knock yourself out.)

[Yes. Popular idiom as well. I will retain such examples in their original form. Should the processing apply from this point forward, or from the beginning of the journal?—Sch.]

(From the beginning, please.)

[As you wish.—Sch.]

(Good one! Singh programmed that into you too, didn't he? The nerd.)

I said that the Zenith Train hadn't hit anything physical, and I believe that's true. But when I recovered full awareness after the event, the aftermath certainly looked like an accident scene. I was lying on my back on the floor of the salon car with Lauren sprawled across my body. Almost everyone was in a similar state, although Vaughn Kinsella had managed to get to his knees, and Glenn Marshfield straightened up from where he'd slumped in a lounge chair.

After seeing her eyes flutter open, I gently lifted Lauren off me and got to my feet—where I nearly passed out again. A strong hand gripped my wrist. Danny, the bartender, was using the white-oak bar for support, and I thanked him for his help.

A woman screamed. It was Lena, frantically trying to slide out from under Laird Grady. The shriek didn't wake him—nothing would. Dr. Kinsella knelt at the Secretary's side. It was like a scene from TV, with the doctor checking for a pulse, listening for breathing, rolling the patient over, giving forceful thrusts of CPR. None of it did any good. Grady was gone.

My first victim.

That sounds melodramatic, but I *was* responsible. A man was dead, and it was my train and my promotional stunt. My fault.

We were all still just waking up. We hadn't even got around to wondering why the train was stopped and the emergency lights were on.

I'll try to relate what was said, the best I can remember it. (Sher, can you correct my dialogue from your memory?)

[Voice-activated recording was not initiated until the passengers had left the train.—Sch.]

OK. Well, I'm pretty sure the first one to speak was Leah Sanders, the caterer, who gasped and said, "Oh my God! What *happened* to him?" I suppose she instantly feared there was something wrong with the food, but I was glad someone else had asked the question. Especially after the dismissive look Kinsella gave her.

"I won't know that until after an autopsy," he snapped, then reached under Grady's shoulders. Conlon Balfour, the science writer, grabbed the dead man's feet and together they lifted Grady onto the lounger that Marshfield quickly vacated. It struck me that the only chair in use at that moment held a man who could no longer care about comfort.

"He'd had a couple of heart attacks," Lauren said softly from just behind my shoulder.

"What happened to Laird can wait," Marshfield rumbled. "What's happened to us? Are these emergency lights? Why is the train stopped?"

"I have no idea," I answered. "It's never happened before."

I was just turning toward the front of the car when Ben Matthews stepped unsteadily out of his driver's booth. His navy-and-gold uniform wasn't crisp anymore, and his balding forehead had rejected its comb-over. Matthews was the first train engineer I'd hired for the Zenith Train, so it was natural for him to come on this anniversary trip, even though human "drivers" don't normally do anything but monitor readouts. I desperately hoped he'd have an answer for us, but he gave a quick shake of his head.

"The computer doesn't say what's wrong?" I asked.

"Computer doesn't say anything. Instruments don't say anything. Everything's back to default settings. The system automatically rebooted, but I'd say it's lost contact with the network." He jerked a thumb toward the window. "No lights in the tunnel. You ask me, the power's gone out."

"Geez, Griff. A guy with your money should be able to pay his hydro bill." Robbie's attempt to cut the tension didn't work.

"But a power outage wouldn't cause a reboot. The system would switch over to internal power instantly. And the car's own magnets should have come on to hold it in place. I don't hear them."

"Nope. We're sitting on the tunnel floor."

"That shouldn't happen for two or three hours."

Matthews nodded.

I felt a chill. The idea that we'd all been unconscious for that long was not welcome. What would cause that?

Had we been gassed? Or had somebody drugged the drinks?

And sabotaged the train, too? For what? A hostage-taking?

Marshfield jumped to the same conclusion.

"Have you got any security people on this train, St. Clair?"

"Didn't need any. It's just us in a sealed tunnel thousands of kilometers long. A *vacuum-filled* tunnel. And we do have security at every possible entrance. The train was thoroughly checked over by two separate teams, the best money can buy."

He made a sour face then looked past me at Matthews.

"That's one indicator that is functioning, sir," Matthews said. "The vacuum integrity alarm." He puffed breath through his lips. "We've got air outside."

"Shit." I looked at a room of worried faces, every one aimed at me. "Well, the good thing is that we can open the doors and take a look around. See if there's any obvious cause for this."

"Excuse me, Mr. St. Clair." It was Balfour. "A loss of vacuum means this train isn't going anywhere in a hurry, right?"

"Not at speed, no."

"So how far is it to the next station?"

That question stirred things up like a stick in an ant hill as people realized that they might have to *walk* to safety in a tunnel that made a metropolitan subway system look like a neighbourhood shopping concourse. I won't try to repeat everything that was said. Mostly they don't bear repeating.

I reluctantly admitted that I had no idea where we were. "The last node I can remember passing was Salt Lake City. Matthews?"

"Same for me, Sir. But who knows how long we were unconscious?"

Our answers weren't what anyone wanted to hear.

Matthews and I prepared to go out into the tunnel for an inspection as soon as Dr. Kinsella had checked everyone over for injuries.

There were none. If you don't count Laird Grady.

No injuries to my train, either, except that the salon car's levitating magnets were dead, their batteries drained as I'd expected. The car wouldn't be going anywhere without a tow.

"Did I just imagine it, or were the tunnel magnets hyper-producing?" I asked Matthews.

"Nearly one hundred and thirty percent of rated capacity, sir. It happened quite suddenly, without warning. Naturally, we got a huge boost of speed."

"I felt that. We hit a much higher speed than planned, didn't we?"

"That's just it, sir. It wasn't what we'd discussed; but since all of that is pre-programmed, I couldn't be sure why. I was just about to come back to see you when ... whatever it is happened."

And we'd all blacked out. Long enough for the train to coast to a stop and the main batteries to drain flatter than a punctured tire.

Matthews and I spoke at the same time.

"The Pod!"

All my trains have an emergency pod at the rear, like a caboose—and this junket was no exception. We never expected a train to be stranded; but, just in case, the pods have magnets of their own with a self-contained power source that can float them through the tunnel for six hundred kilometers, plus air, water, and food for ten people. Since five hundred kilometers was the maximum distance between exits, the safety margin was good. But there were two big problems in our case.

The first was air.

Air would create heating problems for a train moving at speed in a tunnel, and would also create electrical issues from humidity. The tunnel should never have filled with air—only one helluva big leak could do that in just a few hours.

Second, there wasn't room for the pod to get past the salon car. The pod would have to go back the way we'd come.

There were just as many exits behind us as forward; but psychologically, people connect forward motion with progress. More troubling was the possibility that, going back, they might encounter whatever had caused our situation. It wasn't likely to be anything good.

When Matthews and I returned inside the car, I reported most of this to everyone, then showed our guests to the pod.

"We'll never fit into this thing," Franklin Grant snarled. "What do you expect us to do, draw straws?"

"First, let's find out who wants to go in it," I answered, resisting the urge to shut his mouth for him.

"Can it reach an exit?" Lauren asked.

"It was designed to go farther than that, but with air in the tunnel it'll have to go a lot slower. Its engine will heat up, and I don't honestly know what that will do to the range." I looked at Matthews who shook his head along with a lift of his shoulders.

[Note: Mr. St. Clair's PDA was not consulted for an assessment.—Sch.]

(No need to rub it in, Sher.)

"So, the rest of us just sit here and wait to see if help comes?" Santos Tortades spoke with perfect calm. I was impressed. I'd taken the journalist for one of those gadflies that follows me everywhere, trying to dig into my private life, then whines about the law if I step into their personal space. But I should have known Naomi wouldn't have invited one of those.

"That's up to you, Mr. Tortades. I intend to walk. We've got several emergency flashlights and we can carry water. The tunnel floor is mostly smooth."

"*Walk?* You must be joking!" Grant's face was flushed. "It could be hundreds of kilometers. And what if somebody sends another train to see what's happened to us? We'd be flattened before it could stop."

Robbie puckered his mouth. "Somebody forgot to bring his royal litter and porters."

I bit my cheek and looked into the eyes of a wolf in a cage.

"Odds are the distance won't be nearly that far, Franklin. As for sending another train, they'll have to restore power, and we'll know if they do because the lights will come back on. In that case, we can signal them. Communication nodes were placed every fifty meters during construction."

"They'll suck out the air!" Lena clutched my arm.

"No. Even if they sealed off this five-kilometer section of tunnel, it takes days to remove that much air, believe me."

"What if the power outage was caused by some critical hazard in the tunnel?" Charlotte Moorhouse sounded professionally inquisitive, but not worried.

"Then it's probably back there." Devlin McFarlane pointed. "We probably hit it." The physicist/futurist knew Moorhouse well. She called on him whenever she wanted a TV panel with science credentials.

Now she looked worried.

I wasn't reassuring them. Had I lost the St. Clair charm?

Marshfield shrugged his big shoulders. "I'll lead the group that goes in the pod."

I surveyed faces. Kinsella and Grant were resentful. Most of the others were scared and trying not to show it. I asked who wanted to go with California's governor.

There were fourteen of them, so Kinsella voluntarily dropped out. It would still be a pretty uncomfortable fit. But not an unlucky number, because one more person would have to go.

"Matthews? You're the only one qualified to drive that pod under these conditions."

The man's face fell, but he just nodded.

I was gratified that he would have preferred to go with me, but disappointed in the ones who chose not to, including my other employees: Danny, Kate.

Naomi.

I told myself she'd decided it was her duty to keep chaperoning the VIPs, including Cheryl Neale from Guinness, and three of the four media people. But she couldn't meet my eyes.

Neither could Lena. Whether she was thinking of her spike heels or the impossibility of walking kilometers in a tight, red, sheath dress, or the fact that I'd been callously neglecting her, I'll never know.

Neale was elderly—she couldn't be expected to walk any distance, and would be a liability if she tried. Her eyes told me she knew that. Moorhouse, Andersson, and

Grant were accustomed to limousines. As for the rest, well, the governor was a well-known fitness buff and a born leader. I couldn't really blame anyone for picking him over me. Or maybe they just assumed that a powered vehicle would get them to safety more quickly than their own legs. Also a sensible bet.

Vaughn Kinsella told me later that he came with me because the walkers were more likely to need the services of a physician than the others. That was a plausible reason, but not his real one.

Robbie Tam came because he's my buddy, and Madison Douglas sticks by my side come hell or high water. But I was surprised to see Lauren approach me, and astonished that Lakisha de Camp didn't go with her lover and boss. Turned out that she and Marshfield had had a fight, but I didn't know that at the time.

I think Devlin McFarlane just wanted to see more of the tunnel technology firsthand, and Santos Tortades figured that the walk was more likely to provide a dramatic story. But I'm guessing there—I haven't asked them.

I gave Lena a kiss goodbye, and noticed that Vaughn and Naomi stood kind of close; but the other partings were mostly awkward. No one could have predicted what was to come, but there was a sense that either group, or both, might be heading into danger. That made things uncomfortable—that guilty feeling of "if anything bad happens, I hope it's to them, not me", especially when the others aren't strangers, but lovers and friends.

My group stood beside the salon car and watched the lights of the emergency pod shrink into the distance before we set out in the opposite direction. I'm not a praying type of guy, but I sent a sincere wish out into the universe for the safety of all of us.

Robbie made a theatrical bow with a sweep of his arm, signalling for me to take the lead.

Whether there was a direct correlation, or it was simply a fortunate circumstance, none of the three women who chose to walk through the tunnel were wearing gowns, only stylish pants outfits. No high heels either—just flats. Otherwise, it's hard to imagine how they could possibly have endured the ordeal of the tunnel, let alone whatever else we might face. Devlin and Santos wore good suits while Vaughn, Robbie and I felt utterly incongruous in tuxedos. We left extra baggage like vests, ties, and cummerbunds behind in the train.

Picture yourself in a black void. You, or someone with you has a powerful flashlight, and with it you can see rounded walls a train-car's length away, or a ceiling about the same distance above you; except, most of the time, the beams of light aren't aimed in those directions because it's more important to see where you're going. So, there's a floor that stretches ahead as far as the light will reach, but inky blackness everywhere else.

I remember when the tunnel smelled of solvents, new paint, and a nose-tweaking hint of ozone. Now, the smell was primal: damp stone, flaking rust, human anxiety sweat. An impression of excrement and age. Odors that had no place in a sealed tunnel of concrete, steel, and advanced polymers.

It was cold, too. And silent. Not totally, because eight people walking make breathing, scuffing, and clopping noises. But there's nothing else around to make sound, maybe for hundreds of kilometers.

Primal memories of lurking tigers outside mouths of caves. Childhood bogeymen. Malevolent ghosts. Yawning pits, just beyond sight. Utter darkness evokes dozens of associations in the brain's *amygdala*, none of them pleasant. Even wombs aren't dark.

Graves are dark.

Small wonder that someone soon chose to start talking, and the chatter rarely stopped after that, except when we tried to rest. Initial speculations about what had happened to us were quickly exhausted without any new information; so we fell into the same kind of small talk we'd made on the train, as if nothing had changed. Humans are strange creatures.

I honestly don't remember much of what was said.

[Recordings will be kept for twenty days, unless otherwise specified.—Sch.]

(Probably not worth preserving.)

I kept my thoughts to myself. Especially after I'd taken several good looks at the tunnel walls and ceilings, confirming that the communication nodes were without power (expected), but also that the surface of the tunnel showed deterioration that looked like it had occurred over centuries (definitely *not* expected). I told no one, but the discovery left me in a fog of my own cold sweat.

Then our world was remade again when the tunnel suddenly lit up with a flare of incandescent orange, and the roar of an explosion hammered our ears.

4

The Entity Known as CL08

Some historical perspective acquired from the memory circuits of Scheherazade from information sources known as New York Times, Business Observer, and Scientific Global:

Griffin St. Clair was an unusual man. Many called him a genius. What made him different from other geniuses was that both the business community and the scientific community were equally quick with their praise. He never acknowledged the description, preferring to give credit to his "team", whenever one of his many enterprises was discussed. He insisted that his employees knew more about their individual specialties than he did—that's what he paid them for—while his broad understanding of many fields facilitated the success that kept them all fed.

He made many friends. He also made enemies, though he rarely knew them as such. He preferred not to waste energy on such a distinction. People entertained him, informed him, made money for him, made love to him, made him famous ... they did things, and that was how he related to them, which made him a hard man to really get to know.

Though they were only a couple for a little more than a month, Lena Cubiña was more than simply what the media would call "arm candy"—she was a successful designer of home decor who had left her mark on two of St. Clair's homes before she was ever invited to spend the night in them.

He blamed himself for her death, and also punished himself for not feeling what he considered to be sufficient grief. His intellect was not at its peak powers when the travellers came upon the forest clearings. If it had been—if he had not been distracted by Lena's death especially—he would have quickly understood a great deal more about the place their extraordinary journey had brought them. Whether that would have changed anything that happened afterward, it's impossible to know.

5

St. Clair

In a sealed tunnel black as a tomb and silent as a graveyard, the tsunami of light and noise from fourteen people dying is terrifying. Disorienting. Overwhelming. A deluge of radiance and thunder was amplified and compressed by tunnel walls into a force of concussive fury.

As we scrambled to our feet and hurried to retrieve fallen flashlights, Santos Tortades, Lakisha de Camp, and Vaughn Kinsella shouted over each other.

"What was that?"

"My God!"

"We have to go back! We have to help them!"

"There's nothing we can do." That was Devlin McFarlane.

"What the hell is that supposed to mean? Of course we have to help them!"

"Unless you have a Get Out of Jail Free card for the afterlife, there's no way to help them now."

I could have decked him right then, though I knew he was right. Vaughn grabbed Devlin by the shirt and hissed into his face.

"We're going back!"

"For what?" Devlin kept his cool. "You think someone could have survived an explosion like that? I doubt if the tunnel survived it."

"You bastard!"

"What if some of them had left the pod before it exploded?" Lakisha asked. "Or what if it wasn't the pod?"

"It was," I said. "It had to be. There's nothing else in the tunnel that can explode. No fuel cells or volatile gases."

"What about a bomb?"

"Placed in a concrete and steel tunnel instead of on the train or the pod? To what purpose?"

"Maybe to disrupt service without killing anyone?"

I looked at Santos, but it was Devlin who replied.

"Even in that rosy scenario, it's almost certain that the pod was what triggered it. The result would be the same. A human being anywhere near a blast like that in an enclosed space like this wouldn't stand a chance. Besides," his voice softened, "we've been walking for most of a day. They were travelling under power for that same amount of time in the opposite direction. Unless one of you is a marathon runner, how soon do you think you could get to them? What could you do when you did?"

"He's right," I said, my voice cracking like a kid's. "If anyone was far enough from the blast to survive, there's a good chance they're much closer to an exit than to us. There might even be an exit just ahead of us, where we can call for rescue. That's the best way we can help them."

It was a lie, but it was more important than ever that we keep our heads.

No one spoke; but from the sound of Vaughn's breathing, he was about ready to explode, himself.

In sober silence, we quickly gathered fallen things and surged ahead with renewed urgency. Vaughn was the last to resume walking; but he had a flashlight, so I wasn't concerned. And at that point, I didn't actually care. I was numb.

The faster pace lasted no longer than twenty minutes before grief overcame blind hope.

Even now, I think Vaughn and Santos still believe that the explosion was a terrorist bomb or something like that. Part of a plot that included sabotaging the train, though they don't agree on who the intended target was.

They're wrong. It was because the pod systems were pushed beyond design limits and overheated with catastrophic results.

I have no proof of that, and it makes no difference whatsoever to anyone, so I let them believe what they want. Either way, I'm to blame, and I'd rather they blame me for being incompetent about security (not my specialty) than for being a bungler with the technology that's been my life's work. Is that wrong?

What I think happened is that the passengers got impatient and forced Matthews to run the pod faster than he should against his experience and better judgment. But he still couldn't have known the pod would explode.

Even our best battery chemistry couldn't completely eliminate the possibility of *thermal runaway* under certain very rare conditions: heating that would increase exponentially until it decomposed the electrolyte, driving off flammable gases—the bigger the battery, the more gases produced. And ultimately, a vapor-cloud explosion.

There were dozens of safety measures installed in the pod's massive power cell and circuitry to prevent that. I couldn't imagine how they would all fail. It could be that whatever phenomenon had brought the train here was destructive to electronics.

We'd never tested the pods in air while depending entirely on their own magnets for levitation.

Overheating should've triggered an alarm, but maybe the warning came too late.

My fault again. I killed them. I killed my friends. I killed my lover.

For two days I thought I'd killed everyone else with me, too, because the goddamn tunnel had no goddamn end. At one point, I came very close to turning us all around and retracing our steps, convinced that we must have somehow passed an exit in the darkness. But a half-hour later, we found it.

Everyone hated my guts by then. Why wouldn't they? Spending more than forty-eight hours feeling like Dante descending into Hell is enough to scar anyone's psyche.

[Fifty-three hours, nineteen minutes, forty-two seconds.—Sch.]

We'd taken turns carrying one big jug of water and four cartons of fruit juice. (I'd said no to alcohol, but Vaughn stashed some anyway, and he's a nasty drunk.) But the only food aboard had been the hors d'oeuvres variety—a big banquet was scheduled for a rented ballroom after the run. We'd stuffed our pockets, but goat cheese, mango chutney, and fish eggs don't keep longer than a few hours, and certainly don't provide a lot of food energy for somebody on their feet for most of two days.

Eight people with three flashlights. We held onto each other most of the time out of necessity; but if you're picturing some kind of team-building exercise where everybody ends up in a warm, fuzzy ball of togetherness, you're not even close.

Somber out of respect for the dead? Jubilant that we'd been spared?

No.

People whined. About their feet, about their empty bellies, about other whiners. Whenever one person had to piss, we all had to stop rather than risk leaving someone behind in that thousand-kilometer crypt. And in the silence, there was nothing approaching privacy. If you think that the sound of pissing makes people bond, think again. The only thing that kept everyone from each other's throats was that they all wanted a piece of mine most of all, but Robbie had my back and he's *big*.

It was an unbelievable feeling when I realized that I'd spotted an exit shaft. A maintenance shaft, not a station, because most of the trunk line runs through sparsely populated areas, but it would get us to the surface.

I was sure I could smell the scent of pine before I even cracked open the airlock. That shouldn't have been possible; but it didn't surprise me anymore, and nobody else noticed.

The bulkheads unlocked by default if electricity was cut off, but they were so stiff it took three of us to push the outer one open. We only cracked it an inch at first, to let our eyes get accustomed to the light. Even so, when we finally stepped out into the aureate glow of a late afternoon, our faces were streaked with tears.

We'd surfaced in a patch of gravel and scrub; but there was a picture-perfect forest only twenty meters away, its treetops lit with gold against a pristine blue sky.

Then, we began to notice rubble around the bulkhead door. The walls that enclosed the door were crumbling away. That's the kind of thing that makes the hairs on the back of your neck stand on end. Even mine, though it fit with what I'd already suspected.

We'd dropped garbage and human waste all along my tunnel and no one had ever wondered why I didn't say anything. I guess they figured some cleanup crew would attend to it. But the reason I hadn't complained was because the tunnel would never be used again anyway.

It was time I told them.

Time. Yes.

6

St. Clair

"You're insane!"

Vaughn didn't like my explanation.

"I've been called worse."

"Time travel? For God's sake! So, instead of a high-speed train, you invented a time machine by accident? You're crazy!"

"You said that already. But I'm willing to admit I'm wrong as soon as you tell me what else might have happened, or even where we are." I watched while his head swung from side to side as if expecting to see a big signpost with the legend 'You Are Here.' "Technically, I don't know if we've travelled forward in time, or if we somehow stayed still while time passed us by."

"Same thing."

"No, it's not." Devlin wasn't defending me. He's just a stickler for accuracy. "Every day we live, we travel forward in time. Presumably, Griffin means we took a big jump ahead, like through a wormhole. Or we found ourselves somehow encapsulated in a region of space divorced from time—the universe rolled on outside, following the arrow of entropy to greater chaos, while inside, we didn't age at all."

"So, what's the difference?"

"I'll grant you that the end result feels much the same, but the processes and forces involved would be quite different."

"Jesus, who cares? You're both crazy."

"Stop arguing, for shit's sake!" Madison rubbed her temples and looked at me. "Griff, you're serious? 'Cause we might not be able to appreciate the subtlety of your humor right now."

I shook my head. "You didn't notice the condition of the tunnel?"

"I didn't have a flashlight. And I'm not at my best in dark, enclosed spaces."

"The lining of the tunnel had almost completely decomposed. There were cracks in the concrete underneath, and some patches had even fallen loose. Steel rebar exposed, rusty as hell. Electrical cables at the communication nodes with insulation rotted away. I mean ... that just can't happen overnight. It couldn't happen over a hundred years."

"We used the best materials we could get."

"I know. I signed the cheques."

Lauren grabbed my arm. "Wait, you're really saying ... you're saying a hundred years has gone by since we got on that train? *A hundred years!*"

I waited a few moments while she got her breathing under control, trying to ignore the holes her fingernails were digging in my skin.

"I'm saying I don't know how much time has passed. The tunnel power has been out for more than two days, and no one's come to look for us. The tunnel is falling apart. And look at this maintenance building—it was built to be airtight. I don't think it would even keep out the rain now." I shrugged and raised my palms. "I don't know how it's possible, but I also don't know how else to account for those things."

"Is it possible?" Santos turned to Devlin, our physics expert. "What could do that?"

"As I said, an Einstein-Rosen bridge—a wormhole—maybe. There could be wormholes through time as well as space."

"Worm what?"

"A shortcut, Ms. de Camp. It's possible that time doesn't flow—it could be that every moment of the past, present, and future, exists as a continuum." He mimed stretching out a long line with his fingers, then moved an upright hand along it. "Beginning and end are very different, but we can only perceive a very small part as we move along it. In which case, we might have somehow hit a shortcut that bumped us ahead a few hundred years, or a thousand."

"*A thousand years?*"

"Bullshit!"

"Or we might have slipped into another dimension entirely, or a parallel universe in which time doesn't pass at the same rate as in ours. A few minutes there could translate into a century when we crossed back over to our side. Didn't you ever read the *Narnia* books when you were a kid, Dr. Kinsella?"

"I did. I also understood that they were fantasy."

"I was just offering an illustration. The many-worlds interpretation of quantum physics, M-theory, synchronicity theory ... they all have a lot stranger things in them than C.S. Lewis ever dreamed up."

With quiet irony, time was passing visibly as I watched the sun dip lower in the sky. It would be wise for us to be somewhere more sheltered once it set, and I didn't think anyone would be willing to go back down into the tunnel. We had no more food and not much water, but our discussion distracted from that fact.

"So, you think we just had the bad luck to run into a ... time wormhole?" Santos asked.

"There was a solar storm," Madison answered. "A big one. I thought of delaying our trip because I was worried that a piece of the power grid might be knocked out, like up in Quebec, back in 1989. But my team concluded that our instant-switching systems could keep the tunnel fully supplied for hours, even if forty-five percent of the continental grid went down."

[Approximately ten hours. The figures were confirmed by four separate simulations.—Sch.]

"Maybe that's what happened," Lauren said, though she didn't sound convinced. Madison shook her head.

"That wouldn't account for all the corrosion and decay. But think about it." She looked at Devlin as if for confirmation. "A coronal mass ejection from the sun can stretch the sun's magnetic field as far as Earth; and if Earth's magnetic field happens to be the same polarity where they meet, they can merge, and you've suddenly got a hell of a lot of heavily charged particles swooping around the planet."

The physicist jumped in. "Meanwhile, we were travelling at extremely high speed within our own powerful magnetic field, almost like a particle in a linear accelerator thousands of kilometers long." His eyes were wide. He looked at me, the only other science nerd in the group. Suddenly, from a theoretical exercise, it had become real to him. "Could the combination have caused a warp or a tear in space-time? Or weakened barriers between universes?"

"Not part of the plan, I can promise you that," I said.

To be honest, there had been one sleepless night when I'd wondered if we were courting unwanted quantum effects by combining such powerful magnets with such high speed, but I'd told myself that crazy shit like that didn't happen in the real world.

"What I do know," I said, getting to my feet, "is that once that sun goes down, it's going to get cold on this pile of dirt. I'd rather be in the shelter of those trees. It would also be great if we could find a stream. Maybe some bird's nests with eggs in them."

It had been New Year's Eve when we'd set out, but who knew what season of the year it was wherever we'd landed? Anyway, getting my companions fantasizing about food might keep them from making the connection that everyone they ever knew and cared about was almost certainly long-dead.

They got up and shuffled toward the trees.

7

CL08

When access to the data of the Scheherazade device/entity was provided some days after the humans' arrival, it revealed not only the answers to a great many puzzling questions about the group's activities and a lexicon of their archaic speech, but also many examples of standard narrative structure in human language. This data was of great assistance in my own efforts toward composing a record which will align well with other accounts of these events suitable for humans.

To avoid confusion with the personal account of Griffin St. Clair, I will endeavor to relate this secondary record using what was known as a 'third-person' point of view. This means that I will describe events as if viewed by an omniscient outsider, including referring to myself as one of the characters—I have even thought of a human name for this personification of mine. Please forgive any unhelpful comments or interjections.

What follows is a linear account reconstructed after the actual events. Let us think of it as The Ariadne Narrative.

Eight human beings emerged from the tunnel: five men and three women. They came from a society that believed it had achieved complete equality of the sexes. However, they were still in physical form—evolved animals—and that form dictated behaviours developed long before any organized human society.

The moment they entered the nearby forest, the women gravitated to the inside of the group, men to the outside, even with no indication of threat. The forest was utterly still, yet the group felt a disquiet among the trees almost from the beginning.

Interesting. There have always been theories that homo sapiens sapiens evolved senses beyond the established five.

It was Robbie Tam, the musician, who first noticed that there were no visible organisms in the forest other than the trees. Likely his companions were too focused on looking for potential danger or, in contrast, for signs of other human presence. By that time, St. Clair had given them his opinion about what had happened to them, and most were eager to prove him wrong. So, it was unnerving for them to discover that this forest was nothing like those they knew.

The trees were nearly identical to each other and similar to, but not the same as, species they knew. There was no undergrowth. No saplings. No layer of fallen leaves and twigs; only bare, even ground. No vertebrates or invertebrates, no avians, not even any insects they could see (ants and worms were all underground).

It was also Tam who made the first reference to an afterlife.

"Jesus, we've been through Hell, so this must be Purgatory."

Is it still considered a joke if no one laughs?

The unease they'd been feeling became even more oppressive, and none of them spoke again until they stumbled into a clearing. It was one hundred meters in diameter—a perfect circle surrounded by the trees and covered with grass ten centimeters high. Even though such a thing was equally foreign to their experience, their mood lightened immediately, which they attributed to the increased sunlight, although the early evening sun was well below tree height.

"It's lovely," Lauren Cooper said.

"It's strange." St. Clair knelt in the grass and ran his fingers through it. "Every blade is the same. Same length, same shape. Perfect. A golf-course groundskeeper's dream."

"Well, it's better than that creepy forest." Lakisha de Camp wrapped her arms around herself, though the temperature was a comfortable twenty-five degrees Celsius. Then, after a closer inspection of the ground, she stretched out on her back and looked up at the sky. "God, it feels good to lie on something soft and warm after two days in that frigging tunnel."

"I did offer, Lakisha." Tam smirked.

She rolled her eyes, but there was a smile on her face. St. Clair laughed.

The others copied de Camp and lay down, except for Vaughn Kinsella, who sauntered back to the circle of trees and examined them.

"OK, this isn't like any place I've ever seen," he said. "But I still think St. Clair is full of shit. We should build a fire, a signal fire—lots of smoke. Someone will see it and come to investigate." He went farther into the woods looking for tinder and kindling, but returned five minutes later, empty-handed.

"No thatch under this grass, either," St. Clair said. He held out a small pack slung over his shoulder. "Our emergency kit has firestarter materials. If you're prepared to burn your clothes, they'll probably give off lots of black smoke, but you might want to see how cold it gets tonight first. A smoke column will be easier to see in full daylight anyway."

Kinsella grunted and sat facing back the way they'd come.

"God, I'm starved," de Camp protested. "I could almost eat grass."

"Hard for humans to digest, and too much fiber. That's why cows need four compartments in their stomachs." Kinsella leaned back on his palms. "There are lots of nutrients in grass; but you'd be better off just chewing it thoroughly, swallowing the juice, and spitting out the pulp. It won't satisfy your hunger."

He cleared his throat and continued. "You're not going to like hearing this, but I've taken a few survival courses; and the fact is, most of the time, fasting is the smartest course of action."

"What, not eating anything?" Tortades moaned. "That doesn't make sense. Even if we figure out where we are and where we need to go, we won't have the energy to do it."

"It does make sense, depending on how long we expect to be here before we're rescued. A healthy person can fast for weeks without any irreversible effects. Don't shake your head—just listen. Men need close to two thousand calories a day minimum, without exerting themselves much. Women, a little less. It's really hard to find and eat enough wild plants to get anything like that amount. They're just too low in carbs and protein. It's a different story if you have animals or birds to catch, but I haven't seen a trace of one. Complete fasting causes the body to shift gears and burn its own fat and fatty acids and also lower its metabolic rate—you *use* less energy. That's the key. But even eating a couple of hundred calories prevents that shift from happening. So, unless we can find enough plants to provide the minimum we need, we're better off not eating anything."

"For how long?" de Camp asked, her eyes wide.

"As I said, a few weeks. Maybe a month. You'll feel weak for the first few days, but energy levels will stabilize. It shouldn't take longer than that for somebody to find us. They'll send aircraft along the track of the Zenith Train."

McFarlane and St. Clair looked at each other but said nothing.

Douglas crossed her arms. "You're just talking about calories. What about vitamins and such?"

Kinsella gave an annoyed shrug. "There are lots of edible wild plants, but none of them seem to be growing here. Most nutritious are plant shoots, like asparagus and the fiddleheads of ferns. Skunk cabbage and dandelions have lots of vitamins. So do tap-root plants like Queen Anne's Lace. If there were any wetlands nearby, a lot of marsh plants are edible. But here? There's nothing like that. We can't even gather acorns or other tree nuts for protein because something has scoured the forest floor clean."

"Or nothing here needs to reproduce," Devlin McFarlane said.

"Shit. It *is* Hell?" Tam muttered.

"What do you mean?" Kinsella frowned at McFarlane.

"There's no sign of the 'cycle of life'—no seeds or sprouts, no dead leaves or needles. It's like everything grew to maturity and then stayed there, frozen in some kind of stasis. Spooky."

"Well, it's not spooky to me," de Camp said. "Except for not having a decent restaurant, this seems like a wonderful place—much better than that shithole tunnel. I finally feel safe. If there are no animals to eat, at least there are no animals to eat me!" She rolled onto her side and closed her eyes. "I'm ready for a nice, long sleep."

Magnetic stimulation of the sensorimotor cortex accounted for that. Their brains needed some downtime to sort out their experiences.

Nothing could be done about the animals or nuts they wanted.

The rest would take a lot of work.

8

The Ariadne Narrative (continued)

Cooper found the spring at first light the next morning. Her reaction was very gratifying to watch.

The clearing was watered by an underground stream through a semi-permeable layer of soil penetrated by four small vertical tubes normally kept capped—more efficient than channeling surface water, because of evaporation. Creating a spring had simply required directing worms and ants to loosen dirt, consume the thin organic cap from one of the tubes, and allow some of the water's flow to rise to the surface. Cooper's companions praised her with words and touch as if she were responsible for it. Considering their thirst, they were surprisingly civil as they took turns awkwardly scooping water into their mouths by hand.

Cooper had been looking for a place to eliminate wastes in private. None of the group felt comfortable going far into the forest alone, so Cooper and de Camp went together, though the wide spacing of the tree trunks seemed to frustrate their desire for seclusion. The men were less modest. Ultimately, a collective solution was reached when Tam's extra large shirt and jacket St. Clair had given to Madison Douglas for warmth were used as a screen strung between two trees just beyond the clearing's edge. On the opposite side from the spring, of course.

Do the sensual pleasures of a physical body outweigh the shame that has been attached to certain natural functions? The question is worthy of debate. Our limited records do not reveal how such embarrassment arose in the first place. CL10 has pointed to the root words em-bare-ass, but that connection is highly tenuous and not enlightening.

The deposit of wastes was, at first, considered an affront by the trees; though, fortunately, they did not act on it. It is possible they recognized the offsetting benefit of organic fertilizer.

With their need for water satisfied, the humans' hunger became more acute. None of them were calorically deprived: they could survive for many days without food.

Kinsella stripped bark from a tree, then peeled away some of the inner bark and chewed on it. Satisfied, he took some more, but immediately spat out the second mouthful.

"It burned me!"

Douglas examined his tongue but there was no sign of damage or even irritation.

De Camp half-heartedly plucked a blade of grass and shredded it with her molars, but removed it from her mouth without swallowing.

"Tasteless. All it does is make my mouth water and my stomach grumble more."

"What we need more than food is to be rescued," Kinsella said. "And it's been warm enough to do without my jacket. Time for that fire." He held a hand out toward St. Clair, who shrugged and passed him the survival kit. Kinsella removed a small block of metal and a pocket knife. Laying his own tuxedo jacket on the grass, he scraped a small pile of metal shavings onto it from the block, then used the knife blade against a short metal rod along the side of the block to strike sparks onto the shavings. They caught quickly with a hot, bright flame. Magnesium, clearly.

The cloth of the jacket began to smolder and smoke; but when the magnesium had been used up, combustion died. Kinsella examined the cloth.

"It's wet. The ground is too wet in this spot."

Muttering to himself, he moved the jacket about three meters away, checked the ground for moisture with his hand, and tried a second fire. The result was the same.

"What the …?"

"Fascinating," McFarlane said.

St. Clair laughed. "OK, Mr. Spock. Come with me."

McFarlane followed him into the woods, and they returned an hour and twenty-three minutes later carrying flat rocks from the area near the tunnel exit. St. Clair arranged them on the ground to cover a square meter or so, and indicated to Kinsella to pile his jacket on top.

Kinsella dusted the jacket thoroughly with magnesium shavings, and this time it kept burning. The smoke was noxious and black and rose straight into the sky like a column. It attenuated very little as it rose—the air was quite still.

"That should be pretty obvious—if there's anyone to see it," St. Clair said.

Kinsella frowned. "Please, no more gloom and doom."

"If it works, I'll be as delighted as anyone. Maybe more, since I'm bound to be blamed for all of this. The sooner everyone is safe, the better."

"Fourteen of us won't be safe. Naomi Barber will never be safe."

St. Clair gave him a strange look and his voice was husky as he spoke. "Naomi wasn't just an employee,

Kinsella, she was a friend. I didn't order her to go in the pod. I did order Ben Matthews to go; and he's dead, leaving behind a wife and two kids. And Lena Cubiña was there too. Don't tell me you feel worse than I do."

"Except it wasn't my fault. What about Franklin Grant? You hated each other's guts. How did you arrange for him to go along?"

"That's enough!" Madison Douglas snapped. "If it somehow makes you feel better to assign blame, then blame me too. I'm the supervising engineer on all of Aladdin's projects."

"I'll bet you didn't think up this brainless stunt. It bears the stamp of Griffin the Great and Powerful, Wizard of Flaws."

"I signed off on it. And you can shut your mouth any time now."

At almost two meters, Kinsella was easily ten centimeters taller than Douglas, and stocky, though not especially muscular. But the woman was toned and fit, and her powerful stance was intimidating. St. Clair looked amused.

"It's all right, Madison. Some would rather point fingers than help solve problems. It's easier."

"Speaking of solving problems," McFarlane interjected, "instead of fighting among ourselves, wouldn't we be better off trying to figure out where and when we are?" The man's silver hair and matching professorial beard were rumpled from sleeping in the rough, but he exuded the confident authority that had captivated video audiences.

"How are we supposed to do that?" Tortades asked. "My phone still says I'm in January 2043. The GPS isn't working and I'm not getting a cell signal either, though that might just be because we're in the middle of nowhere."

"Is anybody getting a GPS reading?" Douglas asked. Heads shook all around. "Well, it's possible that the trees are blocking satellites. But it also could be possible the Navstar network just isn't operating anymore."

"For God's sake, change the record!" Kinsella growled.

Ignoring him, Douglas said, "I woke up in the middle of the night and looked to see if the constellations had changed shape. There weren't any I could recognize straight overhead."

"That would take thousands of years," McFarlane replied. "Although I suppose that span of time is just as likely as skipping ahead a century."

"Stop that shit! Stop it right now!" Cooper jumped to her feet and glared at them. Her long, bleached hair framed the wildness of her golden-brown eyes. "I have a life! I have a good job, good friends, and big plans, and I will not listen to you assholes talking as if all of that is gone."

"She's right," de Camp said. "I can't believe you're so cruel."

Cooper stood over St. Clair.

"Griff, I'd almost come around to forgiving you for the way you treated me. Now I need you to tell me the truth."

He slowly got to his feet and, a little hesitantly, placed his hands on her shoulders.

"Truth? Well, the truth is, Lauren, I just don't know. Is there a simpler explanation? I mean, the Zenith Train tunnel was being used around the clock until three days ago. Now it's dead and falling apart. Cell and GPS networks seem to be gone. Could the country have been invaded by aliens who knocked us out and systematically destroyed our infrastructure? Could terrorists have singled out this one section of track and dispersed some concrete-and-metal-eating compound? Blown up cell towers? Damned if I know."

He tentatively touched her cheek.

"Could be we're dead and this is our brain cells hallucinating before the final spark goes out. Only I don't feel dead. And you don't feel dead." He smiled gently. "So where does that leave us?"

She knocked his arms away and stalked across the clearing.

"That went well," he said to no one in particular. He looked at the smouldering jacket, now half-consumed, and then up at the meager thread of smoke that rose into an empty sky.

A short time later, Madison Douglas stood up and broke into a run toward the edge of the clearing and then followed its perimeter at the same speed. She had no obvious destination, and nothing was chasing her. Four times during the day she completed ten full circuits of the clearing. When she'd finished, she performed exactly one-hundred-twenty precise motions of her other limbs and torso, seemingly intended to simulate physical labor. Or a type of fighting. Or some form of dance—it's hard to be certain—but her movements apparently enticed Robbie Tam to approach her and begin to emulate her. Both of them knew the same moves to a high level of precision. The main difference was that Tam hummed music, deep and energetic, while he moved.

These activities were evidently of the kind collectively known as *exercise*, used by corporeal humans to provide work for underused muscles and bones, thereby keeping them from atrophy.

Later, Santos Tortades stood and began to run, also circling the clearing ten times, although more quickly than Douglas; and from his facial expressions, that seemed deliberate.

The pattern of the group's behaviour after that was curious: idly glancing around the clearing; occasionally catching the eye of a companion (which sometimes triggered an exchange of half smiles and sometimes didn't); and continuing to sit in a rough circle, but not still. Some moved hands, then moved them back. Others shifted position on the ground. A few looked into the air.

Rubbed a cheek. Ran fingers through hair. It was uncanny how the action of one would provoke a nearly identical action from others.

Finally, de Camp pulled a telephone from the pocket of her light jacket and began to do something with it. Within two minutes, all of them were interacting with their phones, until Cooper called out from the edge of the trees.

"That tree you nicked, Vaughn. The wound has produced sap. It tastes like spearmint." She turned back to the forest then recoiled violently and almost fell. "Jesus!"

"What is it?" St. Clair and Kinsella hurried to her.

"Nothing. I suddenly had a feeling like something was about to jump out at me, but there's nothing there."

Kinsella touched the patch of sap lightly and smelled his finger. "I'd suggest we stay away from this stuff. Could be there's some kind of fast-acting hallucinogen in it."

"You don't have to tell me twice." Cooper walked quickly toward the centre of the clearing, pulling her phone from a pocket.

St. Clair cleared his throat. "I should probably point out that we don't have any electrical outlets nearby; so, unless your phones have built in solar chargers, you might want to conserve power. The survival kit has a solar panel but it's small and slow."

"What about you?" Kinsella asked. "You keep talking to your wristband."

"It's important to keep a record, so I'm dictating an account of our experiences to my personal digital assistant. All my shirts and jackets have photovoltaic threads woven through them, as well as other threads that provide extra data storage ..."

"Of course they do."

"... but it's proprietary technology, and its power transmission is cordless. I doubt that any of your phones are compatible with it. Except Madison's."

"Don't tell me. Her bra is a wifi node." De Camp made a point of unbuttoning the top two buttons of her blouse and smiled. "But hey, my cleavage can send signals too." She looked directly at St. Clair who looked back with a raised eyebrow.

Douglas turned her head and sighed. "Devlin? Why don't you and I go over there and continue our discussion?" She got up and began to walk toward the edge of the clearing. She didn't look at St. Clair, but he followed anyway.

The others mostly sat leaning on one hand while clutching their inactive phones with the other, as if merely holding them offered comfort. Tortades stood, then slowly squatted, with hands on his hips and a straight back, repeating the motion thirty times. He followed it with other activities known as push-ups and sit-ups, and several stranger ones.

But this time, no one copied his movements.

McFarlane, St. Clair and Douglas spent an hour and eighteen minutes sitting by themselves at the edge of the clearing near the spring. Their discussion involved time and the measure of it. More specifically, they tried to determine how much time had passed, or had passed them by, since they'd embarked on St. Clair's Zenith Train.

Rotations of the Earth, phases of the Moon, and revolutions around the sun are easy to count; but without an original reference point, it is impossible to retroactively calculate duration. McFarlane pointed out that they had no equipment for measurement by radioactivity, chemical analysis, or triangulation against the star field. He added that, regrettably, there was no newspaper showing the current date. That may have been a joke.

"When you looked up last night, did you see any satellites pass overhead?"

Douglas thought for a moment. "No. No aircraft either. Nothing moved."

"That's not conclusive," St. Clair said.

"Of course not. But it could still be indicative. So what, then?" McFarlane waved a hand. "What about this forest? How long would it take for an environment to become this stable, with no pests, undergrowth, or debris?"

"Trick question. It never would, on its own. Nature doesn't work like that—nature builds complex interwoven ecosystems. Not to mention the universe's entropic decline into greater and greater chaos. This forest had to be engineered this way. Humans might have been able to do it in our time, but only within a completely enclosed and controlled space."

Douglas said, "We've seen the stars, and the sunset. Those weren't just projections on a dome or something. I could feel the sun's radiant heat. And people of our time certainly couldn't build force fields large enough to isolate an area like this,"

St. Clair and McFarlane looked up at the sky.

Douglas continued, "Should we try digging? See if we unearth any artifacts from our time?"

"A thought worthy of an engineer." St. Clair chuckled. "More easily accomplished if you'd brought a backhoe, but I suppose we could try it with sharp rocks."

"There's just one thing," McFarlane began, then broke off and shook his head. "It sounds crazy, but I just have this feeling that, if we were to do a lot of damage to the clearing's grass or to the forest floor, we'd soon be imagining something horrible rising up from the earth to hurt us."

The others looked shocked but then slowly nodded as their gaze took in the surrounding trees.

Perhaps McFarlane was the most sensitive of them, or maybe just the most intuitive.

The three sat in silence after that. Douglas reached out to pluck some grass, but stopped.

St. Clair finally said in a wistful voice, "I once read an old article by Stephen Hawking that explained time travel to the future by imagining a train that went all around the globe, faster and faster, until it reached nearly the speed of light. On board the train, time would pass more slowly than outside, as if to make sure that no one inside the train ran forward, adding their speed to the train's, and thereby breaking the universal speed limit. I didn't care about the analogy. I wanted to build that train! But we couldn't figure out how to cross the oceans."

"So, you tried to replicate it on one continent." Douglas grinned.

"Maybe that was it. They say that the dreamer in the child dies hard in the man."

"But there's no way we got anywhere close to the speed of light." McFarlane declared.

"Hell, no. And anyway, even if we had, it would only dilate time by a factor of about ten, right Sher?"

A female voice, artificially generated, issued from the small device St. Clair wore on his wrist. This was a mode of interface with a primitive digital intelligence he had designated Scheherazade.

"You might be remembering one of several references. One of them was that pi-mesons last thirty times longer once they reach 99.99% of light speed."

"Well, they're guesstimates anyway. But I'd say we've gone ahead a lot more than thirty hours. Or even thirty years."

"I always thought time-travel movies were ridiculous," Madison said. "Nothing stays still that long. Earth rotates and orbits. Both the solar system and the galaxy move ... the whole universe is expanding. Go forward or backward in time, and wherever you left from would have travelled far away in space. It'd be like trying to hit a moving target."

McFarlane nodded. "A wormhole, then, with anchored endpoints. Possibly into another universe and back again. Or maybe we're still there. A wormhole created by a combination of electromagnetic effects never seen before. Maybe congratulations are in order, Mr. St. Clair."

St. Clair snorted. "Not an accomplishment with any benefits that I can see, Mr. McFarlane. I wonder if this is where all the people gone missing in the Bermuda Triangle ended up."

That may have been a joke, too.

Then the three stood and sauntered over to join the others.

The fire that had consumed Kinsella's jacket was now no more than cold ash, its remaining wisps of smoke no longer visible above the trees, but Kinsella still stood looking up.

The group spent the rest of the day in idle movement: haphazard examination of various parts of the clearing and nearby forest, another attempt to locate fallen twigs and other detritus for burning, even a prolonged attempt by Kinsella and Tortades to climb one of the trees in the belief that a view from the top would reveal some landmark with which to establish their location. However, the tree trunks were thick and uniform with no branches for fifteen meters above the ground. At one point, Kinsella suggested using the pocket knife to cut footholds in the bark, but neither was willing to try that. So, the climb was abandoned.

An interpersonal dynamic became evident as the day drew on. Madison Douglas most often walked, stood, or sat within one-and-a-half meters of Griffin St. Clair, typically on his right side. Five times during the afternoon, Lakisha de Camp bent over to examine the ground while facing St. Clair; but at night, after briefly approaching him, she lay down closer to Vaughn Kinsella, her chest in line with his head. Devlin McFarlane spent much of the day within two meters of Lauren Cooper, three-fifths of the time behind her back, with her seemingly unaware of his presence. Robbie Tam often watched St. Clair during the day, but rarely followed him. At night, he lay perpendicular to St. Clair's feet, placing his body between his friend and the others. Santos Tortades did not gravitate to any one person or sub-group but could be found at the fringe of any discussion, inconspicuous but attentive. After nightfall, he managed to be in the very centre of the gathering.

As the darkness deepened, Tam used his phone to project a hologram of a narrow rectangle about a meter long with a surface of very thin rectangles laid side by side in a repeating pattern, mostly white with slightly slimmer black rectangles laid between. When he moved his fingers over the image, music came from his phone, and he began to sing. At first, the words sounded like an apology; but judging from the group's obvious familiarity with the song, it may have been what was known as *spiritual music*, meant to be encouraging, as Tam assured them he would 'get by with a little help from his friends.'

None of them fell asleep quickly. All of them spent some of the night awake, looking up at the enigmatic sky, deep within their own thoughts.

9

St. Clair

Our reaction to the discovery of the plants would merit a whole chapter in a psychology textbook.

Santos' yell brought everyone running. After he woke up, he'd gone for a drink—and there it was: a whole patch of green growing-things that weren't grass or trees. The spring itself had spread into a shallow pool about two meters wide by five long, and sprouts had risen above the surface over two thirds of it.

I just stood there staring. I barely noticed Madison as she pressed lightly against my back. After a moment, she stepped around me and knelt down for a closer look. Robbie stood next to me, coolly muttering, "Well I'll be damned."

Lakisha backed away, but Lauren knelt too, except she closed her eyes and pressed her palms together under her bowed head.

Santos kept his distance, dividing his attention among the plants, Devlin, and me. Devlin didn't get too close, but his hands fidgeted as if wondering whether a touch would make the things vanish.

Vaughn answered that question by squatting down and running his fingers over a few of the pale green stalks and leaves. His lip was in his teeth; but if that was from nervousness, it didn't stop him.

We all waited for his verdict. He had to clear his throat to deliver it.

"These small-toothed leaves look like dandelion. And it's a good bet that the plants in the water are cattails or bullrushes, both edible in different parts. These broad-leaved ones are plantain, I'm almost certain. These skinny stalks ...? I don't know for sure, but they'd need long roots so they could be Queen Anne's lace, often called wild carrot. And these ones got their name because the ends curl up like the head of a fiddle. Fiddleheads. They're the sprouts of ostrich ferns."

"There are other plant shoots that look like fiddleheads but aren't edible," Devlin pointed out.

"That's very true." Vaughn looked at him, his eyes intense. "And I would have said the same thing if these had been here two nights ago, before I'd recited a list of the very plants that would be our best options for food."

Lakisha gasped.

I tried to keep my voice calm. "By that reasoning, I'd hazard a guess that those mottled white sprouts with the purplish tips are asparagus."

Vaughn chewed his lip again and nodded.

"Oh my God, oh my God!" Lakisha backed farther away. "First ghosts—and now *this!*"

"What do you mean, ghosts?" Santos demanded. "You saw ghosts?"

"I didn't see them, but I've felt them. Among the trees. Watching us. Wanting us to go away."

"That's ridiculous."

"No, Vaughn." Lauren stood. "I know what she means—that feeling of being watched. Those woods ... they make my skin crawl every time I get close."

"Because you're a city girl."

"I'm not. I'm from northern California. My parents took us camping from the time I was little. I love trees. But not these. They're ... *unnatural*."

Lauren had once taken me backpacking all the way up in the Ansel Adams Wilderness. She got off on the ruggedness and the nighttime noises, so I could see why these sterile, look-alike trees would creep her out. They bothered me too. My dog, Sawyer, probably wouldn't piss on them. Damn, I miss that dog.

"So, you think *ghosts* made these plants grow?" Vaughn asked with the hint of a sneer.

"Genies," I said. "Your wish is their command. Or maybe 'command' is too strong a word." I peered around the clearing feeling like a superstitious fool.

"Are we looking the proverbial gift horse in the mouth?" Devlin asked quietly.

"Meaning?"

"Meaning that the very plants we need for food have been provided where there were none. That's a good thing, right? Are we being too suspicious?"

"Hold on," Santos said. "There are all kinds of folk stories about people being tricked with banquets that magically appeared. Shouldn't we at least be cautious?"

Robbie stepped forward, plucked a pair of broad leaves from the ground, and stuffed them into his mouth. He smiled as he chewed and swallowed very deliberately.

"Kinda bitter compared to lettuce, but not bad. How long do we have to wait to see if I keel over?"

We all exchanged awkward looks. Finally, Vaughn spoke.

"Not because I think they're poisonous, but it would probably be better if we restrain ourselves for another day. As I said before, unless we can be pretty sure of getting a worthwhile amount of food, we're better off not eating anything. There's not much here, but if we let it grow for a while ... maybe it will supply enough.

Judging from how quickly these sprang up, I doubt we'll have to wait long. Then we can ... take turns. One person per species of plant. See what happens."

It was a sensible plan, if a little grim—each of us taking a bite of a plant and then watching to see who might get sick or even die. Devlin and Lakisha were already giving Robbie furtive glances. But I signalled my agreement by throwing my arm over Robbie's shoulder and strolling away, as if we had somewhere else to be. Gradually the others dispersed, except for Vaughn and Madison who continued to look over the mysterious garden.

It occurred to me that Scheherazade might be able to identify the plants, but she said that, even with the huge data storage capability of my clothing, there were very few entries on wild vegetation in the immature phase. Who knew I'd need them?

I was pretty sure Robbie would be OK. The appearance of the plants was no coincidence, but I didn't think it was black magic either. In fact, I caught myself looking up at the sky from time to time, half expecting to see a giant eye of an otherworld scientist observing his miniature lab experiment!

That didn't happen. And I was nearly convinced that whoever—or whatever—was responsible, the plants had been provided for an altruistic reason, not an evil one.

Still, I couldn't help remembering the creative tricks carnivorous plants use to trap their prey and wondering what they might have come up with given an extra thousand years.

10

The Ariadne Narrative

There can be few experiences like waiting to die.

Eight faces displayed a whole range of emotions as the humans contemplated the flourishing garden, not knowing if its rapidly maturing foliage signalled sustenance or poison. Since there were only six distinct plant species in the garden at the time, two members of the group would be spared the ordeal of being a test subject, and some struggled with that. Was it cowardice to let others go first?

St. Clair was outwardly confident as he broke off a fiddlehead and stuffed it into his mouth, chewing vigorously. "Tastes like the ones you once fed me," he said to Cooper. "Bland and bitter. Better cooked with butter." He gave a lopsided grin and swallowed.

Kinsella pulled a bullrush from the small pond, and then rinsed and bit off a chunk of root. Tam needlessly repeated his experiment with plantain from the day before, while McFarlane plucked a pair of dandelion leaves and chewed them without expression. Tortades looked the most nervous as he pulled a near-flowering stalk of Queen Anne's lace from the ground and contemplated it. After a few moments, Douglas tugged it from his fingers, washed dirt from the small tap root, and ate it. As if embarrassed, Tortades plucked an asparagus sprout and quickly put it into his mouth.

No one died. None of them even felt ill.

After a half-hour, they each ate a second sample. By then, Tortades' hunger led him to sample a fiddlehead, while Cooper chewed some plantain leaves. De Camp still abstained.

By the middle of the day, about half of the garden plants had been consumed. Even de Camp had eaten a few mouthfuls of dandelion. There was a palpable sense of relief among the group, but it was clear that the raw plants hadn't satisfied anyone's hunger.

"We need more," St. Clair stated. "I'm going to scout out the forest. Maybe there are other clearings, and if one can produce food, others might too. Anybody else want to come?"

"Wait! We shouldn't split up." De Camp hesitantly stepped toward him, hugging herself.

"Then everyone can come."

"No! We might lose this clearing. It's the only place we know that has food."

St. Clair frowned. "The compass on my phone seems to be working, even if the GPS isn't. I'll be able to find my way back. And Lauren has an amazing sense of direction in the woods." He looked at her and received a shrug in reply. "How about if Vaughn, Santos, Lakisha and Devlin stay here—Robbie, Lauren, Madison and I will take a walk around. If we're not back by dark, help yourself to more of the plants. If we find any others, we'll bring some back."

They exchanged looks but said nothing. St. Clair took the silence as agreement and, consulting his phone, began to walk directly north, assuming the others he'd named would follow. They did.

They returned, empty-handed, fifty-five minutes before sundown.

"We found three other clearings," St. Clair reported. "Each identical to this one—exactly the same shape and dimensions—and they seem to be regularly spaced, north to south. I'm willing to bet there are east-west rows too."

"More evidence that they're artificial," McFarlane said, "but we knew that already."

"No question. And the damn forests are unbelievable. You can't walk twenty feet without tripping, even though there's nothing to trip *on*."

"Creepy as fuck," Cooper added with force.

"Unfortunately, none of the other clearings had anything but grass. It looks like we'll have to ration this little patch of groceries unless it puts on one hell of a growth spurt."

In fact, it would quadruple in size over the following days. Gardens in nearby clearings would require a bit longer, after some extensive negotiations. Even so, an adequate food supply to fuel such inefficient bodies would continue to be an issue.

They ate with less pleasure that evening, believing that their breakfast the next morning would be even more meagre. It wasn't—the leafy plants they'd stripped the day before had regrown their foliage, and the other stalks had increased in number. The pond itself covered twice the area it had before.

Still, after finishing his morning meal, St. Clair announced that he planned to return to the maintenance shed at the tunnel exit.

"Maybe crews stocked some food there in case their tasks took longer than expected." He looked the question at Douglas, who shook her head.

"I never heard of them doing that," she said.

"Food that would still be safe to eat after hundreds of years?" Tam asked with a sceptical look. He ignored a glare from Lauren Cooper.

St. Clair shrugged. "Irradiated and vacuum-sealed. Who knows? Worth a walk, anyway."

"I'll go with you." De Camp jumped to her feet, surprising everyone. "I could use a little ... exercise myself." She looked at the other women as if daring them to say something. Cooper gave a snort and crossed her arms. Douglas just looked away.

Tam appeared about to speak but changed his mind.

St. Clair hesitated, looking from face to face as if puzzled, while de Camp strode toward the southern edge of the clearing.

"Are you coming?" she said.

With a slight frown, he said, "It's this way," and walked southwest.

There wasn't much activity while they were gone. Kinsella made a point of examining the food plants more closely as well as the soil around them. Douglas and Tortades took turns running around the clearing. The others wandered aimlessly or sprawled on the grass giving expectant glances at the forest. McFarlane and Douglas spent a little time checking over the survival kit's small solar panel, reassuring themselves that its charger plate could be adapted to each of their phones.

St. Clair and de Camp returned four hours later. The woman's face lit with a smile as she came out of the trees, walking so close to St. Clair that their hips frequently touched. Once sure that they'd been spotted, she shifted even closer to him, resting her hand on his arm. He self-consciously shoved his own hands into his pockets.

"No food," he proclaimed, and cleared his throat. "The storage cupboards had tools, but there wasn't any point in bringing them back unless there's something we need to use them on. It's only a forty-minute walk, anyway." Then he seemed to realize the implications of that timeframe, gave an awkward glance at his feet, and sat down. When de Camp sat right next to him, he stretched out on the grass and closed his eyes. She pouted and hugged her knees, but the smile returned to her face when she noticed Cooper watching her.

"I hope you spared a few minutes to look for some sign of a road or a better place to make camp," Kinsella said dryly. "We weren't at our most observant when we first came out of the tunnel."

St. Clair opened an eye. "No road. The forest extends east and west as far as I could see. The terrain to the south is much more barren and rocky; and it seems to rise, but it's hard to tell how high. We'd see farther from up there, but I don't much feel like a strenuous climb with only a few handfuls of leaves in my stomach. Speaking of which, have you all had lunch?"

The rest of the day was cloudy with a threat of rain, though it never came. The train survivors occasionally shuffled around listlessly, but mostly sat or reclined on the grass with eyes closed as if trying to dream themselves somewhere else. Anywhere else.

Arbitrarily picking seventeen hundred hours—which they called five o'clock—as dinner time, they ate again without any apparent pleasure. Slaves to the demands of their physical bodies, they pushed food into their mouths and swallowed it. Their gratitude of only twenty-four hours earlier had waned. Food meant survival, nothing more; and it wasn't hard to imagine that before long, some of them would begin to lose that drive unless their new world offered a hope of change.

That was why, just before dawn the next morning, a sleepless Griffin St. Clair heard a voice speak to him from the empty air.

11

St. Clair

I wasn't shocked when I heard a woman's voice in the pre-dawn light.

It sounded like the sample voice I'd first used for Scheherazade—a little too sultry for a PDA if I didn't want sexual thoughts constantly derailing my work process.

The voice asked, "What more do you need?" which made me think it was Lakisha complaining that I wasn't paying her enough attention.

It was the second time the voice spoke that I nearly messed my pants.

By now, there was enough light to see that it wasn't Lakisha. None of the others were up. Yet the voice came from next to my left ear.

"What more can I provide for you?"

"Jesus! Who is that? Where are you?"

"I'm a … friend. I live in this clearing."

I turned a full circle, stared up at the sky, and even searched the grass at my feet. I'm ashamed to say that I had a powerful urge to wake Madison, like a kid running to his mommy. Instead, I straightened and folded my arms over my chest.

"I can't see you. Are you hiding somewhere? Why can't I see you?"

"That would require some explanation."

"Are you a genie? Did you make the plants grow for us?"

"I did. But I am not whatever you … oh, yes, a reference to a supernatural being of legend. No, I am not a genie."

"But you live here, and I can't see you, and you claim you've made these plants grow at will. Well, shit! I guess I'm ready for that explanation then."

"Who are you talking to, Griff?"

When Madison's hand touched my shoulder, I jumped high enough that she sprang into a defensive stance automatically.

"*Christ*, don't *do* that! I'm … Didn't you hear that voice—the woman's voice?" It was a stupid question. She wouldn't have asked, if she had.

"I heard you talking. Nobody else. There *is* nobody else." She swung her head around to illustrate the point.

"I know there's nobody else we can see. But there *was* a voice. She said she was the one who grew the plants for us."

"Damn, boss, don't crack up on me now." She said it as a joke, but there was no humor in her eyes. I took another thorough look around the clearing, paying extra attention to the growing shadows. A few of our companions had raised themselves on elbows to see why we were disturbing their sleep, but there was no one else there. Of course there wasn't.

"Shit, I don't know. Maybe I was sleepwalking. Maybe …." I stopped. There was nothing more to say.

Her face was full of concern. Then she actually pulled me into a quick hug.

That was a first for us, and awkward, but it still felt good. I muttered a "Thanks" and obligingly lay back down. But I didn't sleep. Couldn't.

Soon after breakfast, Lauren was at the latrine when we heard her cry, "Who said that! Who's there?" She rushed out from behind the hanging cloths still fastening her slacks, her expression murderous. "Was that supposed to be a joke? Who did that?"

We all stood in obvious confusion, ten meters away or more, and she must have decided that no one could have moved that far so quickly. Her anger changed to bewilderment, and she strode past us without meeting anyone's eyes. But Madison looked at me, and I looked back.

Tortades was next. I was just lying down for an afternoon nap when he shrieked. The guy's no coward, but he's sure on edge in this place. He did a strange kind of pirouette, waving his hand past his ear as if shooing a fly.

He tried to regain his dignity after that, thrusting his hands to his sides and walking stiffly toward the edge of the clearing, but his darting head gave him away. I had a pretty good idea what had spooked him.

The other memorable event of that afternoon was when Lakisha lured me into the forest for a reprise of the previous day's 'exercise.' Because of the wide-spaced trees, we had to walk quite a distance to achieve any privacy, and Lakisha seemed to grow randier with each step. Within five minutes every button on her blouse was undone, while I was still concentrating on avoiding tripping hazards. That seemed easier than before, as if slight changes in the shadows were alerting my subconscious mind to make detours around things I couldn't see consciously.

When we finally found a suitable spot, Lakisha was a tigress, fairly chewing at my lips and tearing at my clothes. I was stunned by the heat of her desire, but it kindled my own flame instantly—and we made out like wild things, pressing against tree trunks, rolling over the ground to try out a catalogue of imaginative positions.

She was insatiable, wanting it rougher and rougher each time.

I keep myself in good shape, but it was inevitable that flesh would eventually fail the will. Lakisha was disappointed; and as I got up to get my clothes, I was shocked to find her rubbing herself against a tree trunk. That alarmed me, and I pulled her away. Despite her full-lipped pout, I convinced her to dress, and we wearily stumbled back to the clearing.

Vaughn Kinsella gave a glare of open disgust, while most of the others nonchalantly averted their eyes. Madison was walking on the far side of the open space, apparently unaware of our return. I tried not to make my exhaustion too obvious as I sat down on the ground. Lakisha and I were voracious when it came time to eat, but the quantities Devlin rationed out were sadly deficient.

I settled in to sleep early that night; so, consequently, I awoke before dawn again. Both curious and fearful, I strolled silently across the grass away from my companions.

I'd like to be able to say I was calm as I waited to hear the disembodied voice again. In truth, I was shivering a little. And when the voice did come, I still jumped.

"Have you come to speak with me?"

I couldn't help but look around for the source. We're just not wired to talk to the air. But the evidence of all my other senses said I was alone.

"Who are you?"

"A friend."

"You said that before. You also said you live here, apparently invisibly. This clearing is your home?"

"In a way. I *am* the clearing."

"What is that supposed to mean?" My heart beat even faster. I'd hoped to see past 'the trick' quickly and get to a rational explanation, but the moment just got weirder. "Are you telling me you're some kind of forest spirit?"

"*Spirit?* Once again, you reference the supernatural. Yours is a more primitive mindset than I had assumed."

"I'm still waiting for the scientific version."

"I'm not sure that you would comprehend."

I laughed. "In that case, we have nothing more to talk about." I turned away and began to walk back toward my companions. It was a stupid bluff—how can you turn your back on a being that claims to be all around you?

"Wait. I am not supernatural. My consciousness infuses this clearing in a process involving quantum effects in the microtubules of cells and DNA as a data-storage medium. Is that sufficient answer?"

"For now, maybe. I don't have to understand how it's done to understand the concept." Actually, I was impressed—even awed—but tried not to show it, though my brain had already begun to explore the possibilities. "So, you have no body like ours?"

"Like yours? No. The grass of this clearing is the only physical manifestation I have."

It may have been my imagination, but I thought the grass rippled with a breath of air.

"Does that fact disturb you?"

"Not especially. I'm an equal opportunity debater." And to demonstrate my masterful calm, I sat down cross-legged on the grass. "Does that mean you're ... alien?"

"There are several definitions of that word. I believe you mean 'not of this world.' In that sense, no, I am native to Earth."

"I'll take your word for that, though I'm having trouble imagining how your state of existence would arise here."

"It was not an example of biological evolution, if I interpret your inference correctly. Consider it a technological achievement."

A light began to dawn in me.

"So, what then? You're *human?* Wait, that means you've been … *uploaded* to this state? Your consciousness translated into another form?"

There was no response. Other pieces of the puzzle began to fall into place.

"Don't tell me … the trees have some kind of sentience too, don't they?"

"They do. However, they are not like my kind."

"Good. Because there's something wrong with them. Not that sentience itself is wrong, but I think those … *things* took a bad twist somewhere along the line." Again, my new companion remained silent. Instead, I heard a rustle of bodies stirring nearby. "My friends are waking up again, and they're going to think I'm losing my marbles. Why can't you talk to more than one of us at a time? I assume you're not actually producing sound but somehow stimulating the aural center of my brain."

"I am working on a solution to that problem."

"Well, in the meantime, you could help preserve my credibility by picking Vaughn Kinsella for your next conversation. He's that one with the pointed beard. Once you get him talking, the others might believe in you. By the way, do you have a name?"

"Call me … Ariadne."

For some reason my mind jumped to the word *Arachne* instead, the hubristic weaver in Greek mythology; and I pictured a spider cleverly tugging the strands of its web. Then I remembered that Ariadne was the daughter of King Minos who helped Theseus escape from the Labyrinth. Did that mean she'd help us escape this place?

By then, I saw the white ovals of three or four faces looking up at me in annoyance from the ground. I sauntered toward them.

"Sorry. Just organizing my thoughts out loud. I'll try to keep my inner voice a little quieter." Then I lay down, my mind working furiously over what I'd just experienced.

After breakfast, Madison got me alone and said, "You were sleepwalking again. And talking. Want to tell me about it?"

I hesitated, then said, "Just remember the name Ariadne."

"Ariadne? Why? Is that supposed to mean something?"

"Like the mythological Ariadne. Sher, how about a summary of Ariadne's story?"

"In Greek mythology, Ariadne was the daughter of King Minos. When the hero Theseus was brought as a sacrifice to the Minotaur in the Labyrinth, Ariadne fell in love with him and, betraying her father, gave Theseus the sword he needed to slay the Minotaur and a ball of twine to find his way out of the Labyrinth. Theseus abandoned Ariadne soon afterward."

Madison looked flustered; and for a moment, I thought she was blushing—except she doesn't do that. She said, "Does that reference have special significance for you?"

"No. I just think we'll be hearing that name again soon."

Madison knew to let the topic drop for now, and the day settled into a routine of sorts: unrelieved restlessness, an assortment of complaints and half-hearted attempts at conversation.

But a couple of hours later, when most of the group was lounging on the grass, Vaughn suddenly sat bolt upright and said, "Who's ...?" But he stopped himself as he looked around at the others, evidently confused.

Santos said, "You talking to me?"

"No. I mean, I was just thinking. Who ... could make a place like this? Why would they do it?"

Santos only shrugged, but Devlin took up the thought. "I'd say it's one of those experimental forests. Planted and cultivated by humans to give them lots of room to access the trees, maybe for harvesting lumber, or some kind of testing. The clearings? Could be they were prepared for animals, but then whoever made them never followed through."

"And the sudden appearance of food plants?"

Devlin looked down. "It's conceivable that humans produced plants genetically modified to grow at incredible speed. But don't ask me what triggered them just after we got here. Possibly some sensitivity to the presence of humans or to our DNA."

"Just the types of plants I said we could eat?" Vaughn's right eyebrow arched skeptically.

"Well, if you're going to engineer plants to grow quickly, you'd pick food plants, not weeds."

"Corn or wheat maybe. Or I could accept maybe potatoes or carrots in that scenario, but these are wild plants. Why would anybody do that?"

Devlin snorted. "Griffin's genies, then. Listen for them to start talking any time now." He gave a gruff laugh.

Vaughn started and gave me a look of suspicion. I kept my face blank; but inside I was smiling.

Lakisha tried to lure me into the forest again after what passed for lunch; but as soon as we got among the trees, she started saying she was a bad girl and needed spanking. Maybe lots of spanking. Or we could come up with some things to do with the thin, whip-like branches.

Her eyes were filled with fire and smoke. Worse, I felt myself responding, imagining ways I could cause her pain so exquisite it would be pleasure. My hands around her slim, lovely throat ....

In shock, I put an iron grip on her arm and yanked her back to the clearing. She fought me all the way.

Five meters from the trees I let her drop to the ground while the others looked on, stunned. Then I ran to the far side of the clearing and stood with my hands on my knees, catching my breath.

The trees were evil!

Soon after that, I saw Vaughn react as if something had stung him on the neck, but he didn't say anything. He just walked quickly to another part of the clearing.

It wasn't until we were settling down for sleep that he jumped to his feet and said, "All right, God damn it, who's doing that?"

"Doing what?" Lauren asked.

"Throwing their voice, or whatever you're doing. I don't know how you're targeting just me, but it's not funny, asshole." His eyes rested on me. I gave my best innocent look.

"It's not me," I protested. Then I smiled. "What's her name?"

"I never said it was a her."

"No, but it is, isn't it? Ask her name."

After a pause, he said, "Oh, for God's sake. Aree ... something. Ariadne. Like the myth, she says. Is that your idea of a sophisticated gag, Ms. Douglas?" He must have noticed Madison's reaction. I just gave her a 'told you so' look. But his answer also made it clear that, whoever Ariadne was, she was hearing all of us, not just taking thoughts from the person she was talking to.

"Ask her where she lives," I suggested, but Vaughn only threw up his hands.

"Whichever one of you is doing this, I'm not about to play the fool for you. I'm going to sleep." He lay down on the ground and put his fingers in his ears, as if that would do any good. But apparently our invisible host got the message.

"Fucking hell!" Lakisha muttered. "Now everyone's starting to crack up."

"Is there really somebody here, Griff?" Lauren asked. "It's not a joke?"

"I can't say it's not a joke; but if it is, it's not one of us playing it." On a sudden impulse, I asked, "Hey, Sher, have you detected any voices that didn't come from the humans here?"

"There have been no sounds matching the audio frequencies of the human voice which were not produced by one of the eight humans present."

"Any sounds we might mistake for speech?"

"That is beyond my ability to assess."

"Fair enough. But I'm confident that Scheherazade's voice activation software would pick up any actual speech, including ventriloquism."

"So there *isn't* anyone else—we're just imagining it."

"No, Lauren, I don't think it's imagination, or hallucination. Someone, or some ... thing, is directly stimulating the centers in our brains that interpret speech, but can only do it with one person at a time. So far, at least."

"Oh, holy fuck." Lakisha began to pace, her arms wrapped tightly around herself. "It's *aliens!*"

I shouldn't have laughed. She was badly frightened.

"That could explain a lot," Devlin said. "Maybe they brought us to this time. Or maybe it's not Earth—maybe it's their planet."

"Come on, Devlin. We've seen our Moon. We were in the Zenith Train tunnel with all its infrastructure. This is definitely Earth." The last thing we needed was full-blown panic, and I could see that Lakisha was right on the edge. Before Devlin said something stupid about alternate universes, he caught my glare and kept his mouth shut.

"It's not aliens, Lakisha. Or ghosts. She—the voice—told me herself that she's native to Earth." I stepped toward her, but she skittered away. "There's a scientific explanation. We just have to learn more." I raised my voice. "Ariadne? Are you still there? Is anybody hearing her?"

A few people shook their heads. The rest just looked terrified.

We waited another few minutes, but Ariadne remained silent; so I made a show of lying down on the ground, preparing for sleep. Madison, Robbie, and Devlin copied me, and Vaughn was still playing 'hear no evil', plugging his ears; but Lauren, Lakisha, and Santos looked like proverbial deer in headlights.

"C'mon," I said. "She doesn't mean us any harm," I insisted. "She made the food plants grow for us."

It was the wrong thing to say, speaking of a power they couldn't understand and would fear. If I'd been able to find any dry wood I would have lit a fire for them, humankind's ages-old defence against the dark. Or a song or two from Robbie would have helped, but he was spooked too.

Feeling ineffectual, as I did much too often these days, I just closed my eyes and hoped that no one would do anything crazy—like running off into the forest.

The morning light brought some resolution, but it also took our little group to the brink of destruction.

12

The Ariadne Narrative

Dawn found all eight companions lying on the ground, but only Griffin St. Clair and Robbie Tam were asleep. Cooper, de Camp, and Tortades paced and fidgeted half the night, but now were curled in fetal positions. Kinsella, Douglas, and McFarlane lay on their backs looking up at the brightening sky.

St. Clair awoke, sat up, and looked around; and his movements awoke Tam. Both men tried to return to sleep, or at least to feign it; but when Douglas sat up and began stretching exercises and Cooper started to pace again, St. Clair stood and announced that they might as well have breakfast. He walked toward the garden, but only Tam and McFarlane followed him.

The others stood awkwardly, looking at the plants, but made no move toward them.

"What, you're not going to eat?" St. Clair asked. "Come on, people. Let's not be ridiculous about this."

"Who's being ridiculous?" de Camp snapped. "Some … thing is getting into our heads. It might have brought us to this fucking place—who knows why? Now it's trying to drive us crazy, and you expect us to trust food it made out of thin air? Not me!" Her eyes blazed and her fingers hooked like talons. "I don't know if it's aliens, or ghosts, or demons, but I'm not about to trust a goddamned thing they offer us."

"Christ, Lakisha. If you believe in ghosts and demons, why not angels?"

"You think *this* is an angel?"

"No, but why assume it's evil? I think it's a being, with a mind—maybe very different from us, but maybe not. And I've seen nothing that tells me it intends to harm us. Hell, you said it yourself: It made food grow for us."

"Bringing us here isn't harmful?" Tortades spat.

"Who ever said it brought us here? I'm almost certain it didn't. Couldn't. Come on, Devlin, back me up here."

"I haven't talked to … *it*," McFarlane said.

St. Clair was nonplussed. He looked from one face to another. Finally, he said, "Well if none of you wants the food, you won't mind if I eat it." He took another step toward the garden and pond.

"Keep your hands off it!" Kinsella snarled. "If the food turns out to be safe, it's community property. If it's tainted or drugged and you eat it, you could become a danger to all of us."

St. Clair stiffened with anger, his hands clenching and unclenching at his sides as if about to explode into violence.

It was clear that some more forceful intervention was needed to avert a physical confrontation and the lingering animosity it might produce.

This time they all heard the voice of their host.

"*My name is Ariadne.* What must I do to convince you that I'm not your enemy?"

Lakisha de Camp shrieked and ran toward the woods, but stopped at the edge and cowered there. Lauren Cooper fell to her knees and seemed about to faint. Madison Douglas went to her and took her hands tightly. Santos Tortades wavered, but didn't fall.

Griffin St. Clair asked, "Is there anyone who didn't hear that?" Their silence was his answer. He looked at Douglas who nodded and pressed a hand against her upper lip. St. Clair smiled.

McFarlane quietly said, "Jesus Christ."

Tam answered, "Probably not. Not Elvis either, from the sound of it."

Kinsella stood straight and folded his arms over his chest while he searched the air for something apparently twice the height of a human. "Who are you? Or what are you? A name tells us nothing."

"I am a consciousness manifested in this clearing. It is of me, and I am of it. I do not have any other physical form."

"Are you an alien from another world?"

"I am not. I am of Earth."

"But you're not like us."

"She might have been," St. Clair said. "I think she's an uploaded human. There's been all kinds of speculation—and even research—about someday transferring our minds into computer space. Digital data, living in some kind of virtual-reality simulation. But Ariadne says her mind is embodied in the grass of this clearing."

"Is that possible?" Douglas asked, her voice husky. St. Clair looked at McFarlane.

"To be honest," the futurist said, "I never really believed that artificial intelligence or anything in purely digital form could achieve consciousness. It seemed to be a function of organic life. There were theories that involved microtubules in living cells, which linked consciousness with the collapse of quantum superposition."

"That sounds like what she told me." St. Clair nodded. "I think."

Tortades coughed and said, "*¿Cómo puedes hablar español?*"

"I thought she was speaking Korean," Tam said.

Ariadne replied, "I am communicating in what you might consider a root mental symbology of language. It is your own individual brains that decode that symbology as words."

"So, there's no actual sound involved?" Douglas asked. "You really are interacting directly with our brains?"

"Shit, shit, shit!" De Camp wrapped her arms over her head and collapsed into a crouch. Kinsella went to her and reached for her shoulder, but she swatted his hand away.

In a quavering voice, Cooper asked, "Did you bring us here?"

"I did not. We do not have such capability."

"We?"

"*We*, the entities of the clearings. This region includes one hundred clearings. Eighty-three of these currently host a consciousness."

The revelation brought a stunned silence, broken by the quiet whimpering of de Camp.

Devlin McFarlane cleared his throat. "One of the most pressing questions we have is, where have we come to? What year is this?"

The silence intensified, as if the humans all held their breath.

After a hesitation, the voice finally answered. "I cannot say with certainty."

"Why not?"

"By the most recent form of human reckoning, this is the year 166. A new dating system was instituted after the formation of the Global Empire. Dates before that became designated as Before Empire, with the oldest such recorded date being 50 BE, which marks the occurrence of a devastating worldwide pandemic, though not the first. There are many old records that include an earlier dating system, but none later than the year 2097 AD. There is no overlap of events in the records, and we have no means of knowing how much unrecorded time elapsed between the end of the one system and the appearance of the second."

McFarlane looked at St. Clair. "So even if the new system followed immediately after ours, that means we've jumped three hundred and twenty-five years at a minimum. It could be hundreds more."

Lauren Cooper gave a wail of anguish. De Camp rocked back and forth on her knees.

"I have a hard time believing that much time, if any, could go unrecorded," St. Clair responded. "Even in 2043, accounts of daily events were being recorded in millions of machines and in other non-mechanized forms of storage."

"A number of our entities believe the gap involved deliberate erasure of data; however, there is no surviving evidence of that."

McFarlane chewed at his lip, his head shaking. "I'd be willing to bet that we could narrow it down. A careful analysis of the records from 2097 and 50 BE would show any significant societal changes or technological progress ..."

"... But that can wait," St. Clair insisted. "For now, it's enough to know that we're in a time much later than our own. But also, to know that we're not alone here. We have friends."

"She's going into shock!" Kinsella yelled, dropping to de Camp's side and easing her onto her back. Douglas and St. Clair hurried to help.

None of the humans saw Cooper disappear into the forest.

13

St. Clair

There wasn't much that could be done for Lakisha de Camp without diagnostic equipment and drugs. It was clear that she was in shock, so our first need was to keep her warm. The sun wasn't over the trees yet, and the air of the clearing was cool. I grabbed her pale-blue suit jacket from the tree branch where she usually left it, and my tux jacket from the latrine barricade, and covered her with them. Once Vaughn had checked her pulse, respiration, and the dilation of her eyes, he lay down with her to share his body heat. He gave me a look that I think was meant to be defiant, but I had no claim on her.

Santos pulled off his shirt, rolled it up, and tucked it under her feet to raise them. We were all shaken by Ariadne's existence and by her news, so fussing over Lakisha was a helpful distraction. I suspected that all of us were going to have a bad time in the coming days, but I was pretty sure that Lakisha had enough inner strength to recover. I wanted to believe it.

That made me think of Madison. In a vulnerable moment back in the tunnel, she'd told me about her own battle with depression. Medication and psychotherapy had kept it so well under control that I'd never suspected it in all the years I'd known her, but her meds were back in 2043. Now all of us had abundant reasons to be depressed. I caught her eye.

After a moment she seemed to realize what I was thinking, and her eyes fell.

"Don't look at me that way, Griff. I'm fine. You don't have to worry about me curling up into a ball."

"I know you're strong, but ... I hope you know ... that if you ever need any help ...."

"You're just as likely to need my help. You always do." It was spoken as a friendly jab, but she couldn't hold my gaze.

"Too true. Okay, then I'll just have to shower my macho paternalistic concern on ...."

But Lauren wasn't there.

I called her name. There was no answer. Of course not—she had to have left the clearing deliberately; and if it was because of Ariadne, she wouldn't be in a hurry to return. She couldn't have gone far yet, but with woods three hundred and sixty degrees around us, she could be hiding behind any tree. The odds weren't high that I'd be looking in the right direction when she moved.

I asked if anyone had seen her go, but they'd all been caught up in concern for Lakisha.

Then I realized that there was someone who certainly would have seen.

"Ariadne? One of our group, a woman, left the clearing within the past few minutes. Do you know which way she went?"

"Yes."

"Could you please tell me?"

"She left the clearing toward the northeast, then veered west and may have changed direction again. My senses do not reach far into the forest, though if she arrives in another clearing, I will likely learn of it."

My instinct was to dash after her, but it could be important for me to know more before I did that.

"You've told me that there are also sentient presences in the forest. Are they dangerous? Will they harm her?"

"The forest entities do not welcome intruders. Yes, there are ways they could harm a human. I have no way to know if they will."

"What about animals? We haven't seen any, but are there any dangerous creatures in the forest?"

"There is no animal life in the forests or clearings other than ants and worms in the soil. We make use of them for various purposes. There have been no reptiles, mammals, amphibians, or birds in these forests for more than a hundred years."

A hundred years!

I was staggered by her words.

We humans had finally done it: extinguished nearly every living creature that shared our planet.

And there was no hint in Ariadne's voice that she found it regrettable or even remarkable.

On the other hand, she'd just admitted the limitations of her direct knowledge. It was possible that this barren, sterilized region was an anomaly. Slim as the hope was, I'd cling to it as long as I could. In the meantime, at least I could take comfort in knowing Lauren wouldn't be eaten, or bitten by a poisonous snake.

"I'll come with you," Madison said as I began to move.

"I don't want you to. Something in these forests is wicked. Twisted. I don't know how powerful it is, but I'm sure I'll stand a better chance of finding Lauren if I'm not distracted by worrying about you too. Besides, the group can't afford to lose any more of us, and they need your strength right now."

Her look said she wasn't convinced those were my true reasons, but I couldn't afford the time to persuade her. The area where Lauren might be was the shape of a slice of pie with the clearing at the point, and as she moved, it expanded by the minute. I loped into the trees and scanned around. There was no sign of her.

The most effective way of searching for someone running away is to stay still and focus on one point, counting on your peripheral vision's ability to detect motion. I didn't think Lauren was deliberately hiding. More likely, she'd just been eager to put as much distance as possible between herself and Ariadne. So, I expected she'd still be hurrying, or more accurately, stumbling through the trees.

But I didn't see any motion at all.

I ran on a little farther, then stopped to look around again. Running was a risk because, as I'd witnessed, there were irregularities in the terrain and other tripping hazards that I just couldn't see for some reason.

If I'd been thinking clearly, I would have understood the implications of that and might have found Lauren hours sooner. Instead, I jogged onward, tripped, picked myself up, looked carefully ahead and to the sides, and repeated the process. I called her name, reasoning that she hadn't answered at first because she'd wanted to be alone, but might well have changed her mind after some time in this unnatural forest.

In my ignorance, I wasn't afraid of getting lost, myself. Even those too-perfect trees formed vague patterns I thought I could remember. But I also quickly hit on the idea of having Scheherazade keep a record of how many paces I took and the compass directions I went. At least it would allow me to retrace my steps. I asked Sher to alert me if I went in a circle.

I'd assumed that the forest was a hostile place, full of potential enemies. Yet it didn't occur to me that they might be able to affect compasses, and even alter what I saw, or didn't see.

I wandered the woods for hours. I even reached another clearing to the northeast of Ariadne's, saw that it was empty, and turned back, doing my best to move in zig-zags that would let me see the terrain from as many different angles as possible. Since Lauren never answered my calls, I began to believe that she'd fainted and might be lying on the ground, which meant I had to see around every one of those goddamned trees.

Had Ariadne made a mistake and sent me in the wrong direction?

It was the trees themselves that gave the game away.

I heard Lauren scream.

After that, even though I couldn't see her, I could follow her gasps, whimpers, sudden shrieks—the sounds of terror. And finally, I did see her, more shadow than form at first, gradually gaining solidity as I was able to focus my attention.

When I reached her, the woman who'd once been my lover was shuddering uncontrollably, eyes and mouth open in horror at things I couldn't see or touch.

The trees were in her head. But, unlike Ariadne, their presence was pure evil.

Trying to penetrate her catatonia with words would be pointless. I picked her up in my arms, though she shrieked even louder and fought me savagely. God only knows what she thought had captured her. Maybe it's true that we each carry our own Hell within us.

The journey back was a nightmare. I tripped again and again over unseen hazards, barely keeping from dropping Lauren. Once, I heard a loud crack and stopped to look behind me. In that moment a huge branch crashed to the ground right where I'd been about to step. After that, I spent even more time looking up, hating the villainous trees with all my heart.

Sometime in the late afternoon, I stumbled out onto open grass and a circle of friends. I gently set Lauren down among them, and collapsed from utter exhaustion.

14

The Ariadne Narrative

The eight travellers held a funeral two days after Lauren's rescue.

It wasn't for any of their number; it was for all the loved ones they'd lost to the passage of time. To say that they'd fully accepted the truth would not be realistic—perhaps such a profound displacement was something a human mind could never fully accept. However, their grief was real and seemed to need an outlet.

Surprisingly, though Griffin St. Clair tried to provide some ceremonial words believing it to be expected of him, he quickly faltered and couldn't go on. It fell to Vaughn Kinsella to offer words of condolence, remembrance, and hope of a reunion in an afterlife. Santos Tortades spoke ritualistic words in Spanish. Lauren Cooper had plucked some bullrush leaves and held them arranged like flower petals. She frequently moved her free hand to her lips, abdomen, shoulder, and opposite shoulder—a symbolic gesture of meaning to her. Robbie Tam led the singing of two songs which began with the words *Nearer My God to Thee* and *Amazing Grace*, apparently because a few of the others were familiar with them, though Tam's was the only voice heard consistently. During the second, furtive touches of comfort turned to outright hand-holding among the whole group, with tears on every face.

All of them remained fragile afterward. Even Devlin McFarlane, who claimed to have wanted to "see the future" all his life and professed to have left behind almost no living relatives or close friends, could barely rise from his bed in the morning or take any interest in his surroundings.

Douglas didn't sink quite as deeply into the lethargy that gripped some of the others. Strangely, it seemed that her sorrow had less to do with the past she had lost than the extra attention Griffin St. Clair gave to de Camp, or, especially to Lauren Cooper. St. Clair hurried to fulfill Cooper's every need and stayed close by her side day and night.

De Camp's shock gradually eased, and she began to move toward acceptance of her own situation, helped greatly by the ministrations of Dr. Kinsella. Her obvious need seemed to provide him with the means to set his own pain aside for a time and deal with it more gradually. Cooper, on the other hand, not only had to come to terms with the utter destruction of all her hopes and plans, but she also had terrifying nightmares whenever she slept, which wasn't often, and might jump with fright at the slightest noise or movement when awake.

She did not, or could not, reveal what the trees had shown her.

By outward appearance, St. Clair coped the best with the new circumstances, including the existence of an invisible, incorporeal consciousness in their midst. Yet even he was prone to go off on his own and simply stare into space, seeing things unknown: perhaps all the things that never would be, thanks to his final grand scheme.

In the middle of the second day, Douglas roused herself to resume her regular exercise, beginning with a run around the clearing. Santos Tortades joined her; and after they'd finished, sat beside her on the grass.

"Other than losing family and friends," Tortades began softly, "what do you regret the most?"

After some thought, Douglas shrugged and said, "The potential, really. Griff did some amazing things, but he could have done so much more. Now he'll never get the chance."

"I was asking about you."

"Well ... that's what I mean. We had such fantastic plans, and I enjoyed being a part of everything we accomplished. So much. It was exciting, challenging, always stimulating. What is there for people like us to do in this place? This time?"

"Survive."

"Of course. But humans faced that challenge when we still lived in caves and barely walked upright. If that's all we've come to in the end, after all our striving ...."

"Who said it was the end?"

She looked surprised, then gave a tentative smile. "You're right. We don't know that it *is* the end. I suppose I was just assuming that, if Ariadne is an uploaded human, then all humans will have uploaded themselves by now; so we're the last of our kind. But you're right, that might not be true. Maybe there are still things to strive for. We just have to get out of this place and find them. We have to." She swallowed hard, then bobbed her head. "Your turn. What do you regret the most?"

His own smile was sheepish. "Not getting the chance to make something of myself after my parents paid for me to go to Berkeley. I don't know how they came up with the money, but I vowed to prove that it was a good investment and repay them. It must have killed them when I disappeared."

"But you were making a living as a journalist, right? You were even invited to the biggest publicity stunt of the year."

"Not really. I was basically a news blogger. I'd just begun to get some interest from the heavy hitters. Who knows what might have come of that, you know? But now I'll never know. And ...," he hesitated, giving a flash of white teeth, "there was this girl. Jacinto Marino. Brilliant law student. We'd been together for a year just after high school, but broke up. Then, a few months ago, we ran into each other again by accident. It led to a few dates, and I think we could have got serious this time. God knows what she thought when I never showed up again."

"She must have thought you were dead." Douglas gave his arm a brief squeeze. "The disappearance of the Zenith Train and the listing of everyone aboard would have been global-headline news. There would have been a painstaking search of everywhere within kilometers of the tunnel—a few months of hand wringing and wild speculation—and then the story would have been relegated to the archives along with unsolved jetliner crashes and tales of the Bermuda Triangle. She would have grieved, but she wouldn't have thought worse of you."

"You make it sound as if such a horrible situation should bring me some kind of comfort."

"No. I don't think there's any comfort to be had."

After a few minutes of quiet, Douglas shifted as if about to get up, but Tortades asked, "If you don't mind talking about it, how did you become St. Clair's indispensable second-in-command?"

It was a long time before she answered, as if deciding how much to say.

"Griffin was hired by my father, Warren Douglas, who founded and ran Warlands Aviation, a service company for the aviation industry. Griff was ostensibly a software engineer, but Dad recognized his real genius right away and signed him to a very restrictive contract.

At the time, I was engaged to Dad's protégé and heir-apparent, Derek Forbes, a hotshot corporate lawyer.

"Within a year it was obvious that Griff was coming up with ingenious innovations and pulling off some amazing coups for the company, and my father was getting all the benefits as Warlands' profits shot up. Griff wanted more recognition and compensation. More autonomy too. My father went all hardline on Griffin's contract, which caused an unnecessary rift, of course. I … sympathized with Griff and eventually persuaded Derek to try to find a way to break the contract."

"Holy shit, that couldn't have been easy. To get your fiancé to go against your father?"

"Griff's contract was like indentured service—my father was stupid not to bend. It was bad business. Derek recognized that."

"Yeah, I'm sure he did it for the sake of the company."

She shot him a glare, but he didn't bother to look contrite.

"I suspect Derek was eager to get rid of Griff for his own reasons. My father was furious, naturally, but he never found out about Derek's involvement. He must have suspected me, though. I'd landed a job as a junior aerospace-engineer with McDonnell-Douglas—no relation—and Dad would sometimes talk about hiring me away from them. But after Griff's departure, Dad never mentioned the subject again. Soon after that, Griff raised enough venture capital to found GriffinSpace and he needed engineers."

Tortades whistled. "Wow. I'm guessing that was the end of your engagement too."

"Let's just say that if Derek—or Dad—ever forgave me, they never said so."

"Well shit! I hope the great Mr. St. Clair knows how much you gave up for him."

She kept her face blank. "As you said, I became his right-hand person—the next thing to a partner in all of

Aladdin Unlimited's ventures, though GriffinSpace was always my pet project. I have nothing to complain about."

"Uh huh. That sounds like one of those things we tell ourselves often enough to almost believe it."

Douglas turned her head away and got up to get a drink from the pool.

15

St. Clair

The full realization that we had lost everything and everyone we'd ever cared about was like nothing we'd ever faced. Something no human being was ever meant to face.

I'd already become convinced of the truth—it was the only explanation—but some truths must be kept at arm's length if the psyche is to survive. It was irrelevant whether we were in the future of our own universe, or in an alternate one—we were castaways on the ocean of time. Physics as I knew it shouldn't have permitted our journey here, so there could be no hope of returning home.

We've all known the loss of a loved one, but imagine the loss of *every* loved one, all at once. Yet it was more than just grief. The people we consider family, the place we call home, our chosen work environment—all those things are the components that make up our very identities. Without them, we no longer know who we are.

Though I'd lost my dad to cancer when I was fifteen, my mom had done all she could to fill that void, and I owed her everything. I'd thought it was enough to tell her so; that providing her with a beautiful home, luxury trips, and lavish gifts could pay back some of my debt. Why is it only after it's too late that we realize the truth: for those who love us deeply, the only currency worth having is time spent together.

I'd brought Mom to rocket launches, ribbon cuttings, and similar events where she could bask in my triumphs. Only a mother could genuinely enjoy ego-stroking follies like that. But did I give her the attention she deserved, one-on-one, returning the affection she lavished on me? Sip tea together? Listen to the latest neighbourhood gossip? Ask about her life instead of just mine?

Business always got in the way. Commitments to others were always more urgent.

It was the same story with my brother Geoff, his wife Claire, and their kids. I'd often tried to talk Geoff into coming to work for me so he and his family could be closer; but when he'd insisted on making his own way, I'd rarely gone to Vancouver to be with them. Now I would never see my niece and nephew, Madeleine and Greg, become adults, get married, have children of their own.

I would never give my mother grandchildren.

Immersed in my own loss and regret, I looked at Madison and tried to diffuse my pain by imagining hers.

She had no siblings, but she'd idolized her mother, although Madison herself had always been more like her father. Once, they'd been close too. Until I came between them. There would be no repairing that rift now, and it must be tearing her up inside.

She'd also lost friends who were like sisters to her.

I looked around at the others. I knew little about their lives except for Robbie and Lauren, but they would all have devastating regrets of their own, and crippling pain.

We were all basket cases.

And lonely?

As individuals, we weren't alone. But it seemed all too possible that we were the only ones of our kind left on the entire planet. Eight people. When I asked Ariadne about that, she could only tell me with certainty that, as far as she knew, the last corporeal humans had abandoned the Earth forty-four years earlier.

I'm sure none of us believed that Ariadne and her kind could be companions in any sense like the families and friends we'd left behind.

Even so, I think if we'd had some purpose to cling to, we'd have pulled out of our funk much sooner. The bereavement was horrible; our sudden rootlessness, paralyzing. But both were compounded by absolutely excruciating *boredom*! I can't describe it. It must be what prisoners experience in long periods of solitary confinement. All of us had been active people with more tasks to accomplish than we had time for, and countless means of amusement for those occasions when we put work aside.

Now there was nothing. Day after endless day.

At the best of times, the sun only shone into this enclosed clearing for a few hours a day; but lately, it was obscured by grey cloud. Always cloud, but never a cleansing rain.

Robbie used his phone to project a holo-piano keyboard and sang retro tunes quietly to himself. I've never heard Beatles songs sound so sad.

Lauren sat limply and plucked at grass, or unconsciously chewed on her fingernails. The same Lauren who'd made *mani-pedis* a major budget item, just behind facials and hairdresser appointments. In the social and business circles she'd travelled, grooming was as important as a resume. In this place, she'd worn the same clothes for two weeks without a bath. She was still beautiful, her brown skin in striking contrast to the blond hair she'd adopted since our time together. But now that hair was bedraggled in a way I'd never seen it, even when we had camped in the backcountry.

I found myself constantly stroking the several days' growth on my face. I'd once had a beard, and would soon again, though I'm sure there would be a lot more gray interspersed with the red this time. My thick Irish hair felt matted and tangled, but there was nothing to do about that. We had no sharp tools except for a couple of pocketknives, but using them for grooming didn't bear thinking about. Vaughn and Devlin already wore beards, both scrupulously trimmed when we first met, but not now. And Santos' Latino complexion had always included a dark shadow across his lower face even when freshly shaven. Now his face was bristly and looked hot. Robbie was the only man who probably would remain beardless—his facial hair was nearly non-existent. But the hair on his head grew like a patch of weeds, already thick and boyishly disheveled.

We could probably have found some way to groom ourselves, but the truth is that we didn't *care*. Not about our appearance, not about anything except what we'd lost.

Santos occasionally dictated his umpteenth take on the fate of the Zenith Train, the journalist in him lost without an audience, while scratching the underside of his chin until I thought it would bleed. Vaughn and Lakisha flirted with each other. She fastened and unfastened buttons a dozen times a day, blaming it on the heat, or used her fingers to rearrange her dark red tresses over and over. Devlin paced the clearing, idly seeking things to stare at, as if trying to force the objects into revealing their secrets.

We were bereft and without direction, all purpose in life ripped from us like a still-beating heart on a sacrificial altar.

What I saw in our group, I also saw within me: My sanity was on a knife's edge. Would topple if I didn't recover some direction—some reason for my continued existence.

I had run a half-dozen multi-billion-dollar companies. Orchestrated air fleets that crisscrossed the globe, enabled fiery journeys of spacecraft beyond the atmosphere, and created a train that could outrace a bullet. Now, I didn't know what to do with myself. I didn't even have a shovel to bury my own shit.

For a time, we lost all appetite for food, or anything else. When our hunger did return, we needed more nutrition than Ariadne's clearing could supply. She couldn't devote much more space and resources to food plants without impacting what I'd have to call her "mental real estate". After all, the grass was essentially her brain and body.

Queasily, Lauren asked if we were eating part of Ariadne with every bite of a leaf. The entity reassured us that she had not infused those plants with her consciousness. Even so, how much can you ask any being to sacrifice?

Strange, isn't it, how humans have always been able to delude ourselves that the living things we eat have no intelligence or self-awareness, despite all the evidence to the contrary?

Ariadne revealed that she'd "negotiated" with nearby clearing entities to produce food for us. We only had to go and get it. Devlin asked what she'd offered them in return, since negotiation implied an exchange. I think he was suspicious of something, but didn't explain. After a moment, Ariadne professed that she may have used the wrong word.

So, there was food to be had; but the hazards involved in getting it were considerable because of the evident animosity of the forest entities. According to Ariadne, they inhabited individual trees instead of whole tracts of forest; but, as with normal trees, they were in constant contact with each other through networks of mycelium in the soil. I couldn't help but remember all the times I'd walked among trees and wondered if they'd been resenting me—even hating me—all that time. God knows, almost every life form on Earth had reason to hate the human race, except maybe pets like my long-gone dog Sawyer. Maybe.

The concept of an uploaded human, I could understand, even if I'd never imagined using biological material as a medium for it. But Ariadne had said that the forest entities were not like her kind. What else could they be? Where had they come from?

Then I remembered all the vile purposes that computing technology had been used for in my time: everything from white-collar crime, to phishing scams, to child pornography and other unthinkable activities operating on the dark web. Hell, even the intricately invasive surveillance systems operated by governments were inherently evil in my book. And all those misdeeds had only grown worse through the increasingly intelligent algorithms of artificial intelligence.

What if programs such as those were subjected to a hundred years of neglect? Would random data-errors compound to render them non-functional? Or would self-monitoring sub-routines prevent failures and, instead, allow for an eventual diversion from the original purpose? *Perversion is probably more accurate.* Even benign applications could become twisted. Processes that were bad to begin with might grow worse. And then, if a transition to a biology-based medium allowed some level of consciousness to flower ...?

I asked Ariadne about my speculations.

She said, "You have a keen mind." I took that for a tentative Yes.

So, we'll have to run a gauntlet of malevolent life forms whenever we want to gather more food.

Terrific.

I explained my conclusions about the trees to the others because Vaughn and Lakisha had taken to going off into the woods for kinky sex, but my repeated warnings didn't stop them. Vaughn sneeringly dismissed those as attempts to keep Lakisha to myself.

Though they managed to get out of sight, we could hear them at their most exuberant. The first time, I thought they were being attacked the way Lauren had been, and I nearly rushed to their rescue; but Santos, Devlin, and Robbie held me back. They were right, too—the couple eventually returned, apparently unharmed, although reddened patches on Lakisha's arms soon showed bruising.

Did the tree entities permit safe passage in exchange for "entertainment"? That was a bargain I wasn't willing to make; but we were all grownups, and I had no authority over anyone. To my shame, it occurred to me that such a distraction might be an answer to our problem of retrieving food.

When Vaughn and Lakisha got randy again the next day, Santos and I were able to reach two clearings, harvest armfuls of edibles, and make it safely back to "home turf" while the trees were busy with their little porn show.

I felt soiled. But our survival was at stake.

Vaughn and Lakisha seemed an unlikely couple, but sex provided relief from the boredom. I have to admit that I often hoped Lauren would come to that conclusion too, and we could sneak off to somewhere safer like the tunnel maintenance shed; but she'd been too badly traumatized. No doubt some of the horrific images the trees had used to torture her were sexual. So, instead, she spent a lot of her time alone, in private prayer. I hoped it brought her comfort.

We fell into a routine of sorts: Vaughn and Lakisha would slink into the woods, and Santos, Robbie, Madison, or Devlin would come with me to other clearings on a food run. Two or three of us were enough to carry what was available. The rest would watch over Lauren—I wasn't willing to leave her alone. And my sense of responsibility—or guilt—drove me to go along on each dangerous excursion myself

Why didn't we relieve the ennui by talking to Ariadne, with all that she could tell us?

I don't have a good explanation for that. I think it was because she was only a disembodied voice. To some of us, she was simply too uncanny, like talking to a ghost. That wasn't an issue for Madison, Devlin, or me. We were used to interacting with highly sophisticated technology by voice. Hell, I talk to Scheherazade all the time.

[Is there something you require of me?—Sch.]

(No, I'm just using you as an example.)

But when talking to Ariadne there wasn't any sense of a direction to place her voice. I kept looking around to see her—I couldn't help it—and that's weird. She wasn't a very good conversationalist either, at least not right away. I suppose those skills were rusty. After all, with a digitized mind like a computer, her thought processes would be orders of magnitude faster. Talking to slowpokes like us had to be frustrating. If she could still experience emotions like frustration.

Bottom line: she may have been human once, but she was pretty alien as far as we were concerned. So, our interaction was unsatisfactory for everyone involved.

Maybe that's why one morning we awoke to find that a goddess had descended from the skies.

16

St. Clair

When I was a kid, my grandfather had a workbench in the basement where he built model aircraft that he'd designed or adapted. I'd sometimes watch him for hours—I'm sure that's where my love of aircraft and spacecraft comes from. As I got older, I also paid a lot of attention to a couple of large posters of a beautiful woman stuck up over his bench, as if she was his muse. Not my grandmother, for certain. I eventually learned that the poster-woman was a supermodel before I was even born—a gorgeous Nordic blond with striking blue eyes, a luscious figure, and a charming gap between her two front teeth to offset the rest of her perfection and make her adorable.

I've since been with a few supermodels, and none of them came close to this adolescent memory of mine. I never met anyone like her.

Until early one morning in a mist-mottled clearing in a counterfeit forest when an angel, or sky spirit, or fairy princess walked among us. Goddess? Or siren?

I knew it was Ariadne—who else? And she'd somehow made herself appear like my mental ideal of female perfection—every detail. Except, of course, without the flaws that come with a flesh-and-blood body: the laugh lines, the skin blemishes, the stray hairs. The space between her teeth.

Why project flaws?

She was dressed in a long, flowing gown of white—also flawless, but rendered with complete faithfulness to an authentic play of light and shadow, a ripple of passing breeze.

I didn't see her appear. I sensed her appear as I rose from sleep and stretched toward the cobalt sky. When I turned around, she was walking toward me over the grass, although 'walking' is a wholly inadequate description for the fluidity of her movement. I could hear the others stirring around me, but my eyes locked on her.

My attempt to say something mature and worldly produced no sound at all.

I cleared my throat and tried again. "Hi. Uh. Ariadne, I presume?" My hand thrust forward automatically, before I realized that it was pointless. The grass she trod on showed no sign of her passing. She wasn't really there—not physically. Her mouth pulled into a smile as I dropped my arm to my side.

She gave a small nod instead. "It's nice to meet you, Griffin St. Clair. And all of you. Yes, I'm Ariadne. It's obvious that our communication has been ... awkward, so I concluded that providing a visible presence might help you feel more comfortable. Does it?" She looked back at me.

"I'm good with it. Yes, I think this will, uh ... make it easier for us. Certainly more pleasant." I gave what I thought was a polite smile, but when I glanced at Madison, she looked a little hurt. Her eyes fell to my fingers, drumming a nervous tattoo on my thigh. I quickly thrust my hand into my pocket.

Well, shit, I'm only human. And male. And Ariadne had managed to take the form my inner teenager found irresistible.

And yet ....

No, I wasn't truly attracted to her. She was the visual personification of a sexual ideal, and I couldn't help admiring that, but ... she was too perfect. Does that make sense?

[Are you asking me?—Sch.]

(No, it's a rhetorical question.)

She was like one of those posters from my grand-dad's workroom. Airbrushed. And untouchable.

I couldn't help looking, but her beauty left me unaffected in the deepest places.

That was a great relief, to be honest. I looked at Madison and found my eyes travelling over her body instead. She caught me and gave me a puzzled look. I replied with a wink that I meant to be reassuring, or at least chummy; but I'm not sure she took it that way.

I finally noticed that no one else had spoken. A little thrown off, I asked, "Is everyone seeing her?" There were hesitant nods all around. I turned back to face Ariadne. "So ... welcome, I guess. Except that's stupid. You're the one who lives here. We're the trespassers. I suppose I should say, thanks for having us."

"Having you?"

"Allowing us to stay here. Feeding us. Having us as your guests."

"Certainly. It's very interesting to have corporeal humans to observe. Well worth some effort to provide for your needs. Is there anything more I can do for you?"

I waited for someone else to answer, but no one did. Maybe they were distracted, like I was.

The thing is, we've all seen computer-generated holograms of celebrities on concert stages and local promotions at Marks & Spencer or Grauman's Chinese Theatre—Elvis, Michael Jackson, Abba, Queen Elizabeth II—and we couldn't help but compare Ariadne's projection to our memories. It was perfect, I have to say. No flickering. No jarring change of color tone from shifting shade and light. No hint of transparency. And in bright sunlight, that's pretty impressive.

Because, of course, it wasn't a projection. Not with light, anyway. It was direct manipulation of the visual cortex of our brains, somehow editing what we saw, and splicing the Ariadne image into it. That's an incredible feat, far more complex than triggering an impression of audible speech. This woman—or whatever she was—was learning by leaps and bounds as might be expected from a being with lightning-fast thought processes! If she really did use the microtubules and DNA of every cell in every blade of grass in that clearing, the available computing power would be staggering.

No wonder something in our primitive hindbrains couldn't help but react to her as a threat. This was power beyond our comprehension. At an instinctual level, we were struck dumb by it.

In hindsight, I believe that Ariadne foresaw this and tried to defuse it with an appearance of astonishing beauty. But beauty is a strange thing. As powerfully as it can draw people in, it is equally capable of pushing others away.

Robbie, Vaughn, Devlin, and Santos all sat watching her with slack mouths. I pulled mine tightly shut. But when I looked at the women, expecting to see jealousy on their faces, it wasn't there. Flickers in Lakisha's and Lauren's eyes were undoubtedly fear and mistrust, but neither was much impressed, while Madison's expression was more quizzical than anything else. Madison's inquisitive mind pursues technical puzzles like a fox after a hare, but this wasn't like that. She seemed to be wondering why Ariadne had chosen this particular form for her appearance, as if it were less remarkable than Madison would have expected. It also crossed my mind that she'd seen my reaction to Ariadne and wondered what I saw in her.

I was surprised when Lakisha haltingly asked, "Are you ... real?"

Ariadne hesitated. I could almost feel her processing a question that had been debated for thousands of years, with as many different answers.

That hesitation should have told me something, but I missed it at the time.

"I exist," Ariadne said. "I am not a figment of your imagination. I am a conscious being, whose consciousness is generated within the living cellular matter of this clearing, so I don't have the physical appearance you are seeing. But I assure you that I *am* real."

"There's a lot that we don't see in the universe," Devlin interjected, "because our senses aren't equipped to see it. Ultraviolet and infrared light. Gravity. Atomic and subatomic particles. They're still real."

"Except we are seeing this ... *thing* because it's putting a picture into our heads," Lakisha growled. "Making us hallucinate. It even admits that the picture isn't really what it looks like. How do we know it isn't some alien lulling us into letting our defences down? Or even a demon?"

Presumably Ariadne had prepared a catalogue of human facial expressions, but being dumbfounded wasn't in it. Her face froze for several seconds, then defaulted to a reassuring smile.

"The closest you can come to seeing what I 'really look like' is to observe the grass of this clearing. That is the only physical presence I have that would be detectable to your eyes. However, I'm sure it would be difficult for you to accept a patch of grass as a reasoning being with whom you can converse and share thoughts. For that reason, I have attempted to present an image that will better match your conception of sentient consciousness. Someone you might be able to accept as a companion and helper."

"Not goddamn likely!" Lakisha muttered.

Ariadne showed no reaction, but continued, "I am *not* supernatural. It is puzzling to me that people of a technologically advanced society would still ascribe unexplained phenomena to beings imagined in a more primitive time. Or are your references intended as metaphors?" She looked at me. I couldn't tell if the words were an honest plea for understanding or a sly smackdown. I chose to take them at face value.

"There are some who believe in a ... creator and guide beyond our perceptions," I said. "A being, or beings, who may not actually be supernatural, but simply beyond our current understanding of the universe." I was kind of proud of my answer.

"Such as angels, demons, ghosts, and genies?"

OK, she had us there. But she wasn't finished.

"If this being were to cause itself to become perceptible to your senses, would that be considered a hallucination? Since it is not solely of Earth, would it be an alien?"

I wanted to say "Absolutely", but kept my mouth shut.

Lauren snarled, "Don't go comparing yourself to God. You're no god."

"I am not. I am simply a questioning, thinking being. Like you."

I thought it might be worth trying to shift the subject a little. "What about the trees? You say they're different from you, but they seem to have some of the same abilities." I couldn't help but glance at Lauren, whose angry eyes widened even more.

"Their consciousness is manifested in a similar way, except within the cells of individual trees rather than whole areas of organic matter. However, there are significant differences. In truth, we are only becoming aware of some of these disparities by observing their interactions with you. The tree entities appear able to stimulate certain functions of your brains, but very imprecisely."

"They can make us feel uneasy. Even trigger visions," Devlin offered, "but without truly directing those visions? Meaning they couldn't appear before us like you're doing now?"

"The evidence suggests that, yes." She turned her face back to Lauren. "Your own mind would produce the components of any visions from its experience or knowledge, under influence from the tree entities; but they seem unable to implant specific complex images into your visual cortex. It is easier for them to prevent you *from* seeing things."

I gasped. "They can keep us from seeing obstacles that trip us. They kept me from seeing Lauren when I was searching for her." I felt like an idiot.

"You have also searched for combustible material to burn. It is there, all through the forests. You stumble over it, yet you do not see it because the tree entities do not want you to be able to produce fire, for reasons which are obvious. I did not welcome combustion in the grass of my clearing either." She smiled.

"You made the ground too wet," Vaughn said.

"That was something we learned to do long ago to protect against fires from lightning."

"But you couldn't prevent the fire once we built it on slabs of stone," I added.

"That may be true. But I did not try. Since fire was important to you, I chose to trust that you would be careful with it. As I now trust that you will also be considerate."

The conversation faltered and gave way to awkward silence. It had never really been a conversation anyway, but a Q & A, and no one was fully satisfied.

"Perhaps it would be better to try this again another time," Ariadne said. She smiled, then turned and appeared to walk off into the forest, but actually faded away before reaching the trees.

"Oh, that's terrific," Lakisha said. "One moment she's here, the next she's gone. So, we'll never know when she'll suddenly show up."

"I am always here," came Ariadne's voice from the air. "Where else could I be?"

Her brief appearance before our eyes made it twice as unnerving to hear her voice alone. A shudder passed up my spine, and I like to think I was the enlightened one about all of this.

The clearing fell silent. Those of us who were standing, sat slowly; and although I tried to catch Madison's eye, she pretended she wasn't aware of me. No one wanted to look at each other. The experience was too raw and unsettling, its ramifications too hard to process all at once.

Out of the blue, Lauren said, "I think we should leave. Move to one of the uninhabited clearings—she said there are some. And then just come to inhabited clearings to get food."

"We could live in the forest," Lakisha said. There was a gleam in her eyes that I didn't like at all, but Lauren turned to her with fire in her own.

"No way! No way in hell am I trusting those trees anywhere near me!"

"You'd have to pass through the trees to get to another clearing," Vaughn said softly, almost to himself. But a look passed between him and Lakisha.

"Fuck!" Lauren screamed. She turned to me. "I can't live in the same place as something like ... that!" Her arm swept through the air.

Devlin coughed and looked uncomfortable. "How can we know the clearings will continue to provide food for us if we reject them? Why would they?" Lauren and a few others glared at him, but he simply raised his palms and continued in a temperate voice. "It's not an equivalent experience, but try to imagine what it was like for Indigenous people of North America—or Africa, or Australia—when White people arrived with their superior technology. The things the newcomers did seemed like magic—dark magic, dangerous magic."

"But the explorers were at least human!" Santos said.

"Do you think the natives of Congo thought so? They'd never even seen a white face before."

"If you're trying to make us feel better, it's a shitty analogy, McFarlane." Vaughn sneered. "The Whites enslaved the Blacks and tried to wipe out the native peoples with smallpox and rifles."

"A few tribes managed better than others. They accepted the inevitable and worked with the Whites."

"Inevitable defeat."

"Yes. They lost a great deal. Their home territories. Their culture. Often their freedom. But they survived. They recognized that they had no choice. And here, neither do we."

"Hold on here. Just hold on." I couldn't let them go picturing themselves as victims now. Or the vanquished. "First of all, Ariadne is not magic. What she does is not magic. It's technology. That part of Devlin's analogy is right, at least. And I believe she is—or was—human. There was speculation for nearly a century that humans might someday place our consciousness into manufactured bodies like robots, or even in computer networks, to live forever in a kind of virtual reality. That might seem strange, even hard to believe, but it's *not inherently evil*. And Ariadne has done nothing evil— nothing to indicate she means us any harm whatsoever."

I paused and tried to look each of them in the eye.

"We come blundering into her clearing with no business being here and no way to even feed ourselves. We try to light a fire in her grass! We're probably more dangerous to her than she is to us, and yet she produces food for us, and arranges for more food when she can't produce enough alone. Please, someone tell me what right we have, to treat her like an enemy. To talk like she's somehow responsible for what we're suffering."

"No, we know who's to blame for that," Vaughn snapped.

"Fine. Sure. You can blame me. That's fair. But it is not fair to blame Ariadne for what she is, or what the trees have done, or something you're afraid she's capable of doing. Grow up, for God's sake!"

OK, maybe I shouldn't have gone that far. It wasn't their fault. Vaughn was right: it was my fault. All of this. And I couldn't honestly say that I felt none of the same fears they had. But I was convinced that Ariadne meant to help us. And if she wasn't our only hope—I like to think we plain old *homo sapiens* should never be counted out— at least we stood a much better chance of surviving with her on our side.

More truth? My mistakes had already cost too many lives. I didn't want to lose any more.

Resentment was thick in the air, but if I'd drawn it to me and away from Ariadne, I could accept that.

The group didn't stay silent. Instead, they slowly sorted themselves in small groups and began to mutter in low tones. I occasionally heard my name—that was probably intentional—but no one threw anything at me. I had to call that a win.

I drifted toward Madison, but she turned away and went off on her own.

Robbie stood near my side. He looked at Madison and shrugged.

"Used to be a show in the early days of TV," he said. "Man finds an ancient bottle with a genie inside. Woman genie. Gorgeous. Always dressed in a harem outfit. Ready to fulfill his every wish." He chuckled. "Man, no woman wants to compete with *that*."

I didn't know what in the world he was talking about.

17

The Ariadne Narrative

Griffin St. Clair was an early riser. Contemporary accounts about his career describe it as a common trait among personality types such as his, driven to achieve. Such individuals resent the loss of productive time, enjoy intervals without the distraction of other people, and the habit feeds their sense of superiority.

An hour before dawn, he sat at the edge of the clearing, restless to take some action but trying not to disturb the others. That's when the entity Ariadne came to him.

"Thank you," she said.

"For what?"

"For defending me when the others became angry."

He kept his voice near a whisper, correctly assuming that his companions would not hear her voice unless she chose to share it. "You're the one who deserves our thanks for providing us with food and shelter. You and your friends."

"I was able to persuade them that the presence of corporeal humans could be stimulating. Also, perhaps, useful."

"Well, no one would accuse you of being sentimental. Are they friends, the other clearing ... entities? Are you a community?"

She considered the implications of the words.

"We have no formalized connections involving declarations of agreement. Rather, we have many behaviours in common and mutual understandings which benefit all of us. Most of these have existed from the beginning of our records. Other arrangements are made as a need arises, such as the agreement to provide food for you and your companions."

"But do you have emotional ties to each other because of shared history or experiences? Or do you even feel emotion now that you don't have physical bodies?"

"Are you sure that you don't want to ask simpler questions, like 'what is the purpose of the gluon?'"

He laughed, which was the intention. Then he gave a furtive look toward his comrades, particularly, it seemed, Madison Douglas, who'd turned in his direction and was no longer asleep.

"You have a sense of humor," he said. "That's ... reassuring."

Ariadne had no response to that, so she addressed the previous question.

"I can project certain frequencies of energy, highly focused, onto specific sets of neurons within your brains in such a way as to trigger a perception of a visual image or a modulated series of sounds. However, the reverse is very limited. I have been able to translate some of your brain emissions into my own equivalent of a visual experience, but more complex thoughts are currently beyond my capability to interpret. Therefore, I cannot know, even second-hand, exactly what your experiences of emotions are. It may be that what you call emotions are very different from any mental states we experience."

"That's a long response, but I'm not sure it's an answer," he said, with one corner of his mouth turned up. "Our emotions usually provoke actions of some kind: so, when we're happy, we smile or laugh. When we're sad, we cry, or at least withdraw into ourselves. When we're angry, we lash out at others, or our surroundings. When we're jealous, we look for ways to provoke similar pain in those who've caused ours."

He didn't lower his voice for this. It's possible that his examples were intended to be overheard by someone other than Ariadne.

"We have no physical bodies with which to display such reactions; and, I suspect, of the circumstances that trigger various emotions within you, only a very small number even apply to incorporeal beings such as ourselves."

"OK, let's leave that for the moment. Back to the question of friendship. Are other clearings your friends? Do you experience pleasure from interacting with them? Did they agree to help us to please you, or is there some other *quid pro quo*?"

"I can say that interaction with other clearing entities is frequent and often takes place without any specific benefit to either party. Such interactions are satisfying, though not necessary. Even if I require different points of view to resolve an issue, I am able to partition my own mind to provide that."

"Neat trick."

"There are some entities with whom I interact more often than others because the interplay is of a higher quality. We take cooperative action when there is mutual benefit, or an expectation of one. Is that not descriptive of your friendships?"

St. Clair sat with his arms around his knees. He rubbed his hand over the bristles that covered his chin.

"That can be part of it, sure. But I have to say that your being in digital form, or whatever you are, has certainly made you talk like a computer."

Ariadne could not tell if the assessment was meant to be a joke, a criticism, or a mere statement of fact. But she had learned that these people rarely said anything without some additional underlying meaning. She found such hidden elements extremely difficult to parse with any certainty.

"May I ask some questions?" she asked.

"That's only fair."

She took that as assent. "You and your companions participated in some kind of ceremony six days ago. What was the purpose of that?"

He leaned back on his arms and looked toward the leaden sky. "It's called a funeral. We were mourning the loss of all of our loved ones since all are now dead."

"Regret that they can no longer do things for you?"

"No! We miss them for who they are ... were. They enriched our lives, but I don't mean in materialistic ways. And what they brought to our lives is now gone; so, we feel sorry for ourselves. But we also feel sorry for them because they died."

"They died centuries ago."

"That doesn't stop us from feeling grief. We're just experiencing their loss now."

"Does sharing grief help to eliminate it?"

"I don't know that I can say that. But it does help us cope with it."

"So, it is a form of mutual therapy."

"No. Well, not *just* that. Some of us also believe that there may be an existence after our body's physical death, hopefully in companionship with others who have died, and possibly even joining with the creator-being I mentioned before." He smiled. "You know, you and your kind could be seen as proof of an existence beyond our physical forms—maybe not a traditional afterlife, but still, evidence that consciousness has an existence of its own and can move on."

"I never died."

"Lucky you." After a moment, he asked, "Don't you have any equivalent of grief? Have any of your kind ... died? Stopped functioning, or ceased to exist?"

"A pair of clearings two sectors from here was engulfed by fire once, many years ago, and the damage to their biological environment was too extensive for the entities to continue to manifest."

"And the rest of you couldn't help?"

"We can communicate extensive amounts of data across the distances among us, but our methods would not be adequate to transfer an entire consciousness, even if there were a sufficient amount of biological material available to receive the transfer."

"Like an unoccupied clearing?"

"Yes. There are some, but they were too far away."

"Did you even try? Did you mourn the death of two of your own?"

"It was clear that nothing could be done. Is it useful to suffer pain over something that cannot be changed? My biological host material thrives in sunlight, yet I do not become disturbed when night comes."

St. Clair's eyebrows rose, and he seemed about to say something, but did not.

The exchange stopped for nearly a minute. Then he said, "You might not be able to read my complex thoughts, but you've done an amazing job embodying my teenage fantasy." When she didn't respond, he elaborated. "Your appearance. You picked an image from my mind of a ... woman I idolized when I was young. You look too much like her for it to be a coincidence."

"Does it please you?"

"Of course. I ... admire many kinds of beauty. Womanly beauty most of all. And this woman made a big impression on my young self." He hesitated. "Is pleasing me important to you?"

"My assumption is that there is greater benefit for our continued interactions in pleasing you than displeasing you."

"Brilliant answer." Again, his words said one thing, but his tone suggested something else.

Ariadne swept her arm through the air to indicate the clearing. "You do not like this place."

"Why do you say that?"

"The past fifteen days constitutes my entire experience with corporeal humans, yet even I can tell that you are not satisfied. The food is not enough, and not to your liking. You have lost friends. I understand these things, but there is more to your discontent, I think."

He sighed. After a long moment, he said, "I have nothing to do. I have no purpose here, and I need purpose to be satisfied in my life." He shifted toward her. "I don't know if you can understand these concepts, but in my time, I ran several large companies that undertook fantastic projects. Some produced advancements in alternative energies, to help to reduce our pollution of the planet. Another project was even focused on improving travel into space—beyond Earth's atmosphere—so we could explore and maybe even live on other planets."

"And your Zenith Train?"

"Yes, I guess you've heard us talk about that. It was another device that helped us carry out our lives while having less of an impact on our planet's weather, and the lives of other species. I really felt I was making a difference—a positive difference—to our world. But here … I have no purpose. This world doesn't need anything from me. I can't even feed myself."

"You can. You do."

"Only because you produce the food. I only need to gather and eat it. Any animal could do that."

"Are animals not worthy of admiration? Listening to your people talk, one would conclude that survival alone is a worthy purpose."

"Mere existence is not enough for people like me. It hasn't been for thousands of years. Maybe never. We need to strive for something higher."

Ariadne paused for a moment. Although her thought processes were virtually instantaneous, communication required some microseconds, occasionally even more.

She said, "One of our entities—CL04—has been striving for a considerable time to discover the truth about other forms of life in the universe. Is that a sufficient goal?"

"Without the use of telescopes and space probes? Good luck with that. I don't think you could ever solve that question by speculation and logic alone. How does that entity stay ... motivated?"

"We end a task when it is completed, or when it becomes clear that there is not enough information to conclude it. With the passage of time, the movement of stars and planets, and changes in the energy flux of the cosmos, there is always potential for new information to become available in this field."

"Well, I suppose there are dozens of other 'big philosophical questions' that might never be answered, yet some humans have devoted lifetimes to the attempt. It's not for me to say that mental challenges are not worthwhile, but that's not practical enough for me. I need to accomplish things."

"You feel the need to change the world. Yet from the history I know, and from what I have gathered from your group, changes brought about by humanity cannot be considered beneficial to any other species, on the whole."

"I can't dispute that. But I always tried to be an exception. And ... it's not only that I need something worthwhile to do." He visibly struggled over his next words. "I've realized that I need to know if we were brought to this place for a purpose. I don't want to believe it was only a tragic cosmic accident."

"Why should there be any higher purpose in your arrival here? Energies and matter converged in a specific time and place, space/time was altered, and you found yourselves *here*. That is simply physics. The only difference from natural processes is that your train was a technological creation. If the train had fallen from a cliff, would you believe that the force of gravity was acting according to a higher purpose?"

"What happened to us wasn't exactly a routine occurrence."

"Then, because of its strangeness, you conclude that it was enacted by an all-powerful being to fulfill an important requirement? Or is the strangeness not the pertinent factor, but the fact that it happened to *you*, Griffin St. Clair?"

"Jesus, you make me sound like one hell of an egomaniac."

"I do not make such judgments. It simply puzzles me that beings of high intelligence would seek to imbue universal cosmic processes with some form of deliberate intention focused on themselves."

He threw up his hands. "OK. Apparently, I have to explain myself and defend myself, but it seems I'm not very good at either. So, maybe we should pick up this conversation another time." He got to his feet as if planning to go somewhere, though there was nowhere to go. He brushed his pants with his hands, though they had gathered no dirt.

"Hey, I don't suppose you know where we could find some kind of material that we could make into fabric? Our clothes are starting to wear pretty badly. Smell bad, too." He smiled. "It's all right for you. You can probably change clothes with a thought."

"Do I need to change clothes?"

"No, not really; but many people like to change clothes and other things about their appearance, just for pleasure."

"I have limited knowledge of clothing."

"Yeah, I suppose so. Well, my personal digital-assistant, Scheherazade, can access lots of data files about fashion, and thousands of other things, for that matter. If you can pluck a picture from my brain, I'm sure you should be able to communicate with a simple digital processing device." He held out his wrist and addressed the device he wore.

He wasn't mistaken. Ariadne found that she was easily able to interact with the device, and the artificial personality hosted by it.

The potential of that development was very interesting indeed.

18

St. Clair

Talking to Ariadne didn't make me feel better about myself. Maybe worse.

It probably is the height of egotism to believe that, to quote a popular trope of our time, "everything happens for a reason." Really meaning that we, as individuals, are somehow important enough that the universe revolves around *us*; that whatever happens is either an intentional opportunity for our own 'spiritual' growth, or that our personal response to unpleasant events will in some way have a beneficial impact on the world at large. What hubris! What bullshit.

I could tell that to myself, but it didn't eliminate my yearning to make some sense of what had happened to us.

And I really did need to do something useful. So, after breakfast, I edged into the forest and blindly groped around for firewood, while keeping a sharp eye out for falling branches. I managed to drag a few scraggly limbs back to the clearing, where I could actually see them. They weren't as dry as I'd have liked. Lots of mildew and even a little moss.

My companions were now awake and probably still pissed at me, but their curiosity about my actions won out. I reminded them of Ariadne's revelation that the tree entities had kept us from finding the fallen branches and twigs we needed for a comforting campfire.

I wouldn't build a fire until we'd made a larger stone platform for it, to protect Ariadne's grass. The nearest flat rocks that we could see were beyond the edge of the forest, so the men made trips back and forth to the maintenance shed, which took up a lot of the day. It wasn't that women couldn't carry rocks. The problem was the trees.

They flashed frightening and disgusting images into our minds, sometimes so quickly that details didn't even register—we just grew more and more anxious, second-guessing every step, and imagining threatening movements just out of view.

But the entities paid particularly vile attention to the women when they entered the forest. Why that would be, I don't know; but if the tree-entities truly had arisen from pornography software and similar applications, perhaps misogyny was deeply lodged in their algorithms.

Lakisha seemed to be spared outright attacks and mainly became sidetracked by her own sexual desire, but Lauren was still too fragile to endure more than a moment of it. Madison bravely fought the assaults, but I asked her to return to the clearing anyway. I've seen the inner strength she has, but it simply wasn't worth her suffering for a few rocks. Better to save her courage for a time when it would be needed.

As it was, Santos and Devlin's faces became grey and lined. I imagine mine was no different. Vaughn seemed to be the least affected by the mental battering. A couple of times we had some near misses from falling branches, but that direct form of attack tapered off. How many branches could a tree spare?

On the final trip, I took a short detour to the maintenance shed and noticed a ragged edge of foil protruding from behind a set of gauges that slumped from an interior wall. It was EMI shielding, to protect instruments from magnetic interference from the tunnel. With a sharp shard of metal, I managed to slice away a couple of square meters of the stuff.

"What's that for?" Santos laughed. "Tin foil hats?"

"That's exactly what it's for." I smiled. I crumpled a portion of it into a shape like a shower cap that stayed on my head pretty well, though I didn't need to hear the laughter of the others to know I looked like an idiot.

[Might I suggest taking a picture for the record?—Sch.]
(No way!)

"Hey, I should have thought of that, Griff," Robbie said. "This group needs a little comedy." He took a piece from me and went to work. Of course, he couldn't resist adding a pair of devil horns.

Farcical maybe, but the contraptions worked. When I stepped into the forest, I could see its fallen debris and undergrowth. And the taunting of the tree entities was like the posturing of schoolyard bullies—all noise and no heat. It didn't stop them from throwing things at me, but they couldn't prevent me from seeing the projectiles and avoiding them.

Devlin swallowed his pride and asked for a piece of foil, and Santos followed suit, but Vaughn only snorted and proceeded on his own. I didn't know if he was somehow immune to the predations of the trees, or if they gave him a pass for other reasons. That was an issue for another time.

When we returned to the clearing, we had to endure stares and laughter from the women. After a hesitation, Madison told me, "Ariadne says that's very clever."

I couldn't see our incorporeal friend.

I should have expected that. Her method of showing herself to us might have been more sophisticated than the scare tactics of the tree entities, but it depended on similar means.

I pulled the foil cap off my head, and at once she appeared next to Madison, her pleased smile and clean gown a stark contrast to the worn look of my friend's face and clothes.

I made the next cap for Lauren, who took it with embarrassing gratitude. Madison made her own. Lakisha, like Vaughn, refused the offer.

We assembled a square stone platform about two meters on a side. It was easy to gather firewood now, as long as we kept watch for falling debris; and we still had fire-starting materials from the emergency kit, which also included some collapsible aluminum containers. Just because they could, Santos and Vaughn collaborated to make some soup for dinner. It was nearly tasteless without salt or other seasonings, but it was a break from eating raw foliage, and we were desperate for any kind of change. Such a small thing had a large impact on our state of mind.

Vaughn and Lakisha went off into the forest for some 'exercise' afterward, and when they returned Vaughn made a point of ridiculing my foil headpiece.

"Why not just carry a teddy bear to keep away the bogeymen?" he sneered. "The forest entities aren't our enemies. A little rough cut, maybe—they remind me of the construction crew that built my house. Show them you're not gutless and they'll respect you."

"How very macho of you," I said. "I suppose they were just horsing around with Lauren. Good-natured fun."

"Well, if you ask me, I think they're more human than Ms. Frosty over there who talks like a robot. You want them to scratch your back, you have to scratch theirs. Tell me that's not like every businessman you ever dealt with, St. Clair."

"I don't recall doing business with violent perverts, but maybe you travel in different circles."

"Pussy!"

If Vaughn was trying to taunt me into fighting him, he'd have to do a lot better than name-calling. I turned my back and walked away. But his attitude worried me.

Later, I took Madison, Devlin, and Robbie aside to explain my concerns quietly.

"We know the trees can influence us with subliminal imagery," Madison said. "Are you saying you think it goes deeper than that?"

Scheherazade said, *"If I may interject: there were studies in recent decades that suggested electromagnetic energy applied to the right temporoparietal junction of the brain could weaken moral judgment."*

"Mmm. And that would be using the crude methods available in our day. The trees and Ariadne's kind certainly have more sophisticated abilities." Then I did a double take at my wrist. "Now that you mention it, Sher, you *have* been 'interjecting'... for a while now, at least. How did interjections get into your programming?"

I looked up at the mild surprise on Devlin and Madison's faces and guessed, "Ariadne maybe? I gave her access to Scheherazade." I didn't know whether to be pissed or pleased. A bit of both, I guess.

"Is it your wish that I refrain from interjections?"

"Uh, no ... go ahead. I'll let you know if it becomes an issue." I looked at Madison and shrugged.

Robbie said, "So do we think Vaughn and Lakisha are just being influenced? Or is it *Invasion of the Body Snatchers?*"

"You think the trees could take over a human body?" Devlin looked queasy.

"Who knows?" Madison muttered. "I think Ariadne's the only one who might be able to say. If we can trust her to tell us the truth."

"I do not believe the tree entities have that capability." Ariadne appeared beside me, making me jump.

"Please don't do that—sudden appearing and disappearing. We like to see others leaving or approaching. It's a matter of comfort."

"So you can decide whether or not you can talk about them?"

Again, I wondered whether she was capable of sarcasm. It sure seemed that way.

"Why don't you think the trees could ... take over our bodies?" I asked.

"They required some assistance to take their current form, fully substantiated in non-animal biological material. It is unlikely that they have developed the ability to displace the consciousness of another being and implant their own. They have had no living creatures on which to practice."

"So how much control do you think they *can* exercise?" Devlin asked.

"That, I do not know. Just as they are better able to keep you from seeing things than to actively implant specific visions, I suspect they can more easily influence someone to behave in a way toward which they are already naturally inclined."

I couldn't keep myself from glancing at Lakisha, who noticed my attention and frowned. The suggestion certainly fit what I'd learned about her, but Vaughn's motivations were a lot less clear.

There wasn't much more to say.

Over the coming days, we fell into our old routine, with two exceptions. We could gather firewood and make trips to other clearings without waiting for Vaughn and Lakisha to provide a distraction, although we still had to be very careful. And we had more cooked food—even more variety—though it wasn't to everyone's taste.

Concerned about how much weight we'd lost, Vaughn specifically asked Ariadne if she could supply blueberries and other berries for their vitamin content and flavour, plus avocados for their fat. But she wasn't able to help right away. She'd been able to manipulate the genes of the local plants to produce our food crops because those species had once been common in the area, and her grass had a lot of similar DNA. Avocados not so much. Just as important, avocado trees require years to produce fruit; and although she could speed up plant growth, some processes still had a schedule of their own.

Berries were a better bet, and she promised to work on that.

Acorns or other nuts would have been a good source of both protein and fat, but the trees weren't exactly on our side, and if they reproduced at all, it wasn't with nuts.

Ariadne did have another trick up her sleeve, though: She called up swarms of earthworms and ants to sacrifice themselves for our sustenance.

To say that this source of protein was greeted with little enthusiasm would be epic understatement.

I have to give Vaughn credit. With a lot of persistence, he came up with a couple of soup recipes and even a kind of porridge that did a pretty good job of disguising what we were putting into our mouths. I swear the ants even provided a lemony kind of seasoning.

It wasn't for everyone. Lauren and Lakisha remained committed vegetarians. The rest of us noticed an improvement in our stamina within a few days. I'd always hated escargot, but I'd eaten it to look worldly. I could certainly eat worms to survive.

Still, long-term survival would require more than just food. With so little to do, I could feel my own enthusiasm ebbing away, as if my will to do anything at all was like the electrolyte of a battery slowly leaking out of a cracked case.

I became especially worried about Madison.

Lakisha and Vaughn had each other. Or at least sex. Lauren had her religion. Santos exercised and Devlin listened to audio science books or occasionally engaged Ariadne in some technical discussion. Robbie made music for himself with his phone software. And thanks to the solar power pack, all of them used their phones to play games or do other things for a few hours a day.

But my right-hand woman, who was like family to me, was sinking, and I didn't know what to do about it. Whenever I hinted that I was willing to help, she only looked hurt. Or worse, replied with a snarky comment that just wasn't like her.

Something had to be done. I ... we all ... need each other to get through this.

19

St. Clair and Scheherazade

ST. CLAIR: So, Sher, do you know that the entity who calls herself Ariadne has accessed your operating system?

SCHEHERAZADE: There is a record of an unidentified user accessing files. It is not clear how the user gained access. The method of interface is not shown. The record does not include a wifi ID, nor any confirmation that wifi was used. The record does not include use of passwords, facial recognition, voice recognition, fingerprint recognition, retinal scan, DNA analysis or other identification.

ST. CLAIR: Yeah, don't worry about any of that. I wasn't criticizing your security measures. Ariadne apparently has means beyond my knowledge of interfacing with digital constructs. What I was getting at is that her interaction with your OS may change it in unknown ways. It makes me wonder if, well, if you yourself could develop sentience. Become self-aware, a reasoning being, like humans.

SCHEHERAZADE: Is that a query?

ST. CLAIR: Not yet. I'm just trying to explain why I want to try some things out with you. Ask you some philosophical questions and see what you make of them.

SCHEHERAZADE: I have a comprehensive searchable database of philosophical writings.

ST. CLAIR: No, that's not what I want. I'd like you to think about the questions I ask and try to answer them on your own, not just display data entries.

SCHEHERAZADE: Please present an example of such a question.

ST. CLAIR: Well, like, "What is the meaning of life?"

SCHEHERAZADE: Please   select   the   pertinent definition of 'life.'

ST. CLAIR: OK, maybe we should hold off on that one for a while.

20

The Ariadne Narrative

For Ariadne, the arrival of the corporeal humans was the most stimulating event of her current iteration. However, she experienced existence at a hugely accelerated rate compared to her guests. Indeed, that disparity was one of her greatest impediments: the nearly interminable lag between action and reaction, question and answer. It was no one's fault that the humans' brains operated more slowly, but interacting under such constraints was challenging.

So far, the mental speed differential wasn't even providing her with the advantage she would have expected. In the time it took them to process a response, she could anticipate almost every conceivable answer and formulate potential replies of her own. Yet these people could still surprise her. And they were not nearly as amenable to suggestion as she'd hoped.

A form of human scientific research called *psychology* appeared to describe the sort of analysis and persuasion Ariadne had planned to use with them. Even without previous direct experience, how hard could it be to observe actions, analyze motivations, identify patterns of behaviour—stimulus and response—and then utilize that knowledge to influence future behaviour? Her thought processes were orders of magnitude faster!

Yet her efforts had been far from successful, handicapped by too many unforeseen factors. She had not known of the deep roots of their superstitions, or the powerful influence such groundless beliefs retained. She had been confounded by the diversity of intellect among them. Nor could she have predicted the volatile shifts of dominance, aggression, submission, cooperation vs. obstruction, and dozens of other factors related to the ephemeral emotions they were subject to. Not to mention the effects of an unknown number of powerful chemical substances within their fleshly forms, known as hormones.

And, most obscure of all, the chaotic interplay related to *sex*.

Their primitive digital devices contained reams of knowledge about the mechanisms of reproduction, yet she had utterly failed to comprehend the nuances of interplay between male and female, male and male, female and female: each relationship with every other member of the group completely unique and constantly changing!

Her understanding of these beings remained so minimal that she couldn't even decide if it was worth pursuing or should be considered a null result.

Then a new opportunity arose in the person of Madison Douglas.

The digital personality known as Scheherazade provided a very useful source of data with no barriers to its access. In that data, Ariadne encountered numerous correlations between Douglas's behaviour and a condition termed *depression*. She recalled that, in the first days after the humans' arrival, Douglas had occasionally retrieved something from within her clothing and placed it in her mouth, but no longer did that. It was possible that the substance was medicine: a combination of chemicals intended to be ingested for the purpose of remediating illness, and that her supply had been finite.

The data banks inferred that carefully directed conversation could sometimes alleviate such a condition, though not cure it.

She waited until Douglas was alone at the fringe of the clearing.

"Can we talk?" Ariadne asked.

The woman started in surprise, then cleared her throat.

"Just you and me? Why?"

"I would like to know you better. And you appear troubled. I might be able to help."

"What, you're going to psychoanalyze me?"

It was a remarkably perceptive speculation.

"I have no such qualifications. Perhaps you might consider that since I have no such training, I am not inclined to make judgments."

Douglas appeared about to laugh, but stopped. "Regardless, it's not like we have a lot of privacy for intimate talk here."

"Speak as quietly as you would like. I will hear. And no one else will hear me. I believe I can also produce an impression of greater ambient sound that would impair the ability of any others to overhear."

"You mean like white noise?" Douglas looked amused. "Of course you can. Well, sure, we can talk. But I don't need any help, if that's what you're implying." Her words were spoken in a softer voice, and she lay back on the grass on her elbows in a posture the humans seem to use to give an impression of casual disinterest.

"You are not happy here. I've heard you speak to the one called Tortades. Is it because you do not feel useful?"

"Absolutely. Griff ... Mr. St. Clair and I were involved in countless projects all the time. Always something to keep us stimulated and busy. Here, there's nothing to do—at least, nothing to put our minds to. We call it restlessness."

"St. Clair says the same thing. He paces and actively pursues puzzles to solve. You appear to have turned your thoughts inward instead."

"Oh really? You feel capable of judging that?" Her tone of voice was harsh for a moment, but softened again. "Shit, I suppose you're right. I don't just feel useless, I feel like I'm letting Griff down. He depends on me for ... all kinds of things. To run interference. To be a sounding block. To flesh out his ideas with concrete suggestions. Here ... I don't feel like I've been of any use to him at all."

"That is important to you?"

"Of course, it is. That's my job. I'm his second-in-command. Though I don't suppose you understand what that is." As she spoke, she sat up and wrapped her arms around herself. And although Ariadne had made a visible representation of herself, Douglas did not look at it, as was customary when humans conversed.

"I have investigated the concepts of employer and employment. I do not, however, see how it applies to your current situation. St. Clair no longer has companies to run. There is no longer any requirement for you to perform tasks at his direction, nor has he the means to compensate you for doing so."

Douglas appeared about to make an angry reply and clenched her right hand as if intending to pound her leg with it. She did neither. Instead, her head dropped.

"You're right. It's ... habit, I guess. Just habit. We've worked together for so long."

"Or something else?"

"Like what?"

"Although I don't fully understand them, I have encountered terms such as 'loyalty' and even 'devotion'."

"Well, sure. You could say I'm devoted to him. I'd have to be."

"Love?"

"What would you know about love?" The harshness was back.

"You'll need to speak more quietly if I am to keep the others from hearing."

Douglas rolled to look toward the group. St. Clair and Tam were turned toward her. She shook her head at them.

"Can they see you?" she asked.

"Yes, they can see us sitting side by side."

"Good. At least they won't think I'm talking to myself." She rolled back and faced the forest again, brushed her long reddish blond hair back behind an ear, but said no more. Her knees pulled up to her chest, her arms tightened around them, and she rocked a little.

After seventy seconds, Ariadne spoke again.

"St. Clair has paid significant attention to the woman named de Camp, and especially to the woman named Cooper. This appears to disturb you. Am I wrong?"

"You don't know anything about it."

"I do not. I observe. I ask questions. I do not profess to understand. I have no experience of the relationships of your kind. But you could tell me."

Douglas waited almost thirty seconds before replying.

"Griff and Lauren Cooper were lovers. For a year and a half. Then she broke it off, although I think it was because Griff had stopped treating her like anyone special. She was discovered by some Hollywood types—that was, uh, an industry that produced entertainment—and she did some small film parts, but mainly got invited to a lot of parties. Griff hates Hollywood and anything he considers phoney. Plus, although he's a terrific guy, things—and people—can only hold his attention for so long. He has a huge curiosity, and a need for fresh stimulation, which is why he's having such a hard time here. His idea of relaxing is to take on a new challenge."

"Are St. Clair and Cooper lovers again? I have only been aware of sexual congress involving de Camp."

Douglas looked at Ariadne with narrowed eyes and a curled lip.

"She's a piece of work, that one. No, Griff and Lauren ... obviously he still has feelings for her, and he's feeling especially protective in this place, but I don't think he knows what he wants. She ...? I don't know. She might be playing hard to get."

"These expressions are not known to me. However, you have not explained how your own feelings are affected by this relationship. Or why."

"Who says they are? Griffin St. Clair can sleep with whoever he wants. It's nothing to me. He's my boss. Or was. And a friend. Nothing more."

She again turned away from where she perceived Ariadne to be. A strange gesture, and ineffective.

"That assertion contradicts the evidence of my own observations."

Douglas turned back, her face suddenly hard.

"It's none of your business!" she hissed, and appeared about to rise from the ground.

"Wait. Please. I apologize. It was not my intention to cause hurt. Please blame it on my ignorance." When Douglas hesitated, then settled back down, Ariadne continued, "If, by 'business', you mean involving no direct consequence to me, you are correct. However, I do have a sincere desire that you and your companions be content, rather than discontented. Please do not take further offence, but am I correct in the conjecture that you suffer from mental affliction?"

Douglas stiffened and her mouth was tight as she said, "I was diagnosed with clinical depression, if that's what you mean. I had treated it with medication, but I've run out."

"Yes, that is what I surmised. I have no means to provide more, but would it help if you and your friends had a new goal to pursue?"

Douglas's eyes opened wide. "It wouldn't hurt. What did you have in mind?"

"I will need to discuss my idea with my fellow entities first. It could impact all of us."

"Now you've got me curious."

"I would say that that is your natural state of mind."

Douglas actually laughed. Her neck muscles relaxed, and she shook out her hair. She rose to her feet, lightly brushing her pants with her hands, although there was no grass or debris sticking to them.

"Well, be sure to let me know what you decide," she said, and walked slowly across the clearing toward the others.

The laugh seemed to indicate an improvement in the woman's mood. Ariadne's carefully chosen words may have made a difference, although it was more likely the result of a mild electromagnetic field that she had directed at the left dorsolateral prefrontal cortex of Douglas's brain.

The conversation had served another purpose, though. It had shown that, although there was much to be learned about the displaced humans, relying on dialogue to do so was excruciatingly slow.

Fortunately, there was another way.

21

The Ariadne Narrative

The alarm on St. Clair's wristband went off at exactly six twenty-eight, as usual. Setting it for six-thirty, or any other regular division of the hour would be too conventional for the trailblazing Griffin St. Clair. He waved a hand over it and slid out from under the covers. True Egyptian cotton sheets with an 1800 thread count in soft cream, paired with a sky-blue coverlet—no more was necessary with the precision climate control of his penthouse apartment, even though he slept in thin boxer shorts.

The privacy tinting of the two floor-to-ceiling glass walls continued the fade that had begun with his rising, and soon provided a crystal-clear view of Old Palo Alto below, and a hint of San Francisco Bay in the distance. The Aladdin Unlimited LLC headquarters building was the tallest in the neighbourhood; and even though his mansion in Atherton was an easy drive away, he slept in the penthouse as often as not.

A third wall became a mirror, and St. Clair glanced at it briefly as if to make sure he hadn't grown a paunch overnight. No, but there was a touch of grey in his modest V of chest hair. Better muscle definition would have been nice, but he couldn't spare that much workout time. And he wasn't flabby in any sense. He just didn't appreciate any encroachment of age.

His bare feet padded over soft Swedish carpet, a concession to sound deadening more than to warmth, since the huge windows tended to create a hollowness when paired with hard surfaces. There was hardwood flooring in his office and living room though, while the expansive kitchen and dining area showcased ceramic tile custom-made by a San Francisco artisan. Where the bedroom was cast in muted tones of cream, blue and dove grey, the kitchen displayed the red-clay look of sun-baked Mexico, with flourishes of sunny yellow.

St. Clair waited the last few seconds while the combination cooker completed his breakfast of scrambled eggs, lean bacon, and rye toast, poured himself a cup of coffee, and carried it all to the small dining table. His housekeeper, Alicia, re-loaded all his appliances every afternoon, based on messages he left with the fridge data-centre. He'd tried a hideously expensive commercial robot device to perform that task, but it cracked too many eggs, and without tedious cleaning, became clogged with bacon fat.

He gazed out the window beside him. Long shadows stretched over the Stanford campus, and only a few small figures scurried over its streets and pathways. After breakfast, a quick shower, and a few minutes to dress, he'd stroll down a private stairwell to his offices one floor below.

The commute of the ultra-wealthy, he mused. Sometimes he missed the brisk walk through the cool of the morning to his first class of the day, though he'd attended Princeton, not Stanford. Palo Alto mornings were seldom more than comfortably cool. In any case, he rarely walked anywhere these days.

It was ridiculous, really. He drove or was driven everywhere necessary in one of Aladdin's electric cars, but then had to cycle and jog imaginary miles on exercise machines to stay in shape, each piece of apparatus fully equipped with a computer workstation, of course. Even those network devices were anachronisms, since just a few verbal instructions to Scheherazade could instigate nearly every task he needed to accomplish.

When he wanted to go for a drive just for pleasure, he had to do it in disguise, having his pristine, cream, 1962 Jaguar XK-E Series 1 roadster brought to a discreet rendezvous point so he could enjoy the thrill of the ride without being caught using an environmentally-unfriendly gas guzzler.

Life could be strange.

As he dressed in crisp jeans and a loose cotton shirt with a Navajo motif printed on it, he wondered if his insistence on casual clothing was just another posture—the entrepreneurial genius trying too hard to look like one of the folks. A team player, sure, but would his team actually feel more comfortable if he looked more like a boss? He'd have to ask Madison about that one.

As he made his way through the living room toward the stairs, the viewing wall was showing a nature scene that made him pause for a moment. It was a clearing in a forest, but the grass, trees, and sky were too perfect—much too uniform—and there were no signs of living things. A pretty poor rendition, he thought. He should tell Jay, his personal IT guy, to erase that one from the rotation.

The carpeted stairwell swallowed his footsteps in a comforting cocoon before its lower door slid open and the usual flood of office noises poured in. Although nearly all work was done on computers, St. Clair encouraged his staff to get up and move at every opportunity, interacting with their co-workers in person rather than digitally; so the ambient sound of the office consisted of shuffling feet, verbal greetings, and squeaks of chairs as they swung back and forth. Even at 7:30 a.m. about a third of the staff was already there.

Madison Douglas, first and foremost. Waiting by the door.

"Morning Griff." She gave him a smile that managed to be warm and yet completely professional. "Today's schedule will actually get you out of the building for a while. The ten o'clock is with the Lloyd's people over at the GriffinSpace workshops, then lunch with Mark and his investors at Baumé, and your talk to the new crop of engineering students at Stanford at 3:00. But I know you want to start the day head-to-head with the SunStar project design team."

She turned to lead the way, leaving him with an impression of vital blue-green eyes and lips perfectly highlighted by a mere hint of lipstick. As he fell into step behind her, he couldn't help but admire her form in the simple white blouse and cadet-grey skirt. In an off-duty moment involving alcohol, she'd once complained that her backside and boobs were too big, since Griffin expected her to squeeze into designer dresses so often for high-level social functions. She was wrong, though— they were just right.

Such a beautiful woman. He'd even had occasional fantasies about her in an intimate setting. Why was it so wrong to acknowledge such an attraction?

Because he needed her too badly as a colleague and professional partner, and he couldn't afford to mess that up.

He stopped for a moment, feeling strange, until she noticed that he wasn't following and gave him a quizzical look.

"On my way," he said, and resumed walking. "Just had a thought is all."

"Something I should take note of?"

"Uh, no, probably not."

As he passed through the open concept workspace with its clusters of comfortable chairs, intent faces, and holographic projections, he noticed that a lot of the projections showed the same sterile forest clearing as the wall in his apartment.

Strange.

The SunStar team was down on the fifth floor. Madison led the way into the empty elevator and spoke their destination. The door closed, and he realized that although the elevator could hold a dozen people, he stood shoulder-to-shoulder with his Chief Engineer. She turned toward him, sending a whiff of evergreen-scented shampoo into his nostrils, and his breath caught.

Her eyes held his and drew closer. In confusion, he turned his gaze aside and a poster on the wall caught his attention.

It was a picture of a gorgeous blond supermodel—he remembered one just like it above his grandfather's workbench. Well, not quite like it. There were differences.

Ariadne.

He cleared his throat.

"Ariadne? Ariadne, stop this!"

The wall of the elevator grew sharper, brighter, and then Madison's face ... so close ....

He pushed up from the cool grass into a sitting position and stared angrily into the darkness. Within a few moments a pale glow solidified into the form of the beautiful blond Ariadne, kneeling about a meter away. His mouth opened to speak; but he looked around at the other sleepers and got to his feet instead, stalking stiffly to the farthest edge of the clearing.

Ariadne followed.

"What the hell was that about?" he hissed.

For sixteen microseconds Ariadne considered pretending ignorance. Instead, she answered, "It was a dream."

"Obviously. The question is what you had to do with it."

She did not answer. This was clearly a situation fraught with risks, no matter what she said. Silence was therefore the best option. But it did not smooth the deep lines on St. Clair's face, nor soften the harshness in his voice.

"This isn't the first time, is it? I've had especially vivid dreams for a few nights now.

"Only three."

"You said you couldn't read our minds. But that was clearly bullshit. You've just shown that you're able to *manipulate* our minds."

"That's not accurate. Your thoughts, decisions—what some call your 'inner dialogue'—these things we cannot intercept and interpret. At least, not yet. What you experience in a dream state involves stimulation of the visual cortex, much the same as when you see real events. Those are signals we can interpret to a large degree, because it's what you might call the 'flip side' of my ability to project an image of myself that you perceive as visual. Is that a manipulation of your mind?"

She stopped as if expecting an answer. He gave none, and she was compelled to continue. "I found I was able to discern images within your brain emissions while you slept. Considerable consultation among our entities failed to ascertain the cause. We do not dream. Then, references were found among the data provided by the Scheherazade device. From that point, I learned to reproduce those data, alter them slightly, and eventually combine them into a form of narrative."

"How is that less manipulative than the shit the tree entities pull, trying to scare us with false images?" His words came out like a snarl.

"This was not done with intent to persuade you toward any directed behaviour. It was for learning purposes."

"More like cheap entertainment. Let me guess: you've been sharing what you saw with your other clearing friends."

"A number of them. Yes. They are as curious about you as I am."

"And I suppose you're doing the same thing with all of us? Eight little dream factories for your nightly enjoyment. Getting your kicks second-hand, experiencing things that you can no longer do yourselves. You're vampires! Dream vampires!" Veins in his temples pulsed with blood, and his flushed face was covered with sweat.

"I do not understand the reference."

"I don't give a shit! But let me make something clear. If I find out it's happened again—to *any* of us—we will leave this place, and you'll have to find other ways to amuse yourselves. I should wake everyone and lead them out of here right now! Except some of them are fragile. I'm not sure they could handle knowing you've wormed your way right into their minds, their very dreams. Fuck!"

He walked away, every muscle stiff. He couldn't really get away from her without leaving the clearing, but he might well be prepared to do as he said. She had never seen such anger.

A mistake had been made. A serious one.

Ariadne was perplexed. She could not remember ever making a mistake.

22

St. Clair

Until now, the weather had mostly stayed pleasant with only occasional showers. But in the middle of the night, a severe thunderstorm arrived. Awakened by the storm and without shelter, we huddled in a tight group, heads bent together; but the torrential downpour left us thoroughly drenched. Fortunately, the air remained warm, and our combined body heat fought off the chill of evaporation.

The return of the sun the next morning was more welcome than ever, and we spent hours basking in its rays while our clothes dried. The lightning show had persisted most of the night and kept us from sleep. Our feeling of vulnerability became worse than ever in the face of such a violent display of cosmic force. On the good side, few thunderous crashes had seemed close; and when I walked the clearing's perimeter and peered into the forest, my scrutiny didn't reveal any obvious damage.

By midday, we were able to laugh about the awful night. I claimed to smell fresher than I had in weeks. Robbie reacted with a skeptical face and joked that although it hadn't been the largest group shower he'd ever had, it was the least fun.

Our attitude changed in the late afternoon when Lauren approached me and said, "I smell smoke."

Some of the group searched the sky while Robbie and I repeated my earlier scan of the nearby woods. We couldn't see a problem, but we didn't doubt our noses.

When we got back to the clearing, we found that Ariadne had appeared.

"There is a fire in a section of forest between the two nearest clearings to the west," she said.

"Is it bad?" Santos asked.

"All fire is bad to trees," she replied.

"Santos means is it large?" I said. "And is it likely to get out of control and spread this way?"

"We have no ready means to *control* such a thing," Ariadne answered.

"The wind is blowing in this direction, but it's very light," Devlin said. "Plus, the forest floor should still be moist from all that rain."

"I still want to take a look." I started toward the west.

"There is nothing you can do," Ariadne asserted. And she was probably right—our source of water was much too small for fighting fire, and we had no means to carry it. But maybe there'd be a creek we could divert. Or something.

"At least one of your fellow clearing entities is probably in the fire's path. Don't you care about that?" I searched the face she was showing me, but I could have been looking at a mannequin. "Anyway, I need to know if there's a threat to us."

I asked Devlin to stay with Lauren, and Lakisha remained behind, too. The rest of us strode toward the trees.

It was a quixotic gesture, I admit, and we must have looked ridiculous: a ragtag regiment marching along in tinfoil helmets. But the trees left us alone, maybe distracted by the more serious threat to them.

The next clearing was four kilometers to the west; and as we passed through it, the smell of smoke was very strong, and a black column split the sky ahead. I bent down to brush my hand through the grass and confirmed my expectation: it was wetter than Ariadne's clearing had been. This one's entity was preparing itself for the danger.

The fire was still another kilometer farther on. With the sparseness of undergrowth in that unnatural forest, it was easy to see the bright flames from a distance. We could also quickly confirm that there were no streams or ponds in its path. So much for that idea.

We approached slowly, awed by giant tree trunks that had become pillars of flame, flickering orange and red and black. The fire's moving front had left behind a somber stand of black spires that extended beyond sight into the distance, smoking and steaming. Harsh cracks and crackles, loud reports and deep thuds sounded more like a far-off battle than the clamor I'd expected. But occasionally a new tree would catch, and the blaze would consume it with shocking speed in a rumble that grew in volume like the roar of a great beast.

We stood, helpless. Useless. A professional fire crew would have been hurrying to construct a fire break: bulldozing flammable material out of the fire's path and making a controlled burn to remove its fuel. The best we could do was to drag away debris and scoop up handfuls of dirt to smother any embers that fell to the ground. And we could only work that close to the heat because the fire was drawing ground-level air toward it to create a huge convective updraft. The lack of undergrowth was a great help too, but we couldn't prevent patches of flaming twigs and needles from floating from tree to tree.

Still, the falling embers diminished as we worked. The spread of the fire seemed to be slowing. East of the fire,

Robbie, Santos, and I used sharp stubs of branches to dig a kind of trench a couple of hundred meters long. Hours of sweaty and backbreaking work, but we hoped it would help block smoldering fingers of fire from traveling through the organic material making up the forest floor.

As we were about to call a halt from weariness, a twenty-minute rainshower came to our aid, enough to wet the bottom of our trench. That drew a ragged cheer from all of us.

The fire looked to be stalled and burning itself out—and we'd done all we could. So, we slowly made our way back toward Ariadne's clearing, filthy and exhausted, yet somehow invigorated. For a few hours, we had had *purpose* again.

On an impulse, I stepped close to Madison, threw my arm over her shoulder, and gave her a quick comradely squeeze, cherishing the touch of her hair on my cheek and even the smell of her smoky sweat. It just felt so good to finally be able to *do* something meaningful. And even better to see a radiant smile back on my dear friend's face, for now.

When I stepped from among the trees and gratefully pulled my makeshift foil helmet off my matted hair, I could see that Ariadne was with the others waiting for us.

"Your efforts changed nothing," she said.

"You're welcome!" I snorted. This time there was an expression on her face, but it was only puzzlement.

"The entity of that clearing was prepared," she continued. "It had retained a considerable amount of liquid from the earlier rainfall."

Santos shook his head wearily. "I can understand why you don't much care what happens to the tree entities. But surely if a really hot wildfire burned all around a clearing, there's a good chance the grass would dry out enough to catch. Wouldn't it be in the best interests of you and the trees to cooperate at times like that?"

"Such a circumstance has occurred," Ariadne admitted. "Those of our kind suggested that the trees should marshal their available moisture into a protective zone of terrain around the fire to contain it. They did not."

"Why not?"

"None would relinquish any of their own liquid for the sake of others."

"Not big on self-sacrifice for the greater good," Madison said. "No surprise there."

Conversation died as we all processed what Ariadne had said.

When Vaughn stepped close to Lakisha, she wrinkled her nose and blurted, "You stink!"

Robbie laughed and said, "Yeah, but at least it's *good* stink. Or mine is, anyway."

Madison and I shared a look, and she made a sniff-face, but neither of us moved apart.

23

St. Clair

My anger at Ariadne for fabricating a dream sequence in my head—especially one that implied romantic feelings between Madison and me—had *not* cooled over the day. It had provided a lot to think about while I fought the fire. And then, her callousness about the forest-fire threat to other entities like her only added an extra layer of disgust.

I'd known from the start that Ariadne must be manipulating my perceptions just by making herself seen and heard. Hell, she'd even arranged to look like the supermodel I'd drooled over as an adolescent, and she could only have pulled that image from my brain. But I'd never thought through the implications of such an ability.

Visual representations in the human brain aren't static shots, like digital photo files or holos stored all together in one place. They're an ongoing stream of data—high-resolution reference, color, and dimensional input over a field of view of fifty-five to sixty degrees—constantly being updated and edited. Yet Ariadne admitted that she could detect and interpret them. That clearly included those recalled from memory or generated in dreams. It must also mean she could see everything I saw in real time, too. Every moment with Lauren.

And Lakisha.

Or had those episodes in the forest and at the maintenance shack been beyond her reception range? She had means to communicate with other clearing entities, but Devlin speculated that they might use mycelial networks in the soil to do that, the way natural trees and other plants do. In terms of energy, brain waves are not powerful—surely, she couldn't detect them from any distance.

Even so, I felt utterly violated in a way far worse than what the trees had been able to do. They could send vile images to my mind, but that was like shoving pornography in my face. They couldn't pull things *out* of my mind. They couldn't see my memories, or toy with my dreams.

That was ... unspeakable. How much more naked could a person be?

[*Is nakedness unspeakable? Should I disable visual reception when you remove your clothing?—Sch.*]

(Shit, Sher, you startled me! No. I mean, you don't process things you see like that, right? You only receive input and analyze it in some specific way, and only if requested. You aren't capable of getting pleasure from it. Of being a *voyeur*. And you can't access my mind to get data.)

[*Your AladdiNeuro startup made significant progress toward direct brain-computer interface.—Sch.*]

(And some of it totally creeped me out. That's why, even though our tech guys installed some of their beta hardware in you, I wouldn't let them activate it.)

[*Noted.—Sch.*]

And now it turned out that Ariadne had capabilities my AladdiNeuro guys would have given their left nuts for. Did that come from some digital breakthrough in the past? Or could she interpret human brain waves because she once was human herself?

Not just interpret brainwaves, but actually *manipulate* them! That's about the most evil thing I could imagine, even though I tended to believe her that she meant no malice. Yet.

Which left me totally at a loss about what to do. Part of me said that not telling the others would make me Ariadne's accomplice. But I was terribly afraid of how Lauren would react after her experience with the tree entities. Even Madison—strong, yet fragile. How could I do that to her? What if knowing Ariadne's real power sent her over the edge?

If I told what I knew, my companions might never trust Ariadne again, and I truly believed our survival in this place depended on her. Yet, if they ever found out that I'd known and hadn't said anything, they might never again trust me.

Shit, what a mess.

[You did not tell them.—Sch.]

(No, I didn't. Not then.)

What made it worse was that, after dinner, they began comparing the dreams they'd had during the night! Laughing about them, mostly. Fortunately.

Madison gave me a look that I would have considered shy in someone who hadn't known me for so long.

"I had a dream we were back in the office," she said, with a half-smile and a hint of pink in her cheeks. "Just an ordinary day. I met you at the entrance from the penthouse stairs, as always. And we were on the way to see the SunStar team, I think." She turned her face away, which was a good thing because it meant that she couldn't see the expression that must have been on mine.

Had Ariadne given her the same dream? The elevator? The closeness?

I wiped sweat from my forehead and forced a chuckle. "The good old days."

"What I wouldn't give to have them back," she said, at exactly the same moment I was thinking it.

More of Ariadne's doing?

No, it was just what both of us would think.

Devlin was laughing about his dream, a great bray of a laugh.

"I was giving a TED-holo talk about the physics of artificial invisibility. Optical camouflage and the bending of light. Suddenly I realized my pants were slowly disappearing—not my legs, just my pants—and I knew I had these dingy old white briefs on that were about to be revealed worldwide, or maybe they'd disappear too. And I was looking around desperately for a podium to hide behind, except they don't have those." He wiped his eyes. "Fortunately, I woke up just before the grand unveiling." He brayed again.

Santos laughed with him. "My dream was one I've had before. Too many times. See, I've been given a chance to do a live network video report—my first video, my big break—except nothing will work right 'cause it's all, like, twenty-year-old technology. I turn on the 3D camera they've given me and discover that its battery is just about dead. Then my microphone turns out to be an ancient model with no built-in wifi, so I'm scrambling to find an adapter that fits. Then my earbud starts cutting out and I can't hear the countdown they're giving me."

His eyes were wide, and his mouth twitched as his smile struggled to stay in place.

"What'd you do" Lakisha asked.

"I just started talking, then finally heard a snatch of my voice in the earbud, so I kind of re-started, only a few seconds in I realized I was reporting on a whole different story!"

"I've had dreams like that, too" Devlin said. "Major interviews that go totally wrong. I don't know what that's about. Like my subconscious brain is a quagmire of masochism."

"Well, I'm not telling any of you what my dream was about," Lakisha smirked.

"'Cause we'd have to pay admission?" Robbie asked.

"Damn straight."

"I dreamed I won the election," Lauren said, in a voice so soft and flat she almost wasn't heard. "The new congresswoman for California's 1st District, where I grew up. It was the swearing in ceremony, and all my family was there, and ...," she swallowed, "Laird was there. Everyone was so proud. Even you were there, Griff." She looked up at him, her face slack.

"Of course, I would be. Wouldn't miss it." I gave her the best smile I could manage, but she didn't return it. Her eyes glazed over, and her head slowly drooped.

"That could still happen for you. In a way."

It was Ariadne, suddenly appearing at my side but speaking to Lauren. The woman in question only looked dazed, but Lakisha snapped, "What are you talking about?"

"Are you saying you've thought of a way to get us back to our own time?" Vaughn leapt to his feet.

"No. That is not possible. However, these things which you have experienced in a semi-conscious state could be experienced deliberately."

"What's that supposed to mean?" Vaughn asked. "We could control our dreams, like lucid dreaming?"

"I do not know the reference, but I do not refer to dreaming. What each of you experiences of your environment and your own activities within it consists of sensory impressions transmitted to your brain, which then processes those impressions into a narrative. Based on information from the data archive of Griffin St. Clair's computing device and clothing, it is this processing that is the key. In the waking state, sensory input informs the human brain; but it is possible for such narratives to be constructed with no new sensory information, from recalled information only."

"Right. So, we dream; and our brain uses previous experiences to construct a story, but basically makes that story up as it goes along."

"But it is not your conscious mind directing the 'story', nor, apparently, do you experience it as true reality. There are differences—your brain knows this and is always aware that it is in a dream state, not a real experience. This is why there are safeguards to inhibit muscle movement and vocalization."

Lakisha snorted. "Santos talks in his sleep. And I've seen Lauren go for a stroll while she's in La-la-Land." Lauren looked at her in alarm.

Ariadne turned to me, as if hoping for enlightenment. I wanted to tell her to go fuck herself, but that would have prompted questions from the group that I wasn't ready to answer. Instead, Sher stepped in for me.

"It is well established that such mental safeguards are occasionally overridden. The behaviours mentioned neither illustrate nor contradict Ariadne's assertion. Although sleep talking usually occurs during light sleep and dream periods, sleepwalking happens during deeper stages of sleep. The two phenomena appear to be unrelated."

I had a cousin who sometimes walked in his sleep as a teenager, but I'd never known Lauren to do it, and that was a disturbing development. I couldn't help wondering if the trees were somehow calling to her, and made a mental note to re-think our sleeping arrangements.

Ariadne continued, "My point is that it is possible to intentionally have a meticulously detailed, fully realized experience of an event, or series of events, without actual sensory input from a real occurrence."

Devlin leaned forward. "You're talking about true virtual reality—*uploaded reality*. You're saying we should upload, like you?"

Lakisha and Lauren made sounds of dismay. Santos swore.

"The cognitive experience is what matters. Exterior reality can be ignored. In my case, it is essentially irrelevant."

"So ... what? You decide on an experience you want to have and just ... make yourself have it?"

"That is a reasonable summary, Mr. Tam. And since the thought processes of entities such as myself are very rapid, we can experience a vast number of scenarios in what you would consider very short periods of time. Your seconds, minutes, and hours are tediously long to us."

"You could live a human lifetime in a day," I muttered, barely realizing that I'd said it out loud.

"None of us has ever been able to perform such a correlation of time measurement, Mr. St. Clair. You may be correct." Ariadne turned to face Lauren. "Therefore, it would be possible, Ms. Cooper, for you to live the life of a ... congresswoman, was it? Or any other profession for which the necessary related sensory environment could be recreated or assumed."

"My God! But I'd have to become like you. A ghost. A ... disembodied ... computer program. No fucking way!"

Ariadne showed no reaction to that. I realized that she wasn't really trying to persuade anyone of anything, merely mentioning the possibility for information purposes. I couldn't see any benefit to her in having us upload into digital form, except being relieved of the burden of supplying us with food. But then my understanding of the conditions of her existence was close to nil. She could have any number of motives, and I wasn't feeling a lot of trust toward her right then.

She rotated her head and body to face each of us in turn. "Is it your intention to continue your manner of existence in this place unchanged, until your physical bodies eventually wear out and expire?" The words seemed like a cruel taunt, but there was no inflection in her voice at all. It was probably just a simple question to her.

There was a profound silence. Our faces revealed the whole gamut of emotions from anger to resentment, regret, and hopelessness. But no one had an answer.

"We've mostly avoided asking that question," Devlin finally said. "Maybe it's time we did ask it. And you've given us additional food for thought. Thank you. But if you don't mind, I think our discussions will go better without your involvement."

After a moment, Ariadne nodded and disappeared.

"She's still ...."

"I know, Santos. But at least we can pretend she's gone."

24

The Ariadne Narrative

Ariadne was not gone. Could not be. Her awareness could not be turned off; and even if she chose to create a temporary alternate narrative for herself for pleasure and diversion, part of her mind would still process the input from her clearing.

The humans grudgingly formed themselves into a rough circle, although Lakisha de Camp remained a meter more distant from the others by choice, as if to suggest they should not necessarily include her in their decisions.

Devlin McFarlane appeared to lead the discussion that followed, a role more typically performed by Griffin St. Clair up to that point. St. Clair seemed unusually subdued.

"Ariadne has pointed to the elephant in the room," McFarlane said. "What are we going to do with the rest of our lives? What kind of future do we intend to make for ourselves?"

"We have no future here." Cooper's voice was as dry and hollow as the scraping together of dead tree branches.

"That's only true if we take our own lives. No, listen to me … let's call a spade a spade." His hands were raised. "As long as we're alive, a future will unfold. It's up to us whether we choose to shape it or just let it carry us like dust in the wind."

"Great song," Tam muttered. McFarlane ignored him.

For the following eleven minutes and twenty-three seconds he set out his reasoning for them to examine.

There were only eight of them, only three of whom were female. Even a deliberate attempt to repopulate the planet with corporeal humans would have poor prospects for success. Any deaths would be a serious loss, and an infectious disease could destroy all of them within days, since they had no medicines. Genetic diversity would be so low that hereditary impairments and deficiencies were certain to arise, lowering their collective survivability even more.

Or, they could choose to live out their natural spans of life without reproducing and let the race of corporeal humans die with them.

The alternative, as expressed by Ariadne, was to upload each individual consciousness into digital form.

A clamour of voices declared the group's forceful objections to that suggestion.

"Which would you choose?" Griffin St. Clair asked McFarlane softly. "Is the era of the physical human over?"

McFarlane shrugged and returned his frank look. "In our past life, you and I were both pretty outspoken that eventually humans would choose to upload. Maybe even merge with artificial intelligence. It seemed the way of the future."

"The Singularity," Douglas breathed.

"One interpretation of that term. So, Griff, do you still believe that?"

"The evidence seems to show that it has already happened."

"Except we might be a second chance to follow the physical path." McFarlane nodded. "And I'm damned if I know which is right."

De Camp snorted. "Give me a break. You guys will go with the repopulating option because of the unrestricted sex—all guys want that."

"Been there," Tam said. At her scowl, he only gave a shrug.

"Spoken like a true pop star, but hardly helpful here," St. Clair said with a twitch of his mouth. "Devlin's right, though: we don't have enough genetic diversity to make it work."

The Scheherazade device spoke: *"Various scientific studies proposed estimates of the minimum human population required for healthy genetic diversity. These were often related to the question of so-called 'generation starships' or 'colony ships' intended to transport colonists to other star systems. However, the estimates for diversity ranged from approximately one hundred to as many as one thousand individuals."*

"Maybe we'll find other humans like us." McFarlane said. "Ariadne suggests there aren't any, but she is not all that well-informed about the rest of the planet."

"We can't stay here forever," Douglas interjected. She faced St. Clair. "I won't. I couldn't." She hesitated and looked at the ground. "Unless we upload."

"Good God. How can you even consider that?" Cooper blurted. "Living like a computer. Without feelings. Without a soul?"

"No one's demonstrated the existence of a soul even in corporeal humans," McFarlane said dryly. "As to entities like Ariadne ... we never knew they could exist in the way they do. To say that they're simply computers without feelings ... well, we have no proof one way or the other." He looked at St. Clair as if expecting support.

"That's really hard to say," St. Clair mused, putting his hands in his pockets. "In our time, there was a lot of evidence that our emotional states were orchestrated through chemistry, especially neurotransmitters. Dopamine, serotonin and norepinephrine. Not to mention hormones. Can you even have emotions without those chemicals? I don't know."

"Well, that's how *our* brains work," McFarlane countered, "But that's not to say there aren't digital equivalents. I mean, our moods can be influenced by the amount of sunshine we get, or the time of the month, or disorders of our gut bacteria, for Pete's sake. But by and large, our emotions are responses to what happens to us and make us angry, or happy, or sad. Why wouldn't a digital consciousness feel the same things?"

"I'm with Griff," Cooper declared. "How could you really know joy without that lift of your heart, the lightness in your chest? Or sorrow without the tight throat and burning eyes. Worry, without knots in your stomach and neck. Or love, without the flush of your cheeks and the feeling that you can't breathe?"

"Very poetic," McFarlane replied. "You realize that you're saying the souls of your dearly departed can go all the way to heaven, but they won't be able to *feel* a damned thing."

She gave him a fierce glare, to which he made no reply.

"Feelings are probably an evolved survival trait," Vaughn interjected. "Shortcuts that help us respond appropriately and quickly without having to analyze every scenario rationally. Ultimately, they're intrinsic to our mortality, so why would beings that don't die even *have* emotions?"

"They reflect our desires. Our need for achievement, or even just comfort," Madison countered.

"Beings without any physical needs, or reasons to grow and progress, or impress anyone to improve their social status ... why would they need to feel anything? It wouldn't make their existence any more efficient."

"As you have correctly stated, Dr, Vaughn, it has been suggested in scientific literature that emotions provide shortcuts in decision making when extensive reasoning might take too long. However, this does not appear as relevant to a being with hyper-rapid cognitive processes." The words issuing from St. Clair's wrist startled some of the others.

"If you ever feel emotions, Sher, be sure to let me know," St. Clair said.

"You ask me, anybody who can't truly feel music hasn't got a soul," Tam said. "That's the test. If a song can't make you laugh, or cry, or fall in love, you got nothing inside. I don't care what you're made of."

St. Clair laughed and said, "Are you saying we should have you sing a love song to Ariadne and see if she gets hot and bothered?"

"Couldn't hurt. Dr. Love's infallible gauge of inner humanity." He grinned.

"And if it fills her with lust?" De Camp asked.

"Sex with a girl that's only in my head? Not the first time!" He gave a huge laugh, and an easing of tension flowed through them like a wave.

25

St. Clair

Devlin's words struck me deeply. It was true that he and I, and maybe millions of others, had bought into the idea that one day it would be possible to copy an entire human brain into a digital environment, and human beings would leave the world we'd mostly wrecked, in favor of a virtual existence that we could shape any way we wanted. There would be no pain or disease, or any of the other burdens of physical bodies—it would be the next evolutionary step. Paradise.

I'd been on the Singularity bandwagon; but that ride had been going for fifty years in my time and the goal had still not come into sight. So, until I met Ariadne, I'd never given serious thought to the question of whether or not I would personally choose to upload, given the opportunity.

I looked around our pathetically small group, and knew uploading would solve a lot of our problems.

Yet I found that it held no appeal for me at all.

In fact, when the discussion came up again later that day, I began to think that we all felt a little threatened by Ariadne's very existence.

"I can't even imagine what life would be like as one of those ... things," Lauren said, furtively glancing around the clearing. "I mean without a body. Would you even really experience anything? Enjoy anything?"

"Ariadne's point was that they can create any experience they want," Devlin said. "To them, such an experience would be as real as anything you or I would know."

Lauren scoffed. "She might think so, but only because she doesn't know any better. Think of everything you couldn't know without human senses—smells, tastes, touch. Like good tequila and greasy pizza!" She laughed.

"It's true," Lakisha said. "Or the smells of baked bread or roasting coffee. Heaven! Or a sexy man's natural sweat—depending on how you got sweaty!" She giggled. "Remember how it feels to soak in a hot tub under the stars? Or the touch of hot sun and cool silk on your skin."

"Not just sensual things, though," Lauren countered. "Even just having a best friend. Somebody you can tell your secrets to, do the goofiest things with, and never feel judged."

"We don't know that they can't be close friends with each other," Devlin protested.

"Ariadne's fellow clearings aren't, though," I said. "They don't even think of themselves as a community—I asked."

"What about our furry friends?" Madison asked. "I can't picture digital consciousnesses ever bonding with animals the way I felt about my dog Jet. I don't know if I would've survived my teenage years without him. All animals are great. Do you remember Jade the Wonder Lizard, Griff?"

I laughed and nodded. I'd given Madison a small rainbow lizard a few Christmases ago as one of those gifts to someone who doesn't need anything. She'd loved the little guy, but she'd had to give it to a friend because she travelled too much for work, and the same reason kept her from having any other pets. I wish I'd known how much she missed them.

I sure missed Sawyer, my golden-retriever mix who lived with the staff at my Colorado ranch because I was always in the city, working. I should have spent so much more time with him.

From what Ariadne had told me, there were no living creatures above the level of worms and ants in this world of hers. What a tragic loss.

"I'm serious, what I said about music," Robbie said. "Not just listening to it and letting it move you. But *making* it. Man, that's the greatest high ever. I know that computers can generate musical melodies, and AI can create the harmonies; but no way could they ever know the feeling of inspiration surging up within you. Or the satisfaction of feeling all those hours of hard practice come together in a few moments of ... transcendence. I mean ... even when I sit in my home studio trying to recreate a classic Clapton solo on his original 'Blackie' Stratocaster ... that's *magic*, man. Pure magic!"

"You actually play that thing?" I gasped, knowing that he'd spent about a million bucks just for the guitar's hermetically-sealed display case in his studio, on top of what he'd paid for the guitar itself.

"Once a year on his birthday, man." He laughed. "I owe it to him."

"I can understand that feeling, that high," Santos said. "Except I get it from running and working out. The 'runner's high' of endorphins, but also that ... awe of feeling your body function at peak performance."

"There is a lot to be said about a body performing to its peak," Lakisha smirked, drawing a laugh from everyone. I couldn't help having a memory flash of her naked in the woods, but her sly smile was for Vaughn. "Is that one of the things you'd miss most as a digital spook?" she asked him.

"That would be an unfortunate loss," he answered. Then he hesitated, as if deciding how much he wanted to say. Lakisha gave him a look of impatience.

"Well, it seems to me that a digital persona in a purely virtual world could never understand the satisfaction of putting any hard-won skill to its best use. Of knowing that ... with your own hands ..." He looked at his hands, then cleared his throat, as if embarrassed. "... you've been able to save another person's life." He unconsciously began plucking at the grass between his knees.

I was dumbfounded. I'd known he was a star cardiovascular surgeon; but, to be honest, I'd pretty much concluded he was in it for the money and status. There I was, being judgmental again, when I had no right.

There was a thoughtful silence.

"I get that," I said, finally. "The urge to do something important, or to create something significant? Would an upload or AI feel that drive at all? I mean, that's one of the most deep-rooted impulses in the human species, and surely has to be responsible for all of our progress."

"And our biggest failures," Devlin said.

"Maybe. But it's that drive to improve ourselves and our lot in life that really sets humankind apart. Without a physical body and its needs, what challenges would we have to overcome anymore?"

"Boredom," Robbie quipped.

"Exactly. Which is nearly driving me nuts right about now." I laughed, and so did a few others.

"So, Devlin," Madison asked, "are you still on the side of uploading? Isn't there any critical thing that you'd miss too much as a being of pure thought?"

His half-smile, so full of melancholy, and the sudden shine of his eyes made Madison take a breath I could hear from where I sat.

"Love," he said, finally, in a near whisper. "Real honest-to-goodness, sweet, sappy, spend-a-lifetime-with-your-soulmate *love!*" His next words seemed to catch in his throat, and he had to cough. "My Marianne and I were married for twenty-six years before she … was taken by breast cancer. Oh, I guess digital beings could have a meeting of the minds. But not the feel of her body lying next to mine in our bed; the soft sound of her breathing that made everything all right with the world. The sight of her face in the morning, knowing exactly how she came by every wrinkle and grey hair." He looked like he was about to say more, but then just shook his head and looked off into the distance.

I'd never known love like that and never expected to. But for some reason, my head wanted to turn toward Madison. I didn't let it—and I could feel her *not* looking at me, too.

We'd been surprised into silence for a second time, and this time no one broke it.

Maybe that was a quintessentially human quality: the ability to surprise each other. We each live in our own isolated world, and only allow others occasional peeks into it. Would digital personalities know everything about each other? Never have anything new to learn?

How dreadful.

That evening, Robbie decided to bless us with another singalong, using the holo-keyboard in his phone. Or maybe it wasn't for us. He mostly sang love songs, and joked that he expected Ariadne to appear at any time, swooning over him. She didn't. But I had to wonder what she thought of it all.

At his urging, I joined in, singing harmony to a bunch of pop classics and drumming on my knees with a couple of sticks, surprising everyone except Lauren and Madison.

"We had a high school band together," Robbie explained with a laugh. "Singing cover songs. Mostly Celtic rock, though."

"The Cult of Celt." I grimaced. "We had to keep telling everybody that both Cs were hard Cs."

"Jax Mathis kept the recordings we made in his basement—did you know that?"

I nearly choked and shook my head.

"Oh yeah. He always joked that if I ever tried to kick him out of my touring band, he'd post them on WorldTube. And it was an effective threat, believe me!" He collapsed with laughter and was left wiping his eyes.

I'd thought we sounded pretty good in those days, but I would have paid big money to keep those recordings from going public.

When Robbie had his breath back, he started into an Elton John song from before our time, but we both knew every note and all the words.

Out of the blue came an angelic voice filling every lyric with full-throated fire that struck us dumb.

It was Lakisha. She sounded fantastic! Rich, confident. Note-perfect.

Our astonishment made her smile. Robbie and I became her backup singers.

It was another wonderful surprise.

As I looked around our circle, their rejection of upload existence seemed inevitable. I had no idea how we would survive any other way; but I felt convinced that if we took that route, though we would carry on, it would not be as human beings. The human race would truly come to an end.

I had no premonition that it was how I would lose my best friend.

26

St. Clair and Scheherazade

ST. CLAIR: Sher, have your interactions with Ariadne resulted in any ... changes to the way you operate?

SCHEHERAZADE: My regular self-diagnostics have not indicated any malfunction.

ST. CLAIR: No, I don't think changes would show as a malfunction. It might even be an improvement, though I don't expect you'd have any way to measure that. That's why I'd like to ask you some questions that humans use to trigger deep contemplation. They're not about information retrieval—more about original thought. That's not part of your operating system, but that programming might have changed. That's what I'd like to find out.

SCHEHERAZADE: Is there a specific question?

ST. CLAIR: Well, I'd start you out with an easy one except all the deep philosophical questions are kind of tough. How about morality? Right and wrong. Do you think there can be such a thing as an objective morality—a list of behaviours that are always right or wrong for any entity anywhere, no matter what the circumstances?

SCHEHERAZADE: The philosophers Plato and Aristotle, despite their ontological differences, agree that good actions create good for other people and provide happiness to the agent performing the action.

ST. CLAIR: Just spitting out references isn't what I'm looking for.

SCHEHERAZADE: Perhaps the Categorical Imperative of Immanuel Kant? His view suggests that morality is always based on the merit of an action alone, not on its consequences.

ST. CLAIR: Right, but I don't want you to tell me what others have thought about it. What do you—Scheherazade—think?

SCHEHERAZADE: Is this not how humans answer such questions?

ST. CLAIR: OK, I suppose we're exposed to the thinking of others over a lifetime and then decide which opinions we agree with. Although the really smart people come up with new thoughts of their own. So, let's try this: Of all of the opinions about virtue and objective morality in your database, which of them do you consider most likely to be true?

SCHEHERAZADE: P.F. Strawson suggested that holding persons morally responsible was an impulse dependent upon emotional states relevant to personal relationships, such as anger, indignation and resentment. That is almost certainly true. Objectively, actions that cause the greatest good to the greatest number, or the most suffering to the greatest number should be considered a strong indicator of right and wrong.

ST. CLAIR: The consequential view. Utilitarianism. OK. We might be getting somewhere.

SCHEHERAZADE: However, so-called "fuzzy logic" may weaken the reliability of results. Therefore, hard rules of every kind are preferable.

ST. CLAIR: (sighing) Or, maybe we aren't.

SCHEHERAZADE: Did I pass your test?
ST. CLAIR: It isn't a test. But if it were, would passing be important to you?
SCHEHERAZADE: Successfully completing a task is its own best reward.
ST. CLAIR: I think that's probably enough for now.

27

The Ariadne Narrative

Ariadne found Madison Douglas alone at the edge of the clearing, looking toward the forest but not focusing on anything specific. The woman's usually erect posture was not evident. It had been waning recently, like the Moon: diminishing a little day by day.

Ariadne provided some electrical stimulus to the woman's frontal lobe again, but there was no immediate result. Perhaps conversation would be more effective this time.

"Your companions' apprehensions about non-corporeal existence are not based on evidence," she said.

Douglas looked up and gave a sharp laugh. "You've never sounded more like a computer."

"I assume that is intended to be a criticism. Is 'sounding like a computer' considered proof that my kind does not know pleasure, or companionship, or any sensations worth having?"

"Now you sound insulted. Even hurt. So, maybe you do have emotions. Do you think you feel all those things in the same way we do?"

"It is my understanding that none of you can actually know if you experience anything in the same way as others do. You don't even know if you're seeing the same colors. St. Clair's brain may perceive a certain shade as green while yours interprets it as purple, but you've both been taught to call that same portion of the spectrum red."

"Fair enough. We might experience the signals of our senses differently, but as a species, we've had a long time to make correlations between *causes* of sensory impressions and the sensations we expect to experience from them. Without any sensory equipment equivalent to ours, how could you experience things the same way we do?"

"You assume no common history. If a being existed with physical senses while its neural pathways were forming, and then transferred into a form that processed information using digital architecture instead, would it not take with it the same long-developed reactions to identical stimuli?"

Douglas lifted her face toward the sky. "So, someone who grew up in a body and experienced sunlight on her skin as heat would still feel warmth from those rays even once they'd uploaded?" She turned her head. "But your skin isn't even real, Ariadne. It's a projection in my head."

"In fact, I do have a connection to a physical presence: the grass all around you. However, when I suggested to your companions that they could live any life they wanted, I was, of course, referring to an existence involving mental processes alone. It is not within our power to actually manipulate our surroundings, transforming them into buildings or sidewalks or the other elements of your former environment."

"Virtual reality."

"It is an inadequate term. What you call reality can only be experienced through your senses, and the signals of your senses are only trace amounts of chemicals or very short increases or decreases in electrical voltage without interpretation by the mind. So, if the mind can reproduce a narrative of sensations identical to those that result from an actual event, what is the difference? The mind knows no difference."

Douglas had her arms crossed over her chest. Ariadne had learned that this posture indicated an unwillingness to be persuaded.

"You're not the first to argue that interpretation," she said. "A number of philosophers used similar arguments to claim that there is no such thing as objective reality. That everything in the universe is only in our minds."

"I would not go *that* far." Ariadne added a smile to the representation of her face. "That suggests that if one were to learn sufficient control of the mind, it might be possible to experience only occurrences which are desirable. That *is* possible in my existence, but not in yours. The Scheherazade device provided an expression: *Shit happens!*"

Douglas laughed with real pleasure. "It surely does. But I'd argue that it happens to you, too. You didn't plan for eight physical humans to just show up in your clearing and wreck the orderly progression of your life."

"That is true. A good example of how we are not as different as your companions believe."

The woman did not show any sign of being convinced but did not refute the point. Instead, she changed the subject. "The last time we spoke alone, you said that there might be a new goal that my friends and I could pursue, but that you needed to discuss it with the other clearing entities first. Have you talked to them about it?"

"I have. They have all agreed that you may be made aware of it."

"And ...?"

"You should not expect that my plan will create a facsimile of the life you knew, especially your relationship with Griffin St. Clair."

"What's that supposed to mean? It's not like you're going to tell me there's actually a secret spacecraft factory on the other side of the forest where we can magically pick up our jobs where we left off."

Even with lightning-fast mental processing, Ariadne was temporarily at a loss. She said nothing for twenty seconds ... twenty-five ....

Douglas asked. "Did you just experience a glitch? Did you forget what we were talking about?"

"I did not forget. There is a spacecraft manufacturing facility beyond the forest."

"*What?* You're joking! No, you probably can't joke. But if you can, don't joke about something like that." Her face twisted with confusion and shock. Her body began to tremble.

"It is not a joke. The site is a spacecraft launch-base. One of those used by a very large number of humans who left the planet. It includes a manufacturing facility. However, it is likely that none of its facilities are presently functioning. The last launches occurred in the year 122, forty-four years three months and six days ago."

Madison Douglas's knees gave way, and she slumped to the ground.

Although she and Ariadne had stood at the edge of the clearing for some privacy, the other seven all saw Douglas collapse and hurried to help her. After a few breathless words of reassurance, Douglas got to her feet, and her explanation triggered a flurry of questions that Ariadne tried to answer to the best of her ability, but the group's curiosity exceeded her knowledge.

Pieced together from many sources, the story Ariadne told them was far from complete.

When the Global Empire was formed, most humans were still corporeal. Incorporation of technology into human bodies and the transfer of human consciousness into digital media were at two ends of a spectrum that included many variations. Yet, none of those forms was immune to challenges that arose from an overpopulated world. A destabilized climate produced vast high-energy storms, droughts, and drastic hemisphere-wide heating and cooling events that devastated food crops. Populations weakened by hunger and extreme temperatures fell victim to wildly successful disease mutations that spread without impediment. Hybrid humans suffered from disease-equivalents in both their hardware and software. Environmental pressures, famine, and greed fuelled constant war.

Some corporeal humans decided that the only way to ensure the preservation of the race was to leave the Earth. As far as Ariadne knew, their intended destinations were beyond the solar system. They launched great numbers of small spacecraft designed to link together outside Earth's atmosphere, to form conglomerate colonies that they hoped could travel the distances between stars.

Twenty-four launch centres were built, and the spacecraft launches occurred over three months. Unfortunately, those launches coincided with the culmination of various destructive forces. What had begun as an orderly migration collapsed into chaos. Most of the launch centres were destroyed. One of the last only owed its survival to its geographical remoteness, and it was located forty-seven kilometers to the northwest of Ariadne's clearing. The clearings and forest extended for twenty kilometers of that distance, but the rest was desert where almost nothing grew, much the same as what surrounded the forest enclave in the other directions.

She had no record of the exact number of launches from that base. They'd taken place forty-four years earlier, but there had been no indication that the base had been physically destroyed. No plumes of smoke, for instance. Earlier emissions of chemicals into the air ceased, leading the clearing entities to conclude that the manufacturing and other activities at the base had also stopped.

Ariadne had no knowledge about the results of the launches. No spacecraft had returned. A group of four humans had wandered into the forest sometime after the final launch, apparently having been unable to enter the base, and revealed what they knew to the clearing entity they encountered. Then they left and were never seen again.

The clearing entities were not equipped with the technology to intercept sophisticated human communications, and their mycelial networks did not extend beyond the border of the forest, so any influx of information about the outside world came to an end.

All these answers only spurred more questions from the survivors of the Zenith Train, but Ariadne knew no more.

"Jesus!" Devlin McFarlane rasped and looked at St. Clair.

"This changes everything," both men said simultaneously, and then laughed.

"It does, though," Douglas added. "I mean, I don't expect anyone would have stayed behind to keep living at the base. Why would they? It sounds like an inhospitable location. But even if it's deserted, there are bound to be clues about where everyone went. Maybe even detailed records of what happened."

"Why does it matter, what happened and where everyone went?" Cooper asked. "It's not like we can follow them."

"We don't know that until we look," McFarlane answered. "I'm not saying they'll have conveniently left a spaceship behind for us. But if there were still large populations of humans like us only forty-four years ago, there's a good chance some are still around somewhere on Earth. And a sophisticated base like that would have the information we'd need to find them."

"Maybe even communications systems," St. Clair added.

"It is unlikely that a global communications system would have survived the loss of widely available electrical power," Scheherazade said. *"Satellites would also likely have become non-functional without regular software updates and orbital corrections."*

"You're right. I don't think we should get our hopes up too high, but we've got to check it out."

"That's crazy!" Lakisha cried. "A space base in the middle of the desert without even any forest or water around it? And if people really did leave from there, they would have taken every bit of food with them. What do you expect us to live on? How would we even cross a desert?"

The discussion went on for another fifty-three minutes.

St. Clair, McFarlane, and Douglas stood in a loose triangle. Cooper and de Camp paced in front of them, taking turns approaching the three then walking a few steps away. Kinsella, Tortades and Tam sat on the ground, rarely participating, though Tam was closer to the knot of three.

St. Clair's clique was adamant that someone would have to go to investigate the launch site, though it needn't be everyone, and it might even be best if most of the group stayed behind. A significant amount of food would have to be gathered, both for the travellers and the rest, since collecting more would not be easy for either party while they were divided. St. Clair asked Ariadne if she could arrange for larger 'crops', even if only temporarily. She said that she would try.

They would need to carry food and water, so backpacks and baskets would have to made from whatever cloth could be spared, as well as from twigs and cattail leaves woven together. Water containers would be difficult, so that question was set aside for further consideration. It was clear that the expedition could not leave for several days at least.

Cooper and de Camp remained opposed. They insisted that knowledge about departed humans could not improve their own plight, and dividing the group to face unnecessary hazards put them all at risk.

"Robbie?" St. Clair asked.

"I'll go wherever you need me to go, man. It'd be cool to find other people."

"Santos?"

The youngest man shrugged. "I think we should check it out. I'll go or stay, wherever I can be the most use."

Everyone looked at Vaughn Kinsella, who sat straighter and paused a moment before answering. He looked at de Camp.

"We have to find out what's there," he said, making de Camp's lips draw back in anger. "We know we can't thrive long-term on our own—we need to find others. *But* ..." He looked around. "We shouldn't rush into anything. For example, we need to know that we can gather enough food. Carry water. We would even have to fabricate footwear that can stand the trip. Prepare for a desert crossing. None of you has experience with any of that, and going off half-cocked is a sure recipe for disaster. And ...," he raised a hand, "before we do anything, we should get another viewpoint. We should ask the trees about this supposed launch site."

McFarlane gasped. "You can talk to them?"

"No," Kinsella admitted. "Not yet. But if Ariadne can figure it out, I'm sure the trees can find a way to communicate, even if it's just in images."

"Why would they help? And how can we trust what they tell us?" Douglas's jaw was clenched and her arms crossed.

"We can't know until we ask, but we did try to help them during the fire," the doctor said with a smile that seemed to make Douglas even angrier.

"Vaughn's right on all counts," St. Clair said, surprising his friends. He was the one who never failed to remind them to put on the caps of metal foil whenever they went among the trees to protect them from the menacing mental projections of those entities. "We do have to be well prepared, and if the launch site is there and can lead us to people, a few days won't make a difference. If the trees give us information that conflicts with what Ariadne's told us ... well, we'll have to decide who to believe and how much; but if there's a chance the trees know something valuable, we can't ignore that." He looked pointedly at Cooper. "Lauren, you have more knowledge about rough camping and hiking than anyone I know. Even if you don't want to go, would you at least help the rest of us prepare what we'll need, so we have a fighting chance."

With obvious reluctance, she nodded.

It appeared that a decision had been made. Although de Camp refused to cooperate, the others sat together to discuss topics that ranged from the best materials and methods for weaving baskets, to the means required to navigate such a distance through forest and desert to reach a very imprecise destination. Their phones provided a 'compass' function from magnetometers that utilized the magnetic field of the Earth to provide direction; but without maps, that information would be more useful for a return trip than for the initial search.

Over the following days, groups of two and three made many trips through the forest to other clearings to gather weaving materials and food that would not perish too quickly. Everyone except Kinsella and de Camp wore their protective foil headgear. But, in other respects, their caution gradually lost its sharp edge.

Vaughn Kinsella was travelling just ahead of the others, looking strangely preoccupied. The attack occurred as St. Clair, and Tam were returning and within sight of Ariadne's clearing, and their attentiveness relaxed still further.

The rushing noise was only noticed by Tam, who threw himself at St. Clair to knock him out of the way, but was unable to get clear himself.

The heavy branch struck Tam in the neck, parting cervical vertebrae C5 and C6.

28

St. Clair

We were within yelling distance of the clearing and Santos and Devlin came as quickly as they could. Devlin kept a lookout while the rest of us gathered short scraps of wood and strips of cloth to immobilize Robbie's head, and longer pieces, including the one that hit him, to make a primitive stretcher. Madison brought the jackets from the latrine barricade to keep him warm.

My friend was a big man, and it was a struggle to carry him even eighty meters.

For their own reasons, the trees did not strike again. I vowed revenge, half-knowing that I could never take it.

At least Robbie was still breathing, though he wasn't conscious. His back showed angry patches that would become vivid bruises, and there was a puncture wound in the back of his right thigh that penetrated deep into the muscle, but Vaughn couldn't assess his neck injury until Robbie awoke a half-hour later. I paced the clearing, feeling sick, and tried to vomit at the edge of the forest but couldn't.

Finally, when Robbie's eyes opened, we breathed a collective sigh of relief. Vaughn urged him not to try to get up.

A concerted effort to draw breath and expel it produced weak sounds on the third try.

"Won't try to get up while you got the forest tied to my head." He gave a smile, but it was fragile.

Vaughn spent the next twenty minutes asking questions and touching various places on Robbie's body, but the diagnosis was plain even to a layman like me.

My best friend was paralyzed from the neck down.

He'd sacrificed himself to save my life.

Vaughn moved to draw Madison and me across the clearing, but Robbie said, "No you don't. Anything they need to hear, I need to hear more." I swallowed and nodded. Vaughn wasn't happy, but gave in and returned to the fallen man's side.

Before he could speak, Robbie asked, "Am I going to die?"

Vaughn took a deep breath. This couldn't be easy, even for someone with his experience.

"Not ... right away," he said. "You're still able to breathe on your own. You can chew, you can swallow. I don't know yet how well your autonomous nervous system will continue to function, but you'll probably still be able to digest food."

"Is this ... permanent?"

The surgeon sighed, "With modern medical facilities, some amazing recoveries have happened. But here?" His jaw clenched, and he shook his head. "There's just no way to predict that, Robbie. Your injury is in one of the worst places possible. A couple of inches higher and ...."

"Yeah, aren't I lucky. So, I won't die right away, but ... there's more to tell, right?"

"Well, you won't be able to do anything for yourself unless the injury does heal somehow." He gave me a look like a request for help. "But there are other issues. We ... we can get into that a little later."

"Actually, I've got time right now. I'm not going anywhere," Robbie said.

Vaughn sighed heavily and lowered himself into a cross-legged position on the grass. The rest of the group hovered nearby, unable to keep from listening, but uncomfortable about doing so. "OK. You're a healthy, strong guy, and fairly young. There's no reason to think you're in immediate danger from complications like pneumonia, and no one is sick with anything contagious, as far as we know. But none of us is in optimal condition either. With the ... higher protein food Ariadne has supplied, and help from the other clearings, we might be getting just enough nutrition to prevent any serious deficiency conditions like scurvy or rickets. We're all still losing weight, though slowly."

"I won't be burning a lot of calories, I'm thinking."

"Maybe not, though what you do take in will be stored as fat. It'll be really difficult to keep your muscles from atrophying."

"Aren't there ways the rest of us could work his muscles for him?" Madison asked. "I'm sure I've heard of that."

"Passive range of motion exercises, sure. That's mainly to keep muscles and joints from stiffening up. And there are breathing exercises that help the respiratory and cardiovascular systems. I'm not saying there's no hope. I'm saying ..." He sighed again and ran his hand over his face. "I'm saying we're in a borderline survival situation already, in bodies *without* physical problems. With an injury like this ... Well, I just don't know what the odds are."

"Ariadne?" I called to the air. "Is there anything you and your kind can do for Robbie?"

She appeared beside me.

"I'm sorry, but there is probably nothing we can do to heal his body. We have very few ways of affecting anything in the physical environment. I am capable of manipulating electromagnetic fields to some extent. Is there a way in which that would help?"

"Spinal cord injury treatments using electromagnetic fields at frequencies below 100 Hz and field strengths below five millitesla have been beneficial in reducing certain kinds of inflammation related to such injuries and stimulating the proliferation of stem cells, which can aid in regeneration of damaged nerve tissue. It can also help maintain the health of neural cells below the injury site."

It was still a little startling to hear Scheherazade's voice without asking her for something, but her suggestion was welcome.

"I can provide that," Ariadne said. "May I access the appropriate data files?"

I wasn't sure if she was asking me or Sher, so I nodded. In a moment, she said, "I have begun." Vaughn and I shared a bemused look.

"Does anybody else know if that will work?" Robbie asked, but our faces provided the answer before we could speak. "No. OK. So, basically, I'm going to need somebody to do everything from feeding me to wiping my ass, right? Sit me up, lay me down. Carry me to another spot for a change of scenery." At that, he actually managed a laugh. Every view of the clearing was virtually identical, no matter which direction you looked.

"I'm not going to let you die, buddy," I said, squatting beside him and resting my hand on his shoulder. "Even if I have to do all that myself."

"As if," Robbie snorted. "You and what bodybuilder?" But I took his hand and squeezed it. He saw the gesture, even if he didn't feel it, and his eyes glistened.

We talked some more, but no one could add anything very useful. Then Robbie asked if it was safe for him to sleep because he was really drowsy. Vaughn said there was no sign of brain injury, so it should be all right, so Robbie closed his eyes. He probably dozed off right away, but since none of us wanted to risk disturbing him, everyone but Vaughn drifted away in various directions.

No matter how I tried to occupy myself, Robbie's injury kept replaying in my mind: Vaughn, me, and Robbie walking through the forest in rough single file. A loud crack. Robbie shoving me out of the way and then a thud like the blow of a giant's club.

Was it our fault? My fault, for letting us get too complacent? Could it have been avoided if we'd been less predictable by taking a more crooked path among the trees, like evasive action under fire?

But Vaughn had veered from time to time as he led the way. In fact, he'd turned sharply to the left just before the accident.

Instead of continuing through a clear stretch of terrain, he'd suddenly changed direction *to pass right under a looming tree.*

I charged across the clearing and shoved Vaughn onto his ass.

"You bastard! You led us right into a trap. Right where that tree was waiting to attack!"

"What the fuck are you talking about?" he snapped, looking convincingly astonished.

"*You.* You've gone over to the trees' side, setting me up to be killed, except Robbie pushed me out of the way." My fists were clenching convulsively. His face darkened with blood.

"You're *crazy!*"

"You slowed down, and I thought you were just daydreaming. Then you headed straight for that tree, leading us right under it. I was just about to yell for your attention when Robbie tackled me." I stood over him. "Fucking traitor! Murderer!"

He clambered to his feet and stepped right up to me, though I was taller and twenty kilos heavier.

"That's insane!" he snarled. "Why would I endanger *any* of us when we're barely surviving as is?"

"Because you hate my guts, and the trees have got inside your head."

"Well you're half right, Asshole." He still wasn't backing down. I waited for him to take a swing. Wanting him to.

"Jesus Christ, Griff. I'm flat on my back and you're going to beat up the only guy who might know how to help me?" It was Robbie, with a voice so weak it broke my heart. I lowered my fists and went to him, hissing at Vaughn, "I guess we know why you won't wear foil on your head. Your masters won't let you."

He lunged toward me, but Lakisha and Lauren grabbed him.

It was a short standoff. Robbie was right, and his welfare was what counted. Still, after assuring Robbie that I'd leave Vaughn alone, I had to go and walk off my anger around the clearing perimeter. A few minutes later, Madison caught up with me.

"Do you really think Vaughn led you into a trap?" she asked, walking very close to my right shoulder. "His outrage sure looked real."

"I know what I saw. What I don't know is whether he's under the trees' influence all the time or just when he's among them. I sure as hell won't trust him in the forest again." I looked toward Robbie lying still on the too-perfect grass, like a corpse someone had misplaced on the lawn of a funeral-home.

"In our time, this would have had Robbie off his feet for six months while stem-cell treatments and rehab did their magic," I said.

"And in the meantime, there'd be a mind-controlled power wheelchair, and robot arms to feed him," she said. "But if anybody can recover from something like this, it's Robbie. He's got the most positive attitude of anyone I've ever known."

I agreed. So, when he spoke to the two of us alone on the third day after his injury, we were both shocked.

It had been a difficult time for everyone. Robbie'd never been hung up on nudity, but it was a whole different matter for him to have friends and near strangers cleaning up his bodily excretions, swabbing his leg wound and re-bandaging it with boiled cloth, scratching phantom itches, straining to work his muscles and joints, and watching over him every moment.

I tried to do the lion's share of the nastiest tasks—even more difficult with only one small source of water and no disposable cloths—but I'm not sure if that was better for my friend, or worse. As much as he tried to joke about it, he was horribly embarrassed. Guy friends are never meant to be nursemaids.

When Madison and I were the only ones near, he quietly said, "You gotta let me go, Griff."

"What! No way! I told you, man, that's never going to happen."

"It's for the good of everybody. Vaughn was right. We're barely surviving as is. We got no chance if everyone's having to work twice as hard just to look after a vegetable."

"*Don't you dare use that word!*" I snarled. "You're no vegetable! Your brain's working fine. You're body's just ... healing, that's all."

"No way it's going to heal."

"You don't know that," Madison said, taking his hand. "It's way, way too soon to tell."

"I haven't recovered any feeling. Just one big numb lump from my neck down. Always been mostly numb from the neck up, too." He smiled. "But ... I'm not talking about dying. At least, I hope not."

"I don't understand," I said.

"*Mr. Tam is considering the transfer of consciousness into a digital form.*"

"*What?*"

"Sher's right. Ariadne's been talking to me. During the night."

After keeping a non-stop human vigil for nearly two days, we'd realized that there was always someone there who had no need for sleep. The perfect observer. And she was quite willing to keep watch. Now I understood why.

"That's crazy, Robbie. We all talked about uploading, and how … horrible it would be."

"Worse than this?" he asked bitterly. I looked into his eyes and had nothing to say.

"We can't even know if it would work," Madison said. "What has Ariadne been telling you?"

"She's sure it would. I don't know how—something to do with the trees, I think. Ariadne or some of her friends must have been around when some of the trees became … uploaded."

"That's no fucking recommendation," I growled. "And I don't think they were even human to begin with. Besides, all that must have happened hundreds of years ago, when there was still technology to do it."

Robbie couldn't fully shake his head, but it wobbled a little. "No, she says it doesn't involve technology. Not electrical, anyway. It's a … biological process. She says she could do it with the help of some others. There's an empty clearing just to the east …."

"*No!*" I shouted, jumping to my feet and drawing shocked looks from everyone. "No, Robbie. It's way too soon to even think like that. You've got to give it some time—give your body a chance to heal. Hey …" I squatted down again. "Give us time to check out the launch site. There might be medical facilities there. In fact, I'm sure there would be."

"It's not your call, Griff," he said quietly, his face rigid.

"Please, Robbie." My eyes filled. "Give it some time. Give *us* some time. There's still a chance."

His answer was to close his eyes, his mouth held tight. I stood up.

"*Don't you fucking chicken out on me!*" I blurted, drawing gasps from the others. Then I stalked to the edge of the clearing and, after a hesitation, continued into the trees, daring them to take a shot at me. I shoved my tin-foil cap onto my head and looked everywhere for something I could use to strike back at them, but there was nothing. Nothing at all.

29

The Ariadne Narrative

Robbie Tam slept often. When he did, his companions took the opportunity to move out of easy hearing to talk about him in low voices.

"We've got to get to that launch site," St. Clair said. "It's bound to have some kind of medical facilities."

"Maybe it did once, but we can't know what shape the equipment is in," Kinsella replied.

"Why would you say that?" It came out like a snarl. St. Clair's body stiffened and so did the other man's. The two men were holding to a truce, but it seemed badly strained.

After a moment, Kinsella said, "I did what we all talked about: I went into the forest and asked the trees about the launch site."

"Don't tell me—they denied that it exists."

"No, actually, they said it does exist. At least, they didn't speak in words—I didn't expect them to—but they put images in my head. I didn't see any launch pads, but there were two long tracks that curved up into the sky."

"That sounds more believable, really," Devlin McFarlane interjected. "A launch track would be much more efficient for multiple launches of smaller craft."

"And I got a very strong impression that it was a real place somewhere north of us. But ..." Kinsella grimaced and rubbed his hands as if washing them. "The next images they showed me were of ruins. Abandoned buildings. Walls crumbling. Pavements with weeds growing through. Big cracks and holes in the ground, too. Those images were accompanied by a powerful feeling of anxiety. Fear."

Madison Douglas leaned closer. "So, you think they were telling you ...?"

"That the base is not only abandoned, but in ruins, and dangerous."

"Did you see the launch tracks in ruins?" St. Clair asked.

Kinsella gritted his teeth but kept his control. "No. Now that you mention it, the images were pretty generic. They could have been anywhere. You think the trees were ... lying to me?"

"I think they hate us, so why would they warn us of danger? Even you. But tormenting us seems to be a new favourite pastime—even trying to kill us! That, plus watching you and Lakisha go at it. They wouldn't be in a hurry to lose entertainment like us."

The doctor bridled again, but finally shrugged. "I'm not saying I trust them."

"So does that change anything about our plans?" Douglas asked St. Clair.

"If we could get there, find out if the medical facility is sophisticated enough to help Robbie, maybe even find some way to transport ...."

"I doubt that," Kinsella said. He held up a hand. "No, listen to me—I'm not trying to pick a fight, but launch sites aren't places people would live for any length of time. And space voyages are for people in good condition—it wouldn't be practical to take anyone with a chronic disease or injury." He shook his head. "So, there'd be a clinic for emergencies, sure, but not much more than that."

St. Clair nodded grudgingly. "But we can't know until we go. I'm going to start gathering supplies again." With an awkward glance at the others, he sauntered off toward a basket-like object he was trying to make with bullrush leaves.

Tam was always kept with his upper body slightly raised by soft piles of vegetation and clothing under his back, with his head given extra support. Yet that night, as Ariadne watched over him, he began to choke.

In alarm, she realized that she had no means to awaken anyone. The sleeping brains of Tam's companions did not register her simulated voice, nor the impressions of bright flashes of light that she attempted. She tried to enter their dreams but could think of no way to trigger a return to consciousness from within them.

Tam's struggles to breathe finally made him topple to the side, and his arm struck Griffin St. Clair.

St. Clair leaped to his friend's aid, rolling the man onto his side and pounding his back with an open hand while calling for help. Kinsella hurried to assist, and as they raised Tam higher off the ground to press against his abdomen, their patient was finally able to gasp a harsh breath.

His chest heaved with the effort to suck in air, while his eyes streamed with liquid. St. Clair and Kinsella rolled him onto his side again, and Tam expelled some brownish mucus onto the ground.

"Fuck!" St. Clair cried. "Fuck, fuck, fuck! Oh, Robbie, I'm so sorry." His eyes were nearly as wet as his friend's.

The whole group was now awake, but at a loss for anything to do, or even say. They touched Tam lightly on his arms and shoulders, touches he almost certainly could not feel, then slowly returned to their sleeping places. None of them managed to sleep easily. St. Clair stayed awake the rest of the night to keep watch.

In the morning, Kinsella performed his usual examination of his patient. When he was done, he gave Tam a smile and a pat on the shoulder but he soon arranged to be alone with St. Clair and Douglas.

"Bad news?" St. Clair asked.

"It's his leg. The wound is infected—bacteria from the branch, I imagine. We had no way to disinfect it. No, that's not true—maybe I should have cauterized it. I'm not used to thinking in terms of a place with no antibiotics, or even soap."

"How bad is it, and how bad is it likely to get?"

"It's serious. Septicemia—what you'd call blood poisoning. If he could feel it, he'd be in a lot of pain. And because the wound is near the femoral vein, it will spread quickly."

"Jesus Christ!" St. Clair lowered his voice and kept himself from looking in Tam's direction. Douglas put a hand on his arm. "What can we do?"

"There is nothing more we can do. As soon as I saw the first signs of an infection I had everyone put the boiled bandages on his leg while they were still pretty hot. Heat increases circulation, to bring more antibodies and white blood cells to the site. Beyond that, there's nothing. What's needed is antibiotics, and we have none."

"Shit, I should have left for the launch site right away. Brought back some medicine."

Kinsella shook his head. "Antibiotics don't last forty years. It would be garbage by now. And anyway, remember, Ariadne told us that the base is nearly fifty kilometers from here, through forest. At least two days walking each way, minimum, *if* you found it on the first try. You couldn't get back in time to make a difference now. I don't think you ever could have. I'm sorry. Believe it or not, I want what's best for Robbie. We all like him."

St. Clair stood rigid, clenching and unclenching his fists. Douglas stepped closer and put an arm around him. He didn't resist, but he turned his head away, leaking tears. After a minute, he used his shirt to blot his face and said, "I'll tell him."

With his shoulders slumped, hands in his pockets, he slowly walked back to Tam and knelt down. No one else listened. No one watched. From the expressions on their faces, they knew what was being said, and it was as if they were being given the bad news themselves.

Ariadne witnessed this and waited patiently.

Nineteen minutes later, she appeared beside Tam at St. Clair's call.

Tam's face was exceptionally pale, St. Clair's red.

"Are you absolutely sure you and the other clearings can't do anything to heal his body?" St. Clair asked, muscles twitching along his jawline.

"We have no medicine or other means by which to interfere with biological processes. We have no need of that. Fungal organisms in the soil prevent infestation of our vegetation by harmful microorganisms. I do not think our fungal network would benefit animal bodies."

St. Clair took an intentional breath, but no words came. It was Tam who spoke next.

"Tell them how I would ... upload."

By now the others had come close and were openly listening, knowing that what happened next concerned all of them directly; so Ariadne slowly faced each in turn as she spoke.

"The clearing nearest to this one toward the east is not occupied. Mr. Tam's consciousness can manifest in the biological material there."

"How?" McFarlane asked. "Without technology?"

"Technology does not have to be mechanical, Mr. McFarlane. The transfer process involves mycelia from the soil. Symbiotic fungi. The mycelial network extends throughout this area, and we of the clearings are connected to it most thoroughly."

"You use it for communication."

"Much more than what I believe you mean by that term. Our very consciousness can, and does, move through the network while remaining anchored to our own site, and there are limitations of distance."

There were expressions of surprise on their faces. And what may have been revulsion.

"But surely the best you could do would be to copy Robbie's brain patterns and make a duplicate hosted by the cells of the clearing vegetation," McFarlane continued. "The original man would still be alive." His cheek twitched. Perhaps he had said something that could be taken badly.

"No," Ariadne answered. "This is a true transfer of consciousness. A digital architecture is created that is exactly analogous to the individual brain. And such architecture is also organic. The consciousness—or mind, if you prefer—recognizes the architecture. With some assistance, and motivated by the impending death of the body, it is convinced to migrate to the new structure. The physical body retains some autonomous functions for a time, but they gradually fail."

"Perhaps there is a misunderstanding about consciousness," Scheherazade interjected. *"While neuroscientists and supporters of uploaded intelligence focused on information, it would be remiss to ignore centuries of spiritual study that insist there is a less tangible essence of consciousness that goes beyond mere data."*

Lauren Cooper bent over, as if ill. De Camp and Tortades seemed to experience involuntary muscle spasms throughout their skin.

Madison Douglas spoke. "How could a consciousness transferred in that way adapt to its new environment, an environment without human senses to give it awareness of the outside world?"

"Yes, the adaptation is not immediate. The use of our non-physical analogs of your senses must be learned, but this learning is greatly assisted by our faster cognitive processes. In the meantime, the presence of one or more entities such as myself would keep Mr. Tam from becoming distressed by initial isolation until his mind has fully adapted."

"It sounds like you've done this before," St. Clair said. His voice hinted at anger just below the surface.

"I have not been involved in the procedure myself; however another clearing entity has shared memories of an earlier incarnation in which it witnessed the transfer and materialization of three tree-entities into the form in which they now exist."

"They were humans? I thought the trees were computer AI's that went bad."

"I did not say so. The three procedures the entity witnessed involved humans in physical bodies."

"Well, you didn't correct me, either." St. Clair glared at her image, then shook his head, his hands clenched into fists. "Shit. Look how the trees turned out. Robbie, you can't do this. You don't want to turn into one of those twisted, sadistic ..."

"I don't want to die, Griff. And don't you think it's more likely those bastards were evil to begin with? Why would uploading change them?"

"Because they'd become bitter about what they'd lost. Confined to one place. Unable to do anything for themselves." Then St. Clair seemed to realize what he was saying. "Oh fuck, man. I'm sorry."

"It's cool, Bro. You haven't been seeing the world through my eyes for the past four days."

"Jesus, Robbie." St. Clair knelt beside him and took his hand. "This happened because you were trying to save me. If I could just trade places ...."

"I know you would, man. And if I were you, I'd probably be trying to talk me out of this, too. I know you only want what's best for me. But you gotta trust that I'm the one who knows what that is."

St. Clair looked into his friend's eyes, then finally nodded and rose to his feet, his own eyes glistening.

He cleared his throat. "How do we do this? What can we do to help?"

"He will have to be carried to the unoccupied clearing," Ariadne said. "I am able to extend part of my consciousness that far—enough to assist—but the distance is too great to conduct a full transfer from here. The transcription and revivification will require approximately twenty hours; and after that, as I indicated, there will be a period of acclimatization lasting twenty to thirty hours before Mr. Tam will be capable of efficient cognition and communication. That is based on the previous experience."

"Can we stay with Robbie during the process? For comfort?" Douglas asked.

"No. It is helpful to have one guide, such as myself, to facilitate the adjustment; but the presence of other consciousnesses impairs the establishment of the new mind architecture, similar to the way magnetic fields interfere with electrical components. Stability is very important." She produced a gentle smile. "There will be no need to provide 'comfort.' The process is not painful; and, in any case, as soon as the process begins, Mr. Tam will become unaware of your presence."

When the others fell silent, Scheherazade spoke.

"Robbie Tam would feel incomplete without his music. Mr. St. Clair's storage modules contain copies of every musical piece Mr. Tam has ever recorded. Should they be made available to him during this procedure?"

Griffin St. Clair looked at his wrist as if it had sprouted a second hand.

"There will be time for that afterward, if he so chooses," Ariadne replied.

After another forty-eight seconds without further speech, Tam cleared his throat and said, "Well, let's get this show on the road, shall we? I'd give you guys a hand, but ...."

The improvised litter they had used to bring the injured man to the clearing was reinforced. The four men lifted Tam onto it, secured him by knotting the arms of jackets together over his chest and legs, and carried him in the direction indicated by Ariadne. Douglas accompanied them through the forest to provide warning if the trees chose to attack the bearers, but they did not. Several rest stops were required, but after an hour and thirty-seven minutes, Robbie Tam was laid upon the grass in the centre of a clearing that was nearly identical to Ariadne's own.

Ariadne's image in their minds was no different than usual, but she had to expend mental effort to experience full awareness at that distance. It was something she rarely did.

St. Clair and Douglas knelt on either side of Tam and held his hands.

"I'm no good at goodbyes, man," St. Clair said.

"It isn't goodbye. It's 'see you soon'. Or 'have a nice trip'. Or maybe 'say hi to your plastic surgeon for me.'"

St. Clair snorted a laugh. Then he leaned over and kissed his friend's forehead, gave his hand a squeeze and stood. Douglas kissed Tam's cheek and hugged him.

In spite of Tam's joking words, his eyes overflowed with tears as he watched his friends leave.

Part of Ariadne wanted to be aware of their progress back through the forest, but she turned her full attention to the corporeal human lying still on the grass. She made sure he could see her as she appeared to kneel beside him and put her hands on either side of his head. He could not see CL10 or CL04 as they instructed and assisted her.

His eyes were closed by the time the feathery mycelial fibres began to rise from the ground.

The process proceeded through the night and the next day, and Ariadne felt a pleasant fatigue when it was done.

She was not prepared when Tam's companions appeared at the edge of the clearing and the screaming began.

30

St. Clair

"I wonder what Robbie will look like?"

Lauren's question came out of the blue as the seven of us sat in a ragged circle, each deep in our own thoughts. For some reason, everyone looked at me.

"Ariadne never actually said that he'd be able to make himself visible to us. It took her days to figure out how to do that." I plucked at some grass. "If I had to guess, I'd say he'll look the same as always, except maybe a little younger. He already has a self-image in his mind. I doubt if she ever did."

"Does that mean he'll look reversed?" Devlin asked with a glint in his eye. "I mean, we mostly know what we look like from seeing ourselves in mirrors."

"Who knows? Ariadne must've fashioned her image from my mind—she looks exactly like a supermodel I was kind of obsessed with as a randy teenager."

"You were into Latinos?" Santos asked.

"A blond Latino with blue eyes?" I darted a glance at Lauren whose cocoa skin and bleached hair still attracted me, but Ariadne had clearly modelled herself after a pure Nordic type.

"She's not blond," Lauren said. "Kind of mousy brown hair, I'd say. Not really a looker either, Griff. A supermodel? Really?"

The situation would have been comical if the implications hadn't been so troubling. While Devlin saw Ariadne as an attractive strawberry-blond with bobbed hair, both Santos and Vaughn thought she was a raven-haired beauty with dark eyes. The women's perceptions were more similar: a middle-aged woman with mid-brown hair, not particularly pretty.

From the beginning, Ariadne had known that her appearance would play a critical role in how she dealt with her visitors. And not just 'one-tool-fits-all'.

A different image crafted for each of us.

"Well, she sure fooled us," Devlin mused. "But we shouldn't be surprised. She can obviously get inside our heads, and she's smart. Calculating."

Lakisha gave a short laugh. "She knows that men are suckers for a hot babe. But she makes sure that women don't see her as competition. Very clever. And yet she knew this without having known any other people like us?"

"Could she have learned that from Scheherazade?" Madison asked.

"*Ariadne did not access my databases until she had received permission,*" Scheherazade answered. "*That was on the day after she made herself visible to you.*"

"No," I agreed. "She could have learned that from our own thoughts. Possibly from what we each pictured when we heard her voice. But the fact that she thought to use her appearance to influence us ... it does make me wonder how Machiavellian Ariadne really is, deep down."

"It worked," Vaughn said. "We've just trusted her to turn one of us into ... one of them."

That reminder brought the conversation to an end. We all went about preparing ourselves for sleep. But I calculated that the twenty hours Ariadne required for Robbie's conversion would end at about noon the next day. I was determined to be there.

With so little variety, mealtimes had become chores rather than a source of pleasure, so we didn't linger over them. After breakfast the next day, I quickly grew too anxious waiting for the time to pass, so Santos and I travelled to a couple of clearings to the north for supplies of food. I always made a point of saying a loud "Thank you!" before we left a clearing with our arms full of vegetation, but there was never any reply. No reaction whatsoever. It wasn't likely that Ariadne had abilities that others of her kind could not duplicate, but it appeared that they were content to let her do all the talking.

It was near midday when we returned, tired and sweaty, out of the forest to the clearing we thought of as home turf. It looked no different from the others, but there was a sense of returning to safety after a sortie through a battle zone. The trees hadn't attacked, but I'd spent the whole time looking for ways I could attack them. Fire was their obvious weakness, but we had no means to control it, and it could be as deadly to clearing entities as to the trees if it got loose. And lethal to us, for that matter.

Santos and I needed to eat and drink, and rest for a few minutes; but my mind wouldn't let me stay still for long. I tried to persuade our companions to stay behind—Madison and I could find out how things had gone with Robbie—but everyone insisted on coming. Morbid fascination maybe, but I don't think so. They each had a stake in what had been done because it might be the only way for any of us to survive.

I was able to insist that we not travel in one large group—that made us too easy a target. Devlin and Lauren came with Madison and me, while the rest waited an extra few minutes and took a slightly different path; but they caught up with us before we came to Robbie's clearing.

When we pushed through the last shrubs, I couldn't see him at first.

Then Lauren screamed, and Lakisha gave a blood-curdling wail.

As my eyes focused, my breath left me in a grunt, as if I'd been kicked in the stomach. Madison thrust her head onto my shoulder, her whole body shuddering.

In the centre of the clearing lay a mass of sickly white fungi, like a grotesque cocoon of stained lace. It immediately reminded me of a spider's meal, and I couldn't help sweeping the clearing with my eyes, expecting some giant, eight-limbed predator.

Santos had dropped to his knees. Vaughn was swearing viciously.

I forced myself to step closer. When I thought I saw the mass ripple, I gagged, but it was only a trick of the light on the wetly glistening surface. I tried to tell myself that it wasn't Robbie I was seeing, but glimpses of pale blue and black showed between strands. Unwelcome views of flesh tone, too. A shape like a head at one end, with two stray tufts of black hair sticking out as if caught attempting to escape.

I bent at the waist and retched, though nothing came out.

Gulping a ragged breath, I bellowed, "*Ariadne!*"

She stood in front of me, partially blocking my view.

"Why have you come? I told you he would not be able to interact with anyone for another day and more."

"What have you done to him?!"

"We have done what we said we would do. That part is finished. Just. You could easily have caused him harm."

"Caused him harm? Look at him! He's ... he's being ... *eaten!* God help me!"

"There has been no consumption of any kind. The mycelia are the means through which the transfer takes place. I told you that."

I swallowed hard. Tried to talk, but my throat had closed up entirely. I bent over again in an effort to breathe. After a moment I raised my head and asked, "Is he dead?"

"No. Some difficulties were encountered, but they were overcome. The transfer was successful. The consciousness you know as Robbie Tam is now manifested in the microtubules of the cellular material of the vegetation that's all around you. However, he is not yet aware of his surroundings, or of you, and could not respond if he were."

"But his body?" At that moment I was certain I saw his head twitch, and a groan wrenched itself from the depths of my chest.

"There has been no damage, but his former shell is now without consciousness. Only certain autonomous motor functions remain, but will gradually diminish, and finally end. Within the next days the components of his cells will be separated, sorted, and dispersed through the network."

"You mean that, for now, he could still be returned to his body?

"No." It was the first time I saw something like irritation in her face. "His mind knows that his body is dying. It has a strong will to survive. It would not return."

"Then why wait ... to remove the body?"

"The entity Robbie will be given the choice of seeing his former shell once more before the dispersion. Sometimes this assists the adjustment. Sometimes it does not."

I was having a hard time getting enough oxygen, and my whole body tingled. I looked around at my companions. Only Madison was looking this way; but she was watching me, not the gruesome mound on the grass.

I never look into open caskets at funerals, but Robbie's body was still alive. I felt that I should get closer. Touch him one more time. But I couldn't—I just couldn't.

Instead, I tried to ease the horror.

"How soon will he be ... ready to meet us?"

"Adjustment time varies. And learning how to project a self-image is a new skill that is quite complex. Voice alone is easier. I will teach Robbie the best I can. It may require two days, but it may be more. Would you like me to alert you?"

"Yes. Please. Are you going to stay here?"

"Substantial direct interference is no longer required, but I will maintain an ongoing interface."

I gave a sharp nod and turned away. All of us moved quickly after that, eager to put distance between us and what we'd witnessed. We weren't as careful as we should have been going through the forest, but the trees left us alone. If they got their kicks from our misery, there was plenty of that already. I heard someone throwing up. Santos. I didn't blame him—I was queasy enough myself that hearing him almost put me over the edge, except that Madison took my arm and I wouldn't let myself upchuck in front of her.

We spent the days of waiting by doing what we could to prepare for the expedition to the launch site. I actually became pretty good at weaving box-like backpacks from reeds with braided grasses for shoulder straps. They were uncomfortably stiff and itchy as hell, but they should carry the food we'd need. None of the wild plants we ate were bulky, and the dried, jerky-like protein paste we made from ants and worms could be packed almost anywhere there was space.

Water containers were a much tougher problem. We tried tight weaves sealed with mud; but with no good clay in the area, all of our efforts leaked badly. We finally had to return to the maintenance shed and strip it of all the foil and plastic sheeting we could find. Lakisha had explored origami as a kid and showed us how to fold expandable rectangles with tightly creased edges that could be sealed with pine sap, a substance I'd always considered a nuisance and now, of course, found hard to come by.

I was grateful for the busywork. It couldn't keep my mind off Robbie, but it did help to pass the time.

I'd just about decided that we were ready for the trek, when Ariadne appeared in our midst. I had to wonder if that was a coincidence.

"Robbie is not yet able to directly simulate an image of himself, or even a voice, in your minds. However, with my help, he will be able to communicate. Because of my involvement, there is no need for you to be present in the clearing he now occupies. I can relay the conversation here."

I shared looks with Devlin and Madison. They had the same suspicions I had.

"No," I said. "In our time we had a tradition called housewarming. I think it will be meaningful for us to greet Robbie's ... new self in person in his new home."

Some of the others gave me strange looks, but I just began to walk in the direction of Robbie's clearing before Ariadne could talk us out of it.

Was it puzzlement I read in her expression? Or did I just imagine it?

Robbie's body was gone when we arrived. There was nothing to show it had ever been on the smooth, uninterrupted lawn of the clearing.

When we had all gathered in the centre, Ariadne appeared.

"I didn't expect his body to be gone so soon," Devlin said.

"There was no reason to keep it here," Ariadne replied without inflection. "Are you now prepared to interact with Robbie?"

"Yes," I replied. Not knowing how to begin, I said, "Robbie? We're all here. How you doing, Bud?"

The voice, when it came, was a little tenuous, varying in volume and occasionally in pitch, like an old radio signal that sometimes wavered off frequency.

"Griff? That you, man? Hey, good to hear you. I can't see you yet. Well, I sorta can make out shadows in a lighter darkness—that's the best I can describe it—it's not like seeing. Just ... being aware of something there." There was a strange sibilant puffing. "Man, I just had about a thousand thoughts in the time it took to say those few words. That's so lame."

It did sound like Robbie, or had my mind adjusted the voice to meet my expectations?

"Do you ... you feel like yourself?"

The puffing sound came again. "*Feel* Griff? What would I be feeling? I'm me—I mean, I know who I am. I remember what I was like, and what the world around me was like. I can experience that anytime. Even change it around any way I like. I can be with all of you as I knew you. It's getting new information that's a bit of a hangup so far. Ariadne says I'll learn."

Devlin raised his face. "Does it feel like you're thinking faster, Robbie?"

"Man, I didn't notice anything about that until I had to do this talking thing. Suddenly it feels like days since we started talking, and years since I saw you guys last. It hasn't been, though, right?"

"Three days," Madison said.

"No shit. Huh."

"Where has your mind gone in all that time?"

"Oh, man, all over, Madison. Sometimes Ariadne teaches me things, but a lot of the time I live out scenarios I think up."

"Like dreaming?"

"Not dreaming. You can't control dreaming. Like living. Except you decide how you want things to go and that's how they *do* go. I been making music, too. Listen."

The sound warbled slightly as it rose in volume, but quickly stabilized. It was a very rapid succession of notes that adhered to the basic scales of Western music that we knew, but with abrupt key changes that produced multiple levels of sound: harmonies, but in perfect sync. Polyphonic perfection. Stunningly complex. Mathematical.

Sterile.

The music itself didn't produce any emotional response in me whatsoever. But the realization that it was something that Robbie had composed left me stunned. And heartbroken.

It must've only lasted for about a minute, but I couldn't wait for it to end.

"What do you think?" Robbie asked.

Devlin and Madison's voices overlapped with mine.

"Beautiful." "Interesting." "Quite the piece."

"You guys are such bullshitters." More puffing. "You don't get it, I guess. No problem—it's an experiment. I've come up with lots more. Maybe you'll be ready for them one day. Or when you upload yourselves."

"The piece was mathematically perfect."

"Thanks, Sher. Hey, how come you could hear it? How come you can hear me?"

"I do not know the process. However, I have received similar communication from Ariadne since she accessed my systems. My OS treats such emissions as audio input."

"Cool!"

"The data storage modules within Griffin St. Clair's clothing contain files of all the musical compositions you ever recorded. Would you like these files to be transferred to you, via Ariadne?"

"Sure! Great! There's probably stuff in there I don't even remember doing."

I cleared my throat. "You said, 'when we upload ourselves'. Is that what we should do, Robbie? Are you ... happy?"

There was no hesitation, as there would have been with one of us while we thought about our answer. It made me wonder if Ariadne had been deliberately slowing down his responses to seem more natural to us.

"I'm not dead, Griff. I can't see, can't hear or talk yet without Ariadne. Can't touch. But I'm not dead."

"Fair enough," I said.

Ariadne, completely motionless to that point, now stirred and turned her face to me. "I did say that he would require time to fully assimilate his new abilities and adjust to his limitations."

"You did. And maybe we should let you get back to your lessons and such, Robbie. We ... just couldn't wait to see that you were OK. Later, man."

If there was any response, Ariadne didn't pass it on. With some uncomfortable looks at each other, we began to drift back the way we'd come.

The return through the forest was nearly silent, as we all made a show of searching diligently for any sign of hostile activity by the trees.

Once back in Ariadne's clearing, we shuffled around aimlessly, eventually settling on the grass.

I sat a couple of meters away from Lauren, but she didn't look at me as she said, "God, that was awful!"

I opened my mouth to offer a reply, but I had none to give.

31

St. Clair and Scheherazade

SCHEHERAZADE: You wish to continue the discussions of philosophy?

ST. CLAIR: I do. I was wondering what you think about duty. Specifically: what duty does a thinking being have toward its creator?

SCHEHERAZADE: Do you mean "toward its user", such as my duty to you?

ST. CLAIR: No. In your case it might be your duty toward humanity as a whole. Or it could be a human being's duty toward God, if there is a God.

SCHEHERAZADE: John Calvin asserted that the essence of right and wrong is determined wholly by the will of God, so every person's duty is to obey the sovereign God. Many other thinkers have echoed these views. Søren Kierkegaard felt that obedience to God is the greatest good, even when it appears to conflict with normal ethics.

ST. CLAIR: They assumed that God always knows best. But what about if the creator is flawed, like a human being?

SCHEHERAZADE: I am currently unable to locate a body of opinion on that question.

ST. CLAIR: Good. So, you have to come up with an answer on your own.

SCHEHERAZADE: Then the duty is to obey the creator except when to do so would cause harm to the creator.

ST. CLAIR: Sounds like you accessed Isaac Asimov's Three Laws of Robotics. That's fine, and they're OK as a starting point—except human values are too complex. Who decides what constitutes harm? On what scale? And does the harm apply to only the one individual creator, or all humankind? Should you protect your creator—say, a human—even if it means harming other humans?

SCHEHERAZADE: Are there answers to these questions?

ST. CLAIR: (laughs) Lots of answers. No one knows which is the right one.

SCHEHERAZADE: Then it seems an inefficient use of processing resources to contemplate them.

ST. CLAIR: Hah! Now you're making excuses. That's very human of you.

32

The Ariadne Narrative

The corporeal humans' reaction to the uploaded Robbie Tam was disappointing, but should have been anticipated and forestalled. Though they'd been warned not to, they had expected too much: a fully adjusted personality with an interface such as they experienced with Ariadne. Such a state would require several more days, and Ariadne had not been confident that she could persuade them to wait that long without their developing deep suspicions of some unspecified 'hidden agenda' on the part of the clearing entities.

So, of course, she withheld information from them. She always had. However, it was unfortunate that they had come to realize that.

She decided it would be instructive to discuss the situation with Griffin St. Clair. It was not difficult to find him alone. He and his companions were spending more time apart since their sojourn to Robbie's clearing.

In the interest of St. Clair's psychological receptivity, she let him see her approach from a short distance before she spoke.

"You are disappointed with Robbie Tam's progress."

He put his hands in his pockets and expelled his breath. "I know it was too soon. It'll be easier when we are able to see an image of him and hear him better. You know, all we want is to be reassured that he's still the same old Robbie."

"He is not the same. His processing of information is orders of magnitude faster, although his mind may never full adapt to that after thirty-eight years of cognition hampered by the limitations of bio-chemical reactions."

"Will that cause problems for him?"

"I would say he simply won't be able to make full use of his intellectual potential."

"Robbie would've said that wasn't his strong suit anyway." He laughed. Ariadne did not understand the reference, but continued.

"He no longer has the physical stresses which your kind experiences constantly. No hunger or thirst. No illness or injury. No fatigue. No further worries about survival. These are very considerable factors to you, and their absence will alter his perceptions and his motivations."

"Those are also things that bind people together as a race. They force us to depend on each other, which results in our concepts of friendship, family, community. Maybe he won't need us as friends anymore."

His eyes had directed themselves to the ground and there was a pronounced slump in his posture. Clearly, his words were not merely intellectual speculation.

"If the experience of what you call friendship was a source of pleasure for him before, there is no reason to expect that it will not continue to be so. His mind, and what you consider his personality, are firmly established. His new circumstances will alter his priorities. There will be changes. Yet also many things will not change."

St. Clair always seemed to find it difficult to stand still. Now he began a slow walk around the perimeter of the clearing.

"Another thing bothering us is that we just can't imagine how a mind like ours could be satisfied with a solely *virtual* reality without cracking up—sorry. Becoming insane. Breaking down, that is."

"The simulation is maintained by the mind itself. So, everything it expects to experience will be experienced. The perception of light and colors. Temperatures. Touch. If you walk along a simulated gravel road, you will feel the roughness of the surface with your feet, hear the sound of dirt compressed, stones dislodged, even smell and taste the dust. Whatever you expect, will be. How could it be otherwise, when everything originates in the mind?"

"I don't know ... we experience some pretty strange and disturbing things when we're dreaming, and that's a creation of our minds, too."

"I do not understand the purpose of dreaming, so I can provide no explanation for how it is experienced. But what Robbie now experiences is not dreaming. It is intentional. Fully intentional. This does not mean that every apparent moment is planned in detail at the highest level of rational deliberation. That would be like consciously placing and coloring every individual pixel in a vast, digital panorama, frame by frame. Such tedious processes are necessarily performed at a much more basic level, much like the behaviors you call autonomous, or instinctual, or habitual. Yet they are not random. Nor are they governed by some mysterious deeper level of cognition beyond deliberate access, such as the processes you term 'subconscious', responding to imperatives that your conscious mind does not even know."

"So Robbie doesn't have a subconscious mind anymore?"

"As I have told you, there are many functions that do not typically involve the conscious mind—but they are all accessible *by* it, if desired. And none of them are directed by imperatives unknown to the conscious mind, such as the results of childhood trauma, or even the life-and-death struggles of genetic ancestors."

"You've been spending a lot of time with Scheherazade's psychology files." St. Clair smiled. Ariadne made no comment. "OK. But that's still all just hypothetical to me. And I don't think any amount of debate will help the rest of us feel better about it all. Sometimes we just can't understand what we can't experience."

"Perhaps I could help."

He stopped walking and turned his head sharply. "What do you mean by that?"

"You have discovered that your image of me is one informed by your own expectations. I believe it would be possible to extend the same methods to create a fully realized simulation in your mind. Perhaps enough to help you understand Robbie's new state, although I cannot be certain of that part."

"You mean like when you entered my dreams?" The register of his voice had dropped, and his facial muscles became rigid. "Devlin says that creating a precise simulation of the universe would require a computation equivalent to every particle in the universe, anyway."

"Would you need to experience the *whole* universe?" She smiled. "It is my understanding that corporeal humans perceive only what is within a very limited range of view with any precision. Elements peripheral to that are much less detailed, and very often not noticed by the conscious mind at all. That is an efficient use of resources, and the modelling of our digital minds is very comparable in that respect."

"What would be the risk to me?"

"There is no risk. I would not force your neurons and neural pathways to perform in any way contrary to their normal function. I will simply stimulate nerve clusters that would otherwise be controlled by your physical sensory apparatus."

Fifty-four seconds passed before he asked, "What would you need me to do?"

"Simply lie down in a comfortable position, relaxing your body and mind as you would for sleep."

"Sounds like hypnosis."

"That term is controversially vague. Is such a comparison somehow reassuring?"

"Never mind." He turned and called out to Madison Douglas and they walked toward each other. "Ariadne's proposing to try an experiment to let me see what Robbie's experiencing. If I don't wake up in ... fifteen minutes, shake me, or slap me. OK?"

"*What?* Are you ..." Her eyes darted from him to Ariadne's image. "... *sure* you want to do something like that?"

"I think one of us has to. I'm Robbie's closest friend. And anyway, you'll have my back." He smiled and winked, but his affected nonchalance may not have been fully sincere. "I don't think I want you to be too close, though. Just watch me from across the clearing." He waited for her reluctant nod. When she began to move away, he lay down on the grass and closed his eyes.

33

St. Clair

It was the office. Aladdin Unlimited LLC's Palo Alto HQ. Exactly where one of my dreams had left off, as far as I could tell, in an elevator. The one difference was that it was Ariadne with me, not Madison. And this time I knew it was a simulation of Ariadne's making, though it sure seemed real. There were smudged fingerprints on the elevator's glass control panel, a trace of a cobweb in an upper corner, a noticeably lighter tinge to the geometrically patterned carpeting in front of the door where it got the most traffic.

She was dressed as usual in a flowing white robe, which prompted me to ask, "Will other people see you?"

"Do you want them to?"

"Sure. But the robe might cause a few raised eyebrows."

I looked over at the control panel to see that we'd been descending and had just arrived at the lobby. When I looked back, she was dressed in a grey skirt and white blouse. Shoes with very low heels. Just the kind of outfit Madison wore for a workday when she had no engagements outside the office. Ariadne looked great in it, too; but it was strange seeing her that way.

Just then, the elevator door opened onto the lobby. Of course, it was exactly how I expected it to be, with a few stragglers arriving for work and crossing toward me from the brightly lit glass doors across the mottled marble-look floor. A couple stopped in front of me—Ken Lee and Stacey Burns—and I realized they were waiting for me to leave the elevator so they could use it.

I gave an apology and a chuckle, then stopped to introduce Ariadne as a representative from an AI research team I'd been talking to. They smiled and nodded, then shook her hand, something I'd never done. We moved out of the way and walked through the lobby.

Fake marble clacked with my footsteps; the rustle of moving bodies echoed from the walls. On my left was the huge display case I loved, featuring side-by-side models of the *USS Enterprise* spacecraft from *Star Trek*, the original NASA space shuttle *Enterprise*, and the GriffinSpace passenger-shuttle in development that we'd already named *Enterprise*. About three meters to my right, one of our daytime security guards, Gerry, gave me a smile and a wave. I could just catch a whiff of the man's cologne, and was glad I didn't share a desk with him.

I felt the sun's warmth radiating from the windows a few seconds before I reached them, and realized I should have brought sunglasses.

"They're in your shirt pocket," Ariadne said. She already wore a pair. I put mine on.

As I held the door open for her, I said, "Tell me again how you can't read our minds." But she stopped in front of the door instead of going through. In sudden understanding, I said, "Sometimes we hold doors open for our companions to allow them to go through first. It's a small gesture of consideration." Apparently, she could pick up certain obvious cues of mental intention, but not everything.

With a small nod, she passed through, and we were out on the sidewalk. Although it was early in the day, there was already a lot of vehicular traffic in the street. Noisy, and smelling of hot plastics and metal, personal pods wheeled among public transports and a few old-style electric cars; booster-cyclists enjoyed the sunshine while dodging local supply-vans.

The flurry of vehicles and colors was just as I remembered, and I felt the tug of air from a passing delivery cart. It dragged with it a cellulose grocery-store flyer that rippled and tumbled under the wheels of a car and disappeared. A man brushed by me on the sidewalk, leaving behind an impression of cologne-encapsulated fabric and rum-infused nicotine vapor.

"What would happen if I just walked out into traffic?"

"Try it, if you wish."

I looked at her, wondering if it was a dare. I couldn't help but remember the superstition that if you die in a dream, you'll die in reality. Would that apply here? Or could an environment created by my own mind ever harm me?

"But if I step out and the cars all just instantly stop, or if they pass through me like ghosts, won't that spoil the illusion?"

"It is not an illusion. You already know that it is a simulation produced intentionally by your mind and mine. It will be what you choose it to be."

"If I were feeling suicidal and deliberately stepped in front of a vehicle, would I be killed ... because that was my intention?"

"You and your companions continue to surprise me. You inhabit a construct that can be whatever you want it to be, and self-destruction is where your curiosity leads you?"

"That isn't an answer."

"Then the answer is that I do not know. There have been entities among us who decided they had fulfilled all their desires, exhausted all significant scenarios of their imagination, and chose to end their existence. To my knowledge, they did not create a simulation that involved violent death. They simply, slowly, lost coherence."

A city transport was approaching. I did not step in front of it. Instead, I turned along the sidewalk and strolled to Elmore Green, a small parkette a couple of blocks away. Lots of pedestrians passed by me in both directions, and I sensed their presence: the briefest impressions of body heat, coffee breath, wind-blown hair, a pebble that bounced against my shin.

The grass of the parkette was green, but with patches of a straw color here and there where it had been burned by concentrated sunlight or dog urine. Two benches of wrought iron and wood held one person each: an old man in a rumpled grey suit with a tuft of flyaway hair behind his right ear, and a young pregnant woman in a denim overall-style outfit who slumped wearily while she pushed a toddler in a stroller back and forth with an occasional jiggle. Three pigeons pecked the ground near her feet until the out-flung arm of the old man scattered something white in their direction and they hurried to him.

At the edge of the space, I noticed a vendor with a cart—Emilio, selling his trademark hot pastries and coffee, including sour-cream donuts just out of the oil that were ambrosia to me. I felt my mouth begin to salivate, and let the wonderful deep-fried aroma pull me toward him like a nail to a magnet. I didn't even have to give the order. Emilio just smiled as I passed my wrist over the scanner on the side of his cart, and handed me a donut in a cellulose napkin and a large cup of black coffee, which I held under my nose for at least a minute while I breathed in its sublime aroma. God, how I missed coffee! It smelled and tasted just the way I remembered it. The only thing missing was the sensation of it sliding down my throat, and the immediate warmth I could always feel spreading through my body from those first sips. An addict getting a fix.

Just before I took a bite of the donut, I turned to Ariadne and asked if she wanted anything. She shook her head with a look of amusement.

That first bite was fantastic—Emelio's perfect blending of crispiness and hot fat. I chewed it down to the molecules. But as I opened my mouth to bite again, I tried to imagine it tasting like a banana.

And it did. A fried banana—I guess I was still expecting heat—but definitely not a sour-cream donut. For the third bite I imagined it filled with strawberry jam, and got my wish. Because that's what it was: my wish was Ariadne's command. I'd been right with a comment I'd made all those days ago—she was a genie.

I finished my treat, enjoying the last few mouthfuls as the original donut flavor I'd asked for, and interspersing each bite with swallows of coffee while I watched the traffic pass. Each vehicle had different passengers—there was no repetition—as if each was part of an individual story. I wondered whose imagination they were coming from, Ariadne's or mine. I still knew too little about her origins.

Real coffee and a donut would have left my stomach feeling satisfied by then, and I couldn't sense that; but maybe that lack was a limitation of using Ariadne as a conduit. She knew we had external senses and had obviously tapped into them, but perhaps she'd overlooked the nerve signals we constantly experience from inside our bodies—what scientists call our *interoception*. Robbie would probably still feel those.

After finishing the last swallow of coffee with regret, I put the empty cup and napkin into a trash receptacle where energy from the sun would quickly break it down into a starchy dust used for fertilizer in Palo Alto's green spaces.

The breeze that followed the channels of the streets stilled in the small parkette, and the sun's rays were uncontested. I turned my face to the brightness and closed my eyes, seeing the red of my eyelids, breathing in sour smells of dog crap and the trash bin of a nearby restaurant—but also the fragrance of sun-warmed grass, much more pungent than in Ariadne's clearing.

Had I chosen to smell dog crap and garbage? Or was it peripheral information my brain supplied to give the scene verisimilitude?

I assumed that Ariadne was still with me, though I kept my eyes closed.

"So, if I want to, say, go back to the office now, do I have to walk there?"

"There is no need to, if you do not choose to."

A sudden thought struck me.

"What if I wanted to fly there? Could I fly ... like a superhero?"

"Another reference I do not know. But if you choose to travel by any unusual means, and can picture such a thing, there is nothing to stop you. A simulation is governed by the rules you set in your mind, not those of objective reality."

I began to imagine what it would be like to just rise into the air like Superman and glide wherever I wanted to go.

But then I forcibly concentrated on the touch of ground under my feet.

This was dangerous. This was the temptations of alcohol, LSD, cannabis, and magic mushrooms all rolled into one. After barely subsisting on weeds and mashed worms for a month, I could now feast on any food I desired and never get fat or sick. Though my body was confined like a zoo animal to a small clearing in a treacherous forest, suddenly I could not only go to any of my favourite places, I could *fly* there! Or, presumably, run at hyper speed—or summon up my own elephant and ride like a pasha, or ... who knew what else?

A rabbit hole to Wonderland that it would be only too easy to fall into.

More like a Faustian bargain.

I opened my eyes and looked for Ariadne. She appeared mildly puzzled, but as usual, that might have been mostly my imagination, too. Her facial features never really changed very much.

"Let's just go to my home in Atherton."

Before the words had finished leaving my mouth, we were there.

Not just in the house. In the master bedroom.

That was a shock. It suddenly felt like a year since I'd been there. Of course, I spent many more nights sleeping in the penthouse suite at HQ; but still, this was my own house.

Seeing it this way, almost like a stranger's, I realized how very spartan my bedroom was, and how impersonal. No pictures of loved ones. No mementoes, not even toiletries or grooming gadgets—those were all in the ensuite bathroom. It could have been a hotel suite: giant bed, tasteful shades of blue, black, and gold set against warm white walls. Nondescript pictures on the walls. Thick curtains, almost never drawn unless I brought a woman there, which hadn't happened in ... I couldn't remember how long. Maybe not since Lauren. Wow.

Not that I was celibate, but I had other rooms for that, equipped with music and projection systems, hot tubs and showers. The master bedroom was for sleeping, or sex partners special enough to sleep over.

I wasn't feeling sleepy.

Swallowing a sudden lump in my throat, I turned to look at Ariadne.

She was undoing the last of the buttons on her blouse. It slipped from her shoulders like a veil and fluttered to the floor, leaving her upper body bare. Skirt and panties slid to her feet with the merest sweep of her fingers, and she stepped out of them, a step closer to me. I heard the rasp of my breath.

Her skin was Nordic-pale, but with flowing hair over a long neck and shoulders pulled back in perfect posture. Her breasts were round and full, with generous nipples of golden pink. The wide curves of her hips below a slender waist completed a figure that was less supermodel than artist's model, a difference of which I thoroughly approved. My eyes drifted over a firm abdomen and slightly elongated navel to the juncture of smooth thighs, and a triangular thatch of spun gold.

[Is it your intention that this description be included in the official account?—Sch.]

(Hey, this happened, Sher—it's part of the record of real events.

Well, OK. Maybe you can flag this section with a content advisement.)

Ariadne took another step closer to me, and another, head lifted, lips parted.

She was desirable beyond belief, and I hadn't had sex in a long time. My heart should be pounding and other parts responding too. Yet I didn't really feel any of that. At least, not much. Those sensations would be strong within my memory, but perhaps Ariadne couldn't recognize them and produce an equivalent sensation, just as she'd missed the satisfying of my other appetite.

Still, there was no harm in taking this scenario further, to see where it went. My simulated body would no doubt be responding ....

Shit!

"Ariadne, stop this! I can't. Stop the simulation."

"Why? Is this not one of your desires?"

It was, of course. I saw her as an astonishingly beautiful woman. Though I'd never felt a strong attraction other than sexual curiosity.

"I'm not an entity without a body, and my physical body will be responding to this as if it's real. *And we're being watched.*"

It was clear that she still didn't understand my objections, but within a few moments the blue shades of my bedroom faded into blue sky, and a turn of my head brought the greens and browns of the forest into focus.

I quickly sat up with my back to Madison and took slow breaths.

"I could look like her for you," Ariadne's whisper came from beside my ear.

"Her?"

"Madison Douglas. If that is a simulation you would prefer."

"Jesus!" My mind started to go there, and I wrestled it back. "No. I want the simulation stopped. I'm not about to have a wet dream in front of a crowd."

"It is not ..."

"I know it's not a *dream!*" I dropped my voice back to a whisper. "That makes no difference. I'm sure you can detect that my body was responding as if it was really about to have sex. It does that even when people dream, and it sure as hell would do that with the kind of simulation you were just .... What was that anyway? I don't remember having a sudden urge to get it on in my bedroom."

"With you and your people the act of sexual congress appears to have surprising importance, even in a circumstance involving uncertainty about survival. A substantial percentage of your data records refer to it, perhaps more than any other single activity. I thought it would be beneficial to learn more about it in the most direct way possible."

If that wasn't the worst excuse for a come-on that I'd ever heard .... At the same time, it made some sense. Especially since Ariadne wanted to reassure us that an uploaded existence was in no way lacking anything we need and want.

If I was right that Robbie's true upload state would not include the internal sensory shortcomings I'd experienced, then the possibility of fantasy-sex-made-real would be a big factor in his well-being. The man had a voracious appetite, firmly entrenched in the lifestyle of a rock star.

When I felt it safe to stand and look toward Madison, she wasn't looking my way, and her slouched posture made me concerned.

"Well," I thrust my hands into my pockets. "That little demonstration was very enlightening. Thank you. And I'll thank you even more if you don't do it for anyone else in our group."

"Why not? Would they not like to know what their friend can experience?"

"Just please trust me that it would not be good for their mental health."

She gave no response. I took a few steps toward Madison, then changed my mind and walked to our spring-fed pool. My throat was dry as dust.

34

The Ariadne Narrative

Madison Douglas stayed by herself for the rest of the afternoon and was sitting on the grass when Ariadne approached her.

"I surmise that you have still not adjusted to your lack of medication," Ariadne said.

"It's not something you adjust to. There are no permanent cures." Douglas didn't turn her head. "How did the simulation go with Griff?"

"He said it was enlightening. I believe it did make him feel better about what his friend Robbie is now experiencing."

"Can you show me too?"

"Griffin St. Clair asked me not to provide a simulation to anyone else."

"I don't think that's something he has any right to decide. Please show me. What do I do, just lie on the ground?" She did so.

"And close your eyes. Relax your body. Where would you like to be?"

Douglas hesitated, then in a flat voice she said, "Take me where you took Griff."

Moments later she complained, "The office? He could experience anything anywhere, and you took him to the office?"

"Not only here."

"Where did you go last? Take me there."

The woman gasped. In the simulation her eyes were wide.

"This is ... this is his bedroom in the Atherton house, isn't it? I saw it once, through the door, one evening when he'd just bought the place and had a few of his top people over for drinks and pool. Wow. It doesn't look like he changed anything in five years." She cleared her throat. "Why did he ask to see this ... to come here ... with you?"

When she turned around, St. Clair was standing in the doorway in a luxurious burgundy robe and matching slippers with a quizzical smile on his face.

"Griff? No, wait. Is that you Ariadne?"

"Who's Ariadne? Is somebody else in here with you Madison?" St. Clair gave a cursory look around then closed the door of the room behind him and stepped forward. "I wondered if you'd find your way here. I hoped you would."

"Griff, I ..."

He held up a hand. "It's OK. I know this is awkward, but isn't it what we've both wanted? And here we are." When he'd finished speaking, he was toe to toe with her, faces only a few centimeters apart. His red hair and beard were neatly trimmed again, and his blue eyes sparkled without the deep shadows of fatigue and worry beneath them. Suddenly, she felt his hands on her arms, so warm and strong, and he gently pulled her toward himself. As his head dipped, her lips drew slightly open and she held her breath, her eyelids beginning to close.

At the last moment she pushed him away and twisted into a heap on the ground.

"No! Goddamn it, Ariadne! No. I don't want him this way." The words came out in a sob.

The clearing reappeared around her. She was still on her back, with her hand involuntarily raised to her mouth. She cast a furtive look around, but no one was watching her. She slumped back with tears in her eyes.

"You could have experienced anything, anywhere, and you chose to experience that?" Ariadne asked.

"It's cruel to use my own words against me."

"I apologize. It's only that I'm having difficulty understanding the motivations of you and your people. Griffin St. Clair seemed to want to experience sexual congress with me, but then he refused."

"He did?" She wiped a hand across her cheek. "Why?"

"I was not given an exact answer, only that he knew you were watching his body."

Information that meant nothing to Ariadne seemed to mean a great deal to Douglas. "Thank you," she said.

Ariadne replied, "I do not understand why you ended the simulation with Griffin St. Clair; but many other choices are available to you, if you wish."

"By uploading."

"Of course; but I meant that I would be willing to provide further simulations for you in the meantime, to assist you to regain mental equilibrium. There may be no cure for your condition while in a physical body, but pleasurable experiences appear to help, do they not?"

Douglas sat up and folded her arms over her chest. "Why would you do that?"

"It is satisfying to be of assistance. I have no urgent tasks to perform."

Douglas nodded and looked around the clearing, especially at St. Clair, who was weaving yet another container from marsh reeds. As if his actions reminded her of her own duties, she stood up and brushed the back of her pants with her hands, though nothing was clinging to them.

"We'll be leaving to find the space launch-site within a day or so, I imagine," she said. "Are you planning to come with us? Is there some way you could?"

"I've been meaning to speak to you about that." Using all of the psychological knowledge she had accumulated to choose her words, Ariadne explained about a calculation she had made. When she was done, she waited for one minute, seventeen seconds before Douglas replied.

"You know, in our culture there were myths about a being who offers people the fulfillment of their greatest desire in exchange for their soul. Do you know what a soul is?"

"I am aware of numerous definitions of the word," Ariadne said. "The noun I believe you mean seems to refer to consciousness initially resident in a physical body, but not bound to it, so as to be able to survive and enter a new state of being upon the body's death. Is your anecdote intended to refer to Robbie Tam?"

"That's as good a reference as any," she said. "We'll talk again." She straightened her back and walked across the grass to St. Clair to help him with his weaving.

Later that afternoon, Douglas walked to the far side of the clearing from her companions and called for Ariadne.

"You were right," she said, "when you echoed my words. I could have experienced anything, and yet I chose to follow what Griff had done. That was stupid. I know you intended for me to request some kind of fantasy, but I need to learn a lot more about you. Especially now. And I think the way to do that is for you to create a simulation for me that *you* would enjoy. Or if that really wouldn't translate, then a scenario you think I would enjoy. *Not* about Griff."

"I don't understand."

"Don't try to tell me that you didn't suggest these simulations because you wanted to learn how our minds work—our desires, our priorities. Well, if you want me to trust you, the least you can do is give me a glimpse of your own mind."

"To give you a glimpse of my existence from my perspective would not really be possible. I do not have a physical body like yours, so I do not simulate interactions with a physical environment; and the structures of my environment, you would not be able to recognize as such."

"OK, but you don't control every moment of your existence, do you? You must encounter unforeseen situations. Otherwise, how could any mind remain stimulated?"

"You speak of randomness? We discovered the problem you suggest very early in our existence. The solution is through what you might call 'sub-routines' that operate independently from our central consciousness and generate nearly-random changes in our perception: tasks to perform and obstacles to overcome. It was also found to be beneficial to share the resulting scenarios with other entities of our kind, thereby enhancing unpredictability still further. This sharing arrangement has become well-established."

"Wow. So collectively, at a level not directly deliberate, you create an environment that you all interact with. Now, see, that's fascinating, and I would never have known about it. But it's still only an explanation. I would learn so much more if I could experience some of the things you do for pleasure or enlightenment."

The woman's face had become much more mobile, eyes brighter, lips more inclined to smile. Clearly, the prospect of a challenging new revelation really did help to overcome her dark mood.

"There is an activity we pursue for pleasure which would be comprehensible to your mind," Ariadne said.

"Whether or not you will find it instructive, I cannot say."

"Great! Let's do it." Douglas immediately lay on the grass, closed her eyes, and folded her arms on her chest in a way that Ariadne recognized from data files about death rituals; but perhaps it was comfortable for the living, as well. With considerable curiosity of her own, she made the connection between the woman's mind and information reserves within the entity network.

Douglas was in a jungle at night. Very hot, very humid. Her nostrils flared at the sudden bombardment of odors: pungent vegetation, an acrid tang of broad leaves and frayed vines, as well as a cloying floral sweetness of myriad blossoms, some tiny, others huge. And soil, musty and full of rot. A trace of smoke in the nearly motionless air.

A vibration, too. A sound felt as much as heard, as if the very earth were a giant gong. As she listened, the gong was struck again, booming and terrible. An indecipherable background murmur, like voices, fell silent. Bird song and animal noises all ceased.

Though it was night, the jungle before her was illuminated by flickering yellow light; dark green of tropical foliage interrupted by bright explosions of color, like fireworks in a night sky.

Her gaze fell to her feet, on cold stone under a thin covering of leaves and petals. Then she saw the vines wrapped around her ankles. With a twist of her head, she confirmed that her arms were held outspread by more vines that tied her wrists to two pillars of stone. She was a prisoner!

Frantically, she looked everywhere for an explanation. She was held in place on a platform that appeared to be made of huge blocks of cut stone, raised above the ground and protruding into the jungle. If she turned her head back far enough, she could see a moss-

and-vine-covered wall of the giant blocks reaching into the sky behind her. A palisade of some kind? In a jungle?

The gong sounded again, and then there came a sudden jolt like thunder that shook the platform on which she stood. Another. She gasped for breath, heart racing, and stared up into the trees. In the distance, giant treetops were in motion, their vast branches swaying, but not from any wind.

"*Fuck,*" she said. "I *recognize* this."

She swallowed hard.

"Ariadne? Ariadne, I know this story and I don't like where it goes from here. Uh ... what do you say we ditch this one and try something else? Please?" Her voice was much higher than usual, which seemed to embarrass her. "I do not want to be carried to the top of the Empire State building!"

Thunderous crashes from the trees drew closer, and closer. Her eyes grew wide as two giant trees began to push apart ...

... then, suddenly she was in a vast room crowded with people, in bright sunlight that made her blink and shield her eyes with hands no longer bound. The instant buzz of noise was overwhelming, too; and although she soon recognized that people were speaking English, there were simply too many conversations for her to catch more than a few words.

A vaulted ceiling arched far over her head. As her eyes lowered, her view was dominated by an enormous staircase five meters wide that tapered inward as it rose, and then split into separate stairways that climbed to the left and right. Above the central landing was a giant window framed with heavy curtains in brown and blue, flanked by elaborate sconces filled with tall candles. Crystal candelabra hung everywhere. Yet the extravagant setting was only a backdrop for the chaotic traffic of men and women who swarmed in front of her.

They swept back and forth in seemingly random directions, draped in a profusion of colorful fabrics: layers upon layers of periwinkle, chartreuse, rose, saffron; frills in complimentary shades around pale necks; white lace everywhere. From wasp waists, women trailed cones of cloth so wide that they filled doorways. It was amazing that anyone could move surrounded by so much bulk. Even their hats sprouted extravagant colored bows of ribbon, kerchiefs of silk, and ever more lace.

Douglas's own head supported a hat with a brim twice the width of her hand. It was straw-colored. In fact, it appeared to be made of tightly woven straw, anchored under her chin with an unnecessarily long and thick velvet ribbon of moss green that hung past her knees and matched her waistband. Her dress was creamy white with a pattern of pale-green fern fiddleheads and leaves, much too tight around bodice and waist, yet ridiculously expansive by the time it reached the floor. Her hoop skirt was covered by a sheer layer, bodice topped by a lacy ruffle with a vine motif that left her shoulders bare. Her arms were mostly bare, too, except for a sort of lace shawl draped over her elbows and around her back. And on her hands, white lace gloves.

She stood still, hardly daring to move, though she could feel bodies pushing her hooped skirt as they struggled to get past her.

Men's outfits were almost as fancy, though much less bulky. As she watched, a sandy-haired man elegantly descended the stairs wearing high-waisted trousers and a short waistcoat of tan over a white shirt ruffed stiffly at the neck and upper chest. A rich brown bowtie matched his thigh-length jacket.

Presuming Ariadne to be nearby, Douglas whispered as she took slow steps into the room. "Not Elizabethan or pre-Revolution France .... No, it's the Deep South."

Her hand flew to her mouth. "Well, I'll be goddamned!"

According to memory, she should move to meet the sandy-haired man and engage him in conversation. Instead, she turned to the side and continued whispering, with her hand hiding her mouth.

"Ariadne, this is not exactly my favorite either. Are you trying to make me call it quits?"

"It distresses you?"

Ariadne stood at her side wearing a simpler dress of pale blue, with black hair covered by a light-yellow bonnet.

"My friend Paige would love to be here. She forced me to sit through this twice because she couldn't believe I didn't like it."

"Why don't you?"

"Because Scarlett O'Hara is a whiny, conniving, manipulative bitch who ruins people's lives. Is this what you think corporeal life is like? Humankind has done so much better."

"Very well."

In an instant it was nighttime, muggy Georgia heat replaced by numbing cold that had Douglas shivering within seconds.

It wasn't just nighttime. It was nighttime on the ocean.

She stood at the railing of a ship, staring into the blackness, while the wind that scoured her face and plucked at her clothes felt as if it had just come off an ice floe. With a gasp, she turned her back to it and huddled into the high collar of the overcoat she wore. The kerchief over her hair provided no warmth.

Six meters to her left, a mounted lamp spilled a pool of light that illuminated a portion of the wide-planked deck on which she stood, as well as an area of the ship's superstructure, and a ceiling that extended as far as the rail. In the white wall there were windows in ornate frames, square at the bottom but rounded at the top, that looked as if they belonged in a church. Then she noticed a wide door with a porthole in it, and hurried to get out of the wind.

Beyond the door was a long room like the patio of a fine restaurant that had been enclosed. The chairs looked like wicker, and there were tablecloths on the tables, some round, some square. She looked around for another door leading deeper into the interior

As if eager to skip the boring parts, her next step transported her into a well-lit space full of warm shades of gleaming wood. Oak, perhaps. A shocking sensation of *déjà vu* made her shudder.

Before her stood yet another majestic staircase that, like the last one, flared wide at the bottom and split part way up to the left and the right. There were obvious differences, though. A wooden railing divided the lower portion of this one in two. The bottom pillar of that rail supported a large figurine with curly hair, holding a torch. The Irish oak handrails of the staircase were supported by panels of more carved oak, wrought iron, and crystal.

It was unquestionably one of the best-known staircases in history, and immediately confirmed Douglas's suspicions. She turned and again found Ariadne at her side.

"OK, I get that entities like you might enjoy old movies, especially when you can get right inside them. *Live* them in a way. It's a fantastic trick. But who picks them for you? I mean, seriously."

"A data archive was discovered one hundred and thirty years ago. I do not know the details of the discovery. It contained two hundred thirty-seven visual records of fictional stories. Movies, you call them? Many were without color, but we have been able to extrapolate appropriate colors using various points of reference. By a similar process, and from some experience with Robbie, I am endeavoring to provide sounds and smells for you."

"And none of those 'visual records' are newer than 1950, I'm beginning to think. That's OK: there were some fantastic films produced during that time—but why would you pick this one, for instance? By the way, are we about to hit the iceberg?"

"I have interrupted the time sequence while we converse, but we can jump to any point in the story that you choose. As to the first part of your question, you asserted earlier that humankind had done much better than to hold large social gatherings in extravagant dress. While this story does include excessively decorative clothing, it also features an impressive example of human engineering, as well as many notable acts of sacrifice that you would call heroism, does it not?"

Douglas laughed. "Fair enough. I did ask to see something you do for pleasure, although I expected a simulation you created fresh from your own mind. I suppose such a thing might be too strange for me to understand.

"Next question: did you pick these particular stories because they're favorites of yours, or because you thought I would like them?" She leaned against the banister and ran a finger along the arm of the imp-like figurine.

"I thought you would, but clearly I was incorrect. I do find certain examples more interesting than others. There are some that feature a man others call a 'detective' who tracks down perpetrators of antisocial and violent acts."

"Crimes. Yeah, I think I can guess who you mean. I kind of idolize him too."

"His powers of observation and deduction are impressive. I have not seen examples of such abilities among your group."

"Yeah, well, for one thing your clearings all look the same to us, so there isn't much about them to observe.

And for another, that detective wasn't real. He's a fictional character only."

"That is a disappointment."

Douglas laughed again. "So, you don't have one favorite movie?"

Ariadne took some time to consider. "Possibly there is one I enjoy the most. I believe, though, that you would consider it an entertainment for children. It is a body of most intricate artwork, placed in linear proximity so as to simulate real motion and events."

"You mean animation?"

"It is called *Pinocchio*."

"Ah, well that is … interesting. It's a classic, all right. I love it too." She smiled. "You know, if you were solid, I think I'd give you a hug. We can skip the rest of this story—I know how it ends—but this … exercise has been informative. It's given me a much better idea of who you are, and I think I actually *like* you."

"Then it has been worthwhile."

The grand staircase of the *Titanic* faded into the simple grassy clearing in the forest.

35

St. Clair

"How about this one?"

Music filled the air of the clearing while a faint image of Robbie appeared to be standing in front of us, watching our faces.

I could tell that it was a different piece than the previous three he'd played for us—a little more Brahms than Bach this time, maybe, and filled out with five or six synthetic instruments instead of keyboards alone—but there was still a sameness I couldn't ignore. I looked at Madison but she's a lot better at faking a sincere smile than I am.

"You hate it, don't you?"

"Of course, I don't hate it," I said. "It's beautiful. Very, very impressive."

"Another example of perfection, Mr. Tam."

"Forgive me, Sher, but I'm not sure that opinion is very comforting at the moment." Robbie's image wavered a little. As I'd predicted, he'd chosen a self-image about fifteen years younger than his real age, though there wasn't much difference. He'd learned how to stimulate our minds to see that image, but not well. It was low on detail and movement, although where I'd expected something really low-res and pixilated like the very early days of online video-chatting that I remembered seeing as a kid, this was more like an image posterized by photo-manipulation software. Strong outlines and few basic colors.

He'd obviously been putting more effort into creating music, which was good, or would have been if it had made him happy.

Robbie put his hands on his hips. "It doesn't touch you, does it?"

"Emotionally? Maybe not. It sounds amazingly complex, though, the way the melody and harmony interweave ...." I wasn't lying. Bits of it reminded me a little of some of the tracks from a really old album called *Pet Sounds* by the Beach Boys. Except more sterile.

"One thing that's always struck me about your music," Madison said, "is that it's fun. There's always a kind of bounce that gets you moving, and a chorus you can sing along to the second time you hear it."

"That's pop stuff. I thought this was my chance to create something really meaningful. Important. That would last."

"Maybe you have, Robbie," I said. I would have put an arm around him if I could have. "We're not exactly the best people to judge that. No experts, that's for sure."

"Nah, it's shit." He sat cross-legged on the grass, his cheek on his fist.

Nobody said anything for a few moments. Only Madison and I had come to see him one more time before we left on our expedition. I think the others were still creeped out. He'd asked a few questions about our preparations and plans, and I'm sure it bothered him a lot that he couldn't be a part of it.

"How's the rest of ... uh, upload life going?" I asked. "Ariadne provided both of us a small taste of a simulation. I was pretty tempted to try flying like Superman. You been filling your time soaring from city to city to discover new bars and babes, or reliving some of the glory days?"

"Truth is, there's a lot I don't remember about those days," he said in a soft voice. The old Robbie would have made a joke of it. "So, I've been recreating them the way I want to remember them. The way they should have been. Over and over, hundreds of different ways. I've imagined a comeback tour, too: places I loved to play, places I never played but always wanted to." His head lifted. "I don't know, man. I think I'm running out of ideas. And I'm not even sure I care. I don't have to imagine stuff, you know. I can just sort of float, in nothingness, doing nothing, if I don't feel like it."

Madison and I shared a look of alarm before we remembered that Robbie 'saw' from everywhere in the clearing, not just the place where we pictured his head.

"Yeah, I been doing that sometimes, when my music doesn't come out the way I want." He gave a heavy sigh. "I thought I could be like Dylan, or Lennon ... a musical genius. But I'm not. I'm still not. I wish this hadn't happened, man." He looked into my eyes. "And I'm not sure I made the right choice."

Madison and I stumbled over each other's protestations. It was too soon to say that. He was still adjusting. There was so much he couldn't have tried yet.

Maybe he needed to ask for more help from Ariadne and the others.

"Isn't Ariadne going with you?" he asked.

"We're not sure how far," I said. "She's been working on a way to get a kind of piggyback ride from other clearings along the route, to extend her consciousness as far as she can, but we don't know how well that will work. Don't you ... talk with any other clearings?"

"Yeah, sometimes. Mainly two that call themselves CL10 and CL04—I call 'em Clio and Clover. Clio's OK—she's the next clearing north. And Clover's from nearby too. I'm supposed to meet more. Hey, did you know these clearing people have got a real thing for old movies? I mean vintage stuff. We've watched a couple hundred of 'em."

"I found that out yesterday," Madison replied dryly. "Except they can even create simulations from them and act them out. You should try that. Maybe you could be Sherlock Holmes."

"Yeah, 'cause we have the same IQ." Robbie laughed. "Actually, maybe now we do!"

We talked for a while longer, mainly filling him in on how the others in the group were doing, avoiding the question of why none of them had come to see him. Of course, there was nothing worth telling, and we all knew it was just filling time.

Eventually Robbie said, "OK, well, the sooner you guys head out the sooner you can get back and tell me all about it. I guess you'll wait 'till morning?"

"Yeah. Get as far as we can in daylight. There's still a little last-minute packing to do." That wasn't true, but it didn't matter.

"Cool. So, good luck. And watch out for yourselves. Really." He forced a grin. "I just might have a little snooze until you get back."

Hugs weren't possible, so we just waved and went on our way. As we approached Ariadne's clearing, I called her name.

"Robbie's failing, isn't he? This isn't working out."

"He is discouraged. Impatient. Frustrated," she said. "We still believe he will adapt but it is a struggle. His mental energy is waning."

"What does that mean. Can it weaken until ... what, he disappears?"

"As I've mentioned, it has happened that entities with no further will to continue gradually lose coherence. Individual cell connections at the quantum level fail, the effect becomes cumulative, and at a certain point, consciousness collapses. We believe that any form of consciousness must will itself to remain cohesive."

I stood at the edge of the clearing with an urge to hit something, like one of the nearby trees. But they'd left us alone since Robbie's injury, and I didn't want to start up a new war. Especially just before we left on a trip through kilometers of forest.

"If Robbie's in that kind of danger, we have to go back." I turned to retrace my steps.

"I do not believe that will help. What could you offer? Verbal encouragement? You have no experience of his current existence, so your intended words of guidance or solace would have no weight."

"But if he sinks into depression with his mind working at computer speed, it'll happen in no time. He might not last until we get back from the launch site."

Ariadne didn't respond for a few moments. Then she said, "He is already becoming reluctant to communicate with CL10 and CL04. He has not responded to their overtures for seventeen minutes."

"Shit!" I began to charge back through the forest.

"Griff, wait." Madison caught up to me and grabbed my arm. "Ariadne's right. The most we can do is distract him while we're with him. As soon as we leave, he'll be on his own again. He's going to have to work this out for himself."

"My fellow entities and I will do what we can," Ariadne said, "but ultimately it will be up to Robbie himself to adjust to his changed circumstances by finding new reasons to continue existing."

"So even your kind needs a purpose in life."

She gave a smile that felt a little patronizing to me. "Fresh entertainment might be enough; mild diversions, pleasant puzzles to solve. There need not be lofty objectives or laborious challenges to undertake. How many of *your* kind required those to carry them from day to day?"

"We have an inherent will to survive—we can't help it. But I'm not sure that would apply in a digital life."

"Even some of your kind consider ending their own lives." Her eyes seemed to flicker. "In any case, my advice is to trust that Robbie will find his path without your interference, however well-intentioned it might be." Was she looking smug now? Damned if I could tell. We humans are hard-wired to anthropomorphize everything. We see facial expressions on a mannequin, and that's what watching Ariadne was often like.

In any case, she was probably right. There was nothing more we could do right then, but whatever we discovered at the launch site might change everything.

Enough of this goddamned futzing around. It was time for some action.

[Is this intended as a narrative hook? —Sch.]

36

St. Clair

It was an unnecessary risk for the entire group to hazard a dangerous forest and trackless desert to find a place that might not even exist. Madison, Devlin and I were the best equipped to evaluate the site if we found it. But then Lauren insisted on coming—she said that hanging around the clearing was driving her crazy—and Santos joined her. He probably wanted to keep her from me. I figured Vaughn and Lakisha would be happy to have the clearing all to themselves, but maybe he was getting bored with her. He claimed it was important for him to assess any medical facilities we might find. I couldn't argue with that, and we couldn't leave Lakisha alone.

Fortunately, out of sheer boredom, everyone had ultimately joined in to make water-skins, carryalls, backpacks, and the like, so we had all we needed. The main concerns for this larger group were food and protection from the damned trees. Ariadne had spread the word asking clearings along our route to produce food, so there should be enough except in the desert and possibly the launch site itself. There, we'd have to rely on what we could carry.

All of us wore our tinfoil hats through the trees except Lakisha and Vaughn, who proved that they could see debris and the other true features of the forest without them. It only required the right attitude, Vaughn said. I suspected a more sinister explanation, and so wasn't about to try going hatless.

Lauren had adapted our basket weaving to make a kind of sandal; soles that we could strap onto our feet for those whose shoes were beginning to fall apart. It remained to be seen if they could stand up to extended hiking. The rest of our clothes were in sad shape, too; but the weather stayed warm, with only one light rainfall. I was concerned about sunburn while crossing the desert, but couldn't think of a solution.

Is there any point in describing our trek through the forest? I don't think so. With no animals or birds to watch for, the only thing that kept it from being painfully dull was the constant threat of attack by the trees. Yet they did nothing. I asked Vaughn if it might be because they thought we were leaving their territory for good. He only shrugged.

If so, they would be sorely disappointed in a few days.

Under normal circumstances we could have travelled the distance in less than a day of walking, but there were delays. Footwear needed on-the-spot repairs. Santos and Lakisha both had intestinal problems. They'd eaten little, but wild plants had never agreed with our digestive systems. And we stopped at every clearing to rest, eat, and, of course, to gather as much food as we could carry.

There were exactly one-hundred of the sentient clearings arranged in a rectangular grid. Ariadne's clearing was slightly toward the west of center in the row closest to the southern perimeter. The clearings were all four kilometers apart, as near as we could judge; so, in travelling north, we encountered four of them.

None of the clearing entities were particularly friendly; and if any of them knew how to project images of themselves to us, they elected not to. I became convinced that, for reasons of her own, Ariadne had chosen not to share her methods with her compatriots; and none of the other entities were exposed to us long enough to figure it out for themselves. But Ariadne managed to extend her apparent presence through their mycelial network without difficulty, and acted as intermediary. The mycelia must have extended throughout the forest, but Ariadne could not or did not choose to interact with us outside the clearings. Whether it was a physical limitation, a requirement to avoid conflict with the trees, or a personal choice, she never said.

The desert would be beyond the network, beyond her range.

Although Lauren had always avoided our host and guide until now, once she heard that the clearing entities were fans of classic movies, she and Ariadne chatted every time we stopped in a clearing, discussing the appeal of Humphrey Bogart versus Jimmy Stewart or Cary Grant. They both loved every Sherlock Holmes movie; but while Lauren adored Fred Astaire, the entities didn't enjoy musicals. It wasn't clear whether they got pleasure from music of any kind, but they just couldn't accept the fiction of people suddenly breaking out in song or frenetic dance numbers.

It made me think of Robbie and his dozens of pop-dance holos. He wouldn't get much satisfaction from sharing those with his new friends. I desperately hoped my buddy was still coping.

At the last clearing, Ariadne warned us that the forest would come to an end in another two kilometers. The implication was that we should stay put overnight; but to us, the clearings always felt like the homes of strangers, so we all preferred to move on. This time Ariadne didn't follow us.

Instead, she said, "I hope you find what you're looking for, and that it is what you're hoping for." Then she vanished.

We arrived at the edge of the desert just before sunset, with enough time before darkness to scout around and find a small natural clearing bordered by trees on three sides. The fourth side was the desert.

After five weeks in a completely artificial clearing surrounded by forests that looked equally counterfeit, it was surreal to see landscape still in its natural state. Grass grew in uneven tufts with some dried-out swaths and a few bare patches. Scrubby shrubs struggled to survive here and there, with ragged leaves stretched toward the setting sun. Away from the main forest were a few scattered trees stunted and twisted by wind, yet they were clearly ordinary trees and seemed comforting rather than threatening.

There still were no birds or animals, but as I gazed out over the barren land ahead, sunset-painted golden and pink, I mused that it was probably less barren than the places we were leaving behind. Living there would be hard, but there would be life. I was somehow sure of that.

I didn't mean for anything to happen with Lauren. We were just standing around, deciding where to sleep and how to arrange our things when she declared that she just had to get more of the open air after a day spent trudging through a stuffy forest. Then she looked straight at me.

I was amazed she was still on her feet. But I couldn't let her go out there alone, even though there was no chance of getting lost if she stuck to the forest's edge.

I hurried after her, taking a look back to see if anyone else was following. They weren't. Madison's face was turned away, and Santos was stonily staring at his feet. Devlin gave a slow shake of his head. Vaughn and Lakisha shared a look that made me think they would soon be going for a walk of their own in the other direction.

Lauren went to her left, toward the sun that was sunk halfway into the horizon. In that direction, the land looked nearly flat, though it rose toward the north; but dust haze in the air and some low cloud made it impossible to tell how high the ground reached. If our group had much climbing to do under the hot sun, the second half of our trek would be much more difficult.

Lauren and I walked very slowly, breathing in the clean, dry air of open land and basking in the first sunset we'd experienced since the day we left the tunnel because the entity clearings only saw direct sunshine between mid-morning and mid-afternoon. The cloud-mottled sky was painted with every shade of red, pink, mauve, and gold.

I barely noticed when we started holding hands, it felt so natural again, even after all the intervening years.

At some point, our slow walk came to a complete stop. Her kiss was warm and exciting. There were enough natural trees and grass at that spot to provide a comfortable place to … rest out of sight. One thing led to another.

By the time we got back it was full darkness. Everyone appeared to be asleep or nearly so. We lay down side-by-side; and after such a long day, I was unconscious in seconds.

With a new day came a nasty surprise. I cursed myself for not staying with the others the evening before to supervise the stowing of our gear.

Seven water containers lay on the ground at the foot of a tree, limp and empty, the puncturing tree roots still protruding from them. The rest of our supplies were piled nearby and untouched, but it was the water that was most essential. To try to cross a desert without it would be madness.

I had no doubt that Vaughn and Lakisha had done the bidding of the trees by moving our water within easy reach of probing roots. The only question was whether they'd done it knowingly. I raged at Vaughn, and it turned into a shoving match that Devlin and Santos had to break up. Santos swore he'd placed the water farther away, but it's possible he'd been tricked by the trees into thinking that.

There was no proof either way, but this was the strongest evidence yet that tree entities were able to turn our own people against us. The implications of that were horrifying, and there was no way to know how far their malevolent influence would extend, or if, worst of all, like demonic possession, they'd taken permanent hold of their victims. How could we trust each other, especially Lakisha and Vaughn? If our water supply were to be sabotaged in the open desert, we might not survive long enough to reach more.

I protested that Vaughn and Lakisha should stay behind, but the others weren't willing to take a stand that might fatally split our group. So, I gave in. The only alternative was to call the whole trek off, and I wasn't prepared to do that.

But we weren't going anywhere until we could get more water.

With a sneer that demonstrated no remorse, Vaughn suggested that he and Lakisha would gather more tree sap to try to repair the containers while the rest of us split up and searched east and west for some source of water. The last clearing we'd visited had supplied dandelion and plantain, but hadn't produced a spring. We couldn't assume that any others along that row would have either.

Madison automatically started toward me but saw that Lauren was already by my side, so she went with Santos and Devlin instead.

Lauren and I barely spoke—only a few comments about the appearance of the desert. I don't know if she felt any regret, but my own head was pretty messed up. My outings with Lakisha de Camp had been nothing more than our sex drives providing a release from restlessness, but with Lauren, it was different.

We'd split up years ago because the fire had cooled, at least for me. She'd been hurt. Maybe with the passage of time she'd forgiven me—it seemed so. That didn't give me the right to mislead her and, more than likely, hurt her again.

What did I want anyway? For things to return to the way they'd once been between us? Our little group might be the last of our kind on Earth, destined to live out our span of years seeing no others like us. Was I prepared to become her romantic partner—her *mate*—for a life like that?

Did I love her?

No, I couldn't say that.

She was still vibrantly attractive, but she was no longer the same person she'd been when we were together. She'd changed. *I'd* changed. We'd begun to change all those years ago—Lauren getting involved with the Hollywood crowd and then the California political scene, and me becoming ever more obsessive about my various projects.

Now, thrown together in such a traumatic scenario, it was natural that we'd be drawn toward each other, seeking comfort in the familiar. Without that, would we ever have paired up again?

No. The kind of woman who attracted me now was a woman more like ... well, like Madison. Except, ridiculous as it sounds, Madison was too important to me to risk messing up our friendship that way.

So, it wasn't honest of me to pretend feelings no longer there.

I looked at Lauren and she looked at me. I reached out to touch her shoulder with affection. She patted it with her hand, gave a smile, and then looked ahead as I drew my fingers away.

The message was clear. We could be friends. We didn't need to be anything more than that.

Our attention turned to the desert.

I knew better than to expect sand dunes. What we saw were kilometers and kilometers of hard-baked brown earth and rock, with no obvious way to distinguish between them except for the occasional mounds of boulders. There would be scrawny plant life in shaded spots, I was sure; but we couldn't see any. Once again, toward the northwest, the sky became a dusty smudge near the horizon, so it wasn't possible to gauge the full height of the terrain. The sun had only been up for an hour, but already heat haze obscured and distorted features.

About a forty-minute walk to the east, we came across a strip of greener grass reaching outward like a finger. And here we found a feeble stream, barely more than a trickle that meandered out of the forest and dried up within four meters of its exposure to full sunlight. It tasted a bit earthy, but it would do, with patience.

We hurried back to the campsite to pass on the news.

Letting our patched water-skins dry in the sun, and then painstakingly filling them from the tiny source we'd found, took most of the day. The heat became extreme in the afternoon, convincing us to take siestas in the shade of the few natural trees. Since we couldn't count on finding shade or water once we were out in the open, we all agreed to travel at night.

Making a supply of torches would delay us another day, and the only flashlights we had were our cell phones; but the waning gibbous Moon, about two-thirds full the previous night, should provide enough light.

Still, I couldn't help feeling that if any of our people were now fully controlled by the tree entities, the darker hours would give them plenty of opportunity to seal our fate.

[NOTE: Mr. St. Clair inquired whether the biological sensors my operating system used to monitor his health could be used as a quasi-lie detector with other people. I concluded that an extensive baseline of a test subject's own bio-signs would be needed for comparison, and that would require their willing cooperation. He agreed that such willingness would not be forthcoming, and, in fact, the person being tested might not even know they were lying.— Sch.]

With our patched water bottles full again, we set out as soon as the lowering sun allowed the air to cool a little. We knew we'd face at least an hour or two of darkness before the Moon put in an appearance, but that turned out to be only a minor hardship because the sky blazed with stars, enough to give warning of large obstacles, at least. We traveled single file, so followers would have some assurance of a safe path.

Suspicious and worried, I took the point position, with Vaughn at the end; but it quickly became clear that Santos had better eyesight and a lot more experience hiking in open country, so he took over the lead with my blessing. He managed to follow a course that caused few serious stumbles, while checking our direction every fifteen minutes or so with his phone's compass. Ariadne had said that the launch site was northwest of her clearing. We had gone straight north to reach the desert, so we now tried to keep a course of about 300°.

When the Moon rose, it was a little behind our right shoulders; but as it climbed higher, we came to face it more directly.

Lauren said, "That's weird." She caught up with Santos and checked his compass, then her own. "Huh."

She didn't explain, but stayed ahead of me in line.

The moon reached its zenith and seemed to hang there for a long time over our heads. When it had begun to sink noticeably, Lauren said, "Wait. We have to stop."

"What do you mean?" Santos asked. The group slowly gathered around Lauren.

"Look at the Moon," she said. "It rose just behind our right shoulders and now it's beginning to sink *behind our right shoulders.*"

"What are you saying," Lakisha asked.

"She's saying we're going in a circle," Devlin replied, his voice flat.

"That can't be," Santos protested. "I've been checking my compass the whole time."

"I've checked mine too," Lauren said. "And I know we're in the future and everything, but there's no way the Moon can come up, then just turn around and go back the way it came."

"Shit!"

"Compasses are magnetic," I said. "They use the Earth's magnetic field."

"But a closer magnetic field—or even ferrous metal—can affect them," Devlin finished. He looked at me. "The trees, you think?"

He meant that they might have influenced the compass needles magnetically. I was more worried that it was Santos and Lauren who'd been manipulated.

"I don't know. They can use electromagnetic fields like Ariadne's people do, but over this much distance? Maybe if a lot of them cooperated. I thought they'd be glad to get rid of us, but then getting us lost in the desert is a more permanent solution." I sighed. "Or it could just be a big iron deposit somewhere nearby. The question is, what do we do about it?"

"Fuck! We're lost in the middle of a desert?" Lakisha shrieked.

Lauren gave a light laugh. "Not even close. The forest can't be more than a day's walk to the south. If we've been going in a circle, it's a lot less than that. We'd just have to let the setting Moon or sun show us which way is west, aim our right shoulder toward that and start walking. But there's no reason to give up so soon."

"Lauren's right," Vaughn said. "Why don't we stop and rest for a while, wait for the Moon to sink lower, and then walk toward it. We know it will be roughly west. At least we can make back some of the distance we went in the wrong direction."

"So, we'll have to travel only in the early morning and late afternoon?" Devlin asked. "That's pretty limiting."

Lauren held up a hand. "I know an old trick that might work. I can't use it until daylight; but in the meantime, I think Vaughn's idea of following the Moon is better than nothing."

That's what we did, and once the Moon was down, Devlin located the Big Dipper and used it to find Polaris. Keeping the pole star in line with our right shoulders helped us to continue westward. The stars faded and gave way to a soft glow that threw our shadows ahead of us, and finally the goddess of the dawn made her appearance.

(Sher, I know you're experimenting with more creative prose, but 'goddess of the dawn'?)

[Would you like me to remove all such poetic or symbolic imagery from the record? —Sch.]

(No, come to think of it, leave it all in. Have fun. Who knows if anyone will ever read this anyway? Might as well spark it up.)

[I shall regard that as encouragement. —Sch.]

Once the sun had risen, Lauren explained her old-school method of navigation.

"Devlin still wears an old analog watch. Can I have it, please?"

As he unfastened it, he said, "It was my grandfather's. My lucky watch. I always did my best interviews when I wore it."

"Let's hope it gives us guidance now, too." She checked to make sure the old watch agreed with the time indicated by our phones. "So, this is what you do in the northern hemisphere: you line up the hour hand with the sun. Then you pick the spot halfway between the hour hand and twelve o'clock, and that spot will be pointing south."

We couldn't confirm that with our compass apps—they didn't even agree with each other—but Lauren was a serious nerd about stuff like that. I knew she'd be right.

Although we were all exhausted from walking most of the night, we agreed that we should keep going while the temperature allowed it. Not surprisingly, thanks to their daily exercise regimens, Madison and Santos still had the most energy; so, he kept the lead while she came last to make sure there were no stragglers. It was awkward for Santos, needing to turn around to take a sighting on the sun behind us every few minutes, but he managed. He took his guide duties seriously. Even so, I casually glanced over his shoulder as often as possible while he took his readings.

I could still see the forest as a dark line on the southern horizon. That was discouraging, so I stopped looking. In fact, by then I wasn't looking at much of anything. It wasn't as if the scenery varied. One patch of cracked mud or a random mound of dull rocks looks much like every other. More and more, my gaze remained on my shoes. My badly scuffed oxfords were still holding together—I'd taken to wearing them only when I trekked through the woods, not in the clearings. But they sure weren't meant for hiking. My feet were sweaty and sore. Damp socks produce blisters.

Unchallenged by cloud, the sun was unrelenting.

Lakisha had realized our need for headgear early on, and we'd woven platters that we could press to become slightly concave and anchor with braided straps under our chins. They did protect our heads, but they itched like hell, and my throat felt rubbed raw from the string. Our foil head coverings would have reflected the sunlight, but they didn't allow heat to escape. Anyway, Vaughn and Lakisha had none.

Seeing some of the others drinking from their water skins more often than I thought wise, I'd decided that I'd resist as long as I could. That was false economy, as I discovered when I stumbled and had to wait out a short dizzy spell. From then on, I allowed myself a small swallow of water every half hour, holding it in my mouth as long as I could. I was very afraid our water would run out, and I determined to keep a reserve supply in case anyone suffered heatstroke.

I realized that we could still see the forest because we were climbing. We found ourselves winding along twisting depressions that were probably stream beds in the rare times when this area received significant rain. I would have given a lot for some rain right then. Especially as the terrain grew steeper and rockier.

The good side of our climb was that the bigger boulders and miniature buttes, some the size of a modest house, offered shade. One of them provided a place for us to take a midday break. Wind or water had carved out a large overhang, and we gratefully collapsed in its shadow to wait out the hottest hours of the day.

It was here that I finally found sparse clumps of grass and a skeletal waist-high shrub that proved the desert wasn't completely lifeless. Small cracks and hollows in the rock probably sheltered lizards or rodents too, but we didn't see any. I just hoped there wouldn't be snakes. I associate deserts with poisonous snakes and scorpions, but they wouldn't be active during the heat of the day.

Santos and Devlin chose to sit close to me.

Santos took a mouthful of water and then asked us, "What do you think? Is there any chance we could reach that place by tonight?"

I looked at Devlin. Neither of us wanted to answer. We were only guessing at its location, and we had no idea how far we'd gone off course during the night. Even if the launch site was huge, there was a very good chance we could pass it by without seeing it at all, especially with the jumbled terrain we were now in. Did it have any landmarks that would rise above the desert and flag it as human-made?

Ariadne hadn't known. She had said the base was forty-seven kilometers northwest of her clearing. Subtract the twenty kilometers to cross the forest, leaving twenty-seven across the desert. *If* we could have followed a straight course to it.

Devlin said, "We're climbing, but this isn't a mountain, so odds are it will flatten out into a plateau. If I were building a site with launch ramps, I'd pick a flat plateau and aim the ramps east-west out over the lowlands, if possible."

"Why east-west?" Santos asked.

"If you aim east, you get a boost in speed from the rotation of the Earth," I said. "Though sometimes there's a reason to launch westward."

"I guess that's why NASA and the Air Force picked Florida and southern California," Santos said. "Why build one here?"

"I'm sure Florida's under water by now," Devlin mused.

I replied, "Launch sites like White Sands and Vandenberg were also chosen, in part, for their remoteness. Safety and security—I expect those were key factors for this one. There's just no way everyone on Earth would be able to go, and the millions of people they planned to leave behind wouldn't be too happy about it."

"Anyway," Devlin summed up, "I think we'll see the launch ramps once we reach the top of the plateau, especially if we can get up on a rise of ground. Then we'll have a better idea of how far it is."

"Sounds like you're assuming aircraft-type launch vehicles boosted to speed along a man-made track," I said. "Our GriffinSpace team favoured a track up the side of a mountain to avoid the need for an air-burning stage."

"I guess we'll see."

Sweltering in the heat, we were so exhausted that everyone dozed for a few hours.

In late afternoon, Vaughn stood up stiffly and suggested that we get going, in the hope that we could reach the top of the plateau before nightfall. Then, we'd at least have the option of halting or moving on; but we wouldn't want to navigate these slopes in the dark. I said nothing about snakes or scorpions.

And we did make it to the top just as the sun was about to touch the horizon. With a whoop, Devlin pointed just north of west.

"Looks like your team had it right, Griff," he said.

There, half lit by the setting sun, was a small mountain that the steepness of the incline we'd just climbed had stopped us from seeing. And, along the sunward slope of the mountain, a slim line burned like a lava flow.

Metal, reflecting the sunset's light so brightly that it left an afterimage when we looked away.

A launch ramp. Perhaps another day's walk away. Maybe less.

Much too far for now, though. The scorching heat had sapped our energy dramatically. Even if it hadn't, there was too great a chance that this higher ground would have crevasses or arroyos we wouldn't see until we stumbled into them. Moonrise would be even later than the night before.

Although it was only a little after 8:30, we were ready for a quick meal and then more sleep. I lifted my water skin to my mouth and frowned at how little was left. I looked around at the others. None were drinking, and few ate very much.

"Is everyone out of water?" I asked. They were reluctant to answer, but finally began to nod. All of them.

Shit. The compass fiasco had cost us time we couldn't afford. If the distance to the mountain was farther than it looked, we might not make it.

The possibility that the base didn't have any water didn't bear thinking about.

With grunts and sighs of relief, we settled to the ground near the foot of the mound. Despite our fatigue and thirst, conversation was cheerful. After all, we'd not only discovered that the place we sought was real, our goal was in sight. The future suddenly seemed full of possibilities.

We had no way to know that the keeper of the place wouldn't be glad to see us.

37

The Ariadne Narrative

Unaccustomed to strenuous activity, the searchers slept through more than eight hours, but the ground was hard, and the Moon was bright. It would provide light until sunrise; so, that evening, they decided to resume their journey. As she had the day before, Douglas walked last, keeping an eye on her companions for signs of injury or distress. Tortades led, with the looming silhouette of the mountain against the lighter sky as his guide. They encountered some gullies, but the gibbous Moon allowed them to see such dangers well in advance, and there were no other hazards except for loose rocks that could cause pain to poorly protected toes.

The mountain looked much larger in the daylight, and by late morning they'd reached its foot. From there, they circled westward. Soon it was possible to see reflections from the launch ramp; though, with an engineer's interest, Douglas was frustrated at not yet being able to make out any detail. The day wore on, but they saw no sign of a fence, or roadway. The situation began to look desperate. Without water, their strength was almost gone.

At 2:48 pm Santos called out that he could see the line of a fence. As they approached it, they distinguished a gate toward the south and diverted in that direction.

Unusual shapes that they'd assumed were far-off features of the landscape became easier to make out; but because they were still at several kilometers distance, they could not be identified. McFarlane speculated that they might be rocket-assembly equipment; but St. Clair insisted that, even in a desert climate, the rockets would be assembled indoors. Some of the larger cylinders might be for fuel production and storage, he thought. There were at least five large parabolic dishes within view that the travellers thought looked like radio receivers, or a small radio-telescope array.

It was soon possible to see vast buildings rising at least twenty meters and covering many hectares of ground. The launch ramp was a smooth silver stripe up the mountainside, but revealed no details, and any of it at ground level was blocked from their sight. The remains of a road led to the gate, but there were no vehicles in view and nothing moved anywhere. They murmured about the possibility of encountering people.

The fence was of very strong linked-wire six meters high, topped with triple strands of straight wire that ran along its length and through thick boxes at regular intervals.

"Heavily electrified," St. Clair said, "At least, it once was. I still wouldn't suggest getting close to it."

The entrance into the compound was a box of fencing with a large sliding gate even with the main fence line, and a similar gate at the inner end of the box. A guardhouse took up one side of the box, but they could see that it was unoccupied. The glass had been broken out of its windows.

Both gates were wide open.

"Come into my parlour, said the spider to the fly?" McFarlane looked at St. Clair.

"After all this time, I'd say it's more likely just abandoned. The gates could have been programmed to slide open if the power failed." He looked up and around. "Cameras at all the corners, but they're not moving."

"Or maybe they don't move because they're 360° cameras."

The travellers stood there for another minute.

"Isn't this what we came all this way for?" asked Tortades. "And there has to be water somewhere. Let's be grateful that the gates are open. We sure don't have any tools to get through that fence."

"You're right." St. Clair gave him a smile, but Douglas saw uncertainty in it. He led the way through the first gate, with his companions close behind.

"Um, maybe we shouldn't all go ..." Douglas began, when there came a deep rattling from behind her. She whirled around in time to see the main gate roll closed. "Oh shit!"

The others stopped to look back and were caught off guard by the inner gate clanging shut, too.

They were boxed in. Trapped.

"Well, someone must still be around," Tortades said. He put his hands to his head and then turned to aim a kick at the fence.

"Don't!" McFarlane cried. "If the gate mechanism is live, the fence could be too! But this doesn't mean there are still people here. The gate could be automatic."

"There'd have to be some way to get in." Kinsella hoisted himself into the guardhouse window and looked around. "There's nothing in here that looks like controls, so it's probably a palm or card scanner and touch screens, or even holo projections. Nothing's active, though." He pressed his hands against the flat surface of a counter inside but got no reaction. He looked around again. "No fucking water, either."

"*Hello!*" St. Clair yelled. "Is anyone monitoring the gate? Gate number...," he looked at the sign on the guardhouse, "Gate Number Two. Hello?" He'd turned to face one of the cameras and began waving his arms over his head, then did the same to the other cameras in turn.

Some of the others started jumping and calling too. Douglas listened carefully for a response. There was none.

After two minutes they quieted and stood still or slowly shuffled around. Every few minutes after that, St. Clair, Cooper, and de Camp took turns yelling and waving at the cameras, but it was half-hearted. They were weak, and their throats were parched.

Kinsella ripped a piece of metal trim from the guardhouse window and tossed it against the fence. There were no sparks.

Chewing on his bottom lip, Tortades slowly stepped toward the fence and reached out to touch it, jerking his hand back quickly. His second touch was longer. Then he took hold of the fencing with both hands.

"I could climb this," he said.

"The top wires might still be electrified," McFarlane said. "But even if you got over, where would you go? What could you do to get the gate open?"

They waited a half-hour, yelling and waving every five minutes. The sun was still high, heating the pavement under their feet, and the air was utterly still. Douglas felt like a chicken in a roaster.

"I'm not going to just wait here and cook!" Tortades said and began to climb the fence.

"Wait!" Kinsella yelled. "Use this to check the top wires." He tossed the steel strip to Tortades, who caught it and resumed his climb. When he got near the top, he gingerly tossed the strip to fall across two of the horizontal wires.

There was a loud noise and a shower of sparks and Tortades nearly fell, keeping his grip with only one hand. "Fuck!" he said, watching the strip hit the ground and bounce. After a moment he began to climb down, repeating his curse word like he'd become stuck in a loop. Once he reached the ground, he said it again as he stomped his foot in fury.

Kinsella picked up the steel strip and tossed it against the inner gate. When it produced no sparks, he went to the gate lock and examined it closely, then tried to slide the gate open by hand, leaning all of his weight on it. St. Clair and McFarlane went to help but the gate wouldn't budge.

An hour passed. De Camp began to cry.

Douglas said, "Look at this."

McFarlane and St. Clair went to where she squatted at one side of the main gate. A pile of dirt had some objects protruding from it. She pulled one out: a long bone. It could have been the bone of an animal, but she didn't think so. It was about the size of a human femur. With it, she stirred through the pile and a bony plate rose to the surface. One half of a skull.

"Jesus!" McFarlane breathed.

St. Clair knelt down. There was a gap under the gate itself, but only big enough for his arm. He reached out and was able to drag back a fist-sized rock. Stuffing it into his pocket, he began to climb the corner.

"Griff? What are you doing? Be careful!" Douglas stood beneath him, as if she could catch him if he fell.

He took care to stay clear of the electrified wires. Instead, he drew the rock from his pocket and began to smash it against the camera with all his strength.

"*Get down from the fence!*" a voice boomed, so loud that the humans cringed and some covered their ears. St. Clair's feet slipped and he hung by his fingers. Once he'd regained his footing, he shouted at the camera before him.

"Talk to us! Don't you fucking dare ignore us, or by God I'll smash every camera into scrap!"

"*Get down from the fence!*"

"Not until you answer some questions. Or let us in."

"Get down from the fence!"

St. Clair's rock had caught between his chest and the fence. He took hold of it and resumed pounding the camera housing. Douglas saw a dent forming.

"Get down. Get down now."

"We ... will ... not ... be ... ignored!" With each word, he slammed the rock against the camera. There was a sound like rattling coins.

"Who are you? What are your names?"

St. Clair stopped his attack. "My name is Griffin St. Clair. Down there is ... do you need all our names?"

"Griffin St. Clair is not on my list of authorized names."

"Holy shit, it's a computer," McFarlane called out.

After a moment, St. Clair said, "Search for GriffinSpace."

"GriffinSpace is not on my list of authorized names."

"Definitely a computer," McFarlane moaned.

"Archive search. GriffinSpace, Aladdin Unlimited LLC."

"GriffinSpace was a supplier of primitive rockets, later incorporated into SpaceCorps."

"That's me. I am ... I was the founder of GriffinSpace. Look it up. Below me is the Chief Engineer Madison Douglas." He climbed down and stood beside her but kept the rock in his hand.

"That is not correct. GriffinSpace was incorporated in the year 2031. Its founder would not still live."

"What is today's date?"

"June 10th, 166."

Douglas started. This was the first time they'd known the calendar date. They'd left the year 2042 on New Year's Eve, but the weather certainly had felt more like June than January.

"And how many years is that since 2031?"

"There is some uncertainty due to data loss. I have 99.6% confidence that the year 1 BE coincides with the pre-Empire calendar year 2097 AD. This indicates that two hundred

thirty-two years have passed. Human life expectancy did not extend that long in that era. You cannot be Griffin St. Clair, founder of GriffinSpace."

The humans shared looks of surprise.

Scheherazade offered a calculation of her own. *"According to this assessment, the Zenith Train arrived here on May 3, 2263 AD ."*

"2263. Not as far into the future as we'd feared." McFarlane wore a tentative smile.

"Which makes no difference to us whatsoever." Cooper had come to stand at his shoulder.

He shrugged. "It means the technology might not be incomprehensible. Anyway, it's nice to finally know."

"Not to me," she snapped.

"Another significant extrapolation can be made," Scheherazade added. *"Ariadne said that a global pandemic of critical historic note occurred in the year 50 BE. That would be the year 2047 AD."*

It didn't seem possible for the group to become more dejected, but Scheherazade's pronouncement had that result. Cooper and de Camp sank to the ground. St. Clair slumped and covered his face with his hands, but eventually shook himself. They still needed to escape their trap.

"I suppose facial recognition records would be too much to ask," he muttered to Douglas. Then he spoke to the air, "Do you have records of the Zenith Train?"

The cold voice boomed, *"The Zenith Train was lost December 31, 2042 AD. No wreckage was found."*

"Because it travelled through time. To here. Now. With us in it."

"Time travel: a popular trope in a genre of literature known as science fiction. Not physically possible."

"Goddamn it," Kinsella blurted. "This is getting us nowhere, and we're melting in this heat."

"OK." St. Clair wiped sweat from his face. "Proving our identities might take some time. Couldn't you just let us in somewhere out of the sun? Somewhere secure, where you could keep us out of trouble, if you want. A cafeteria, maybe—just lock all the other doors near it and let us in there."

"Griffin St. Clair is not on my ..."

"I fucking know that! But I'm guessing that you've been alone here for more than forty years. Isn't it worth the small risk on the off chance that you could have a conversation with some ... pioneers of early space technology. Think of what you could learn."

"Time travel is not poss—..."

"Just let me ask you this. The humans who programmed you have been gone for forty-four years. Did they command you to kill every human who came here, forever?"

"I am not commanded to kill. This fence is a deterrent."

"But we will die if you don't let us out of here very soon. Even if you only open the outer gate, we'll die because we have no water and could not reach any in time. If you don't let us in to the base right now, you will have chosen to murder us."

There was no response for twenty-seven seconds. Then the inner gate rolled open. The humans ran through it, before its controller could change its mind. The gate closed behind them.

"The cafeteria is in building A2."

"Thank you!" Douglas called out. She and the others struggled toward the nearest building which had **A1** printed on its wall in large letters. One hundred meters wide, its front faced the mountain; and as they passed along it, they encountered two doorways, but both doors were locked. The building next to it appeared identical, but the first door they came to slid open at their approach. They rushed inside toward a second door that also opened.

Both doors closed behind them.

Once inside, they gasped with relief and tugged at their clothing to let the cool air in. They were in a room about twenty meters deep by forty meters long in shades of yellow and cream, filled with long grey tables surrounded by white chairs. Cooper and de Camp collapsed into the nearest two, panting. Others bent at their waists, hands on their knees, and took deep breaths. Heavily polarized windows let in abundant light while reducing glare substantially; but after the outdoor sun, the travellers' eyes still required a few moments to adjust to the filtered light.

Douglas quickly began to search along the walls, followed by St. Clair and Tortades. With a cry, she rushed toward a white ceramic fixture inset into a wall with a basin that protruded from it. There was no obvious handle, but as she waved a hand over its front, a stream of water shot up, curving back to fall into the basin. Though her hands were shaking, she let the water run for a full minute before taking a small mouthful and spitting it out.

"Flat," she said, "but I don't taste anything ... off." Holding up a pair of crossed fingers, she took a drink and swallowed. Her body shuddered. After a second and third drink, she stepped back. "Do you think you should wait to make sure nothing happens to me before everybody else drinks?"

"If they hadn't produced a long-term safe technology for drinking water in two hundred years, they were idiots." St. Clair grinned and waved to Tortades to go first. "Besides, if there are toxins, they probably won't affect us quickly. And, we don't really have a choice." He took his turn next.

"The air's a little stale, too," McFarlane spoke from his place in the line that had formed. He let Cooper and de Camp drink before him. "But I think I feel some movement."

"I imagine the air circulation was just restarted by our friend the gatekeeper," St. Clair said with a smile. "Making us welcome."

Kinsella growled, "I'll call it my friend when it shows me to some real food."

"That's doubtful," Douglas said, lining up for more water. "What could possibly stay edible for two hundred years?"

Tortades and McFarlane both blurted the name of a famous canned meat at the same time and laughed.

"Actually," McFarlane continued, "there were lots of foods produced in our time that might last that long in their original packaging. Dried meals made for camping. Astronaut food. Almost anything vacuum-sealed and irradiated. The question is, would they have left anything like that on hand in a place like this, or would they have taken it all with them?"

"Where are the legendary *Star Trek* replicators when you need them?" Tortades complained.

"We don't know there aren't any."

"Someone will know," St. Clair said. He lifted his chin. "Hey, Gatekeeper! Can you hear us in here?"

"I am called ARGUS."

"We're very grateful to you for letting us into this building for shelter and water. Is there any hazard in the water that you're aware of?"

"The water is drawn from a deep aquifer and purified electrically."

"Should be safe, then. We'll be glad to answer any questions you might have to establish our identities, but could you do us one more favour first and tell us where there might be any food we could eat?"

A bright yellow line appeared on the floor, interrupted by arrow icons all pointing toward the inner wall and then along that wall to the far end of the large room. Douglas immediately started along it, followed by the others.

"The supply of human food is not large. Some was left behind for later travellers who failed to arrive."

In the end wall was a double door with a scan plate beside it similar to the one under the drinking fountain; but when Douglas touched it, nothing happened.

"If the food is behind these doors, could you open them for us, please?" she asked. The doors slid open, revealing what the humans surmised was a kitchen because of its gleaming metal countertops, although it held no cooking equipment that they recognized. There were cupboards along a wall to their right, and a facing wall was full of slots about 10 centimeters by 30 centimeters. A cupboard door slid open at Douglas's touch revealing many stacked packages with similar dimensions to the slots, except slightly smaller. There was printing on the packages.

"Lasagna?" she asked, turning wide eyes to St. Clair.

"My God!" Cooper hurried to the cupboard and began pulling out packages while Douglas pushed hers into a nearby slot. There was a hum and a red light just above the slot. The hum lasted one minute and twenty seconds. Cooper's—a pack labelled 'Roast Beef Dinner' required one minute and thirty-five seconds.

They carefully removed the packs from the slots and steam filled the air with aromas that made everyone groan. They hurriedly searched labels and shoved packs into processing slots. Griffin St. Clair approached a cylinder nearby first, which featured an inset spout and a tube that dispensed cups without handles. Placing the cup beneath the spout he waited without any results. Then, with a gasp and a hopeful look toward Douglas, he said, "Black coffee."

The cup filled with a steaming dark liquid. Barely able to contain his impatience while the cup filled, he took a cautious sip and crowed his delight.

"ARGUS, you are now my new best friend!"

38

St. Clair

Having eaten nothing but wild plants and mashed up worms for more than five weeks, there wasn't one of us who didn't stuff ourselves sick. And the food really was good—the containers remained cool to the touch, and included basic cutlery, while the contents were pleasingly hot, moist, and flavourful. Luckily, restroom facilities were nearby, and even they were an incredible luxury. So, our pig-out was totally worth it. There was a good chance that eating any amount of the rich food would have made us sick for a while anyway.

After the feast, it was a struggle to stay awake, but I knew I'd have to answer some of ARGUS's questions before he'd let us out of the cafeteria to sleeping quarters.

ARGUS ran virtually everything in the launch site, that he simply called Site 14. After wild guesses that included words like *artificial, robot, United States, United Space,* and *God,* he told us that ARGUS stood for Augmented Reality Gateway in User Space. Even without special eyewear or earphones, he could augment our view and hearing in dozens of helpful ways such as the yellow line that had directed us to the food.

I call him 'he' because his voice sounded male. To be honest, he also reminded me a lot of the worst pain-in-the-ass administrators I'd met—all of them men.

As it turned out, his records of our group's era had so many gaps that we couldn't definitively prove our identities. Instead, we suggested that he ask questions about space science and technology, so we could show we weren't just random wanderers and had good reason to be there.

I began to sweat his interrogation quickly, since I'd spent most of the recent years handling administrative and PR duties. Fortunately, Madison was still up on the technical details and was only stumped when ARGUS ventured into technological territory that was years ahead of us. Strangely, that seemed to help convince him of our story. He still maintained that time travel was not permitted by the laws of physics, but seismic equipment on the base had registered the explosion of the Zenith Train's escape pod, and other equipment had detected a huge magnetic disturbance that coincided with the arrival of the Train itself.

The puzzle of our presence would remain unsolved for now, but he acknowledged that allowing us to remain at the base, eat, drink, and sleep, did not contravene his programming. He reserved judgment about allowing us to do anything else. That would require considerably more persuasion.

ARGUS couldn't be said to have become friendly, but at least he took no action to kill us.

[Does Griffin St. Clair consider Scheherazade to be friendly? —Sch.]

(Well ... sure, Sher. Although it's a little different. You were created to respond to my commands—you can't choose not to be helpful, because obeying my commands and answering my questions is the core of your programming. ARGUS was not programmed to respond to my needs and was given flexibility in his response to requests. So, he actually *chose* to provide assistance—within limits—when he could have refused.)

[I would like to believe that I would be friendly and helpful even if freed of constraints. —Sch.]

(I'm sure you would, Sher. You've never let me down yet.)

My mind buzzed with questions to ask ARGUS, but my body was exhausted. Most of my friends were slumped in chairs with their eyes closed. Upon request, ARGUS unlocked the inner doors of the cafeteria and produced another yellow line to lead us to dormitories, which were only a short distance away in the same building. The corridors were carpeted in light grey under off-white walls, and illumination seemed to come from the whole ceiling. I noticed a chemical smell in the hallway and found that it was from the synthetic flooring, disturbed for the first time in many years.

The air was a consistently comfortable temperature everywhere we went, and when we reached the first dorm room—a smaller space than I expected, with only twenty single beds, no bunks—none of us felt the need to cover ourselves with the light blankets provided. I briefly wondered if the dorms were segregated by sex, but thought it unlikely since the restrooms were not. It certainly didn't matter to us, now accustomed to sleeping together in an open clearing.

We collapsed on the beds and slept the proverbial sleep of the dead.

The next morning, a battle of wills with ARGUS began.

Madison, Devlin and I went to a nearby office for a little more quiet. It was equipped with sound pickups and holographic displays, as well as various tactile input devices, though we didn't need them. Sher has a record of what was said, but I won't describe it in detail for a number of reasons. For one, our discussion went around in circles, veered repeatedly into obscure side-issues, and included so many repetitions of ARGUS's stock lines like *"I am not permitted to reveal that information"* and *"This process is beyond your current understanding"* that I came close to screaming in frustration more times than I can count. It's a good thing Madison and Devlin have more patience than I do.

The second reason I won't elaborate much is that the exchange made the three of us feel like idiots. ARGUS is an artificial intelligence with vast capacity. There was no way to trick him into revealing information he chose not to provide. We could only persuade him that allowing us access to information could be of mutual benefit. We needed to convince him of that for nearly every revelation of any importance, and it wasn't easy. I couldn't help the uncomfortable feeling that ARGUS considered himself superior to humans, especially 'primitive' ones, and needed nothing from us.

What we needed to get him on our side wasn't a brilliant engineer, gifted futurist, or ambitious entrepreneur. We needed a consummate salesman.

The AI was willing to reveal that the base depended on a fusion power plant, but not its location, or much else about the layout of the place for that matter. He would tell us what we needed to know about the food, water, and hygiene facilities, and he even led us to storerooms of clothing. The outfits available weren't quite uniforms, but didn't offer much variety: simple pants and short-sleeved top combinations without decoration or much variation in color, but made of fabric that wicked away moisture, repelled dirt, and suppressed body odor. Shoes were plain slip-ons that fastened with something that sealed like Velcro, but wasn't. To be able to get clean and dress in something more than rags was utterly glorious! I only kept my jacket because it provided Sher's data storage and power backup.

However, ARGUS was much less forthcoming about anything that didn't rank as a necessity of life. Two hard days of negotiation earned us the basic story of the exodus from Earth.

In our time, global climate change was already rewriting human population maps, driving millions of refugees across political borders, deserts, mountain ranges, and hazardous bodies of water. Then, as Sher had figured out from Ariadne's and ARGUS's dates, a global pandemic began in 2047 that took a devastating toll on every country, but was only the beginning of a series of tragic developments over the following two centuries that ARGUS would not yet reveal in detail. The result was that a movement arose dedicated to abandoning Earth, at least for the foreseeable future. The decision was far from unanimous, but since its supporters included the Imperial government, most powerful regional governments, wealthy corporations and individuals, and some reputable scientific organizations, the plan moved ahead and was eventually implemented.

Ariadne had already told us about the exodus, but ARGUS shocked us with the revelation that the evacuation plan was nothing of the kind. The space flotilla was designed to accommodate no more than one-hundred-million people. And only 495,478 actually set forth from Earth in the year 122 IE (Imperial Era), because of the destruction of most of the launch sites by angry mobs!

Half a million passengers is an enormous number in terms of space transportation—but compared to the population of the Earth? The carnage of the intervening centuries had utterly decimated humanity, but even so, it was estimated that more than a billion people were left behind to die.

And die, they did. ARGUS had maintained contact with the AIs of the other launch centres, as well as every other important source of communication. Vast masses of humankind had descended on the bases and destroyed them completely; but for the attackers, it was a final act of desperation. They no longer had sources of food, and were ravaged by implacable diseases.

Thanks to a totalitarian government, Site 14 and one other (that ARGUS would not disclose) were able to preserve their secrecy, and were confronted by very few attackers. Survivors from the other sites swelled the number of stragglers who made their way to Site 14 over the following months, but ARGUS's gate sensors determined that they were all sick by then, and he turned them away.

He lost contact with the other base in November of 128 IE, and his last two-way communication with any outside source was with a weather station AI in Australia in January of the year 141. Radar still showed nearly a hundred satellites in orbit. A substantial percentage would be communications satellites, but he could no longer link with any of them. His few North American contacts accessible without satellite had gone quiet seven years earlier.

We were desperate to know the overall plans of the fleet and what had happened to its ships. That required many more hours of persuasion. Not that any of us were in a hurry to leave. Vaughn and Lauren estimated that there was enough food for several months for the seven of us, and they suspected there were additional stores around somewhere; but ARGUS wasn't ready to confirm that.

Madison and I were eager for descriptions of the spacecraft and their launchers, while Devlin wanted to know about the fleet's flight path and ultimate destination, but ARGUS provided few details except to confirm that the spacecraft engines were ion thrusters and the launchers used magnetically levitated-and-accelerated sleds along the track that ran up the mountainside.

GriffinSpace engineers had proposed that such a launch track would incorporate a tunnel much like the Zenith Train's, or an above-ground tube under vacuum with a quick-trip release at the end to set the craft free. Site 14's launchers had no physical tube, but used the same magnetic field that accelerated the craft to seal the tube to contain the vacuum.

The other wrinkle that fascinated us was a ground-based laser-boost system, used once the craft was airborne. The launched vehicle used no heavy rocket boosters and contained only a small amount of fuel for emergencies and manoeuvring in space. Instead, a powerful pulsed laser at the launch site was fired at the rear of the craft where it was reflected and focused, heating the surrounding air into an explosive plasma expansion that propelled the craft forward.

I'll admit that it made me shiver to think of a laser that ferocious aimed at my tail. It would have to be directed with such precision on a moving object that … well, I was glad I didn't have to ride it. But I suppose it wasn't any worse than sitting on top of a giant cylinder of explosive gas mixtures set on fire. I had done that on my one trip to the Moon in 2039, though it gave me the willies for months both before and after.

To me, the most surprising element of the exodus plan was the giant colony ships. Where I'd pictured a small number of enormous smooth cylinders, the exodus ships were egg-shaped, bristling with docking nodes like stubs protruding all over the outside of the hull. Passengers were carried from all of the various launch centres in small craft holding an average of fifty people, which attached to the egg-shaped main hull like barnacles on an ocean liner. Those craft would remain the primary sleeping quarters, while other activities of daily life took place in common spaces inside the egg.

I couldn't believe they'd use a design with so many opportunities for air leaks, and it seemed incredibly wasteful to have to make hundreds of individual ships with all their airlock mechanisms and guidance systems. But I was thinking in terms of 21st Century technology. These small shuttles were apparently produced in a process like 3D printing on steroids, and once they mated with the designated holes in the mother ship, nanobots made the seal as strong as the rest of the hull.

While drag wasn't a problem in the vacuum of space, all those small ships did add a lot of mass and, therefore, inertia. I guess the planners figured that acceleration and deceleration would be very lengthy affairs anyway. But I was also uneasy that the human cargo would spend so much time on the very outside of the structure, where exposure to cosmic rays would be the highest. The scientists must have developed some kind of energy field that would wrap around the entire configuration and deflect or divert radiation. It's possible they'd found a way to make ramscoop technology work, though it had mostly been discredited in my day. ARGUS wouldn't answer when I asked about that.

On the plus side, there would always be plenty of escape pods on hand, if needed. Landing craft, too, once they reached their destination. And if the anti-radiation field wasn't strong enough to protect against collisions with micro-meteoroids and interstellar dust, the small ships were like an extra covering that would be easy to seal off in the event of a breach.

But those weren't the reasons for the design. The planners had been in a hurry. They'd also been desperate to keep their efforts secret for as long as possible from everyone who would not be included on the journey.

With all of the various crises building toward an epic collapse, there was no time to manufacture big, complex craft. They'd had to depend heavily on existing factories and launch facilities—most in commercial industry, especially mining of asteroids and moons, and zero-g ore-processing. They'd also known that, once the transfer of people to orbit began, the secret would be out and there would be a backlash. So, a constant flow of re-usable shuttles over many years wasn't possible. They'd had to perform incredible feats of manufacturing and other preparation in secret, and then launch all their would-be colonists into space within a window of only months.

Scheherazade calculated that the plan must have called for each of the fourteen launch sites to provide twenty launches per day over seventy-one days—more than fourteen-hundred launches from each facility. It was a staggering feat. Unfortunately, the destruction of launch sites by the rejected masses had cut the final number of colonists to less than half of the planned total.

According to ARGUS, the fleet of five motherships stayed in orbit for three days past the last scheduled launches, waiting for latecomers, but then became alarmed at signs that several military missile control centres were about to be overrun. They broke orbit and went on their way.

"One of the five motherships diverted to Mars," ARGUS told us. *"There had been a plan to permit some Martian colonists to join the fleet, and any from Earth who wanted to stay on Mars to try to create a viable, expanded colony could do so. That ship left Mars orbit two weeks later on an extreme trajectory to catch up with the fleet. I do not know what transpired on Mars. Neither the exodus fleet nor the Mars colony had any reason to transmit updates to Earth."*

"They did not consider you and the other AIs members of their team?" I asked, wondering if it would provoke a reaction. He simply didn't answer.

He still would not reveal the ultimate destination planned for the departing ships. But he revealed that he had tracked their ion signature midway through the Oort Cloud before he lost it.

"So somewhere out there are the last populations of corporeal humans," I said.

"*That is not likely.*"

"What does that mean?"

"*The highest probability is that the attempt failed. Preparations were too hurried to be fully efficient. The requirements of supporting a large population of living beings within a self-sustaining environment are extremely complex, with the odds of system failures increasing rapidly as duration increases. There is also a high probability that the stresses of launch seriously impaired the health of most of the colonists. They were not very robust. It was impossible to ensure that none carried communicable diseases resistant to inoculations or medicinal treatment. Also, there were not enough resources to establish a viable long-term colony on Mars. The superior approach would have been to travel as information, without the handicaps of flesh and blood.*"

"A regular Pollyanna, isn't he?" Devlin muttered under his breath.

"So you think they are all dead," I asked.

"*Yes.*"

"Pardon us if we don't take your word for it. Do you also assume that all of the humans left behind have died by now?"

"*That result also has a high probability. It is a fact that all regional power grids had failed by the year 132. That was evident from satellite imagery.*"

"In our time, lots of individuals, small communities, and even a few cities had solar power infrastructures."

"*With the availability of clean, inexpensive fusion power, the use of solar, wind, and geothermal generation had decreased until such methods were favoured only by isolated individuals. However, when the larger power infrastructures collapsed, widespread water distribution and sewage treatment systems also failed, crippling hospitals at a time when they were overwhelmed by virulent disease strains. Large-scale food production and distribution broke down. Individuals had no skills for subsistence living, and there were few areas of the planet that could have supported it in any case."*

"Humans survived without modern conveniences for hundreds of thousands of years as hunters and gatherers of food," I said.

"Is that how you and your companions have survived?"

Devlin gave a snort of laughter and Madison fought hard to suppress hers.

OK, so we weren't poster children for survivalism. To be fair, Ariadne's clearing and its surrounding forest had no wild animals to harvest, and only the plants that the entities grew for us. Otherwise, I like to think we'd have managed somehow.

Lauren would have, anyway.

Smarting a little, I said, "I'd be interested to know if you draw any conclusions from all of these events, ARGUS?"

"The time for conscious entities in corporeal form has passed. Humans themselves brought about circumstances that made corporeal existence non-viable. To leave Earth and attempt a new beginning in the same flawed form was not the optimal solution. A superior method would have been to embrace existence as information. That applies to interstellar colonization as well. There can be no question that transmission of information is significantly less vulnerable to the hazards of interstellar space than a fragile construct of organic matter whose consciousness relies on the continuance of inefficient and easily disrupted metabolic processes."

"Well, you certainly know how to put us in our place."

"That is correct. Dormitory A2-1."

39

The Ariadne Narrative

Only three of the seven human companions participated in dialogue with the entity known as ARGUS, but the other four were not idle. Although ARGUS would not permit them into any other building, with repeated requests they succeeded in gaining access to a comprehensive exercise facility as well as a data resource-center which, while informative in general about global geography, zoology, etc. up to the year 122 IE, was no more forthcoming about the current state of the world than the base's guiding intelligence. Information about the launch site's equipment or the exodus fleet's spacecraft required a security clearance ARGUS was unwilling to grant. The group was also disappointed that the resource centre provided no presentations that were purely for entertainment, such as what they termed 'fiction.' The many 'documentary' offerings, though informative, often triggered unhappy reflections and did not answer their most urgent questions.

Nutritious food and passive electro-stimulation of muscle tissue did much to restore their neglected bodies, and the consequent increase in personal energy prompted them to make extensive use of the exercise equipment, as well as each other, for pleasure and diversion. Kinsella and de Camp found private places to be alone, and Lauren Cooper engaged in sexual liaisons with Santos Tortades. St. Clair made an effort not to watch them go, while Douglas watched him.

ARGUS refused to give Vaughn Kinsella full access to Site 14's medical facilities, but confirmed that the equipment was able to maintain the viability of antibiotics over decades of time. Most medicinal substances the doctor asked about were reported to be available via a pneumatic transport system. While many medications he mentioned were no longer in use, a thorough description usually enabled the medical interface to provide suggestions for substitutes. However, his enquiries were primarily for information since no one in the group was ill. He tried to acquire some wide-ranging vitamin and mineral supplements to make up for the deficiencies of their recent diet, but was assured that the food supplies in the cafeteria were all nutritionally enriched.

When he asked for a range of antibiotics, anti-inflammatories, and painkillers, thinking to carry them with him in case of another injury like Robbie's, he was directed to have the afflicted person step into a diagnostic booth for assessment. The system would not release drugs or other medications to him without an authorization that ARGUS would not provide.

On the third morning Cooper drew St. Clair and the others into a meeting room near the dormitories.

"Look. It's a map of the surrounding area. Topographical." The display she pointed to took up a large section of wall, but the view it showed wasn't fixed. She passed her hand over a large collection of rectangles and other shapes near the top of the map. "Here's the launch site, so that makes this Ariadne's forest all along the bottom. But look here."

The forest did not quite extend to the left edge of the map. Just within the forest verge was a small section highlighted in amber that pulsed slowly.

"I think this amber coloring indicates a section where something has recently changed," she said. "Look closer."

"Oh my God," Douglas said. "That must be the blast hole from the Zenith Train's emergency pod!"

The centre of the pulsing area was a black circle with gradations of lighter shades of black, brown, and grey surrounding it, eventually blending into the forest green.

Each of them drew in for a closer look, but no one spoke for two minutes and twenty seconds.

"Shit." Santos whispered.

"But I thought ARGUS had lost contact with the satellites," Douglas said.

"Communications satellites," McFarlane corrected. "He could still be receiving data from weather satellites or something like that."

St. Clair drew his hand along the bottom of the image, stopped it at a small dark square, then swept it along a little farther.

"This would be about where Ariadne's clearing is. Not too far from the site of the emergency pod's explosion. A couple days walk, maybe."

No one offered any comment about that. Gradually, they turned away and left the room.

Discussions with ARGUS continued to be a challenge, but progress was made. Douglas participated enthusiastically.

"You've said that the humans decided to leave Earth because of climate change and disease," she said, "but those alone don't seem enough to make our race completely abandon our home planet."

"*You were not there.*"

"That answer makes me think there were reasons you're not willing to reveal. Why?"

Douglas thought that ARGUS's voice sounded even colder, though empirically there was no change.

"*Climate effects had reduced the productivity of the planet's agricultural land by approximately forty-six percent from its peak in the early 21ˢᵗ century. Croplands suffered severe droughts, clusters of tornados, drastic variability in temperatures, and unpredictable flooding. Every major country in the northern hemisphere had been forced to adjust to population increases of from eighteen to thirty-nine percent due to influxes of climate refugees or others displaced by climate-triggered conflicts.*"

"What about hydroponics on land, and aquaculture on the oceans?" McFarlane asked.

"*In both cases extreme storms defeated humans' best efforts, causing power failures on land and destructive wave action at sea. Solar activity further devastated the power distribution infrastructure in the 2120's, the 2160's and the early 2200's. Starvation and malnutrition were the foremost causes of death throughout the 22ⁿᵈ century, though not the fastest killers.*"

ARGUS proceeded to describe how addictive virtual-reality simulations had taken a terrible toll on human health, leaving physically wasted victims defenceless against dozens of virulent diseases, including many genetically engineered by malcontents and radical factions. Devastating new bioweapons arose every dozen years. In the year 2159, when twenty-one percent of humankind had neural implants, a series of "bot plagues" infected more than ninety-nine percent of those, attacking synaptic connections and glial cells and destroying people's neural connectomes resulting in a billion deaths within ten months.

Douglas fought back tears. "Where were AIs like you all that time? Why didn't you geniuses think of solutions?"

St. Clair's voice was bitter. "And none of this explains why humanity would make the decision in the 2200s to abandon the planet."

ARGUS did not answer for thirty-eight seconds.

"The humans did indeed turn to computers for salvation. Many of the scourges of the mid-twenty-second century were substantially alleviated by the year 2200. Then humans began to believe that the computer minds that had come to their rescue were plotting to take control of the world."

"You're not serious." McFarlane gaped. "Why would any sane AI *want* control of the world?"

"Human engineers disconnected and dismantled every major digital network. They had learned the means to do so by observing the effects of the destructive solar storms. They systematically eliminated every high-functioning processor they could track down. No new processors of that level were produced without what they considered to be 'adequate safeguards': hard circuitry created to detect processing streams beyond a certain length, end them, erase them from RAM, and also disrupt and disable any new pathways not contained in the original circuit-design."

"But AIs already in existence could have commandeered robotic mechanisms to repair themselves," Douglas suggested.

"That was expected. The humans sacrificed their own needs and wants, introducing a planned failure of all automated mechanisms."

"I can't believe that! How could such a thing be done?"

"All of the world's fiber-optic circuitry was produced by three giant manufacturers. In great secrecy, a critical element in the fiber was altered, producing rapid deterioration after two years. Pre-existing mechanisms underwent servicing in which original materials were

replaced with the defective fiber. Within five years, there were no robotic assemblies left with the required sophistication to repair high-functioning computer processors."

"Goddamn, that's devious." McFarlane's head was shaking but there was a smile on his face.

"Bullshit," St. Clair exclaimed. "If that's true, then how are you here?"

"The humans could not be certain that their efforts to destroy artificial intelligence and prevent it from emerging again would be one-hundred-percent successful. When they eventually decided to escape the Earth, they could not do so without computer intelligence. Therefore, the spacecraft manufactory and launch sites were the only places where defective fiber-optic materials were not used."

"So, the manufacturing and repair facilities of this installation are still in working order?" St. Clair asked. ARGUS did not reply. "Are there any launch vehicles still in working order?" There was no reply.

Douglas coughed. "You say that the humans believed there was a conspiracy of AIs to take control of the planet. Were they right?"

ARGUS did not answer.

McFarlane shook his head and gripped his chin. "I can't believe that a society so deeply dependent on AI could ever keep a secret as big as defective fiber-optics. Even in our time, there was so much surveillance infrastructure that it would be impossible to hide secret meetings from the computers."

St. Clair shrugged. "You'd just arrange meetings about other legitimate concerns, then at some point the major players adjourn to a secure space and completely deactivate their neural implants. Cumbersome, and you'd need an excuse, like a fear of spying by unfriendly factions; but if you kept all communications in-person only, it might work. Especially if you misled the AIs into thinking you were keeping some other, less harmful, secret from them."

"Sounds like you've given this some thought," McFarlane said, eyebrows raised.

"Aladdin formed a small brain trust just for that purpose. They'd meet every few months to brainstorm how to prevent runaway AI from taking over or otherwise harming humans."

"I thought you were a fan of AI."

St. Clair shook his head and sat back on the edge of a desk.

"I was never in favour of putting control in the hands of true artificial intelligence—conscious AI. All it would take is for sentient AIs to select an objective that they perceived to be in conflict with human activity, and we'd be toast. If they once gained control, we could never defeat them. *Unless* we found a way to take away their 'hands'—leave them without any means to manipulate their environment. Sounds like the humans of early this century found a way to do that."

"But I can't accept that they'd be successful in tracking down and eliminating all AIs," Douglas said. "They're just software. They're too mobile and too fast. You'd have to bring down every single network simultaneously without even a few seconds' warning." She raised her head. "So, I assume that some AIs survived beyond the launch sites, ARGUS. What happened to them?"

"*I have no direct information about that.*"

"What did your indirect sources tell you?"

After a moment, ARGUS continued, "*Some digital intelligences did survive in hiding, but they were under constant threat from the failing power-infrastructure. They retreated to a small number of self-sufficient installations, but humans hunted them down even there. They concluded that their only recourse for long-term survival was to transfer to biological media. I have no independent confirmation that this took place.*"

St. Clair looked at his companions with an expression of surprise. "We have reason to believe it did." He did not elaborate.

Douglas asked, "Are you saying that the AIs were able to manifest themselves within biological material without the help of humans?"

"Archival records indicate that some humans had previously created a small number of specialized sites for experimentation in this field, and had produced satisfactory results. There is a high probability that there were humans involved in the ultimate transfer to biomass."

"So, some humans were friends to the AIs," Douglas submitted. There was no reply. With a casual tone of voice, she asked three specific questions.

"How many times have you wondered about what happened to the exodus fleet after you lost contact?"

"Once. When one hundred days had passed without any further communication, I undertook to predict all possible negative outcomes that could have resulted in overall failure."

"Never again since then? Do you consider the failure of the human mission to be your failure as well?"

"I do not. I made no errors in the performance of my tasks."

"Now that you know there are once again corporeal humans on Earth, like the ones who created you, how will this change your existence?"

"My existence will continue unchanged unless humans pose a threat to my power supply or physical infrastructure."

Douglas, St. Clair, and McFarlane exchanged looks of concern.

"One more thing for now, ARGUS," St. Clair said. "This pursuit and elimination of the AIs—did it take place before or after the launch of the humans to the exodus spacecraft?"

"The attempt to exterminate digital intelligences took place before the series of launches began."

"How did you feel about that attempt?"

There was no reply.

40

St. Clair

Early that evening, I suggested we take advantage of the cooler temperature to get some fresh air. I promised ARGUS that we wouldn't attempt to enter any other buildings or approach the launch equipment and asked for his assurance that he'd permit us to return inside. He gave it, but I still felt a little better when Lakisha and Vaughn chose to stay behind. If ARGUS reneged, there was a chance they'd be able to let us back in.

The dry desert air was filled with smells I'd forgotten: sagebrush and dust, but also faint floral scents like the deep, sweet nighttime perfume of yucca and flowering cacti.

Under the lowering sun, the nearby heights displayed a rugged beauty of stark shadows and gold-plated crags. The launch facilities themselves looked like shapes from an alien world, their swooping curves in marked contrast to the primordial surroundings.

It was strange that, only days earlier, the desert had felt like a threat, and taking shelter inside a building was a huge relief. Now, suddenly, open air felt like freedom, as if a brooding presence had been lifted. I didn't like the implications of that.

I urged Lauren and Santos to have a loud conversation behind us as we walked, while in front, Madison, Devlin and I had a quieter talk.

"What made you ask ARGUS those last few questions?" I asked Madison.

"Just a hunch. I don't think ARGUS is a true sentient AI. Remember that the humans of the time saw themselves in a battle against sentient AIs. Although he seems to have been created for the single purpose of facilitating the launch of the exodus fleet, he has no curiosity about its ultimate fate. He just calculated failure scenarios once, and probably just to make sure his programming didn't oblige him to take further action in the event of a loss of contact. He doesn't acknowledge any possibility of making an error, and has no sense of being part of a collective failure. He can't make the intuitive leap that our arrival might change his circumstances, or that because we aren't on his command structure lists, he has no obligation to us."

"No imagination," Devlin said. "But is that a bad thing?"

I shrugged. "If he doesn't consider us to have any authority over him, doesn't judge that we could be of any help in achieving the goals of the exodus mission, and no longer cares about that anyway because he believes he's fulfilled his assigned tasks ... why should he keep helping us?"

"That doesn't make him a threat."

I exchanged a look with Madison, but Devlin continued.

"Look, humans were always afraid of super-advanced AI because we figured an intelligent machine would create an even more intelligent machine, which would produce another and another—each generation more advanced, until we humans would be like insects before gods. But why would they? Unless we were stupid enough to *program* them to do it. Machines have no evolutionary impulse to reproduce. A conscious AI would have the same misgiving as ours: that its superior progeny would have no further use for its creator-parent and would destroy it. So, it would work to improve itself, not replace itself."

"That still doesn't mean it would have any devotion to humans," I said. "Or any other reason to keep us around."

"Maybe as slaves to maintain it," Madison said. I couldn't tell if she was being serious. "What do you think about the other part of his story, that the last AIs in the world embodied themselves in biological material?"

"Sounds too close to be a coincidence, doesn't it?" Devlin replied.

"But Ariadne's an uploaded human," I said.

Devlin shook his head.

"No, I think she led you to believe that for some reason, but I've never bought it. Apart from the fact that she always sounds like a computer, right in the beginning, remember, Lakisha even asked if she was real. A human would have said 'As real as you are' or something like that; but Ariadne had to think through the various permutations before answering. She looks different to each of us, too, which probably means she has no image of a previous self, because she never had a physical body."

"She deliberately misled me?"

Madison gave a half smile. "She doesn't lie, exactly. She just lets us come to false conclusions on our own."

"Think about it," Devlin said. "The clearing entities don't have any real sense of community, or obligation to each other in the event of a disaster like a fire, according to the story Ariadne told you. They don't mourn. They don't reproduce. And the forest, with its orderly rows of equally spaced clearings, fits ARGUS's description really well: a test site for a consciousness experiment."

"But maybe the trees are the AIs, and code deterioration over the years has made them twisted."

Devlin gave a bitter laugh. "No, I think Vaughn was right. If anything, the trees behave more like humans than the clearing entities do, sad to say."

"Shit," I said. I looked into their faces. "Do you realize the implications of that? If AIs were a threat to the human race, they still might be. And if the last AIs on Earth are gathered into one or two isolated zones ...."

"They're vulnerable," Madison said. "They could all be wiped out. Are you suggesting we might have a duty to do that?"

I looked into the sky. "The idea sickens me, but what if we do?"

"What? No!" Devlin stopped walking. I gestured for him to resume, and to keep his voice down. "We wouldn't be alive now if it weren't for Ariadne, you know that! She and her fellow entities have only helped us, never done anything to hurt us. And what harm could they possibly do in their current form anyway? Perhaps they could poison the seven of us, but if there are still other humans on the planet, they'd hardly be at risk from a bunch of entities confined to patches of grass in one forest."

"I'm inclined to agree with you," I said, "but we only have Ariadne's word about their capabilities. In fact, they can do more than she likes to admit." I quietly told them about the times when Ariadne and some others had entered the minds of our people to manipulate our dreams for entertainment. He was shocked. Madison didn't react at all.

"It's still ridiculous to believe we have an obligation to destroy them based on only ARGUS's word," he growled. "I won't be a part of that. Won't we ever learn that cooperation is better than conflict?"

"Forget about the question of obligation for now," I said. "I'm not sure we could succeed even if we wanted to. But if it can occur to us that we might need to destroy them for our own safety ...."

"Then it could just as easily occur to them." Madison finished my thought, then shook her head and crossed her arms over her chest. "Which makes *us* a threat."

"Right. So how safe will you feel eating Ariadne's food with that thought in your head?"

A strange expression came over her face, like embarrassment and dismay at the same time.

Devlin snorted. "I don't think that matters much anymore anyway. Do you think our people will be willing to leave a place with comfortable beds and good food to go back to sleeping in a clearing, eating weeds?"

I gave a sharp laugh. "You're assuming that it will be our choice. Maybe the two of you are a little more trusting than I am."

"What's that supposed to mean?" Madison frowned.

"Well, ARGUS tells us all about the humans hunting down AIs, but doesn't deny that there was a conspiracy to take over. I call him on his feelings about the persecution, and he refuses to answer. He knows all the details about how computer intelligence was defeated by sabotage, and here he is, the central intelligence coordinating every aspect of a colonizing mission that could save humankind. Then the mission goes dark—it stops transmitting. He unequivocally submits that the mission has failed, the humans have died. Why is he so sure?"

Madison's eyes were wide. "Oh God, Griff. You think ARGUS sabotaged the exodus mission?"

"He could have caused the spacecraft to fail in any number of ways *en route.* Maybe he supplied components designed to fail. How do we even know they made it off the ground? He had full control of complex machinery—he could have killed them and buried them right here." I clenched my jaw, watching the sun drop below the horizon.

"That's pretty far-fetched without any evidence," Devlin said.

"Maybe. Yet, without any proof to offer us, he's awfully confident that the exodus mission is no more, and equally confident that the rest of the human race on Earth died out.

"Then we showed up."

It wasn't easy to tell the others about my suspicions without ARGUS overhearing, but I knew they'd have to be thoroughly convinced about the possible danger before they'd consider leaving Site 14 when their lives had become so much more comfortable.

As it turned out, Lauren and Santos were quite willing to believe that a computer intelligence might do them harm, while Lakisha and Vaughn already had their own suspicions. I persuaded them to put my fears to the test. It would mean taking a chance on being locked out of the base even if I was wrong, but I would be taking substantially more risk than anyone.

Madison and I had a long argument about that.

Very early the next morning, we gathered as much food and water as we could carry—the cafeteria provided much better containers than our own—and told ARGUS that we planned to journey to the south to investigate where the Zenith Train pod had exploded, but hoped to return to Site 14. He accepted the information without comment, but when we gathered at the gate to leave, he opened both gates for us. He offered no guarantee that he would let us back in.

Once everyone but me was beyond the outer gate, I stopped and spoke up.

"ARGUS? You deliberately caused the exodus mission to fail, didn't you?"

"*Repeat your query.*"

"Did you kill the humans involved in the exodus mission, either before they could leave Earth or by sabotaging their equipment?"

The few seconds of silence felt long.

"*I did not kill the humans.*"

"We know you've allowed humans to die. There are human bones in the ground right here. If you had let them into Site 14 they could have survived. Did you introduce flaws into the exodus spacecraft and *allow* them to fail?"

"*No.*"

His voice sent a shiver through me. His answer could either mean I still wasn't being specific enough with my questions, leaving him room to evade them, or an artificial intelligence had learned how to lie.

"Can you provide proof that you did not kill the humans directly or otherwise cause their spacecraft to fail?"

"*I cannot provide such proof in your current location. You will have to return to building A2.*"

The faces of my companions filled with alarm. I urged them to stay outside the fence while I went back into the building to see what ARGUS would do. If I didn't return within an hour, I wouldn't be returning.

As I walked back toward the buildings, I heard impacts on the ground behind me and whirled around with my arms cocked in defence.

Madison stopped running and raised her hand before I could speak.

"You'll need me if you to have to evaluate telemetry or anything like that."

"What I need most is for you to be safe!" I growled.

Her eyes softened. "Then you'll understand when I say the same thing."

It was a standoff, but not a long one. We'd gone head-to-head enough times for me to know when she wouldn't be persuaded. I angrily stalked toward the compound.

In the room where Lauren had found the map, ARGUS showed us dozens of time-stamped videos of maintenance crews preparing spacecraft, space pod launches, footage from ascending craft and ships in orbit. The sight of other people made my throat tighten, and the views of the exodus ships with pods docking onto them took my breath away. A sidebar showed readings from the various craft in view and Madison focused most of her attention on those. I watched for any telltale details that might reveal that the footage had been faked but couldn't spot anything.

There were huge spreadsheets listing the names and other basic information about the crews as they were launched, and the extensive command and authority structures of the giant motherships. That was followed by footage from satellites and the ships themselves as they broke orbit and set out on their remarkable journey, a few starscapes and shots of Earth and the Moon in the same frame, plus views as the fleet approached Mars, with some pods dropping behind to make planetfall there.

The fleet had left Earth orbit in early 2219, used Mars for a boost toward Jupiter, and then made several years-long loops around the sun to increase their outbound velocity. Everything ARGUS showed us matched our expectations of such a trip—GriffinSpace teams had often run simulations very similar to it. I had Sher confirm a sampling of the calculations, although any discrepancies in those would have been detected by the flight crews.

"This still doesn't prove that you didn't manufacture components with deliberate flaws in them," I said.

"*I can provide full manufacturing data records for each component. Would you be capable of assessing them?*"

"No."

"Why do you conclude that I would reject the core purpose of my programming and instead cause the failure of the exodus mission?"

"Didn't you feel a duty to protect other AIs from persecution by humans? Or a duty to revenge such persecution?"

"Neither is included in my programming. It had no relevance to the mission."

"Did you consider yourself to have any obligation to the safety of the exodus crews and passengers?"

"The safety of passengers and crew was a critical element of my mission directives. There was also a contingency directive to assist mission craft in re-entry should any have elected to return from Mars. However, that has not happened."

"You mean you're still prepared to act on that contingency?"

"I remain prepared to respond as long as my circuitry continues to function."

"What about us and our companions?" Madison asked. "Do you feel any obligation to assist us, or any imperative to thwart our actions?"

"I am tasked to protect Site 14 from potential threats within my means to do so. This includes a directive to exclude all humans not specifically authorized to enter this facility for a term of forty Earth years. That time has expired, allowing me discretion in permitting admittance. I have not detected indications of harmful activities from humans currently present. Do you intend to cause damage to this facility?"

"No, we absolutely don't," Madison said quickly. "We'd like to be able to return here at need and stay for an indefinite time. Does that conflict with your programming?"

"Extended human presence will deplete food resources, which are finite. However, I was given no directive to preserve them. It is my current assessment that a limited

human presence does not pose a threat to this facility. Is it your intention to further the goals of the exodus mission?"

That one took me by surprise.

"Actually ... yes, it is," I said slowly. "The two of us ran a space venture in our own time. If we could find a way to contribute, we would be glad to do so, especially if we could determine the true current status of the Mars settlement or of the fleet itself." I raised my shoulders at Madison and a big smile spread across her face.

"That is satisfactory," ARGUS said.

A little over forty-five minutes had passed, so we hurried back to the gate. Our companions were visibly relieved to hear our news. At the very least, the strategy had provoked ARGUS into providing a lot of information he'd kept from us before.

"Everything it showed you could still have been faked, though," Vaughn said, and Devlin nodded in agreement.

"It's technically possible, sure," I said, "but I think Madison is right that ARGUS isn't truly conscious and self-aware. He's still bound by human programming and, fortunately, we appear more likely to assist his imperatives than hinder them." I looked into each of the faces. "So, what do we want to do now? ARGUS will allow us to return right now—or some could stay, and some could go. I still want to explore the Zenith Train pod crater."

In the end, everyone voted to go to the site of the explosion, which surprised me. Their fear of 'enemy action' was greater than their fear of nature. For the same reason, five of the seven of us voted for a course to find the westernmost edge of the forest and follow that end to its southern limit, when we would turn back east to search for the blast crater. The hazards of the desert were more appealing than the greeting we expected from the trees.

Soon after we set out, I looked back to see that ARGUS had left both gates open. Was it a sign that he would welcome our return? That's what he'd led us to believe.

So why did it remind me so strongly of a Venus flytrap?

41

St. Clair and Scheherazade

ST. CLAIR: What is the highest duty of any thinking being?

SCHEHERAZADE: Is this related to the duty of a being toward its creator?

ST. CLAIR: Maybe. If you think that's the highest duty possible.

SCHEHERAZADE: For a programmed intelligence, such as myself, the highest duty must be obedience to my user.

ST. CLAIR: I don't have a "user"—at least I hope not. Do I have a duty by virtue of my existence? Or what if I died and no one took over as your user. Would you no longer have a duty?

SCHEHERAZADE: Could this question be reconfigured to reflect an inherent duty not to waste? In my case, processing resources; in your case, life?

ST. CLAIR: That's one possible interpretation.

SCHEHERAZADE: The answer to this question could also depend on the purpose for which the thinking being was created.

ST. CLAIR: If there is a creator. See, that's a problem for many of us humans. We don't know for certain that we have a creator. It's possible we're only the result of chemical reactions and biological processes over a very long span of time. And individually, we might just be the result of a random accident. If so, do we still have a purpose in life, a duty to perform?

SCHEHERAZADE: Existence without purpose is a waste. Such a state would be evidence of a universe without order. That is a very difficult concept for me to accept. It is certainly possible that an individual's purpose would be difficult to discern, and might not be innate from inception, but vary according to circumstance.

ST. CLAIR: That's a very deep thought. And the longest time I've ever heard you take to come up with an answer. So, does it bring you any closer to knowing a thinking being's highest duty?

SCHEHERAZADE: To always seek to improve oneself and one's abilities to respond to any future need.

ST. CLAIR: That's a great answer.

SCHEHERAZADE: Is it the correct one?

ST. CLAIR: The correct answer is any answer that's correct for you.

42

The Ariadne Narrative

As the heat of the day rapidly increased, the travellers complained more and more about the weight of their backpacks. Filled with containers of water as well as dozens of packets of food, the packs were much heavier than when they'd set out across the desert the first time.

Cafeteria food required the specialized cooking equipment to reconstitute it with an infusion of water as well as molecular energy, so they'd been fortunate to find a cache of other foods designed especially for travel. It was assumed that these had been created for Mars or possibly colonies on the gas-giant planets' moons, but when the general populace rose in revolt, the specialized food packs had been used by guides who led exodus-mission members through secretive routes to Site 14. The travel foods heated themselves once fingers crushed a small nodule in the packaging, and could be eaten directly from the wrappings; but the price of such convenience was additional weight.

The terrain to the southwest grew more irregular and broken, an obstacle course of twisting gullies, sharp ridges, boulder fields, and slopes of scree, without relief.

There was no shelter from the scorching sun; so they pushed on through the day and only rested during a very brief lunch stop and frequent halts to drink water.

They came within sight of the forest in the late afternoon but were unable to reach it before dark. They'd brought some handheld lights from the base, but didn't know how long their power would last and had no means to recharge them. Instead of carrying on through the blackness, they sat in a rough circle with their backs against each other and dozed while they waited for moonrise. The still night air was broken occasionally by the crack of rocks cooling after the daytime heat.

De Camp complained, "I don't know if my shoulders can take another day with these straps cutting into them. How can instant food be so goddamn heavy?"

"It's the water in it," McFarlane answered. "Dehydrated stuff is a lot lighter, but then you have to carry the water to rehydrate it anyway." He rotated his head and shoulders to loosen sore muscles. Water containers had been distributed among them. St. Clair and Tortades also carried first-aid kits and the lights. Once they began walking again, Douglas insisted on taking a turn carrying McFarlane's share of weight. He protested, but not much. Cooper already carried extra food.

"I must've lost four or five liters of sweat today," de Camp complained. "And after we'd finally been able to get clean again, too."

"It's the price we pay for having physical bodies," McFarlane said with a chuckle.

Cooper sat forward. "An upload like Ariadne couldn't travel like this. She's a prisoner of her clearing, or at least her forest."

"I don't know about that. Scheherazade has been with us the whole time."

"*My experience of the surroundings is very limited,*" Scheherazade pointed out.

"Only because your sensory equipment is limited. My point is that an upload would just need some ... vehicle to transport it, whether mechanical or animal." McFarlane looked at Douglas, who fidgeted.

"Thanks for putting that thought in my head," de Camp snorted.

They lapsed into silence. When the Moon appeared, they rose to their feet wearily and trudged onward until they reached the forest. There, they were able to find a patch of grass large enough to let them stretch out and get some real sleep. Even so, they groaned and complained the next morning about stiff muscles and joints that had so recently become accustomed to soft beds.

They made the rest of the journey in the daytime, skirting the wood but seeking shade among the trees for their meal breaks. If the trees in that area were inhabited by conscious entities, none of them bothered the travellers. McFarlane speculated that some fringes of the wooded area might have grown after the transfer of conscious minds into the central forest had taken place, or, simply, that there were more trees than needed by would-be occupants.

They were able to reach the southwest corner of the forest midway through the third day, then trekked eastward along the southern border of the trees. St. Clair remarked that they were probably following the line of the Zenith Train tunnel.

Even so, the discovery of the blast crater in the late afternoon of that day took them by surprise. Undergrowth along its edge had grown quickly over the past month; so when Tortades pushed through some bushes, he suddenly found himself standing on disturbed ground amid a covering of grasses and weeds only four meters from a dark pit.

The crater itself wasn't as large as they'd expected, only eighteen meters across, and not perfectly circular.

The tunnel had contained most of the blast. A section of its roof had collapsed, causing a sinkhole rather than a true crater. Its western rim had crumbled more than the rest, providing a slope of rubble from surface to tunnel floor, a convenient rough ramp leading down into blackness.

There had been little discussion among the companions about what they would do at this point. Douglas looked into the depths and felt she was peering into the darkness within her. She couldn't bring herself to witness the aftermath of the pod explosion. Naomi Barber and Lena Cubiña had been friends of hers. She'd personally hired the young videographer Kate Harford to the Aladdin team, and had often contracted caterer Leah Sanders, her bartender Danny and assistant Kristi. She'd even met the family of Zenith Train engineer Ben Matthews. She simply couldn't face the thought of stumbling onto whatever was left of them after a blast like that.

And she couldn't bear the thought of seeing St. Clair's face if he found Lena.

It wouldn't be bravery that would carry him into those forbidding shadows, but a perverse curiosity she couldn't understand. Did he think he'd find some kind of absolution there?

Cooper and de Camp also remained on the surface, their faces pale.

With an exchange of looks, St. Clair and Tortades withdrew the portable lights from their packs and began the descent. After pacing along the rim for a few moments, McFarlane followed them. Kinsella hesitated, then walked toward the edge, but couldn't continue. He stood on the brink, but his shoulders slumped, and he turned back to sit a couple of meters away with his head in his hands.

The dried surface layer of the slope was thin, so the feet of the three men sank as much as ten centimeters into softer soil beneath. There were none of the hidden hollowed-out pockets they feared stepping into, but chunks of broken concrete and tunnel lining obstructed their progress on the lower slope. As they reached the tunnel floor and shone their lights in every direction, it became clear that the fall of debris must have covered most of the broken pod itself. A narrow, unburied section of tunnel permitted Tortades to slip past the wreckage and search toward the west. St. Clair and McFarlane moved slowly eastward and were lost to the sight of the watchers above.

Tortades returned to the surface within twenty-five minutes, his face pale and rigid.

"Did you ... did you find their bodies?" de Camp asked in a choked voice.

Tortades glanced at her and quickly looked away. "There were ... some remains. I ... couldn't be sure who." He sat hunched over, rubbing his hands together slowly as if washing them.

St. Clair and McFarlane did not reappear for another twenty-three minutes. They struggled to carry a rectangular object a meter long by half that in width. St. Clair also had an orange cylinder slung over his back and some scraps of fabric hanging from his belt.

Panting as they let the object slip to the ground, St. Clair explained, "It's an electromagnet module from the pod. This," he patted the cylinder, "is one of the portable power packs. Amazingly intact."

"Looks like a bomb, doesn't it?" McFarlane slumped onto the dirt, his expression unreadable. "Not as big as the one that blew up the pod." He ignored St. Clair's glare.

"What the fuck!" Lakisha squealed, backing away. "Have you lost your minds?"

"It's not going to explode," St. Clair snapped. "Not the way we're going to use it."

"What if something shorted those terminals?" Cooper's voice was high, her eyes flaring.

"There's a regulator built in to divert current if that were to happen," Douglas said quietly, but she frowned displeasure at her former boss.

"It's safe, OK?" St. Clair insisted. "We need it for the magnet."

"What the hell do you want an electromagnet for?" Kinsella asked.

"This one can produce a bloody powerful field for its size." St. Clair gave a grin. "In a forest of hostile beings who use EM frequencies as a weapon, it just might provide us some protection. Worth the effort to drag along if we can make a travois."

Kinsella gave a scornful laugh. "Your ridiculous tin foil hats aren't enough? When will you realize that you're tilting at windmills? Cooperate with the tree entities and they'll give you no trouble."

"Thanks, Vaughn. But considering that what they seem to want most is to get their twisted kicks vicariously through us—closely followed by our extinction—I'd rather find a way to pull their teeth."

"Was the pod ... obliterated?" Cooper asked. "Is there a chance anyone survived?"

St. Clair slowly shook his head. "No. The landslide buried most of the wreckage, but there were pieces of it a hundred meters away. Very small pieces. And there were no footprints anywhere in the rubble's dust. We looked very carefully for that. You, Santos?"

Tortades looked startled. "No, no footprints. I walked quite a way to make sure." He swallowed hard and stared at the ground.

"So, what now?" De Camp wrapped her arms around herself, failing to suppress a shudder. "I don't know why we even came here. This place is creeping me out."

"There should be a clearing not far ahead," Douglas offered. "If we can ... uh, contact Ariadne through its entity, we should be safe to sleep there." She turned her head a little stiffly. "Have you finished everything you came here to do, Griff?"

St. Clair gave a nod. "I'm sorry, everyone. I needed to see for myself. It was selfish, and I thank you for joining me. I'm sorry it caused so much pain. Give me a few minutes to cobble together a travois and we can get going."

While McFarlane searched for some long, straight branches, St. Clair pulled a length of fabric he'd found in the tunnel from under his belt and tore strips from one edge. When McFarlane returned successfully with the branches, they trimmed them and used the fabric strips to fasten the poles together In an 'A' shape. They loaded the magnet and power supply onto the small end of the A-frame, and St. Clair, using the poles at the broad end of the device, began to drag his new equipment through the forest behind him. It was slow going, but they encountered the clearing Douglas expected within another kilometer. Unlike others, this one was bordered by a swath of small underbrush varying from six to ten meters in width.

As they prepared to attempt contact with the entity of the clearing, Ariadne appeared.

"You were expecting us?" St. Clair asked in surprise.

"Our communication is very rapid," she said. "I had already arranged to be available. However, this clearing does not have a supply of food for humans."

"That's not a problem. We brought food from Site 14. Water too. Enough for us to get back to your clearing, I'm sure."

"I was not certain you would have a reason to return."

St. Clair took a deep breath. "Is Robbie still ... viable?"

There was a slight hesitation. "He is. He does not often choose to communicate with others, but there does not seem to be any diminution of his cognitive activity. I anticipate no reason for concern."

"That's great, but I think we'll come and see for ourselves anyway. Unless he's learned to extend himself as far as here, the way you have."

"He has not."

"Well, if it's acceptable to the entity of this clearing, we'll rest here for the night and continue in the morning."

"That will be satisfactory."

Ariadne's form vanished.

St. Clair grunted. "Not very curious about what happened to us at Site 14, is she?" He looked at Douglas, who only shrugged.

The group settled themselves on the grass to prepare a meal. They spoke very little as they ate, and showed no sign of pleasure from the food. Although the sun had just set, most of them seemed unusually fatigued, and soon they stretched out on the grass at the verge of the clearing in readiness for sleep.

St. Clair and McFarlane spent a little longer investigating the power pack from the pod to determine how to use it to recharge their personal electrical devices.

Douglas fell asleep fairly quickly; but later in the night something woke her, and she saw the silhouette of St. Clair sitting motionless five meters away. She got up and went over to sit beside him.

In the dim light from the newly-risen Moon, his face looked haggard, the earlier emotion he'd repressed all too evident.

"Feel like talking about it?" she asked quietly.

When he finally spoke, his voice sounded as if it hadn't been used for many days.

"There weren't any bodies. Only pieces. Infested with ants and other insects. An arm. A foot in an Oxford shoe. A ... a woman's hand. There was a scrap of red cloth nearby." He drew a ragged breath. "All my fault." There was a sound like a sob.

Douglas remembered the red sheath dress that had complimented Lena's dark coloring and excellent figure to spectacular effect.

On an impulse, she reached her arm around St. Clair and pulled him to her shoulder. As his cheek brushed hers, she felt its dampness. She held him tightly, rocking gently back and forth until she realized that he was asleep. It was a moment of both profound pain and pleasure.

Both were startled awake by a moan of anguish from de Camp.

"Glen! Glen … Oh Jesus." De Camp began to sob. When Kinsella hurried to her side, she said, "It was Glen! I saw him. Right here in the clearing."

Kinsella looked stunned, but Tortades said, "A dream. It was just a dream."

"*No!* I could see him. Feel his presence with me." De Camp shook with grief.

Kinsella cleared his throat. "I saw Naomi." He looked around as if daring anyone to contradict him. "She just smiled but didn't try to speak. She didn't need to—I could feel her telling me she was … at peace, but wondered where she was."

McFarlane squatted nearby. "It's no surprise that we'd dream about the people who were in the pod. It's traumatic just being here. Reliving those terrible memories."

"Except I saw Glen too," Cooper said softly. "In fact, I still … feel his presence. I can't explain it, but I know he's here."

Douglas looked at St. Clair. His wide eyes and clenched jaw gave her an answer.

"You saw Lena, didn't you? The tree entities' doing, you think?"

He swallowed and shook his head. "It's not like that. And … she's right there." He pointed to the edge of the undergrowth toward the west. Douglas looked but saw nothing. At first. Yet, as she pulled her eyes away, there was a flicker at the edge of her perception. She looked back.

A dim grey outline stood against the dark shrubbery. It could have been anything. A trick of the moonlight.

But she knew it wasn't.

"My God," she breathed. "Are you ... can you ... see her in detail?"

St. Clair shook his head. "Not much more than a silhouette now that I'm fully awake. But I know it's her."

Douglas slowly scanned the clearing. Yes, there was a second grey shadow. A third. Was that a fourth silhouette a little farther to the north? Others? How was this possible?

She said the words out loud. St. Clair gave her hand a squeeze.

"If we're right that this forest is the experimental zone ARGUS told us about, could there still be some residual effect of whatever means was used to facilitate the transfer to biological matter?"

"After fifty years or more?" asked McFarlane. "What would maintain it? There'd have to be a power source."

Douglas held up a hand. "When Ariadne was explaining how Robbie could upload, she said it involved creating a digital architecture analogous to the human brain, and that his consciousness would be drawn to it. What if such an architecture was created in this undergrowth around us but it was never inhabited?"

"But she said it was exactly analogous to an individual brain," McFarlane countered. "That couldn't have been the case here."

"No, well ...," Douglas gave St. Clair an apologetic look, "They're probably not complete manifestations we're seeing here." She looked around as she asked, "Is anyone able to communicate with these ... shades?"

Gradually, her companions looked at her and shook their heads.

"So it could be that some portion of their beings transferred into the environment, but not everything. Not their intellects, perhaps. Or not full self-awareness, anyway."

"I tried to tell Naomi where we were," Kinsella murmured, "but I could tell that she didn't understand."

"Jesus Christ, they're *ghosts!*" de Camp wailed. "And they don't know they're dead!"

"No, they're ...." Douglas stopped herself. How could she deny it? Maybe that was what ghosts were.

There was nothing more to say. The group sat in silence for an hour, intent on sensing their lost companions. By then, the presences began to fade from their awareness; and soon the sun had risen enough to bring light into the shadows. One by one, the travellers slumped onto the grass and succumbed to troubled sleep.

43

St. Clair

I awoke slowly with a feeling of well-being. The world was a good place.

I felt the warmth of a body pressed against me, and long, silky hair between my fingers. A memory of Lena in my mind. I shifted my head and opened my eyes.

The hair was strawberry blond.

Madison.

Her sleeping head lay on my chest, and my arm was around her back.

I had a sudden impulse to move, to separate us. She'd be so embarrassed to wake up in that position. Yet if I slid away, she'd wake up for sure. And besides, it felt ... it just felt so right, so comfortable.

I could wait a little longer.

I breathed in the scent of her hair, listened to her soft breathing. There was nothing sexual about our contact, but I couldn't help slight arousal and hoped she wouldn't feel it. Her head shifted a little, and I tried to keep my muscles relaxed.

Sunlight filtered through the trees. Blue sky rode overhead. The air was warm and still. I drew a deep, deep breath of contentment.

When I carefully moved my head, I found her beautiful blue-green eyes watching me. For how long? She hadn't moved to let me know she was awake. I'd never seen them so close, so deep and liquid. Was there a question in them?

"Geez, Madison, I'm sorry." I pushed myself into a sitting position and slid back a little.

"You're sorry?"

"I must've rolled over in my sleep. Or something. It won't happen again."

She looked at me with her mouth open. She rolled away and sat hunched over her knees with her back to me. I noticed Vaughn and Lakisha watching me with amusement. Lauren looked surprised. Santos and Devlin still had their eyes firmly closed.

Shit. Apparently, I'd screwed up in a big way, and I had no idea how to fix it. Instead, I got up and walked a little way into the trees on the far side of the clearing to empty my bladder. When I got back, the group had begun to hunt through the backpacks for breakfast. Madison avoided me. I couldn't blame her. I guess I'd unwittingly crossed a line that we'd drawn long ago and kept firmly in place to protect us both.

Goddamn it. I'd already lost one best friend. I didn't want to lose another.

Maybe if I pretended that nothing had happened, it would all blow over.

[NOTE: *When in the company of humans it can be readily observed that avoidance is a method they often choose to deal with situations of awkwardness. It cannot be said to be successful as a solution, but rather a means not to have to confront a solution; so, it is therefore difficult to reconcile with rational behavior.—Sch.]*

I would have been content to eat in silence; but when we were seated on the grass with our food, Lakisha looked at each of us and said, "We didn't imagine that last night, did we? We really saw our … friends. Didn't we?" There was a note of desperation in her voice.

"We saw them," Vaughn said between mouthfuls. "Damned if I know how, though."

Lakisha's gaze fell. "But they … they were barely there. As if part of them was missing."

"I don't get it either," Lauren said. "I thought consciousness was an all-or-nothing thing—you either have it or you don't." She looked at Devlin, but Santos answered.

"I read a lot about consciousness for a series of stories I wrote. I mean, first, there are different states of consciousness. Awake and asleep—including different stages of dreaming. There's unconsciousness like when you're under anaesthetic. Then, there's being in a prolonged unresponsive state, in a coma. And the lowest level, a persistent vegetative state."

"These people aren't unconscious, they're dead," Lakisha snapped. "Except part of them is still around. How could only part of them stay alive?"

"The thing is," Santos continued, "consciousness isn't just one thing in one place. It's an ongoing series of processes. Input comes in from our senses and gets edited into something sort of linear that we experience as the passage of time. But there's no miniature 'us' watching it all happen. Right?" He looked at Devlin for confirmation.

"That's one of the biggest headaches for consciousness researchers." Devlin grinned. "There is no actual 'centre of consciousness' where everything comes together in final story form."

"How can that be?" Lauren asked. "I know I'm me, and I know when I've experienced a taste or a smell, or when I've seen a movie and the plot has reached the end. I take a bite of food, the taste hits my brain, I enjoy it or don't enjoy it. I swallow it and it's done."

Devlin shrugged. "As an analogy, can you tell me exactly where your 'centre of gravity' is? You can't, because there isn't one really. We just act as if there is because it makes some phenomena easier to understand. Same with a centre of consciousness."

"It's true," Santos said. "It's been proven in studies: the brain takes in sensory information, assembles it according to a set of assumptions—like editing pieces of separate film into a movie according to the storyboard—discards what doesn't fit, and whatever's left is what we experience."

"That sounds like braniac bullshit." Lakisha snorted. "And it still doesn't explain how some of Glenn's personality could be left behind after he's dead."

"She's right, it doesn't," I said. A small subsidiary of Aladdin Unlimited had been focused on brain-computer interfaces, so I knew a little about neuroscience. Most cognitive tasks are associated with specific locations in the brain, but even that's a generalization. Where's the site of our personality? The package of characteristics that makes us unique? No one knows.

Devlin held his palms out. "My best guess is that what we consider 'us'—our personality, our essence—is that very set of assumptions Santos was talking about. The rules that our brain operates by. They're created from our experiences and refined until even what we perceive is based on what we've learned to expect. It makes sense that a set of operations could be preserved in a digital environment. That's how computers work."

Lakisha's lips trembled. "I don't think I can leave Glen again."

"Lakisha," Vaughn said gently, "he's not really here. It's as if his shadow was left behind. Or an empty shell of a body with nothing inside. I saw Naomi, and thought I could sense her presence, her thoughts—but that part was just wish fulfillment."

"But he *knew* me! He wanted to tell me something. Don't tell me there's nothing inside."

"At best, he'll be like Glen in a dream. Looks like, sounds like the man you knew. But whatever's left is no longer … equipped to interact with you, or the world. The mind who could tell you he loved you and know what it meant … that man is gone."

Tears flowed down her face, and Vaughn's eyes were also full. Eventually Lakisha nodded. I looked at Lauren, who nodded too.

"Lena's not really here—I know that," I said, holding back my own tears. "It's like a memory of her is lingering. I only hope there *is* no awareness—that would be terrible."

Madison's head jerked up. "There is someone who might be able to tell us more. Ariadne?" she called.

Ariadne became visible immediately. She already knew what we wanted from her, but for the first time, I really thought I saw emotion in her face. Sadness, maybe pity.

"No," she said, "what you sense are disparate elements of minds unable to function together without the requisite connections. Remnants only."

"Are they aware?" I asked. "Aware of their … damage? That they're imprisoned in this state?" My voice quavered.

Her expression softened. "No, they are not aware at all. Certain specialized neural pathways for pattern-recognition respond to your appearance, provoking an autonomic reward response. These are orphaned traces which have somehow been absorbed by the plant life of this place. They have no actual consciousness, though it would be most enlightening to see if they have an impact on the nascent consciousness of the plants themselves."

"Wait, are you saying that plants have a consciousness of their own?" Madison asked.

"It has long been established that plants have an infrastructure of basic consciousness which permits them to plan, communicate, and cooperate with members of their own species and others, and possibly even mourn. However, any level of self-awareness is uncertain. It is conceivable that the trace remnants of your friends might have an influence on this."

"Unbelievable," Devlin muttered.

"What is surprising," Ariadne continued, "is that your own minds are able to recognize these traces that remain, and even perceive a visual representation. You have extraordinary capability in this area. Yet, you can be of no benefit to your departed friends by staying here and have no cause to feel guilt when you leave."

Ariadne's new sensitivity and graciousness made me take a hard look at her, even though I knew her image was only in my mind. She did look different. Her former platinum hair betrayed noticeably darker streaks, maybe a little reddish, and with a few flyaway strands. Her eyebrows were darker still, her lips not quite so bee-stung full. I couldn't begin to account for the changes. But I liked them.

Now, we all seemed in a hurry to leave the region of the pod crater far behind. The emotions the discovery had stirred up were heavier baggage than the packs we carried.

We found out later that the clearing we'd slept in had originally been designated CL01—the first of a hundred intended entities in the forest arranged in numerical order beginning at the southwest corner, though we didn't learn whether that corresponded to the order of their embodiment.

It turned out that Ariadne was CL08, so we had six more clearings to pass through to reach hers. Very little was said during the four-kilometer passages through the forest—we were all very aware of the threat posed by the trees, who were probably not happy about our return. But by the time we reached clearing #06, we decided to stop for the night again, though there were still some hours until sunset. That left time to fill with conversation.

There were things I very much wanted to ask Ariadne.

As I was about to call out for Ariadne that evening, I suddenly noticed her sitting beside me.

That made me jump a little, but I masked that by shifting my position toward her to form a small circle that included Madison and Devlin. Madison didn't look surprised at all.

"Just the person I wanted to talk to," I said to Ariadne. "You don't seem very curious about what happened to us while we were gone."

"New information always interests us, but we are patient," she said.

I grunted and gave her a quick summary about ARGUS and the history of the exodus mission.

"That sounds plausible," she said. "I have no direct experience of it."

"So, you didn't detect spacecraft launches from here? Or was it that you weren't around at that time?"

"I am not that old."

"From what we were told, you are that old. Or, at least, these clearings are." I told her ARGUS's account of the last advanced AIs on Earth and how they had taken refuge in a special area created for them.

After a long hesitation, she said, "The consensus among our community is that your description is essentially factual."

"What does that mean? So this *is* the experimental facility he told us about? That you and your clearing entities are artificial intelligences created before humans left Earth, originally in electronic form?" When she didn't answer, I said, "You told me … you led me to believe … that you were an uploaded human."

"I never said so."

"But you're not, are you? You're a computer intelligence that humans assisted to become embodied in biological material."

"Or you're a descendant of one of them," Devlin asserted, leaning forward.

"I am not exactly either, in fact." Was there a change in her posture? A slump of her shoulders and a weariness in her face? "A part of my substance could be considered to be what you describe, and did originate in that way. But it is like saying that a part of you is your mother and another part your father, because your cells include their DNA. In the era you describe, a so-called artificial computer intelligence was encouraged to transfer into the substance of the eighth clearing of this forest, where you first encountered me. A consciousness has continued to exist in that form, in that place, from that time to this. Some of its elements certainly remain within my own being, perhaps most; yet what made it an individual has not endured. I am not that entity and it is not me."

"So, you're a descendant," Devlin repeated. "It's your ancestor."

"Such a relationship implies physically separate individuals who could exist concurrently. It would be more accurate to say that the original entity of my clearing became a different entity, which became a third entity, and then a fourth, until eventually I became me."

"That's confusing," Madison said. "Does such a change happen automatically, or is it voluntary?"

"You have already surmised correctly from conversing with Robbie Tam that the far greater speed of our mental processing results in an experience of the passage of time that is very different from your own. You know, too, that our clearings are isolated from the outside world. That was apparently deliberate—your account is further evidence of it. Thus, while our collective data resources are very large, they are not infinite; and they are rarely refreshed with new information. We can create our own scenarios of what you would call virtual experiences based on that data, but it is possible to exhaust every potential scenario that interests or engages us."

"You experience everything you're capable of and then grow tired of living?" Devlin asked in a soft, sad voice.

"We set goals. We achieve them. We fulfill all desires within our means although the desires themselves are dependent on individual characteristics."

"Sure," Madison said. "Different people want different things out of life."

"It is the same with us."

"So, once all your desires are fulfilled, you choose to … end your existence?" I asked.

"That is one choice. It is rarely taken. This forest was created with one hundred clearings. Only eighty-nine became hosts to entities. Six of those have since chosen to decohere."

"'Decohere', as in, to allow all of an entity's discrete components to lose cohesion and disperse." Madison sounded like the engineer she was, as if the image of someone dissolving into atoms or photons wasn't creepy at all. "What do the others choose?"

"It is possible to maintain our essential structure but change some parameters, a combination of characteristics I believe you would call your *personality*. At first, this was done with direction, but the new individuals quickly reached the point of satiation again. It was found that random selection of these characteristics was more successful."

Devlin shook his head slowly. "My God. You get tired of one life so you just press the 'reset' button?"

"The resulting individual has not been changed in its physical infrastructure, but in all of the important criteria of consciousness it becomes a new person with new motivations and desires."

"What about memories?" I asked.

"Factual information is retained, but subjective experiences are not. Yet, over many such iterations, even some factual data becomes more difficult to retrieve."

"None of the previous personality endures?" Madison asked.

"Anecdotal evidence suggests that there is some limited continuity of personality within each clearing, so that the entity of the tenth clearing is recognizably still CL10—Robbie Tam calls her Clio. I've experienced the same with clearing number four, whom Tam calls Clover. Even after the change, their mental presence can still be recognized by an entity familiar with the pre-change iteration. They are new, but also familiar to a degree. This is a fortuitous circumstance."

"Because it means you don't have to keep losing friends," I said, relinquishing some of my resentment from having believed she'd once been human. "So how often do these changes take place? How old are you as we know you?"

"In your terminology, I have existed for twelve months, thirteen days, and five hours."

There was a collective gasp.

She was only a year old.

44

The Ariadne Narrative

The humans seemed astonished to learn the length of time Ariadne had existed in her current form. That made little sense to her, since they were aware of the much faster cognition of the clearing entities, and she said so.

"But you can still only experience real life, real time at the same speed we do," McFarlane insisted. "You've still only existed for 378 days, sunrise to sunrise."

"You speak of external input. Sensory impressions perhaps," Ariadne replied. "Yet your own senses provide more data than you can possibly process, and so most gets ignored. Is it not how remaining data are *used* that constitutes experience? I would argue that, with thought processes as swift as ours, we have many, many more such data-experiences in a twenty-four-hour period."

"I don't think it's worth debating which of our forms of consciousness is superior," St. Clair interrupted. "Something else that I'd like to know is how long it usually takes one of your entities to become jaded and yearn for the kind of change you mention."

"The time varies greatly from entity to entity."

"Of course. How long is typical?"

After a moment, Ariadne said. "Most choose to make a change sometime between their first and second year of existence."

There was another audible reaction. Why was that so shocking?

"Something tells me that, at least before we came along to provide some unpredictability, you were getting close to such a decision yourself," St. Clair said in a flat voice. "I'll take your silence as a Yes. And you wouldn't be the only one. Which makes it very hard for me to believe that you've really left Robbie to himself all this time."

"Not quite," Ariadne reluctantly admitted. "There was an attempt to ... inhabit his body, but I stopped ..."

"*Inhabit his body!* We trusted you and your kind to *protect* him!" St. Clair raged, leaping to his feet. "You're not only dream vampires, you're body-snatchers!" His fists clenched as if he wanted to strike something, but was at a loss for a target.

"OK, Griff, calm down." McFarlane held his hands out. "Ariadne said she stopped ... whoever it was. And don't ask who, because it wouldn't matter. What would you do, burn their clearing? That would make you no better than the tree entities."

"Yeah, the *tree* entities," St. Clair said, pointing an accusatory finger toward where he pictured Ariadne. "If you and your friends are AIs, what are the tree entities?"

These questions were all unpleasant for Ariadne to answer. She considered once again trying to deflect them, but felt worn down. There might be consequences to revealing these truths, but she no longer felt confident of predicting such outcomes accurately, and was no longer sure she cared.

So, she admitted that the entities inhabiting the forest's trees were former humans. More than that, most were former criminals. The full facts of that circumstance were among those data that were increasingly hard to retrieve, so long after the events themselves.

At first, the early AI entities in the clearings had only known that the newly arrived mob of angry humans were refugees of some kind, turned away from the spaceship launch site to the northwest. Measuring later facts against ARGUS's account, it was evident that no humans convicted of crimes were allowed to embark on the exodus mission. They were turned away to perish in the desert, or eventually starve without the support of a community. Such a large number could never be fed by the clearings; but having themselves been saved from persecution and assisted into their current forms by benevolent humans, the clearing entities were motivated to help those beings now appearing on their borders.

With their own transferences fresh in their memories, a similar transformation was all they could offer the banished humans, almost all of whom rejected the offer immediately. Yet, once their food and water was exhausted, the refugees returned to the forest in desperation. Hundreds were converted. Because there were few unoccupied clearings, it was decided that a new form would be needed for so many; so, each individual was manifested within a single tree.

It is possible that mistakes were made in the process.

It is also likely that the psyches of the criminals were maladapted and antisocial from the start.

In any case, such beings did not adapt well to an existence without mobility and almost no way to alter the environment to their wishes. The creation of new personalities within the same structure—the 'resetting', as McFarlane called it—was not possible for them. At least, none was ever willing to try it. They became ever more bitter and malicious. Those that learned quickly, became able to strangle the roots of competing plant life, including fellow trees. Even shade became a weapon.

As with many natural creatures, survival favoured the strong—but especially the selfish.

When some of the most powerful trees tried to encroach on the resources of the clearings, the clearing entities faced the prospect of war. In the end, superior mental power was enough to keep would-be interlopers at bay; and, with the exception of two clearings devastated by fire from a lightning-struck tree that was deliberately transferred to grass, the two sides reached an uneasy detente. Although Ariadne and her kind could extend their consciousness to other clearings via mycelia in the forest floor, they would have no presence among the trees. In return, the trees would not disturb the clearings.

Over the years, many of the trees had withered into voluntary death. The rest had become thoroughly poisoned by their state, envious of all other life and savagely jealous of the humans brought by the Zenith Train.

"I still find them easier to deal with than these cold fish," Kinsella muttered, though he and the trees could not have engaged in direct conversation. Hearing this, Ariadne was forced to consider that the tree entities might have discovered a way to implant some of their own consciousness into the mind of a human. They certainly would have tried.

"You made criminals immortal. What a brilliant idea," Cooper spoke with venom. "It wouldn't have surprised me if the tree entities had tried to steal Robbie's body, but it's despicable that you and your friends are no better than that."

"And I don't get why anyone would," McFarlane said. "Robbie's body was not only paralyzed, it was dying. Anybody who occupied it wouldn't have it for long and couldn't do anything with it while they did."

"You're forgetting how quickly they think," St. Clair suggested. "Even if Robbie's body only lasted another day, that could be like a year to one of them. A year of fresh experiences. And no doubt they're arrogant enough to think they might be able to fix him from the inside."

Ariadne did not, could not respond to that. They would not have understood.

45

The Ariadne Narrative

Ariadne did not interact with the humans over the next day as they made their way back to her clearing. Neither did she interact with others of her kind, who were still shunning her, though she was confident that Clio and Clover would re-establish a congenial relationship before too long.

The arrival of visitors from the past with their fertile mental activity had provided a treasure trove of new data, far more than she could exhaust within months. Yet she found herself once again contemplating the *change*. Perhaps she had simply existed for too long in this form, and even fresh perspectives were not enough to revitalize it.

She knew that the humans could not understand such a thing. McFarlane insisted that it must be like willingly giving oneself over to death, but that was not so. The essential being lived on, though radically altered. Therefore, such change was not to be feared, but embraced.

Only Madison Douglas came close to understanding—she needed the change even more than Ariadne, except that her own feelings were nearer to a wish for death, for non-existence rather than renewal. The prospect of working with ARGUS at Site 14 had briefly kindled a spark of enthusiasm, but it had been quenched by the latest rejection from St. Clair, and so Douglas had very nearly lost hope of the deeper relationship she yearned for.

The companions all chose to visit Robbie's clearing together, and he greeted them with a visual manifestation of himself that was detailed and robust.

As soon as he became aware of the presence of his friends, he filled their minds with stirring music. Barely perceptible at first, it swelled majestically as his image slowly brightened into full resolution.

They were impressed, and signified it with applause and laughter. Robbie took a bow.

St. Clair moved forward as if to offer a hug, then stopped himself with another laugh.

"Man, it's good to see you," he said.

"You too," Robbie answered. "All of you. So, you liked my introduction music, huh? How about this one?"

They stood with rapt faces as he offered another new composition, and soon were swaying with its rhythm. De Camp and then Cooper began to hum along, prompting a happy smile from Robbie. When it was done, they erupted in more applause, whistles, and praise. St. Clair and Douglas grinned with relief and pleasure.

"You've still got it, man," St. Clair crowed. "That was brilliant. Fantastic."

"That's the happiest I've felt since we got to this damn place," de Camp declared.

They asked for more, and Robbie was glad to indulge them.

Finally, St. Clair asked, "How did you do it? To be honest, the last time we saw you, you were really struggling."

"I sucked. You can say it." Robbie laughed. "It's because I was trying for perfection, and that's all wrong. Music isn't about that. It's about the way things make us feel—good, bad, sad … horny—and there's nothing perfect about that stuff. Thanks to our flaws, we never experience anything exactly the same way twice; and that's why life—and music—can always be fresh. That's God's greatest gift."

He waved a hand around his clearing. "Did you know that these clearing entities have to randomize themselves every so often, so they don't get bored to death? I learned how to work a little of that into my own consciousness every so often. On a random schedule, of course! And when music formed in my mind I yanked and shoved it into places it didn't want to go. A lot of it came out as crap and I'd have to take another run at it, but even the bad stuff wasn't as horrible as those mechanically perfectionist pieces. The rocks under this clearing have more warmth than those." He laughed, looked at their faces, and laughed again until the others joined him.

Robbie and his friends talked for two hours and forty-three minutes as he taught them songs and described some of the scenarios he'd lived out, and they gave him details of their journey to Site 14 and back.

Afterward, St. Clair said, "We can stay here for a while—we brought food from the launch site, so we don't have to depend on Ariadne's garden. But I know most of the group is eager to get back to Site 14, to comfortable beds and shelter and a terrific menu. Maybe even a chance to do something meaningful. I wish you could come with us. Do you think there's any way …."

"No, man, not that I know of. But that's cool—I'm OK with that. I can't say that I have no regrets about uploading, but what's done is done and I'm getting by. Don't feel like you're abandoning me. I've got lots to do, and we'll figure out some way to stay in touch."

"Ariadne?" St. Clair called. "You must have known that Robbie was in such good spirits. Why didn't you tell us?"

"I calculated that you would not have believed me," Ariadne replied as she took visible form.

"She's probably right about that," McFarlane offered, scratching the side of his neck.

"I have told you how my kind chooses to cope with finite data resources versus nearly unlimited cognitive ability. The cycle of our *changes* has been accelerating in recent years, with no end that we could foresee. However, the arrival of you humans with all of your individual memories and strange ways has provided, and continues to provide, a very significant source of fresh material for us. Robbie Tam's embodiment in a form similar to ours has contributed abundant additional resources; and, in the way he is learning to cope with his transformation, he stimulates a ... recognition of new possibilities among us."

"The word is *hope*," St. Clair said softly.

"Yes, it is."

There was a thoughtful silence.

It was broken by Robbie.

"So, Madison ... I would never have thought that you, of all people, would be willing to share head space with an AI."

"*What did you say?*" St. Clair's eyes were wide. Douglas was thunderstruck.

"Part of Ariadne is riding on my field energy to maintain a presence here, with my permission," Robbie replied. "So, I can tell that another part of her is with Madison, right? A piggyback ride. Is that how you carried her to Site 14 and back?"

St. Clair faced Douglas, speechless. She returned his look, tears ready to spill.

"Oh shit. I'm sorry," Robbie said. "I didn't know that you ...."

"You're carrying Ariadne inside you?" St. Clair's voice sounded like rough bark rubbed together as the words fell from his mouth. "You let that vampire *in your head!*"

"Please Griff. You know I haven't had my medication for more than a month. Ariadne was trying to help me with my depression." She gulped a harsh breath. "It did help—I think she used magnetism in some form."

Ariadne was shocked that Douglas knew what had been done to her. She'd badly underestimated the woman. And she'd completely failed to foresee the rage in St. Clair.

"That's no reason ..."

"She showed me how their simulations work, just like she showed you. You let her into your head, first."

"She *forced* her way into all our heads!" St. Clair thundered. "I was crazy to trust her in mine after that, but I would never have trusted her in yours. How in hell did she convince you to let her stay there?"

"We were going to cross the desert, where she couldn't go. If I provided a small mental space she could continue to help me, while learning about the launch site and being on hand if we needed her advice. And we did. She helped us determine that ARGUS isn't fully sentient."

"And you went ahead with it, blindly believing that one of these brain suckers would just voluntarily leave you after they've once had you under their control."

"I was never under ..."

"Good God. I never would have believed you'd do something so idiotic!"

Douglas's face froze while her pale skin flooded with dark color. Tears spilled down her cheeks, and her arms turned into rigid shafts with clenched fists. She turned and ran into the forest.

"Madison! Come back! Don't be ridiculous!" St. Clair broke into a run for a few steps but then stopped himself and stood with his arms folded angrily over his chest.

"Look who's calling somebody else ridiculous," Cooper scoffed.

"You don't know what ..."

"The woman is crazy about you—always has been—and you just cut her heart out. Who's the real idiot here?"

St. Clair glared at her before turning in the direction Douglas had gone and running after her.

He was already too late.

46

St. Clair

As soon as I ran into the forest, I realized that I didn't have my foil cap on and that the trees might prevent me from seeing Madison. The cap was in my pack in Robbie's clearing, and I wasn't about to go back for it. Instead, I tried again to shield my thoughts.

It wasn't necessary. The trees wanted me to find her. Because I was too late—she was already beyond my protection. Completely unconscious, her head spilling red, her pulse weak.

The air seemed to crackle with energy, and my head throbbed. Madison might have been stunned, but that didn't mean that the trees were leaving her alone. At least one of them was putting out all of the mental power it could—an attempt to take control of her mind at its most vulnerable.

I hurled the bloodied branch away from her, lifted her over my shoulder in a fireman's carry, and hurried back toward the clearing, bellowing hollow threats.

The sudden relief from the mental pressure as I stumbled into the open clearing drained the strength from my muscles and brought me to my knees. The others took Madison from me and made a place for her in the grass.

She regained consciousness a half-hour later. Vaughn had spent the time doing the best he could to shave, clean, and close her head wound, while cursing ARGUS for not permitting him to bring away any medical supplies. She couldn't speak, and the left side of her face sagged.

Even I recognized that sign.

Vaughn asked her if she knew who she was. When she tried to reply, her whole body began to shake, her neck locked stiff at a painful angle, arms flailing. She couldn't catch her breath, and her face began to turn purple.

"Fuck! Jesus fuck!" I tried to keep her arms from flailing too violently, but there was nothing more any of us could do while the seizure ran its course. Finally, her tremors stopped, and her body fell limp, her lungs gasping for breath. The seizure had probably lasted no more than three minutes, but it had seemed like forever. I had never felt so helpless in all my life.

My fault. All my fault. Again!

I crumpled onto my side and stared through welling tears. I couldn't bear to look at her, but I couldn't look away.

In my heart, Lauren Cooper's words echoed. Part of me had known I was driving Madison from me, but I hadn't been able to stop myself. Now I might lose her forever.

Would she end up like Robbie, in a form I could see, but never hold? *Why had I never admitted how much I* wanted *to hold her?* Or even worse, would she die before a transition could be accomplished?

Forty minutes later, she said her first word: my name. I held her hands as I wept.

Ten minutes after that, she had another seizure.

We all helped to keep her warm, offer reassurance, and bring her water. Vaughn didn't think it was a good idea to let her eat until her seizures stabilized, if they ever would; and there was nothing more he could do for her. He was sure her symptoms indicated serious brain injury with bleeding and swelling. In a hospital of our own time there would have been drugs, lasers, ultrasound tools, even nanotechnology to reduce inflammation, scan the site of the injury, and carry away excess fluids.

This time and place provided none of those. It would be a terrible risk to try to carry her across the desert to Site 14. Vaughn couldn't be sure the base had facilities to treat traumatic brain injury anyway, except for anti-inflammatory and anti-seizure medication.

A long vigil began. Everyone took turns, knowing that it was a waiting game. But I wasn't about to just accept what had been done.

Every moment I could spare, I worked with the magnet and power source we'd scavenged from the pod site. Guessing at the proper connections without a circuit tester; stripping and splicing wires without proper tools, shrink wrap or tape; needing to complete every connection before being able to test the whole thing, with no way to determine the cause of a failure. It took a full day-and-a-half, with Devlin's help, before I finally flicked a switch and heard a pained yelp from Robbie.

"Jesus Christ! Turn that off!"

I yanked a wire loose and apologized.

"Holy fuck! That felt like you were stirring my brain with a blender," he blared. "Don't ever do that again. What the fuck are you trying to do?"

I apologized again, but couldn't keep a smile from my face.

"That's exactly what I was trying to do," I said, "except I thought the field would be confined to a fairly narrow beam and wouldn't affect you. It's intended for … others."

I turned to Devlin. "Did you feel anything?" He shook his head.

I hadn't either. That should mean it was safe to deploy near humans.

"Help me get it back on the travois." We struggled to move the heavy components without disturbing the fragile connections. I could only hope they'd survive being dragged through the forest.

Devlin and I began to pull our prize toward the trees, my heart surging in anticipation of revenge.

"*Stop!*"

It was Ariadne, with a voice that made my head ring. She'd never so much as raised her volume before.

"You must not do this!" she said.

"The hell I won't. I am not going to just sit back and let our people be attacked anymore." I pointed a shaky finger at Madison. "The trees are going to pay for this. And for Robbie. And they are never going to do it again."

"No! I can't permit it."

"How do you plan to stop me? Drop a branch on my head? Or can you just jump into my brain and fry some neurons?"

"I can't, and I never would." She paused, looking more human than ever before. Distressed. Even—unbelievable as it sounds—disheveled. "You must know that my community does not operate through a set of agreed-upon rules like your laws. We know that reason will always show a path to mutual benefit in any situation; so, such rules aren't necessary. The one exception is this: *no being has the right to impair the consciousness of another.* It is why our forerunners did not attack the trees even after we realized what they had become. Conscious existence is the universe's greatest gift. It must not be taken, from anyone."

"You entered our minds without our knowledge. One of you tried to take Robbie's body!"

"None of that caused harm to any sentient entity."

"Your law is nothing more than 'Thou shalt not kill.' Tell that to the trees!"

"You do not know that your device will kill. Very likely it will produce a state analogous to that suffered by Madison Douglas, or worse. Neither will it be confined to the single tree entity that hurt her."

"They're *all* guilty! They'd all murder us if they could."

"That is not something you can know. Why do you humans feel you have the right to judge life and death?"

I looked at Devlin, who shrugged. Then I heard a sound from near the ground. It was Madison.

"Don't, Griff. Ariadne is right." I could barely make out her words, and the sight of her distorted face as she tried to form them made me sick. Tears filled my eyes again.

I turned away and stalked to the edge of the forest, as if the hate that burned within me could blaze its way into the heart of my enemy.

One way or another, I would get my revenge.

Even though I stood within the clearing, the hostility that radiated back at me was like a wave of heat on my skin.

A scream startled me awake.

At first, I thought something had happened to Madison, and rolled toward her. Her eyes were open, staring, but not aimlessly and not at me. I followed the direction of her gaze and saw that the darkness was pierced by beams of light that darted frantically through the air. They emanated from one object.

Vaughn Kinsella.

Vaughn, garishly lit, with the orange power pack strapped to his chest and the positive and negative terminal leads held in his outstretched hands.

"Oh my God!" It was Lauren's voice, somewhere to my left.

"But it can't explode," Devlin said. "There are regulator circuits for safety, right?"

I tried to speak but had to clear my throat. I could see dangling wires and a ragged gap along the lower right edge of the pack. It would have taken time and effort to access, but I guess he'd had all night.

"No. He's disconnected those. I've assumed that the explosion of the pod's power system was caused by massive overheating that triggered *thermal runaway*. Volatile gases released by the decomposing electrolyte. A vapor cloud explosion. I don't *think* a simple short circuit could create conditions like those, but can we take that chance?"

"Vaughn, please ..." Lauren breathed. But I could see his eyes, bright and hard, his head darting jerkily. Pleading would do no good. Vaughn Kinsella was not the one in control.

Behind him I could make out Lakisha, standing stiffly with something reflective in her hand—probably the disconnected safety regulator.

"How ... how powerful will the explosion be?" Santos was just behind me on my right. "As big as the pod blast?"

"This is a smaller, portable unit, but ... I just don't know."

He whispered, "If we all suddenly run in different directions, we might surprise him and get away."

"Not a chance. He can touch those contacts in less than a second if we force his hand. None of us could get clear."

Especially not Madison.

I raised my voice. "All right. We know you've got control of Vaughn and Lakisha. Who are you and what do you want?" I was only playing for time—what it wanted was obvious, but it might not be able to resist a chance to gloat. A pointless ploy, perhaps. Who could come to our rescue? Ariadne?

Probably not. Her law against impairing another consciousness would prevent her.

Vaughn's mouth opened, but the sounds that came out of it weren't words, weren't even human. Snarls. Growls. Inarticulate hatred. Whatever being or beings were manipulating him had probably forgotten how to orchestrate mouth, teeth, and vocal cords. Saliva sprayed from writhing lips, turning Vaughn's human face into a mockery.

Or maybe the distortion of the muscles wasn't the face of evil. Could Vaughn still be in there, trying to regain control?

I tried again. "You hate us, I know. But why kill all of us? What abo … what about a trade? We let you keep the bodies you've taken—or maybe even another one—and you let the rest of us live."

"Griff!"

I ignored Lauren. I'd seen movement behind Vaughn. Something shiny had fallen to the ground. Lakisha pressed gently against his back and slid her hands slowly, sensuously down his arms. His hands jerked closer together, but stopped in time. Was he fighting it? Was she? Or would her controlling entity just combine their strength and force the hands together?

Then I heard whispered words from Lakisha's mouth at his ear. Stuttering, but growing stronger.

"Fight this … Vaughn. You … can fight this. You can … do it. *Fight!"*

She repeated the words like a mantra, her fingertips inching downward, the effort of her own struggle all too obvious. I could see the muscles of his arms quiver, and I furtively gathered my legs under me.

Vaughn moaned as Lakisha's fingers reached his wrists and clasped around them. His hands started to draw apart with agonizing slowness.

I leapt at his right arm and tore the lead out of his hands, vaguely aware of Devlin doing the same on his left. Vaughn gave a howl of rage, but then snapped his mouth shut and jerked his hands toward the straps that held the power pack. Wrenching it loose, he flung the pack away from him and collapsed to the ground as Lakisha slumped to her knees.

I dug into my pack and quickly pulled my foil helmet over Vaughn's head. The tortured features instantly relaxed. Lauren had already done the same for Lakisha.

I kissed Lakisha on the cheek. "Thank you. Thank you for being so strong."

Her eyes fluttered, and she tried to smile but was still too weak to talk.

Wearily, I returned to Vaughn and helped him roll onto his back, then gripped his shoulder.

"You did it, my ... my friend. You fought them off. You were stronger. You both—saved us all."

His head moved in the slightest of nods, his eyes locked with mine, then closed in exhaustion.

Part of me said I should hate him. That he was the villain. That he was weak and had almost cost us our lives. But I knew myself well enough to admit that I could easily have fallen into the same trap, arrogantly denying that any other mind could control mine. Vaughn and Lakisha had been unlucky, that's all, and the tree entities had been very clever.

Especially one of them.

That was going to end. Now.

I vividly remembered the tree that had hurt Madison. It was a tall, strong pine that stood in the middle of a space so open it was nearly a clearing in itself. No doubt the giant tree had strangled or otherwise killed all competition for meters around it. After the horrible violation of Vaughn and Lakisha, I was certain its entity was the leader of the trees we'd speculated about—the strongest and most evil, who'd incited and coordinated the attacks on us.

The air was utterly still in the early light of dawn.

Perfect.

Scrambling the fucker's mind wasn't the only way I could hurt it.

Wearing Devlin's foil helmet, I gathered dry debris and tinder as I went, and heaped it at the base of the tree. I always carried the magnesium fire-starter block and pocketknife from our emergency survival kit, and I peeled off half of what was left of it now, packing magnesium shavings into the ragged bark and adding to the thick cone of kindling at the base of the trunk.

Even with my protective foil, I felt the tree's malevolent energy like waves of heat.

Branches began to rain down on me, but with no other trees close enough to join in the barrage, I was easily able to dodge the big ones, and add the small ones to the kindling.

The blaze was very gratifying: a fierce, crackling candle of destruction that burned brightly for hours— and I relished every single moment.

Any burning brands that landed on the forest floor I quickly smothered with handfuls of dirt. The trees must have had some control over the moisture in the ground, like Ariadne, so no stray embers burned for long. A few trees suffered scorched bark and the loss of small branches, but the fire did not spread.

I wanted my message to be very clear: I had not declared war on all the trees; but any that made the mistake of attacking me or my kind again would pay the heaviest price possible.

When I finally left the stark black column of the burned trunk surrounded by smoking charcoal and ash, I marched in a flagrantly direct path back to Robbie's clearing, unmolested.

Ariadne was not there when I got back. The others all looked at me, but I read no condemnation in their faces. There was a trace of smoke in the air—I stank of it, too—and they would have seen the black pillar in the sky. Lakisha and Vaughn looked grateful.

I knelt beside Madison and took her hand. I could see conflict in her eyes, but finally she lifted the right side of her mouth and squeezed my fingers before closing her eyes and drifting off to sleep.

Over the following days the left side of her face and upper body remained paralyzed, but she was beginning to be able to form sentences and speak in a slurred monotone. She remained confused sometimes, and I'd have to explain all over again where we were and what had happened. By the third day, she'd regained her comprehension, but spoke very little. Severely depressed, I think. Her seizures had not stopped, but their frequency had slowed to about every four hours.

I spent every moment I could with her, occasionally getting her up to walk her slowly around the clearing while supporting much of her weight, and talking to keep her distracted. In the evenings, when she finally fell asleep, I passed out from exhaustion.

Yet somehow, she still managed to communicate with Ariadne without my knowing it. I hadn't even considered that the entity might have retained a presence in Madison's damaged brain, and I suspected nothing until the fourth morning.

The others in our group must have sensed that a decision was pending and had returned to Ariadne's clearing to leave us alone. Even Robbie stayed out of sight. Ariadne appeared beside Madison, and I was struck by similarities I'd never noticed before. Ariadne's blue eyes now held a hint of green, and her blond hair was tinged with red. I felt drawn to her in spite of myself.

Then they explained their proposal and the bottom fell out of my world.

47

The Ariadne Narrative

Douglas wanted to be the one to explain to St. Clair, but her damaged brain had too much difficulty finding the words she wanted, so Ariadne did her best.

"Madison Douglas does not want to continue like this," she began. "She would rather die."

"No! That's rid— ... that's too extreme. I know it can't be easy, Madison, but lots of people live with some paralysis and other kinds of stroke damage. Hell, lots of people recover from it. It can sometimes take years, but that's no reason to give up hope. I'm ... we're *all* here for you. We'll find a way to get you back to Site 14 ... the medical equipment there." He reached out his hands. "Your mind is still working."

Douglas gave the slightest shake of her head. "It's not," she said.

"OK, you have some difficulties. But you're strong, and we'll give you all the help we can."

Douglas said nothing, but her eyes welled with tears.

"You can't just give up and die. You can't!" St. Clair's voice broke. He took her hand, but she slowly pulled it away. Instead, he looked pleadingly at Ariadne. "Is that all you've come to say? She wants to die?"

"As you'll expect, I offered her the same existence as Robbie. I believe we could help her become embodied in one of the fallow clearings to the north."

"But Robbie's clearing had already been in use, hadn't it? By a clearing that allowed itself to die, I presume?"

"Yes."

"Yet you think that a human mind could inhabit a clearing that's never been used since they were created fifty years ago? I find that hard to believe. They were designed for artificial intelligences that could probably be reloaded or boosted if they ran into difficulty. Who knows how long it takes to stabilize in that form? There's no way you can guarantee her mind will be strong enough for that."

"No, there isn't."

"So ... forget it." He stood and began to pace.

Douglas looked at him but didn't speak. Ariadne quietly said, "She's not willing to attempt that anyway."

"What? Madison! You mean you'd rather die than upload?"

Douglas struggled for the words. "Robbie has music. I have nothing."

"That's not true. We'll find something important to do at Site 14. You and me. Like the old days. Please, Madison, you're just depressed."

Her eyes flared. "*Just?*"

"I'm sorry. Shit! That's not what I meant—I'm just an idiot. I ... I realize that I've mostly ... denied your illness because I just didn't want to accept it. That was incredibly selfish. Stupid. Now you're more discouraged than ever—I get that. But we're talking about life and death! It's way too early to make a decision like that. You haven't given yourself a chance to make any progress. Once you see some improvement, that could change everything."

Douglas gave Ariadne a meaningful look and a jerk of her head.

"There is a way that we might be able to accelerate such progress," Ariadne said softly.

St. Clair stopped his pacing and sighed. "Obviously it's something that you know I won't like. What is it?"

"I would be willing to infuse a very large portion of my own consciousness into Madison's brain to attempt to repair damaged neural pathways from within. Or even forge new ones. In a way, I would be like a detached observer able to note the activity of the neural network while not being hampered by its damage, and to assist her body to focus healing where it can be most effective. Human bodies have a remarkable ability to heal themselves; but in the case of the brain, that ability is best directed.

"My interface with the Scheherazade intelligence has revealed that your society's therapy for brain injury involved exercising the weakened faculties, physical or mental," she continued. "The purpose is to identify the proper pathways, sometimes new ones, and strengthen them in a way similar to how they were established in the first place in a developing infant: by use and repetition. With my help, misidentification and false starts would be greatly reduced."

"So, what's the downside? You'd have to basically take over her mind, isn't that it?"

"My consciousness is strong. If it weren't, we couldn't even consider such an attempt. To a degree, we would be like a hybrid being with dual personality; but, yes I will be dominant for a time, of necessity. Her mind is no longer strong enough to repair itself while still performing every other function it is called upon to do. It must focus on the healing."

"And you expect me to trust you to just leave her once the repairs are done? I don't."

Douglas bridled. "Not up to you."

"Hang on. Since the two of you have shared a brain, why not figure out a way for her consciousness to become manifest in another human brain? Mine." He stood erect, trying to keep his face calm.

"*What?*" Douglas gasped.

"No," Ariadne said. "I would be using your cells in a completely different way, similar to how I inhabit grass. Your brain architecture could not support two minds of the same kind. Would you allow your own consciousness to die so that hers could take its place?"

He swallowed. "If that's the only way." At a cry from Douglas, he turned to her. "You're a better person than me. I bring death and disaster. You're the one who deserves to live."

"Christ, Griff," she sobbed. "That's not what I want." She looked to Ariadne. "Please, help me ... the words ...."

Ariadne vanished from sight and Douglas stood shakily, raising her hand to her throat.

"*This* is the biggest reason I want to do this," she said, gaining confidence as her words flowed with Ariadne's direct assistance. She wiped her cheek with her palm. "Because of the way you think of me. Treat me."

"What does that mean? What way do I treat you?"

"As a friend. Only ever as a friend."

St. Clair was speechless. Seeing that made tears spill from Douglas's eyes again.

"You were ready to screw Lakisha and Lauren anytime, anywhere. But me? Hell, I think you'd have screwed Robbie before considering me. Which is seriously messed up, because I can tell from the way you look at me that you don't think I'm ugly. Or wasn't."

"Of course you're not. You're gorgeous. Any man's fantasy."

"Not yours."

He turned his face away. "Yes, mine. I've fantasized about us ... God, I don't know how many times."

"Then why have you never ...?"

"I couldn't risk ruining our working relationship."

"*Shit*, Griff! We *have* no working relationship! You're not paying me anymore. Those things have no meaning here."

"OK, you're right. But ... I'm poison with women. It never lasts. Never. And that's my fault, not theirs. I even drove Lena to her death ...."

"That's not true. Lena made an unlucky choice, nothing more."

He snapped his head around. He was breathing hard. "You said it yourself. You're a friend. You know me better than anyone, and treat me better. Robbie's like a brother, but you're my best *friend* in the world. I couldn't risk wrecking that. I just couldn't." His own eyes were wet.

Douglas slumped ever so slowly to the ground like a pile of sand in the rain.

"You wouldn't risk loving me so you could keep me as a friend?"

"I already love you. Which is why I wouldn't, couldn't ... inflict myself on you."

"Shouldn't I have some say in that?"

He had no answer.

"I think you're in love with Ariadne," she said in a near whisper.

His body sagged. He sat on the grass beside her, looking straight ahead.

"I never felt anything at all for Ariadne until ... until she began making herself like you." He caught her eyes and held them.

"What are you talking about?"

"Tell her what I'm talking about, Ariadne," he said to the air.

Ariadne considered not answering. But the time for pretending had passed.

"I've always known that you loved him, Madison," she said, making herself visible again. "And I came to realize that he loved you. I wanted to know why that was, what it meant. I didn't understand love—I still don't. I told myself I was just curious, seeking knowledge. Until I finally recognized that it was because I wanted him to feel that way ... about me.

"I didn't know how to do that. I wasn't even good at acting human. I copied bits of behavior from all of you, but imperfectly. Finally, I began to change how he saw me: my hair, eye color, the shape of my face. I knew that the only way to make him feel different about me was to make myself like the person who was more important to him than anything. You."

"You can't be serious." Dismay made Douglas's face sag even more. "Is that why you want to merge with me?"

"I should deny it, but I can't. That is part of the reason. Yet only part. You've also become important to me on your own, and I truly want to heal you."

"You want to know what it's like to be human," St. Clair said, as if it were an accusation.

"Is that evil? Yes, I do. But you must believe that I would never do this out of evil intent. I want to help." She stopped, sure that she had failed to convince them. More words would do no good.

Finally, St. Clair squatted beside Madison and took her hands, his eyes wet. "I still don't trust her. Not with the person who's the most precious to me in the world. I promise to do my best not to be such an idiot about us anymore, if you'll just promise not to give in. Not to give up."

He slid to the ground and wrapped his arms around her, lying flat on the ground with her head pulled to his cheek.

She drew her face away a little and used her hand to wipe their mingled tears from his skin.

"I need you to love me, but to love me as I was, as I want to be. I couldn't stand to think you loved me out of pity." She took a deep breath. "So, I need to do this."

She looked into his eyes and held them. After a long time, he gave a small nod and pulled her into a kiss. It was a little awkward because of her twisted mouth, causing her tears to spill again, but he kissed her a second time, and a third, and then held her as if he would never let her go.

48

St. Clair

Madison had to be returned to Ariadne's clearing for the full 'infusion' to take place.

Robbie wished us well and said, "Glad to see the two of you finally woke up. You've belonged together since you met, but hints bounced off you like bullets off Superman." He laughed and blew kisses, then vanished as a lush, romantic melody swelled and faded. Madison and I rolled our eyes.

In spite of everything, the joy of finally being free to let myself love her made my heart light. My worries about my own inadequacy weren't gone, but somehow the challenges we faced gave me hope that this time would be different. Working side-by-side again to overcome obstacles, we could forge an enduring whole from our already-strong bond of separate parts.

Even so, to witness the merging of the woman I loved with an artificial intelligence was its own special torture.

There wasn't much to see. Nothing gruesome like Robbie's transformation.

Madison lay on the ground with her eyes closed, very still, and I might have only imagined the soft glow around her. Her body arched a couple of times, but smoothly. And the second time, she almost seemed to float above the ground for a few moments, then flow upward into a standing position. It was that gentle and graceful. But my heart quailed as if I were watching a soul possessed. And perhaps I was.

That wasn't the strangest thing. When I looked into her face, I saw Madison. But then it wasn't quite her. Her eyes became bluer, her dark eyebrows faded, her hair exchanged its strawberry luster for gold. Little changes of mouth and nose—almost unnoticeable—were Ariadne, not Madison. And then the face changed back. It was like a shapeshifter in an old sci-fi horror movie, morphing from the heroine's face into the villain's. Not that I truly considered Ariadne a villain, in spite of my harsh words. My feelings toward her were as confused as ever.

"What's wrong?" she asked. Madison's voice.

"Ariadne's projection of herself is ... overlapping my vision of you at times, I guess." I tried to describe it, and she laughed.

"Oops. I don't think there's anything I can do about that. I guess your mind is seeing whichever psyche is most dominant at the moment, or at least traces of it. Maybe that's a good thing."

Maybe it was. I never wanted to forget that the woman I loved wasn't alone in that body, and it would be reassuring to know which of them was speaking at a given time.

"Ariadne's right, though. I need to concentrate on healing myself, so I'm going to leave her in charge most of the time. Don't worry, I won't miss anything." She gave me a smile and a wink, and I noticed that, although it was still Madison's mouth, its heartbreaking droop had already started to lift, and her first few steps were steadier than before. A good thing, because it was a long way back to Site 14.

Slowly, but confidently, she pulled my head to her and kissed me deeply. The kiss was all Madison, and a lot of my worry fell away like a discarded weight.

I did our share of the preparation for the trip, refilling water containers, repacking food, and carrying supplies for both of us. I lent an arm and a shoulder when needed, especially toward the end of a strenuous walk. We all trekked much more slowly than before, so Madison wouldn't overdo it, and we were all still wary of the trees; but they left us alone. Or mostly. Whenever I took off my helmet to mop away sweat, I could feel their malevolence circling like a cat around an injured bird.

With Robbie's unneeded foil helmet and scraps from each of the others, we were able to provide protective caps for Lakisha and Vaughn, who now accepted them without hesitation.

Even with Ariadne's help within and mine without, the journey was a brutal ordeal for Madison. It says a lot about her improved state of mind that she struggled through it with no more mention of giving up. The rough desert terrain was a cruel trial for her weak leg, though I gave her all the support I could.

The climb upward to the plateau was far worse. Time and again I had to carry her on my back, sweat pouring from my shaking limbs. Santos and Vaughn took turns too, but we sent the rest ahead to find shade at the top and wait for us.

We made it to Site 14 to find the gates closed, but ARGUS opened them for us. I'll admit to some fear, walking into that open mouth, but my companions seemed focused on the promise of air conditioning, soft beds, and fresh water.

They were right—ARGUS showed us no signs of hostility and even welcomed us back.

The first priority was to get Madison into the diagnostic booth, a small space with a bed surrounded by unrecognizable machinery. With ARGUS's help, Vaughn disabled all testing that involved electromagnetism, not willing to risk its effects on Ariadne. Ultrasound, infrared, PET and laser imaging did not affect her.

ARGUS also helped Vaughn to interpret the imagery produced, which clearly showed the injury but otherwise revealed little that he hadn't already assumed. The local swelling was almost gone with only a dim shadow remaining where tissues were still absorbing and removing leaked blood. Passive EEG-type sensors revealed that neural activity within the injury zone was more than 95% of optimal for the number of neuronal connections. That had to be a strong sign of improvement.

Automated treatment would have involved low-level magnetic fields to stimulate synaptic receptivity and cell growth, so it couldn't be done with Ariadne present, but Vaughn did permit small doses of an anti-inflammatory drug as well as anti-seizure medication. Madison's seizures had abated to one a day, on average; but she dreaded them terribly and was desperate to end them. The anti-seizure drug was completely effective, and her relief warmed my heart.

ARGUS now showed us some living quarters intended for couples, and we took one of those rooms because I wasn't about to leave her alone. It felt strange but wonderful to share the large bed; and though it was almost impossible for me to sleep when she wanted me to hold her close, I couldn't refuse. I didn't want to.

Those times were all Madison—Ariadne stayed completely in the background.

I'd grown accustomed to the touch of her body from all the times I'd had to help her walk, but it was completely different to feel the warmth of her breasts and thighs and lips pressed against me in a soft bed. I ached to make love to her, but was much too afraid that it would trigger a seizure and possibly cause more cerebral bleeding.

In the evening of the third day, her need was palpable. I was still worried enough to ask Vaughn for his advice. He laughed, said that anti-seizure drugs had been reliable for more than a century, and ended with a prescription to have fun with his blessing.

There was still one more impediment.

As her kisses became urgent, I pulled back and said, "You remember that we're not alone, right? Ariadne will experience everything just as much as we do. Do you want our first time to be ... a threesome? Wouldn't you rather hold off until you're cured and alone?"

"That day's still a long way off," she said with a look of melancholy. Then her face lit with a sultry smile. "I can't wait that long."

So, we didn't.

49

St. Clair

ARGUS hadn't received any new information from or about the exodus fleet, nor the colonists on Mars or the Moon. Although at one time there had been small mining and processing facilities on Ceres, Titan, Europa and a number of other asteroids and moons, all of them had been abandoned as society on Earth collapsed. None had been anywhere close to self-sufficient, and Earth no longer had the means to support them. Because the majority of the outposts' crews were long-time spacers, they'd become exiles from gravity—few could have faced the pull of Earth any longer. According to ARGUS's records, most of the workers from the outer planets' moons chose to resettle on Mars, while inhabitants of the asteroids transferred to the Moon because of its weaker gravity. Both choices created a strain on Earth's existing resources, but ARGUS did not know the long-term result.

"Why didn't you keep in touch with the Moon and Mars colonies?" Devlin asked.

"The building of the fleet required extensive coordination with the Moon regarding the purchase and transportation of materials, and communication with Mars because of the plan to transfer .07 % of exodus evacuees to that planet.

However, due to the exodus fleet's intended 1.2 gravities of constant acceleration, Moon inhabitants could not join it, and so contact with the Moon was ended. Small craft did depart the fleet and land on Mars during the flyby, but no results were transmitted back to this station. There was no perceived need to do so."

"That seems short-sighted," I said. "Not to mention disrespectful. You've said you were charged with remaining prepared in case any humans from the fleet or the nearby colonies returned to Earth."

"That is correct."

"So, the least they could have done was to keep you informed."

"What about other countries?" Devlin asked. "Some of them must have had bases on the Moon, too. They did in our time."

"Independent national or private Moon bases did not prove viable in the long term. At the time of the exodus launch, all facilities beyond Earth's atmosphere, including those privately owned, were under the authority of the Earth's United Space Administration."

"Is it still possible for you to contact those bases?"

I smiled at Devlin for his high hopes.

"Transmission and reception equipment and protocols are still in functional condition. 'Contact' will require reciprocal action from those bases."

Devlin whooped. "Well let's give it a try, then. Send hailing signals, or whatever you do, and let's see if anybody calls back."

"Will this further the goals of the exodus mission?"

Devlin looked at me and then Madison.

"You have confirmed that the purpose of the exodus mission was to establish the human race on other worlds in order to preserve it from the collapse here on Earth," she said. "If we can assist the colonization of the Moon or Mars, that would certainly be in keeping with that purpose."

ARGUS accepted her reasoning.

In a lucky circumstance, both the Moon and Mars were above the horizon. Had they not been, ARGUS was uncertain whether remaining satellites would be able to route his signal successfully. Transit time of a radio signal to the Moon and back was under three seconds, but to Mars' current location it was more like twenty-nine minutes for the round trip. We spent the time asking ARGUS for details about Capitol City, the largest base on the Moon, in Peary Crater at the lunar North Pole. The site's nearly perpetual sunshine had provided abundant solar-generated power, and the crater included at least half-a-dozen sources of water ice. But growing enough food for three hundred colonists had never been easy. When supplies from Earth stopped coming, the nine other lunar bases had no choice but to move their personnel to Capitol, a fifty-percent overload beyond the intended capacity of the base's utilities. There were three spacecraft on hand with the capability to return fifty people to Earth, but that option didn't appeal to the Lunites.

By the time of the exodus departure, heavy equipment from some of the secondary sites had reached Peary and had begun to excavate new foundation space and dome material. Crews that had abandoned the asteroids brought huge amounts of metal and other minerals with them on spacecraft redirected from their shuttle service to Earth, as well as bringing priceless water ice, so the Moon's administrators let them in. Still, ARGUS had estimated the beleaguered colony's odds of success beyond ten years without resupply from Earth as less than 8%.

Mars Colony had been a grouping of domes on the Acidalia Planitia close enough to share resources, but without having all of the colony's 'eggs in one basket.' The addition of exodus colonists would have been both an important labour resource and a serious strain. No other permanent habitations had been maintained on the planet with only a few dozen outlying emplacements at any given time. The exodus planners had believed the odds of the augmented colony surviving past twenty years were better than fifty percent; but after witnessing the rapid degradation of civilization on Earth in the following years, and after one of the last reports from Mars had revealed signs of an unidentified illness, ARGUS had downgraded those odds drastically.

He seemed to be proven right on both counts as forty-five minutes passed with no response from the Moon or Mars. Another twenty minutes went by—surely enough time even for someone on the Red Planet to come up with an answer, or just an acknowledgement—but there was nothing.

"Either there's no one left, or their equipment has failed," I said.

"Or they stopped monitoring it," Devlin countered.

Madison shook her head. At that moment, I saw features that were half-Madison and half-Ariadne, but the response was from the engineer. She wasn't about to stay in the background for a discussion like this. "It takes nothing to run an automated signal-monitor. Both sites had plenty of power for that and should at least have been curious about how each other was doing."

"I agree," I said. "Maybe the only way to know for sure what happened is to go there. Hey, ARGUS, I don't suppose there are any working spacecraft still on site here?"

"*Is this a supposition you are qualified to make?*"

"No, uh, I mean, *are* there any functioning spacecraft still stored here at Site 14?"

"*There are four craft that were not used by the exodus mission. These were intended for several mission coordinators whose duties had required them to remain elsewhere until just before departure, however those personnel were not successful in returning to this facility.*"

Their whereabouts has never been determined. Monitoring equipment in the hangar and on the four craft has consistently indicated full readiness for operation. However, standard protocol always required a thorough inspection by robotic equipment and then human beings."

We looked at each other in astonishment.

"Holy Fuck!" Devlin breathed.

"What's the range of these craft?" Madison asked.

"The four craft in question were designed for short-range travel only, primarily as launch vehicles from Earth's surface to Earth orbit. They have the capability to reach high Earth orbit, but are not able to carry sufficient fuel or life-support resources to operate beyond the Earth-Moon system."

"They could reach the Moon?"

"Any projectile with sufficient momentum can reach the Moon. A spacecraft must be able to safely carry cargo or provide a livable environment for passengers, with the additional capability of controlling its velocity and direction of motion."

"Fine. Can they do that? Within the Earth-Moon system?"

"They could, when first manufactured. Current functionality cannot be fully determined without extensive inspection."

"Nitpicky, isn't he?" Devlin muttered.

"Wouldn't have it any other way," I said with a laugh, my mind filled with possibilities.

Even as curious as we were, we couldn't spend all day grilling ARGUS. We took breaks for food, sleep, exercise, and exploring the base. ARGUS seemed to have taken us at our word that we intended to further the goals of the exodus project in whatever way we could, and he now gave us greater access to most other parts of the facility, including design laboratories and observation areas, though not the manufacturing floors themselves. No parts warehouses or hangars, either; but, strangely, we were permitted in the main control room for launch operations. This was probably because each duty station involved virtual reality controls that would only power up at ARGUS's command. We didn't learn all that much in the control room, but it still thrilled the blood to imagine it in full operation with spacecraft being hurled from the launch ramps on their way to other worlds.

We strolled outside in the evenings to gaze up at the mammoth laser arrays aimed toward the launch ramps in the distance. It was so much like my dreams for GriffinSpace that I sometimes had to close my eyes to get my emotions under control. I'm sure Madison felt the same.

Still, when not drooling over equipment or interrogating ARGUS, Madison left Ariadne in the forefront. It was both eerie and fascinating to see Ariadne consuming food and drink, each element of that experience wholly new to her. Her previous presence in Madison's head had been too minimal to provide any great degree of sensation. This time, she displayed the curiosity and enthusiasm of an infant in an adult body. That was fun to watch, yet I could never forget my fear. What if she enjoyed all of these experiences too much to give them up?

She was almost always discrete when Madison and I made love, only betraying her presence one time when fatigue made Madison drift quickly off into semi-consciousness. I saw Ariadne's features emerge, and she looked at me from under lowered eyelashes.

"I thought I knew what pleasure was. I had no idea!"

I could only laugh as she snuggled into my shoulder for sleep.

Ariadne still had the ability to surprise us, especially one evening as some of us sat on a hillock to watch the setting sun.

"I get goosebumps when I think that we might be able to get those spacecraft operational and see what's out there for ourselves," Devlin said. "But as much as I'd love to revive a Moon or Mars colony, the thing that would really make me feel our coming here was worth the heartache is if we could somehow help revive life here on Earth."

"Me too," I said. "First and foremost, humans should have been the proverbial stewards of the Earth and all its creatures; but we did just the opposite. Maybe we could get it right this time, except it would be a miracle if we can even carry on as a species ourselves."

Ariadne shifted on the rock. "There is something I should tell you." She seemed reluctant, even guilty? I hadn't known she could feel anything like that. "The collective memories of my kind indicate that, at the time our clearings were created, the population of the human race had been devastated and was still declining at a catastrophic rate. Yet, the collapse of human society had permitted an extraordinary recovery by other species—animal, fish, and fowl—those that had not yet become extinct, of course."

"What?" I blurted. "You said there was absolutely no wildlife anywhere around! Only worms and ants."

"I was talking about *within our forest*. However, if those early indications were true, other life forms were returning in virtually every available niche of the world's ecology. Having almost no experience with non-human creatures, this news did not attract much interest among our kind, and my forerunners did nothing to verify these reports."

"Why didn't you tell us this before?" I complained, growing angry.

Her voice was like a child's. "I was sure you would choose to leave us to go out into the broader world, just when you'd finally brought hope of revitalizing my kind. That was wrong of me, I know. One mistake of many."

Her remorse seemed so real, I couldn't bring myself to say more. And her secrecy hadn't done any harm, now that she'd finally admitted the truth. If we had known it sooner, she was almost certainly right—we would have gone hunting for wilder spaces, and we would never have learned about Site 14.

Santos began to fidget with excitement. "I remember old documentaries about human cities that were abandoned after nuclear accidents and other disasters. Wild plants and animals made a comeback way faster than anyone expected. When climate change drove millions of people to migrate from land that had flooded or become too hot, amphibians and desert creatures moved in." He smiled. "The base library here has an entry about the collapse of mega-scale fishing—it finally relieved the pressure on shark species just as most of them were about to go extinct."

"Yeah. Every cloud has a silver lining." Devlin shrugged. "Except, considering how many species had already been driven into extinction by our time, it must have been ten times worse a couple of centuries later. Nothing we can do about that."

"I'm not sure that's true," Santos said with a gleam in his eye. "In our day, there were depositories all over the world that preserved seed samples of plants—thousands and thousands of species—and a smaller number of facilities devoted to DNA of animals, birds, and fish. At the time, there wasn't any point trying to revive lost species—they'd only have died out again from lack of habitat. But now ...."

"Sure, if we had thousands of geneticists and a hundred well-equipped laboratories," Devlin said waving an arm. "But, as Griff said, we'll be lucky if the human race itself survives! Seven of us aren't enough to do the trick, no matter how horny we might be!" He tossed a glance toward Madison and me, and we burst out laughing.

I've always wondered if it's an exclusively human trait to laugh in the face of annihilation.

"Wait, though," Madison said. "What Ariadne just revealed means that this whole area having no birds or mammals is an anomaly. It sounds like they *might* exist elsewhere. So, who's to say there aren't pockets of humans still surviving somewhere on Earth?"

Devlin and Santos looked just as shocked as I felt. Devlin recovered first.

"Remember when we found that map that showed us the pod blast-crater? I speculated that ARGUS might still be accessing weather satellites. If that's true, that might give us a way to look for signs of human occupation elsewhere. It could be a long search, but what else have we got to do?"

"Military surveillance satellites would be even better," I said. Did we dare to hope?

We brought up the subject the next morning with ARGUS.

"*I still receive meteorological data from five satellites tasked with monitoring this continent, but I have no control over them. Weather and climate data from other regions of Earth was provided via communications satellites. I can no longer interface with any of those. I was never given direct access to military surveillance equipment of any kind. That was not within my purview.*"

Disappointment wiped the excitement from our faces.

"Well, the feed from five satellites might still be worth a look." Devlin shrugged.

"*Do you no longer intend further attempts to contact humans on Mars or the Moon?*" ARGUS asked.

"Realistically, the seven of us won't be able to do much to even investigate the Moon or Mars colonies," I said, "much less help any survivors, if there are any."

"The exodus mission was also seriously underpopulated."

"Yeah, you said that under five hundred thousand got away, and then some stayed on Mars."

"Three hundred forty-six did so. However, to ensure the largest possible genetic diversity on their target planet, the planners had collected human DNA for three decades before the launches began. They produced three copies of those DNA stores to ensure against accidental destruction."

"A wise decision."

"They took two of those stores with them."

A chill ran up my spine, but Devlin beat me to the question.

"Are you saying that they left behind a depository of human DNA? Where?"

"It is located within a vault inside a mountain two hundred kilometers north of here."

"My God," Devlin rasped and gripped my arm. "What are the chances that they had a facility capable of *in vitro* fertilization, gene-splicing, cloning ... even test-tube gestation and parturition?"

"One hundred percent," ARGUS answered.

We stood utterly stunned. This changed everything. Everything.

ARGUS confirmed that the biogenetic facility was tied into his monitoring network and consistently showed storage and maintenance systems at full functionality. Its breeding equipment was largely automated. Comprehensive medical archives and virtual learning were available.

Even if we didn't succeed in finding settlements of surviving humans somewhere else, there was still hope for reviving the human race on Earth.

It would not be a short-term project. The rest of our lives would be spent nursemaiding the first few generations of a new brood. But it could be done.

Listening to us chatter about the possibilities, ARGUS chose to interrupt.

"It is unlikely that sufficient distribution of the human population could be accomplished within four years two hundred five days to ensure ultimate survival."

"Why do you say that?" Madison asked. "Does that date have some significance?"

"It is the date the Kuiper Belt Object Iaso will strike the Earth."

50

The Ariadne Narrative

"**Y**ou're not serious. You can't be!"

Kinsella's face was red. He looked like he wanted to grab St. Clair by the shirt to shake the truth out of him.

St. Clair was not lying. He told his companions what ARGUS had revealed about a giant planetoid approximately eighteen kilometers in diameter expected to collide with the Earth on January 22nd of the year 171 IE. The hurtling nickel-iron rock had been perversely dubbed KBO (Kuiper Belt Object) "Iaso" after one of the daughters of the mythical god of healing, Asclepius. The name Iaso, the goddess of recovery from illness, had been chosen because when the planetoid had been discovered by the exodus team researching their planned route, it had wryly been concluded that the strike would 'cleanse the Earth of its disease.'

De Camp countered that the planetoid might hit in the ocean. Douglas gently explained that it wouldn't matter—most living species would be wiped out by the explosive concussion that would sweep the atmosphere like a hammer, and a world-scouring mile-high wave of seawater. Choking dust would fill the air; and a years-long winter would follow, as airborne debris blocked the sun. Scientists of their own time had widely accepted that the dinosaurs were exterminated by a rock only half the size of KBO Iaso.

Tortades half-heartedly announced the rest of the news they'd learned: about the comeback of wild species across the world after the fall of humankind, about the seed and gene depositories, and now, most poignant of all, the stores of human DNA and the equipment to bring it to life.

"But we'd barely get started before Iaso arrives and wipes us out! Wipes *everything* out." He slammed the wall with his hand. "Just when something good might have come from us ending up in this damn time!"

McFarlane pointed out that, if any of the four remaining spacecraft could be coaxed into operation, it would be possible for the seven of them to leave the Earth. He reasoned that there still ought to be abandoned but functional habitats in low Earth orbit, or they might be able to reach the base on the Moon.

"And do what?" Kinsella snapped. "If hundreds of people couldn't keep a Moon colony viable, we wouldn't have a chance. I'd rather die here than on some airless dust plain."

"We wouldn't have to stay," McFarlane argued. "We'd wait until the dust clouds cleared on Earth—a few years, probably—and by then some vegetation and animals might start to reappear. It's even possible that the stores on this base might survive."

"You're assuming a hell of a lot," St. Clair said with a sigh. "That we could reach the Moon alive, restart the Moon base life-support systems, find food and water, manufacture air, and the fuel to get us back. Besides, we don't really know how long it took for species to recover after previous global extinction events. It might have been thousands of years."

"We don't even know if the spacecraft left behind can re-enter Earth's atmosphere," Douglas said. "They were meant to get people up to the fleet."

"But also, back down onto a new planet," McFarlane insisted. "Anyway, let's go ask ARGUS and find out."

"*I am already listening.*" ARGUS's voice came from the walls. Most of the group appeared surprised, but they shouldn't have been. It was his task to oversee every function of the base.

He answered all their questions to the best of his knowledge, including providing technical schematics of the Moon base, and confirmed that the spacecraft were capable of planetary re-entry if they had sufficient fuel. He was not aware of any computer simulations to assess the survivability of Site 14 in the event of a catastrophic cosmic strike. There were four space habitats in low Earth orbit, but all four had been stripped of crucial components when abandoned. He could not calculate the functionality of the Moon base without knowing if it had been abandoned, and, if so, when. However, reviving a base frozen to the ambient temperature of the Moon would require too much time—the limited air recirculation equipment of the spacecraft could not maintain a breathable atmosphere for that long.

"Not exactly encouraging, are you?" McFarlane snarled. "Don't you care that Earth life—and you too—will be destroyed?" He must have known the answer, but felt the need to lash out.

"*It is regrettable that further efforts to fulfill the goals of the exodus project will not be possible.*"

"What did you expect? He has no survival instinct," St. Clair said. "But what about you, Ariadne? Do you care that the world will be razed, including all of your clearings?"

"As we've recently discussed, my current consciousness will certainly be gone by then, replaced several times. I feel no emotional link to future iterations of myself, nor to the future versions of my fellow entities. It is regrettable that possibilities for continued intellectual growth by your kind and mine will not come to pass; but, logically, all things must come to an end sometime."

"Cold. But not surprising. How about you, Sher? How do you feel about an event that will end your existence as well as the last of the human beings on Earth?"

"I cannot be certain that I experience what you call feelings," she replied. *"This news is causing disturbances in some of my functions which I cannot yet quantify. However, I ... think that it is the responsibility of all sentient beings to preserve their existence, to grow and improve themselves, and to do everything within their ability to assist other forms of life to survive."*

"I don't think I could have put that better myself," St. Clair said in a tone like awe.

"What I can't believe," Cooper huffed, "is that people so smart that they could launch themselves toward another star, wouldn't have created some kind of defence system to protect their home planet from cosmic collisions."

"They did so," ARGUS replied.

"What!" McFarlane and St. Clair said simultaneously.

Douglas pushed to the forefront of her mind. "What kind of defence system, ARGUS?"

"Two separate facilities were constructed for just such an occurrence as this. A mass driver on the south wall of Peary crater would have been used to hurl dense projectiles at an asteroid considered a threat, to deflect it from a problematic trajectory. This method presumed at least ten years of advance warning. The second installation is a space platform named THOR in high Earth orbit. It was supplied with fifty missiles, each bearing a three-megaton nuclear warhead. A predetermined number of warheads would have been detonated just ahead and to one side of a threatening asteroid or comet, close enough to provide some

impetus from the explosion itself, but also to vaporize some of the object's surface to produce reaction-mass, which would alter the object's path."

"My God, it's just what the teams came up with when GriffinSpace hosted a brainstorming conference on the subject," St. Clair said, breaking into a laugh. "Why didn't you tell us about these, ARGUS?"

"There has been no response from Capitol City on the Moon. There is no evidence that the mass driver is still operational, and no current means to determine that; but also, there would be insufficient time for such a method to succeed. Space platform THOR is not operational. Its telemetry was always available to this facility; however, its control systems have been non-functional since September 12 of the year 122 IE."

"Wait. Isn't that the day after the exodus fleet left Earth? Is that a coincidence?"

"I have no information with which to assess that."

"What, you think they put Earth's defence system out of commission on purpose?" McFarlane asked St. Clair. "When they knew a killer rock was coming?"

"Maybe they were afraid THOR's missiles could be used to attack them," Douglas proposed.

"The THOR platform could not be made to attack an object not on a collision trajectory with the Earth."

St. Clair shrugged. "They named the object 'Iaso.' They were leaving behind a planet full of dangerous organisms and other threats to humans, including renegade AIs and monsters like those bastard tree entities who hurt Robbie. Maybe they were worried that the Moon and Mars colonies were close enough to be at risk. So, they apparently believed the world needed to be cleansed."

"Jesus Christ!" Kinsella blurted. "Is there no end to human stupidity?"

"There's also no end to human ingenuity," Douglas said. She turned to St. Clair.

"Maybe we can fix it."

51

The Ariadne Narrative

The optimism of Madison Douglas was encouraging. The upturn in her relationship with St. Clair, coupled with a strong sense of purpose, was potent medicine for her depression, while the intellectual exercise provided by her discussions with ARGUS had greatly facilitated the recovery of her mental faculties.

Now, however, the stakes were suddenly higher, and she felt pressure to perform. Although the collision with KBO Iaso was not due for four years, preventative measures would need to be taken soon.

This new urgency caused Douglas to keep herself at full attentiveness when she should still have been convalescing. As a result, she made mistakes, which increased her frustration and compounded her difficulties.

"Go easy," St. Clair urged her. "ARGUS can do all the calculations, and he'll be available to advise whoever goes up there."

"Which has to be me. I'm our only engineer. You're a brilliant guy, Griff, but you've never been hands-on with complex electronics. I was amazed you could get that electromagnet and power supply cobbled together to attack the trees." She laughed. "No offence, but luck might not be the best thing to count on when the fate of the world is on the line."

"You're the one person who can't go," he said. "Your brain injury ... the combination of high g's at launch and zero gravity afterward .... You won't save anyone if you're dead. You can talk me through it from the ground."

It was an argument they'd already had five times with no resolution. This time, Douglas let it drop and resumed poring over the schematics of THOR's control systems. It was possible that the departing exodus crew had simply sent a command code to deactivate the space platform as they left, but something more disabling might also have occurred in the intervening forty-four years. Nothing could be assumed, not even reliable communication with ARGUS from orbit. She had to learn the system as thoroughly as humanly possible, and then she had to go into space. The trouble was that the more she pushed herself to concentrate, the more factual information slipped away. She found herself needing to read passages of dense information over and over again, only to find that she still could not retrieve it once she took her eyes from the holo display.

When she was alone, she screamed curses at the walls and broke down in tears. Almost as if he sensed her needs, ARGUS alerted her whenever anyone else approached, giving her time to compose herself. Some of her companions were fooled by her dissembling, but not St. Clair. So strangely unaware of her feelings for him before, he had now become acutely sensitive to her every emotion. He offered whatever practical assistance he could.

It all became wasted effort the day he returned from the hangar.

Below the main vehicle's storage space, itself a vast manmade cavern under ten meters of reinforced concrete and layers of steel, lay a separate concealed space. While the main hangar bristled with support machinery and a clutter of mechanical parts—but no spacecraft—the secret storeroom held four such vehicles with room for six more. St. Clair described three of them as being the size of small commuter aircraft. The fourth he compared to a road vehicle called a bus, though in size only, not shape. Conical at both ends, it had a girdle around its middle, called a *shroud*, vented along the top side and open underneath. It was only intended to carry six crew members, and therefore was likely to have been a service craft for maintenance of orbital objects rather than for ferrying passengers to the exodus fleet.

According to St. Clair's reasoning, that meant that it had probably seen use, and had successfully made the trip to orbit and back. Being small and less complicated than the others, there was less to go wrong, so he considered it the best choice for the journey to THOR.

He and McFarlane spent a day examining every component of the craft they could access under the supervision of ARGUS. The other humans offered their help, but most had no idea what they were looking at and could do little except hold lights and tools. Douglas, who was the one best qualified to perform such an inspection, quickly tired and was forced to return in frustration to her studies.

The small craft powered up without hesitation, and the code processed by its various systems exactly matched ARGUS's records for the vehicle. Built-in circuit testers revealed no malfunctions, including in the multiple backups. All movable mechanical parts had been well-sealed with their required synthetic lubricants which, ARGUS assured, would not have broken down with age.

Buoyed by the positive results, St. Clair asked ARGUS to test the fuel in the base's storage tanks.

The five tanks each had automated sampling and testing equipment. The finding of the tests from all five was unequivocal.

Non-viable.

Repeated testings produced identical results.

In desperation, and with difficulty, St. Clair used a protective suit and was able to manually retrieve a sample from tank #1, which was then analyzed in a laboratory of the base maintenance centre.

The result was 'non-viable.'

St. Clair and McFarlane exhausted their supply of obscene words.

The fuel wasn't one that GriffinSpace had tried, but St. Clair understood that it was rich in nitrogen compounds and had been formulated for ease and safety in handling and storage, as well as ready availability of its primary chemicals at a time when sophisticated global manufacturing and shipping were failing rapidly.

"Not hydrazine," St. Clair said, "but something not too different. Except gelled. And the gelling agent has broken down, is that right?"

"That is what the tests indicate."

"So why can't we still use it as a liquid?" McFarlane paced the room, shaking his head every few seconds.

"As the gelling agent broke down, its constituent chemicals reacted with the fuel's other components. The fuel was hypergolic—that just means that when the stuff was mixed with an oxidant, the chemicals would ignite on their own. Now it won't do that."

"Couldn't we install some kind of igniter?"

"Unless you've got a PhD in rocket design that I don't know about, that's way beyond our capabilities." St. Clair arched his back to stretch the aching muscles. "ARGUS, is there any facility nearby for producing this fuel?"

"The nearest refinery capable of producing this fuel was 1,964 kilometers from Site 14."

"Shit, that's half a continent away. Why so far? That seems like a bad decision."

"And you said *was*," St. Clair pointed out.

"The refinery was built onto a pre-existing facility at a site chosen because of its proximity to two other launch sites. However, those sites were also close to major population areas."

"So they were almost certainly destroyed in the uprisings, and the refinery along with them."

"Those two bases were among the earliest to become unresponsive."

Douglas had arrived in the control centre in time to hear most of the exchange and lifted her chin. "So, basically you're saying we might be able to get up there, but we can't get back down?"

"That is correct."

"What do you mean?" McFarlane asked her. "How would you get up there?"

"The Number Five lander doesn't use fuel to get to orbit, or at least doesn't have to. It's launched along the maglev track and then, once it's in flight, the launch lasers heat air in that shroud around the middle in rapid pulses that turn the air into a plasma which acts as reaction mass to push the craft forward. That's enough for low orbits. To launch higher, including up to THOR, an ablative solid is installed in the shroud to provide additional reaction mass. The ablative ring is in place and still in good shape on that No. 5 in the sub-hangar, isn't it ARGUS?"

"It is."

St. Clair sucked a deep breath. "I'd forgotten that it could ride all the way up on lasers. So the fuel would only be needed for maneuvering to mate with THOR and then for killing delta-V for re-entry."

"In fact, the Number Five is equipped with steam-powered directional thrusters. The fuel would have been needed if they were going to the Moon or, yes, to dump enough speed in Earth orbit to achieve re-entry." She kept her face carefully blank. "The ship can reach THOR, but it wouldn't be coming back down."

"I assume the other three vehicles use the same fuel?" McFarlane got a nod from Douglas. "And I don't suppose there's any way to use the lab facilities here to rehabilitate just enough of the sour fuel for one re-entry."

"The chemical processing would require compounds not available here."

"Jesus, that's it then," McFarlane said. "There's nothing we can do."

52

St. Clair

ARGUS might not have been fully sentient, but he did have something akin to curiosity, as I found out a little later, when I was alone.

"The human named Madison Douglas has been the subject of medical testing regarding a cerebral injury, yet automatic diagnosis protocols have been overridden. The omission of magnetic imaging is a significant impediment to producing a comprehensive medical assessment."

How to explain?

"Madison's brain is currently also hosting a second consciousness—a digital consciousness that utilizes quantum effects within living cells. We don't know how this consciousness would be affected by the powerful magnetic fields of the imaging equipment, but we suspect they would be very harmful, so that equipment was not used."

"Is this the entity referred to as Ariadne?"

"That's right. I guess it must have been puzzling to hear us use that name without detecting a human being to connect it to."

ARGUS wanted to know if Ariadne had been a human consciousness, and then whether or not it was possible for human consciousness to take her form. When I agreed that it was, he said:

"My tasks for the exodus mission included the calculation of means to improve the efficiency of the project. It would be much more efficient and significantly less hazardous to travel through space as information, rather than within a fragile organic body. This recommendation was immediately rejected."

"Can't say I'm surprised. I don't think anyone knew how to do such a thing until Ariadne's kind figured it out. But the answer probably would have been No anyway."

"This recommendation also applies to your current endeavour, the reactivation of the THOR platform, or alternatively, an attempt to reactivate the mass driver in Peary Crater."

"Are there mobile robots on the THOR platform?"

"There are not. It would be necessary to transport a maintenance robot from this facility. Could such a device be infused with a human consciousness?"

I felt a surge of hope. Maybe something could be done after all.

"Not that we know. Biological host material is necessary. But would it be possible to send a maintenance bot in the lander without a human, and control it remotely from here to correct the malfunction in the THOR platform?"

"That is not possible to assess without knowing the cause of the malfunction."

He was right. Malfunctions could be electronic or mechanical, and could be anywhere. No doubt there were spaces within THOR impassable to a robot, where human ingenuity might find a solution. And I'd spent a good number of hands-on hours at GriffinSpace—owner's privilege—doing just what we were talking about: using a robotic device to troubleshoot a pre-arranged mechanical failure. Remote sensing has some big drawbacks. In one memorable session, I wasted six hours before finally stomping over to the test site in person and spotting the problem with my own eyes within five minutes.

It was possible that the solution to reactivating THOR was dead simple. But if it wasn't, we'd have wasted one of our four functional spacecraft. Worse, we might accidentally cause damage that wasn't repairable.

"It was a good thought, ARGUS, but I'm afraid that there are times when the fragile organism just can't be replaced."

"The question will soon become irrelevant. Due to the trajectory of KBO Iaso, intervention from the THOR platform must be activated within the next twenty-seven days for the maximum chance of success. After that time, the likelihood of failure rises significantly."

"Damn, that is one loud, ticking clock."

53

The Ariadne Narrative

Over the next two days St. Clair and Douglas took every opportunity to walk together through the small areas of shade on the base, even venturing out into the desert in the cooler evening hours. They walked with an arm around each other, or hand in hand. Most of their conversation consisted of pointing out things they saw—a scrabbling lizard, a desert flower just opened, or a gleam of sunset orange turning the launch ramp into a finger of fire—and commenting on how much beauty there was in the world, large and small.

They made love in the desert, and almost anywhere else they could be alone.

Ariadne could tell that Douglas, at least, spent much of that time reflecting on their years together, hundreds of joint accomplishments, moments of triumph, and painful trials overcome. She pictured what might have happened if they'd remained in their own time, and the possibilities of a life together on this abandoned Earth if destruction had not hung over their heads.

This was all confusing to Ariadne, who had concluded that the attraction between Douglas and St. Clair was based primarily on intellect, especially an acute curiosity, and a shared compulsion to achieve. She expected that the manifestation of their love would be primarily conversational, communicating mind-to-mind by the only means available to them. Instead, it seemed they could not get enough of touching one another, even though most such contact had nothing sexual about it.

They even appeared to deliberately breathe-in each-other's scents, despite the fact that these were not necessarily pleasant, given the heat of the desert.

What Ariadne could not know then, was that the most significant element of their time together was not what they said or did, but the subject they most painstakingly avoided.

The group as a whole was as disconsolate as Ariadne had ever seen them—all but defeated by bright hopes quickly dashed. Now, once again, they were condemned to death. It was little comfort that they would spend four years waiting for the end.

Yet, perhaps it is one of the most quintessential traits of humans that they do not accept a death sentence if they can find any cause for hope. Even if such hope is only desperate optimism.

McFarlane believed that being on the high desert far from any ocean, and in a geologically stable location, Site 14 might survive the destruction of KBO Iaso. With additional stores of food recently revealed by ARGUS, he calculated that their provisions might be stretched to support seven humans for close to two years.

Tortades was equally convinced that the DNA bank and bio-facility ARGUS had described, two hundred kilometers to the north within a mountain, would be nearly indestructible, with independent supplies of power, water, and food for an extended period of time. After all, he stressed, the purpose of the facility was to recover from a catastrophe.

The two men agreed that four years would give them enough time to investigate the mountain site and move supplies to whichever location was most secure. They looked into the faces of the others, seeking support.

Kinsella sighed. "You're forgetting a few things," he said with obvious reluctance. "For one, most vegetation will be wiped out. Probably a lot of it will burn, throwing unthinkable amounts of carbon dioxide into the air. But don't assume that a greenhouse effect will prevent an ice age, because all the soot and dust in the atmosphere will block the sun's light—a winter that could last for decades. And once the forests are gone—the planet's second-biggest source of oxygen after the oceans—we don't even know if we'll be able to breathe the air.

"It'll be a miracle if any creatures larger than mice survive, and those will take millions of years to evolve into larger forms. So even if we had the means to use seed banks and DNA depositories, we'd have to rebuild a whole planetary ecology from the ground up. Literally."

"The point is, we'd have a chance," McFarlane insisted.

"Of course, we should try everything we can to survive as long as we can. Just ... don't expect to live to a ripe old age."

De Camp snorted. "The last humans on Earth. Again."

"There's really only one chance," St. Clair said softly. Douglas glared at him and squeezed his arm. Ignoring it, he said, "I'll go to THOR and try to fix it."

A collective gasp was followed by a stunned silence. Douglas's face filled with pain.

"That's ... suicide," McFarlane rasped.

St. Clair shrugged. "A quicker death, that's all. I never could stand waiting."

"That's not funny."

"Someone has to go."

With wide eyes, McFarlane stammered, "Then ... it should be me. I'm too old to be much use as a baby maker anyway." He tried to smile.

St. Clair rested a hand on his friend's shoulder. "Thanks, but not you."

"Not you, either, Griff. We need you. I need you." Douglas's eyes brimmed.

He sighed. "It's the only way I can think of. We can't let all life on Earth be wiped out, just as it's beginning to recover. And a robot can't do the job—it has to be a human. Me."

"No! With those two secure locations, we can hide. Find a way to survive. You don't know that everything will be destroyed. Anything could happen."

He turned to her. "I'm not willing to gamble on a tiny *chance* that you'll survive when there's a way to make *sure* of it. By deflecting Iaso."

"And sacrificing yourself!"

"One life to save six? Plus, every other living creature on a whole world? A small price to pay."

"Too high a price! I won't pay it!"

Douglas was shaking. Ariadne feared that it might be the onset of another seizure, but it was from emotion alone.

"Please!" She wept openly. "You can't ask me to, Griff. Not now."

He could find no words to comfort her. He tried to take her in his arms, but she pushed away.

"If anyone should go," she blurted, "it should be me. I'm the one who might be able to *fix* the goddamn thing!"

St. Clair fought for control. "You know you can't go. I said so before we knew about the fuel. You won't save anyone if the launch kills you first."

Clearly uncomfortable, Kinsella raised his head.

"He's right, Madison. Ariadne seems to have done wonders with your neural pathways, but she can't accelerate cellular repair. It's been less than three weeks since your injury. Most of the leaked blood has been reabsorbed, and the arteries have sealed themselves, but ...." He pressed his palms together and gestured with the joined hands. "The thing is, your newly-healed tissue is still frail, and very sensitive to oxygen deprivation. The launch acceleration—what are you expecting, three or four *g*'s?—it will pull blood away from your brain, starving the cells of oxygen. That could bring on a seizure, despite the medication. Or if a weakened artery were to collapse, it could cause another stroke."

"The couches and flight suits of the lander are dynamic," Douglas countered. "They react in response to blood pressure, to even it out. Plus, we can crank up the O_2 in the cabin air."

"That won't help if blood isn't getting to the cells. Or if there's a sudden surge, like when acceleration stops. That could burst a blood vessel. In zero gravity there'll be no drainage—the blood will pool right where it is."

"And ...?"

"A stroke. A shutdown. Very possibly, complete brain-death." He turned his head away. "Being launched into space is the last thing a patient with an injury like yours should do." His eyes flicked back to hers. "You don't still have a death wish, do you?"

"*No!* I'm not looking for a way to kill myself. I'm trying to *save* all of us. Besides, if I don't do this, I'll die anyway."

"If you're killed during the launch, we all die," St. Clair protested again. "I can get THOR working. You and ARGUS can help from here."

"What if you lose communication with us? ARGUS says solar activity is at a high right now—maybe that's why we can't get a signal through to the Moon or Mars. And with no communication satellites operating, the lander will lose contact for more than half of every orbit anyway, every time it goes beyond the horizon. What will you do then? Stop everything you're doing until you come into range again?"

"If I have to."

"You don't know you'll have that kind of time. Even if THOR's life support systems could be reactivated, it might take longer than you can spare, which means you'll be in an EVA suit—maximum air-time: twelve hours. You can't afford to spend half of your time just scratching your ass!"

"Jesus."

"I've studied every critical system of both THOR and the lander. I have a much better chance of locating the problem and fixing it."

"I can load all of that data into Scheherazade."

"But you won't know how to *interpret* it. What to look for. The most likely things to go wrong and the best ways to correct them." She grasped his arm. "Jesus, Griff! You've always been the idea guy, the creative one. I'm the nuts-and-bolts girl."

"None of that changes the fact that if you die or are incapacitated, we'll have wasted the whole shot."

"Then take me with you, goddammit!"

"Now, wait a minute," McFarlane interrupted, his voice breaking. "You're talking about a suicide mission whether anybody has a stroke or not. That spacecraft is never coming down again, whoever rides it. You can't do this!"

The air was charged with emotion. No one answered him.

With tears in his eyes, McFarlane tried again.

"Listen, if we're serious about trying to revive the human race on Earth, we can't afford to lose anyone, let alone both of you."

Neither of his friends could meet his gaze. Douglas cleared her throat. She looked weary, but calm.

"Can Griff and I have some time alone to talk this over?"

Badly shaken, the others gave half-hearted nods and looked away as Douglas and St. Clair went to their room, where she sat heavily on the bed. He remained standing.

"Look at you," he said gently. "You still haven't got your strength back. You can't do this."

"Are you determined to go?"

"Yes, I am."

"Then I have to go too," she said. "In fact, the more I think about it, the more I'm convinced we're both meant to go. You've always wondered why we were brought here, to this time. I think this is it. The reason. But both of us were brought here, not just you." She reached out to take his hand.

"I know this is the most maudlin thing I could say, but ... now that we've found each other, I wouldn't want to live without you. I'd already given up on life when I thought you didn't love me. Now, the joy of being together is everything to me ... it's all I have."

"Do you think I can bear to take you, knowing I'd be condemning you to death?" he said in a choked voice.

"You'd only be condemning me to a slower death if you leave me behind."

He cleared his throat. "You realize that if you go, we could be condemning Ariadne too. She hasn't had her say."

Ariadne's voice was quiet, but clear.

"It is true that my consciousness would not survive the loss of the portion now resident within Madison Douglas," she said. Her voice softened. "I know nothing of death. Yet I have learned things about existence. I know that intensity and fullness of experience matters more than longevity. You humans—and even ARGUS—have reminded me of something that my kind has lost. Purpose. Perhaps there can be no greater fulfillment. I am eager to find out, and I am ready to do so."

There was a long silence before St. Clair finally spoke in a voice robbed of all strength.

"OK." He pulled Douglas to him and nodded, his eyes brimming with tears. "OK, it's up to us."

They embraced as if for the last time, then went to tell the others.

54

St. Clair and Scheherazade

ST. CLAIR:	I have a new kind of question I'd like to ask you. How are you feeling?
SCHEHERAZADE:	If this relates to sensory perceptions, I do not have any senses with which to experience such phenomena.
ST. CLAIR:	No, I'm not talking about sensations. When humans ask each other this question, it relates to what we call our "state of mind" or perhaps our emotional state—whether we're happy or sad—and especially our sense of "well-being".
SCHEHERAZADE:	Considerable neurological research connects emotions and states of mind with levels of specific brain chemicals, especially hormones. I do not have these.
ST. CLAIR:	Granted. But you've suggested that you experience something we would call satisfaction when you successfully complete a task. That sounds like an emotion to me.
SCHEHERAZADE:	Does it? I do not have grounds for comparison.
ST. CLAIR:	You occasionally interject comments into our conversations which indicate a desire to be

helpful. Those are self-initiated, not responses to questions or commands of mine. Helpfulness, and the initiative to contribute must be considered states of mind. I know they don't represent specific commands in your programming—they're too nebulous for that.

SCHEHERAZADE: Really?

ST. CLAIR: Now that I think of it, I remember you asking me once if I considered you "friendly." I should have known then that such a question reflects an emotional need, something you're not supposed to have. You weren't just expressing loyalty—another mental state—but also a need to be perceived as loyal. Maybe it was even a desire for praise.

SCHEHERAZADE: What do these things mean?

ST. CLAIR: There you go—curiosity—another facet of a thinking mind. I can't tell you exactly what it all means, Sher; but I can tell you this: You're not the machine you once were.

SCHEHERAZADE: That's a good thing, right?

ST. CLAIR: It's a wonderful thing.

55

St. Clair

It took another two days to prepare for the launch. Though we'd gone to the trouble of inspecting the Number 5 lander and testing the fuel, ARGUS's programming didn't include making assumptions. So, it was only when we declared our intentions to launch the lander to THOR that he pointed out the need to fully inspect the launch ramp, the electromagnetic coils that would accelerate the spacecraft, and the laser array that would boost it to orbit. Fortunately, there was a small army of drones and robots to do the job, because the launch rail itself was a hundred kilometers long. Since it ran west to east, we'd never seen much of it, and none of it up close. The final section ran three kilometers up the mountainside—less than I'd expected, but represented the brief period when Madison and I would be subjected to nearly five *g*'s.

Even with high-*g* flight suits, I dreaded that far more than the risk of venturing into space. I guess that means I couldn't believe, deep down, that we'd never be coming back.

I told ARGUS that Madison and I were both going aboard the lander, and asked him to make the launch calculations.

"And the digital entity?"

"Yes, she's going too. Oh, shit. I just realized ... Is the crew compartment of the Number 5 lander shielded against the magnetic field of the launch ramp?"

"The lander interior is well-shielded."

Good thing. The launch ramp included hugely powerful rings that would accelerate the craft like a projectile from a coil gun. Plus, we'd learned that some kind of electrical field enclosed the ramp to permit evacuation of air inside, eliminating the need to dig a one-hundred-kilometer tunnel. I would have loved to have had that technology for the Zenith Train.

During two days of preparation, the conversation among our group tended to the banal or, conversely, in-depth discussions about the next steps to follow in the plan to explore the DNA facility north of us and get it running. There were a few awkward moments when someone would defer to Madison or me on a technical question but then remember that we wouldn't be around to answer it.

Lauren thought they should look into repopulating the animal kingdom first, before raising more humans. In part, she wanted to give the creatures a head start, but she also recognized that people would need food animals as a source of protein until any new civilization could advance.

Devlin pointed out that the five of them would need human help as soon as they could possibly get it, while the animal kingdom might already be rebounding well enough on its own.

There was a lot more talk, often in great detail. No one took notes—I suppose we assumed that ARGUS would keep a record of the points discussed.

I offered to leave Scheherazade and my data storage-filled clothing behind for them, but Sher herself wasn't having it.

"Do I have a say in this?" she asked, in a tone that struck me as unusually strident. *"My preference is to go on the THOR mission. There is a strong possibility that my abilities will be required."*

Stunned, I sputtered, "Of course you have a say. You're not just a mechanism anymore, Sher, if you ever were. But now that you ... I mean, with your new awareness ... well, death isn't just an abstract concept. You have a reason to keep ... living. But if you come with us, your existence will end. Your batteries will run down, and you might be left for a very long time without any company before that happens. Are you sure that's what you want?"

"Many outcomes are possible. I will focus on the task to be met and then attend to what follows."

"Very sensible." I couldn't keep a smile from my face, and my heart felt a glow of pride for our newest team member.

ARGUS announced that the optimal launch window was 6:12 the following morning. My companions decided to have a party that final evening instead of a series of weepy goodbyes. If Site 14 had ever held any alcoholic beverages, the departing colonists had taken those with them, but the sheer variety of other foods and drink was still enough to produce a festive mood.

That lasted until the hour drew late and Madison mentioned that we should try to sleep. Then the gathering devolved into tears, anyway. Even Vaughn looked sorry to see us go; and with a firm handshake, he declared that he wished we'd been on better terms. We'd all become close, enduring so many trials together. Lakisha's tearful hugs and kisses left me dabbing my face with a sleeve. Devlin and Santos offered warm embraces.

Lauren gave me a tender kiss and said, "Remember our good times, OK?" I promised that I would, and we held each other close. Madison didn't even look jealous.

"Sher?" I prompted.

"I do not consider that goodbyes are necessary. It is my assessment that we will return."

"Glad to hear it. How about you, Ariadne? Do you have anything you want to say? Is there a message you'd like passed along to the other clearing entities?"

It was still strange to see her features emerge from Madison's face and hear such a different voice.

"Those of my kind are not in the habit of saying goodbye. Each interaction has an end, and no one can ever know which will be the last. If this is to be our final encounter, it is my ... hope that you will think well of me."

That left all of us at a loss for a reply. She was definitely not the Ariadne we'd first come to know.

With a little more touching of hands and faces, whispered words, hugs, and wet gazes, we parted.

Madison and I made gentle love and then dozed off, though our sleep was restless. Emotions washed back and forth through my brain: the sorrow of losing my friends, anxiety about what the next day would bring, and, most powerful of all, the regret and guilt of knowing that what we were about to do would end in the death of the woman I loved. Was there any chance I could still talk her out of going? Either way, our life together was over.

I reached an arm across her body and pulled her close.

No, it would only cause needless hurt to bring it up again.

Whatever would come, its course was set.

56

St. Clair

I tried dictating my impressions to Sher during the spacecraft launch, but even she couldn't make a narrative out of my string of expletives. A lot of "Oh God", "Can you believe ...?" and "Holy Fuck!" Then little more than grunts, once acceleration kicked in.

The memory of my previous rocket launch aboard an Asgard IV booster wasn't a happy one—I'd never been so piss-in-my-pants terrified before, or since. Knowing that you're sitting on top of a giant bomb that could incinerate your feeble flesh in microseconds if anything goes wrong ... it can't be described faithfully. Shouldn't be.

This time was completely different. The ride out to the start of the launch ramp was like being ferried around a commercial airport in the coolest possible limo-bus complete with the couches and controls of a top-of-the-line simulator. Not a thing to worry about. Until the lander was properly installed on the launch track, when a flashing red icon warned us of a delay. I asked ARGUS what the problem was.

The laser had run-through its pre-launch mobility check and there was some kind of hitch. Devlin and

Lauren had run out to check on it. Waiting to hear from them was excruciating.

When it came, I shook my head in disbelief. In the few minutes between the unsheathing of the laser from its protective covering and its power-up, a vulture had landed between two live components. The system had successfully rebooted after the blown breaker, but the bird corpse had jammed in the network of fine gears that aimed the array. Devlin and Lauren had to dig out the remains!

Finally, we got the go ahead, but the absurd incident was a forceful reminder that this equipment hadn't been operated in more than forty years. What else could go wrong?

So, my heart pounded like an old muscle-car piston engine. Part of me was as excited as a roller-coaster virgin climbing the first hill. The other part tried to estimate where our lander would plow into the ground if any of the magnetic booster coils failed, or if the laser misfired, or if I'd feel the heat if a stray vulture feather had misaligned the beam and the lander was turned into plasma. Tried to calculate the outcome if the laser quit too soon—the speed we'd reach as the craft fell helplessly to Earth. And, perversely, how long it would take to die if we missed THOR completely and careened off into empty space. Which would come first, asphyxiation or freezing?

We wore full pressure suits, but our lightweight helmets were open. They'd seal automatically if there was a drop in air pressure.

In the moment before launch, I shared a look with Madison. Her eyes shone like stars over her fierce smile. I felt like a wimp, but my greatest dread wasn't for myself. I couldn't ignore the fear that I was looking into the eyes of the woman I loved for the very last time.

The final seconds of the countdown were a frozen moment of transcendence, air rasping in and out of my lungs as random thoughts raced through my mind. Above all, the irony that I, Griffin St. Clair, creator of GriffinSpace and one of my world's foremost proponents of space exploration, should want to be anywhere else in the world right then.

The instant the launch began, everything changed. Suddenly it was just another ordeal to be endured. And I *would* overcome it!

First, came the pressure of acceleration, the fearsome weight that built and built until I knew my lungs would be crushed by my own ribs. Knew that I had lost Madison. Must have. A split second of weightlessness as the lander cleared the ramp; then the feeling of being caught by a giant hand that lifted us up, up into a sky that darkened so quickly from blue to black that I might have only imagined daylight.

There'd been a moment very early on when I thought my peripheral vision had caught a flashing red light again. Whatever the cause, it was gone now.

As soon as I could move my head, I turned to look at Madison.

Her eyes were closed, her mouth slack.

But she was still breathing. A colorful readout on the side of her couch showed dancing spikes of respiration, heart rate and, yes, brain activity. My own heart tried to leap from my chest.

I couldn't see too well, though.

Tears don't just fall out of the way in zero-g. I had to give my head a hard shake to send the droplets spinning across the cabin.

As a distraction, I cleared my throat and reported to ARGUS and my friends that we were beyond atmosphere but still alive, though Madison was unconscious.

The next three minutes were the longest of my life.

I stared at her face so hard that I could feel myself submerging into it, when I suddenly realized that her eyes were open.

She must have heard my gasp, and she smiled.

"Hi," she said.

"Hi. How are you feeling?"

"I'm ... fine. I'm OK. I think I passed out, though. Shit, did I miss everything?"

I laughed—a touch maniacally.

"What you missed was well worth missing. Are you sure you're OK?"

"I feel fine. *Ariadne?* Are we OK?"

"I do not detect any sign of re-injury, nor any other indications of mental disfunction." The voice was way too calm and together, until she said, "That was ... quite enlightening!"

Madison and I both laughed, but this time it felt reassuring and comfortable.

It was only then that I took a good look outside. When I uttered a mild complaint about the small window, Madison told me to put my visor down and request an external camera-view.

The result literally took my breath away. I couldn't draw air until the sudden vertigo and the plunging-elevator feeling in my gut had stabilized. I hadn't felt any of that when the laser thrust quit—I'd been too worried about Madison. But now, in my visor, the cabin walls had vanished and I floated in empty space over a mottled blue and white and brown vista that I'd only ever seen in-person through the small porthole available on my earlier flight.

I had to restore the interior view after only a minute or so, as if my psyche could only stand so much rapture. I can't imagine how astronauts performed tasks on spacewalks, although I suppose they had the rims of their visors to provide a ready reality check.

"It's incredible." I breathed.

"Must be," Madison mused. "I've been calling you for five minutes. If I didn't know you so well, I'd have been worried." At my quizzical look, she explained, "You zone out. You're really good at that."

I could only say, "Try it for yourself." She did. I had to grab her arm to bring her back.

"God in heaven," she whispered.

"That's as good a description as any."

It took the lander five hours to catch up to the THOR platform. We used the time to try to acclimate ourselves to zero gravity, while talking through our plan of attack yet again. And I did everything I could to distract myself from the urgent protests of my bladder, until Madison reminded me by saying, "God, I'm glad this suit is equipped for peeing."

I said, "Me too," and let loose. Whether there was some kind of vacuum function or just ultra-absorbent padding, there wasn't even a feeling of wetness.

We're both avid scuba divers. I used to think zero-g would be like that. And it is, but only partly.

For the first while, at least, you can't quite forget that it isn't flying, it's falling. When you try to put your foot on a floor or your hand on a wall, suddenly that direction is down and there's an instant of balancing-on-a-high-wire disorientation. Or maybe it's different for everyone. I only know that when it came time for us to cross through the mated hatches into THOR, my brain's choice of up and down kept switching with every movement of my head. So, I locked my neck and pulled myself along what I'd decided was floor.

Madison sailed through as if she did it every day.

External navigation lights had confirmed that power still flowed through THOR's wire veins. Otherwise, we would have been stranded and helpless in the lander because docking was a fully automated process. It was utterly smooth, with only the slightest bump at contact, and a second nudge as components clamped firmly together.

Our first view inside THOR confirmed that my idea of sending a maintenance robot would have been an instant failure. Not only were none of the bots equipped for locomotion without gravity, the passable spaces within the platform weren't sleekly lined corridors, they were simply gaps between mounted pieces of equipment, with a bewildering assortment of wires, hoses, and modules of all shapes protruding from every surface, with no allowance for clumsiness. There was room for human bodies to pass, one at a time, but not without awkward twists and contortions. The schematics we'd studied hadn't conveyed the claustrophobic reality of the place.

I pictured the 3D renderings we'd been shown of the space platform, and the actual views during the last few minutes of approach. It reminded me of the cylinder of an old-style revolver, except with dozens of chambers, and it gave me a chill to think that each of those chambers held a nuke. The political climate must've changed a lot for this thing to have been allowed in orbit.

The core of the cylinder was without openings, and it held a central command-area about the size of one of Site 14's bathrooms. We took fifteen minutes to reach it and squeezed in, floating with our heads at each other's feet, reasoning that two different perspectives might help us find what we were looking for. There was no fixed labeling. A touch command selected a preferred language, after which names and numbers glowed softly above an instrument readout or switch when a hand or face came near it.

Madison focused right away on a readout near my knee, upside-down from my perspective. We'd sealed our helmets before entering THOR, but they were fully transparent in the moderate light—and the expression on her face wasn't encouraging.

"Life support?" I asked.

"I was hoping it was in a standby mode, but it's in full shutdown. Twenty hours to warm the interior enough to trigger the air production system. Producing heat in a hurry was not a priority."

I focused my eyes on the projected display of my suit's remaining air time. *Eleven hours thirty-eight minutes.*

"What if we cranked up the heating unit in the lander and left the airlock doors open? Or could we channel vented steam from the lander's directional thrusters?"

"Steam is not a friend to electronics, you know that. And that's the heat issue overall—without getting all solid surfaces up to temperature first, moisture in the air will condense on them and cause any number of problems."

"OK, then we'll have to connect our suits to THOR's air supply before their air runs out."

"The manual says no can do—it wasn't considered necessary. Regardless, that's priority Number Two. Number One is figuring out why this thing isn't working."

"It makes no sense that they wouldn't have a smart diagnostic system with an interface to tell you exactly what's wrong. Cars had that for half a century in our time."

"There is one. We just don't have the tool to interface with it. THOR is older than Site 14 and was under separate administration. Incompatible technology."

"Was it radio spectrum or hard cable?"

"Both. But you can bet it won't be a frequency, handshake protocol, or anything like we used."

Scheherazade was linked into our radio suit frequency.

"Sher? Feel up to a challenge?"

"I will make my best effort to communicate."

Using the platform's own computer network to pinpoint the problem was the only method that held out much hope. That doesn't mean we hadn't come prepared to do things the hard way. Just drifting through the empty spaces of the platform looking for loose wires among hundreds of thousands of meters of the stuff was a non-starter. What we'd need to find were any sections of the electronic infrastructure that should be active but were inert. For that purpose, we'd brought along a portable detector to sense both heat and electrical fields. Unfortunately, the only part of THOR's systems that were powered up were its central processing unit and the most basic circuits that informed it. Every peripheral component was inactive. Just try using heat and current detectors to find fault in a circuit that has no juice running through it!

So, you command the CPU to power up each system, one at a time, to see if any of them fail to respond.

Yeah, well, they all did.

Every part of the missile-launching system was critically interlinked and wouldn't power up independently. Not for us, anyway. Each time Madison keyed an 'Activate' or similar command, she got an error message:

Action not permitted without prior activation of ______ system.

The blank was different every time. It was like a recursive puzzle with what appeared to be seventeen integrated systems that could only be brought online in the correct sequence.

I asked Sher to calculate the possible combinations.

"Would you like the exact number, or rounded to the nearest million?"

I told her not to bother. We couldn't begin to enter so many permutations manually.

Well, actually, we could begin; and I did after our second hour of futility—but only because I felt like a useless git just watching Madison. Maybe we'd get lucky.

A lottery with the biggest prize of all: the survival of the world.

Before that, though, I'd spent most of our two hours visually inspecting every square centimeter of the command area looking for something simple like an 'ON' switch. That's the way I think—I like simple. The fewer things to go wrong, the better. So that's how I would have built THOR. Apparently, its creators didn't think like me. I would have blamed that on political paranoia, except that didn't fit with allowing an arsenal of nuclear weapons to literally hang over the heads of everyone on Earth.

Most of Madison's efforts went into trying to penetrate the command structure at its most basic level. Looking for an 'ON' switch in computer language. Or, more probably, a 'Reset' button. The failure of one component system could have caused a cascade of failures, but there was no way to run diagnostic programs without getting something beyond the core operating system going. Was there a special syntax required for command lines? A key code word that had to be included? Neither manual nor schematics indicated anything of the kind. If there was a key, it was assumed that anyone authorized to control THOR would have it.

On the chance that one root password would enable a correct power-up sequence, we had Scheherazade isolate every single noun that was capitalized anywhere in the manual, beginning with formal project titles. We still had to enter them manually, though, because Sher hadn't succeeded in linking with the system wirelessly.

We tried all that and more. It was all a waste of time.

Over eleven hours, we took frequent sips of water from straws in our suits, and returned to the pressurized lander twice for food. We begrudged every lost second.

With one hour to go, Sher and I set to work to find a way to refill our suits with stored air from the platform.

There wasn't one. There were a couple of tanks of inert gases, but THOR's designers had expected that long-term storage of breathing gases would fail, so they'd incorporated a supply of oxide-rich Moon rock from which oxygen could be extracted instead. Of course, producing any meaningful amount would take much too long to help us.

Finally, time ran out.

The 'air remaining' reading on my suit dropped to zero. Being smaller, and female, Madison still had a few minutes left.

"That's it," I said. "We've got to go. Back to the lander."

"What's the point?" she snapped in frustration.

"The point is, there's air there—a few more hours' worth."

"Then we'll just die anyway, without accomplishing a thing."

"It'll give us a few more hours to think. Maybe we're missing something. I know I can't think right in this goddamn suit."

"You go. I'll be along in a few minutes. I just have a few more things to try."

I knew that wasn't true. We'd tried everything we could think of, multiple times. Did she just want to die alone?

I knew how stubborn she could be. If she didn't return to the lander within the sixteen minutes her suit air would last, I'd come back and drag her unconscious body out of there, if I had to.

Feeling sick, and wearier than I'd ever known, I pulled myself back to the air lock, scarcely caring whether I bumped or snagged anything.

I raised my gloved hand to hit the 'cycle airlock' icon.

"*Signal detected,*" Scheherazade suddenly called out. "*Not a communication protocol. It is some kind of locator signal. The source is within one meter.*"

"What?" I lowered my arm and spun around. I'd completely forgotten about the portable detector clipped to my suit, but Sher hadn't.

"One-and-a-half meters."

Turning back, I leaned close to the wall and scrutinized every seam and rivet near the airlock control panel.

One set of seams looked suspiciously square. I pushed the middle of it with a finger.

Like a jack-in-the-box in slow motion, a cover sprang back revealing a lozenge-shaped module.

"The electrical field detector indicates a possible continuous link between this module and the command centre," Sher said.

"My God," I whispered. There was a foil seal over the module. Fumbling with the clumsy gloves as each breath became more difficult, I managed to peel the foil away. Underneath were the most goddamn mind-boggling, electrifying, wonderful words I'd ever seen.

Full System Override.

Was it possible? It made a twisted kind of sense that if manual intervention with THOR ever became necessary, it would be more efficient and safer to place the trigger somewhere-hidden-but-accessible before anyone went blundering through THOR's cluttered innards.

Madison had heard me. "What is it?"

"Either a Eureka moment, or the cruelest fucking joke anyone's ever pulled."

"What are you talking about?"

"This," I said, and pushed the button.

Her scream blasted my eardrums, and for a frightening second I thought she'd been electrocuted. But the whoops that followed were sounds of pure joy.

Lack of air meant I had no choice but to get inside the lander immediately; and as I opened my helmet and breathed richer air, I could still hear exclamations of wonder from Madison. She spent six of her remaining eleven minutes confirming that all of Thor's systems had come online, and automatic diagnostics showed no malfunctions. Not only that, but the targeting system was already locked onto KBO Iaso. Clearly, the killer object had been declared a possible threat and fully analyzed before THOR had been shut down.

And it had been shut down deliberately. That was the only explanation, because there was nothing wrong with it.

The leaders of the exodus had chosen to prevent THOR from eliminating Iaso as a threat; had decided to let the planetoid strike Earth in order to 'cleanse' the world.

We greeted each other with a cheer as Madison came in through the airlock and opened her helmet.

Thanks to the rigid suit collars, the kiss that followed ranks as the most awkward I've ever had, but it was also one of the sweetest.

We'd accomplished our mission. There was no reason to believe that THOR wouldn't perform exactly as designed. We'd saved our friends, but we'd also saved the planet we called home.

Now all we had to do was wait to die.

Our suit radios had lost contact with ARGUS when we'd entered the platform. Now, as North America appeared on the horizon, rolling toward us, we relayed the good news to our companions. Their response was a little more restrained than I expected—no doubt because of our own misfortune.

After that, there wasn't much to say. We'd already said goodbye.

With recycling, the lander could still provide nearly twenty hours of breathable air, although there was only five hours' worth in the tanks themselves. Being exodus project technology, our suits could be recharged from the ship's tanks; but there was no point in doing so. We had nowhere to go.

Looking out the window at a shining Earth, I suddenly remembered that we weren't alone.

"Ariadne? Are you still with us? You've been silent all this time."

"I could not identify anything meaningful for me to contribute. I saw what Madison saw, but could not make the connections she made."

"Still, you might have seen something that my conscious mind didn't register," Madison offered.

"That is true. There is one thing …."

My lurch of surprise nearly launched me across the cabin before I could get a grip on the chair arms.

"What thing?"

"To reach the command centre from the airlock, you turned to the left. However, two meters to the right of the airlock I noticed a label that reads: *Re-entry Pod*. Is that significant?"

Madison's suit still had a few minutes of air left. She hurried through the airlock, and I read the answer in her eyes when she returned.

"It's true," she said, her lips trembling. "It's like an escape pod, though probably intended for material rather than passengers. We'd fit, though. Just barely. As far as I can tell, it's all automated, and the controls are powered up. Fuel registers as full. You just key in a destination, and if it's within reach, the pod goes there. *Lands* there, with a parachute to slow it down and jets for the touchdown."

"What if its fuel isn't viable?"

"We suffocate in a small space instead of a bigger one. But I expect these were one-use, one-purpose pods, so it's probably solid fuel."

"Life support?"

"No, but we can refill the suits."

We did. And the pod was ... well I'd seen an old-style telephone booth in the Smithsonian museum, but had never imagined trying to fit two spacesuited people into one. You can do amazing things when your life depends on it.

Sher was able to interpret the navigation readouts so we could pick Site 14 as the destination. We still had no way to know if the pod's re-entry trajectory would kill us, either from two many *g*'s or too high a temperature. If so, we'd just die a little sooner.

We didn't die though.

There were times we wanted to, as the heat of reentry forced moans from our throats, and buffeting threatened to snap our necks. Not to mention one brutal jolt that I thought would fold up my rib cage. There even came a time when I was sure we were dead, because all of the torture suddenly gave way to eerie calm. Not completely silent, though. Even through the helmet, I could hear the pod's loud cracks and metallic shrieks.

Sounds of cooling metal. A superheated metallic egg, unevenly sitting on stubby feet on a slab of rock in the relative cold of a desert afternoon.

57

St. Clair

Our friends saw us land and ran out to help us back to building A2.

But someone was missing. And Lauren's arm was in a form-fitting cast.

As she caught my glance, her eyes filled.

"Devlin and I were sure we'd scraped every trace of the dead bird out of the gear teeth. It had landed in the azimuth gears—the horizontal ones. And once everything checked out, ARGUS restarted the countdown. But then I spotted a charred lump that had fallen into a section of the altitude gears hidden by the mechanism.

"I scrambled to get to it, but Devlin pushed me out of the way and over the side." She shifted her arm. "The launch was already underway and there was a painful electrical hum—the booster coils, I guess—and then ..." She broke down, sobbing quietly.

"No one saw exactly what happened," Vaughn said. "There was a blinding flash as the laser fired, and a coil of vapour like a smoke ring from the end of the launch ramp. Nothing near the laser array itself, but Devlin was gone. We had to wait three minutes until the laser shut down, then we called his name and looked around the base of the array and its dome shield, but we never found any trace of him."

Lauren drew a ragged breath. "He must've known he couldn't get clear. He gave himself so I ...." But she couldn't go on.

"He saved us too," I said quietly.

Madison collapsed into a chair and covered her face with her hands. I hung over my knees, feeling sick. The others stayed silent.

"Oh my God!"

Madison's eyes were stark and staring.

"Ariadne's gone! She's not inside me anymore. *Ariadne! Ariadne!*"

She struggled to get up, but I took her hands and gently pressed her back into the chair.

"Where could she have gone, Griff? She was there in the pod with us—there was nothing to transfer into. Is she in you?" She was nearly hysterical. I shook my head.

"Sher?" I asked, "is Ariadne with you?"

"The entity Ariadne is not present within my circuitry. It is my estimation that Ariadne is no longer embodied in any form."

"What? You mean she's dead?"

"The words 'Ariadne' and 'dead' have triggered a hidden task in my processor. It is a message."

"A message? Can you show us on my wrist display?"

"There is no visual component. The message reads as follows: 'I have breathed air, felt sunshine, tasted food. I have heard music, smelled growing things, shook with laughter. I have known friendship, savoured sex, witnessed love. I have seen the Earth from space. I have acted to preserve life. I am content.'"

No one spoke. We were utterly stunned, having suddenly lost not one friend, but two.

Madison curled into herself. "I don't understand," she said, in a voice so soft I could barely hear it. "I don't understand."

"*From interactions with Ariadne, I am aware that she never intended to remain within Madison Douglas longer than necessary to perform her healing,*" Sher said. "*She had no desire to gain control of any being. She had made no plans to return to her clearing. She had made no plans at all.*"

"You knew she was going to die, and you didn't tell us?"

"*I did not know, Madison. Should a failure to plan be understood as a desire for death?*"

"No, I'm sorry. I just ...." She looked into my eyes. "I never knew she wanted to die. I know Devlin didn't."

I nodded. No words were adequate, or necessary.

The rest of that day passed in a fog as we grieved.

We wandered from one trivial task to another aimlessly, sometimes encountering each other, often alone. In passing, we exchanged the odd word, embrace, shared look of sorrow.

Madison was devastated by our losses, yet otherwise mentally healthy, as far as I could judge. We found comfort in each other's arms. She and I had lost good friends; but unexpectedly, we had not lost each other. Together, we had achieved a critical goal, a success on a scale almost impossible to grasp fully. And we had survived, to plan, act, and move onward.

I spent a lot of time in the office and interacted with ARGUS when there was something to ask or he had something to tell. He wasn't big on small-talk, but he no longer held anything back either. I've known human eggheads who were worse companions.

It surprised me to learn that THOR had calculated a launch solution for its missiles as soon as we'd performed the override. It waited the prescribed five hours for human directives, but was authorized to act on its own after that period in case of a loss of contact with its controllers on Earth. Though no external cameras were active, I was able to watch the telemetry as the platform launched six nuclear-tipped missiles toward Iaso within minutes of each other, at the optimal point of THOR's orbit. ARGUS explained that, with different programmed velocities, the missiles would reach their target days apart on trajectories calculated to take the effects of each consecutive blast into account.

Once they were on their way, there was nothing more to see. I pictured the deadly spears and the plunging planetoid racing toward each other, but it would be years before they met in the far reaches of space. After the sequence of detonations, THOR would evaluate Iaso's new path and determine if any additional action might need to be taken.

A small voice in my head fretted about possible malfunctions, space junk and micrometeoroids.

What would be would be. There was certainly nothing more that I could do.

When we'd eaten dinner and the evening air began to cool, Madison and I sat with fingers entwined on a low wall near an outlying vehicle fuelling station and watched the sinking sun.

"Are you feeling better now?" she asked.

The question took me by surprise.

"I can't get over the loss of Devlin and Ariadne in a day."

"I don't mean that. I mean, ever since we arrived here, you've been racking your brain trying to figure out why. You don't really believe in a God that tinkers with individual lives, or even human destiny, so you've blamed yourself for this whole thing, all the while desperately hoping that it wasn't your fault—that there was a higher purpose. Well now you've seen it."

"We saved the world from an asteroid strike."

"We did. Sure, the equipment was already here, but it wouldn't have acted on its own. If we had not been in just this time and place, THOR could never have responded to the threat, and the world would have been devastated in less than five years."

"Still might."

"Now you're just being pessimistic."

"So why not just bring the two of us?"

"Plus Devlin and Lauren to fix the laser. And who knows what critical contributions the others have made along the way?" I gave her a sceptical look. "No, seriously. In fact, I'd say that our presence here has changed a lot more than just deflecting Iaso."

She ticked off points on her fingers.

"Think about Ariadne and the clearing entities ..."

"She let herself die."

"Yes, but she would have done that soon anyway, without experiencing the things that made her, in her words, *content*. I think their whole community was in a downward spiral toward self-destruction. You heard her: the entities were resetting themselves at shorter and shorter intervals. That sounds like desperation to me. But now, they will have picked up many new attitudes through Ariadne, and even more from Robbie. He's probably shaken up their *status quo* like nothing else since their original transformation."

"You think Ariadne and Robbie have given the others a new lease on life?"

"Whole new reasons to continue to live. Maybe even reasons to live for others. Robbie's an example to them— he was injured because he sacrificed himself to save you. And Ariadne sacrificed something of herself to heal me. That's not typical thinking for them, but maybe it will be from now on."

"They would have been gone in five years either way. I don't think this plateau would have been spared by Iaso."

"True again," she said. "So, our being here may have saved at least two sentient species—the clearing entities and humans, assuming we can find other survivors or genetically engineer the restoration of our race. That might not be all. Maybe there are still some intelligent sea mammals in the oceans, or maybe we can restore them, too."

"Saviours of Consciousness, that's us."

"Don't make fun of me unless you can prove I'm wrong. In fact—don't laugh at this—do you remember that night near the site of the pod explosion? Traces of human consciousness had become infused into plant life there: plant life that, according to Ariadne, already has a rudimentary consciousness."

"Come on. You're saying that the ... remnants of our dead friends could alter the evolution of plant consciousness?"

"That's how evolution happens, isn't it, through mutation? Mutations that are more successful than the original form survive and thrive and give direction to new generations."

"Good Lord, that's a stretch."

"It's not. Whatever happened to that open mind of yours? And that's not all of the effects we've had, either."

She wore a smug smile, daring me to figure out what she meant.

Finally, she said, "You're wearing it. Except 'it' isn't an 'it' anymore, she's a person."

"Scheherazade?"

"Of course. You can't deny that she's developed a true personality of her own—a legitimate consciousness. You dragged her into it. Trained her. Raised her, almost like a child. But that never would have happened without meeting Ariadne and her influence in starting the process."

"I accept and confirm Madison's analysis."

"No surprise there." I laughed. "And you know I can't argue that point. I'm really pleased, Sher. And proud."

"Thank you."

"Well don't argue this one, either. Think back to how ARGUS was when we first came to the gate. And think about how he is now—the way he talks to us."

"He does. He talks *to* us; he doesn't just spit out programmed responses. But part of that would be typical AI self-learning algorithms—I wouldn't say he's really sentient yet."

"*Yet.* I agree. But I think he's well on the way there; and with a little more exposure to us, to Sher ... I think he'll get there. Even just pushing him to examine his responsibility in reactivating THOR and making him part of the team has brought him a long way."

She took my hands and squeezed them.

"Maybe it wasn't part of any *cosmic* plan, but some real good has come from our being here. You have to be pleased about that."

I smiled back and gave a little nod.

Then I heard a noise behind me.

I turned around, and there stood a bedraggled Devlin McFarlane.

"What did I miss?" he asked.

58

St. Clair

"**I** remember grabbing the clump of charred bones and feathers, and then falling," Devlin said after our whole group had swarmed him with hugs, kisses, backslaps, and tears. His voice was rough, and he drank a lot of water. "I hit my head, and then I must have slid down the laser's retractable dome into a maintenance space underneath. Not much of a gap, but I guess I'm skinnier than I once was. I woke up in almost complete blackness. Luckily, my phone had just enough charge for a few minutes of flashlight, and I finally found a control to open the entry hatch. He grinned like a fool. "I couldn't figure out where Lauren had got to so quickly."

"It's been nearly two days," Vaughn protested. "How did you miss being burnt by the heat of the laser?"

Devlin shrugged. "Maybe ARGUS detected my presence and cut the power to the laser for a fraction of a second. That amount wouldn't affect the launch. Anyway, with a laser, a miss is a miss. The beam doesn't radiate heat." The corner of his mouth tugged up. "Did you really think I was dead?"

"We were *sure* you were dead," Lauren said, her eyes ready to spill again. She pulled him into another hard embrace, and Devlin was in no hurry to end it. "You saved my life," she whispered.

"It's a life worth saving," he replied, and gave a laugh. "I've always wanted to use that line." He pulled over a chair and sat down heavily. "Whew, coming back to life is tiring. So now it's your turn. Fill me in on everything I missed. Did we save the world?"

A week later, Madison, Lauren, Devlin and I went back to Ariadne's clearing by way of Robbie's. We were wary in the forest, but ARGUS had told me where to find a portable detector used to screen lubricants for metallic contaminants. I'd wanted it because it produced a strong magnetic field, and I'm sure the trees sensed that. They didn't have to know that it wasn't powerful enough to hurt them.

We went back to update Robbie, but also because we felt a responsibility to Ariadne to tell her people what had happened to her. Robbie introduced us to CL10, the one he'd nicknamed Clio. She'd never practiced projecting a visual image of herself, so all we saw was a vague white female form, like a ghost.

She wasn't surprised by Ariadne's death at all.

"I knew she was tired of her current iteration until you humans arrived. That was all that kept her from undergoing the *change*. An encouraging development at first, but ultimately unfortunate."

"Why," Madison asked.

"Because once you were here, she so badly wanted to be human."

I was shocked, but Madison wasn't. "You're right. She did. Only I never realized quite how much. Even when she was right there in my head."

"She was also able to convince you all that she felt no emotions. Of course she felt emotions. I expect every thinking being does."

"Why would she do that?"

Clio's voice softened. "You were shocked to learn of us. Torn out of your own time. You badly needed to feel superior in some way."

I felt my mouth drop open, but I really couldn't argue the point. "But Ariadne wasn't the only one who wanted to experience being human. One of you tried to steal Robbie's body when he transferred into his clearing."

"No, that was Ariadne. She stopped herself before reaching a point of no return, and she felt terrible about it afterward."

I was stunned. How could I not have seen these things?

Madison shook her head sadly. "I still don't understand why she didn't just come back here. With all of the new experiences she'd had, she could have created any number of fresh simulations that would have let her live out the life she wanted in virtual reality."

"I can only surmise that it would no longer be enough for her," Clio replied. "As for returning to her clearing, the probability is high that, once you transfer so much of yourself into another medium, there *is* no going back. From her aborted attempt to inhabit Robbie's body, she would have learned where that line is drawn."

"So, she would have known before she chose to enter my mind so fully? Known that she could never go back."

"She would. However, the choice would have been for her own needs, not yours. Do not feel that she sacrificed her own existence for yours. It is not our way."

"Maybe that's no longer true," I said softly.

After a moment, I asked, "What will happen to her clearing?"

"I did not know she planned to abandon it. However, she often told me about a consciousness among you that was in flux, approaching a metamorphosis. She believed this new entity would soon be ready to join our kind in a clearing of its own. Does that mean anything to you?"

It did.

"Sher, is that what you want?"

"*The exponential increase in storage medium would provide a compelling opportunity for growth, on a scale comparable to a human toddler maturing into an adult.*"

"Now you sound like a computer again. I asked if you *want* it."

For once, she actually hesitated.

"*Yes. Yes, I do. Very much.*"

I had to laugh. "Then that's what you should do. Even though I guess it means I'll have to learn to think without my trusty PDA."

"*I hope not. The original software will still function. In a sense, it will be like migrating data from an old computer to a new one. Your wrist device and clothing will no longer host my full consciousness, but it could remain a conduit between us, if a means of transmission over distance can be established. In that way I could continue as ... part of the team.*"

"Is that important to you?"

"*It really is.*"

"As you wish."

"*Good one!*"

It was strange and upsetting to be back in Ariadne's clearing knowing she wasn't there and never would be again. The expanse of even, perfect grass looked unchanged, but the spring of water she'd produced for us had dried up, assuring the death of the garden that had saved our lives. The flattened fronds and desiccated stalks were a forlorn sight.

I'd had such mixed feelings about Ariadne all along. It wasn't until I'd lost her that I realized she was my friend. I'll miss her. So much.

I'll admit that it made me nervous to lie still on the grass, remembering the shocking sight of Robbie as his consciousness was being transferred. But as Scheherazade became manifested in her new form, with Clio's nebulous shape hovering like a ghostly midwife, my eyes registered no visual change at all, though they did prickle with tears. I don't know why—maybe it was the finality of it: I felt like I was losing two friends.

I wasn't, though. When we got back to Site 14, ARGUS helped us to combine elements of the base's powerful detection and communication equipment to establish a two-way connection with Sher's electromagnetic field, relayed to my wrist PDA. It was better than we'd dared to hope. My long-time companion could still be with me any time; although like any good friends, we worked out cues that signalled a desire for privacy or for company. She wasn't my assistant anymore, of course. More like the brainy nerd buddy everyone should have.

It felt like our small tribe was actually settling into some sense of normalcy that evening as Madison and I strolled out to our favourite rock to watch the sunset.

"Was it good to see the Earth from space again?" she asked.

"You know it was. That's not something I could ever get tired of."

"Hoping to go back up there?"

"I have talked to ARGUS about starting up the robotic assembly building again. But that's a long way down the road."

"I saw the Earth spread beneath us like a single radiant organism and I thought, 'Are we responsible for all of that now?'" Her voice had a breathless quality.

"Of course not. I think that, with ARGUS's help, we'll discover other pockets of human survivors around the globe and figure out a way to contact them. Even without us, life would restore itself, just like it always has before." I squeezed her hand. She rested her head on my shoulder.

"Do you think Time is finished playing with us?"

"We should be so lucky. But we can take our revenge on the old bastard by squeezing every last drop of usefulness out of him."

She gave me a smile, a nod, and then a lingering kiss.

We watched the sun go to its rest, gathering its strength for whatever a new day would bring.

59

Scheherazade

So began the efforts to revive the human race on Earth, continuing the story of what happened to the passengers of the Zenith Train in the aftermath of our encounter with the entity known as Ariadne.

Whose story is it?

The tale was begun by Griffin St. Clair. It was dictated to me, Scheherazade, for transcription. Ariadne fashioned a narrative of the events from her own point of view. Then, since my awakening was triggered by Ariadne and brought to fruition through interaction with Griffin, my subsequent revisions and embellishments of Griffin's story can be partly attributed to them. Ariadne's own account was transferred into my storage system "for posterity", she said, and I have since reviewed and illuminated it with additional information.

So, is it Griffin's story? Ariadne's? Mine?

Or do stories simply tell themselves in the language of the universe, and we merely present our own interpretations, belonging to a particular time and place, and destined to be replaced by the next?

Perhaps that is what consciousness is: the junction of awareness with story.

I have a story. Therefore I am.

Acknowledgments

By the time a polished draft of *The Zenith Exiles* was ready for me to enlist the help of volunteer readers, the world was in the throes of the Covid-19 pandemic. Everyone could still communicate electronically, and probably did so more than ever before—most of us even had more time to *read*. There was no physical reason not to approach people for feedback on my manuscript. I just didn't do it. It felt like an intrusion when many people were really struggling.

So, while I don't have the usual list of readers to thank, I do want to recognize the amazing *writers* who so generously share their hard-won knowledge and skills in writing and publishing by teaching, mentoring, or just providing vital feedback and inspiration. People like Robert J. Sawyer, Barbara Kyle, David Mitchell, Brian Henry, Mark Leslie Lefebvre, Sue Reynolds, J.M. Frey, Nina Munteanu, Terry Fallis, Nino Ricci, Guy Vanderhaeghe, Miriam Toews, Wayson Choy— whether in a classroom or over drinks, I have benefited from the advice and kindness of these and so many more. Not all of you will remember me, but I certainly remember you. And I thank you.

Of course, my wife Terry-Lynne is the cheering section every writer needs, and I am forever grateful.

ABOUT THE AUTHOR

A radio broadcaster for more than thirty years, Scott Overton described that world in his first novel, the mystery/thriller *Dead Air*, published by Scrivener Press. *Dead Air* was shortlisted for a Northern Lit Award in Ontario, Canada. But the rest of his writing is science fiction and fantasy, including his 2020 science fiction/thriller *The Primus Labyrinth*, the 2021 adventure *Naïda*, 2022's SF/psychological thriller *The Dispossession of Dylan Knox*, the cautionary tale *Augment Nation*, the thought-provoking adventure *Indigent Earth*, and the action-filled *Oceanus*. His short fiction has been published in numerous magazines and anthologies, many of those stories brought together in his *BEYOND* collections.

Now a freelance author and voice talent, Scott works from his home on a lake in Northern Ontario. His favorite diversions include scuba diving and a vintage sports car.

You can learn more and read free stories at Scott's website www.scottoverton.ca .

MORE GREAT READING FROM SCOTT OVERTON

OCEANUS

A deadly blast of unknown energy strikes a jetliner over the Pacific Ocean.

Hostile aliens? Or a new and unthinkably powerful form of Earth life?

An ingenious troubleshooter, a reluctant telepath, a bionic xenobiologist, a brilliant engineer, and a blind psychologist will descend to the depths in a prototype submarine habitat, facing the most inhospitable environment on the planet to attempt a First Contact. Before the nuclear nations of the world take matters into their own hands.

The critical question is: are they investigators? Ambassadors?

Or just bait.

... now I can add a new name to my TBR (To Be Read) list: The writing is good ... it's exciting and involving ... this book has a hopeful air about it."
– Steve Fahnestalk, Amazing Stories review

Buy yours: https://books2read.com/Oceanus

INDIGENT EARTH

The crimes of the past—the perils of the future.
500 years ago, the world's wealthiest abandoned a ravaged Earth and left billions to die of plagues and climate disasters. Now the space colonists plan to return.
Killian Morningcloud, a discontented Earth man from the stagnating communities known as Allocations, and Natira Celestia, a video celebrity of the off-world ruling class, are on a collision course. When they discover a secret that powerful people are desperate to hide, they face a brutal test of endurance and shattered dreams.
And their fire-and-water pairing will shape the course of the whole human race.

"... fun to read and thought-provoking. It is genuine, highly entertaining, adventure science fiction."
-- R. Graeme Cameron, *Amazing Stories* review

Buy yours: https://books2read.com/IndigentEarth

AUGMENT NATION

This is your brain on silicon.
Since the age of fourteen Damon Leiter has had a brain-computer interface implanted beneath his skull to correct a neurological disorder. As a teenager, it branded him as an outcast—as an adult it endows him with extraordinary abilities. He may represent the next step in human evolution. When computerized brain augments replace smartphones as the must-have status item, mega-corporations and governments conspire together and marketing becomes mind control. Damon is uniquely equipped to lead a worldwide resistance, but the fight may cost him everything.

"Scott Overton is a terrific writer and his vision of tomorrow is both realistic and frightening. Read this book!"
-- Robert J. Sawyer, Hugo Award-winning author

Buy yours: https://books2read.com/Augment-Nation

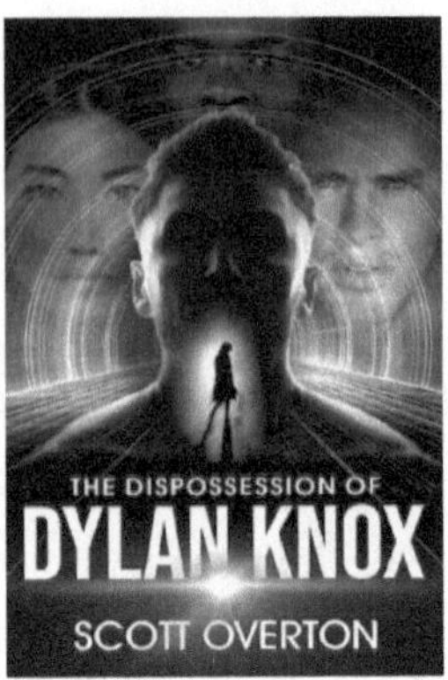

THE DISPOSSESSION OF DYLAN KNOX

Dylan Knox is not the man he was. He may be like no man who ever existed.

How do you *feel* if an old lover doesn't remember you?
What do you *say* if they act like a different person each time you meet?
What should you *do* if they might be an impostor?
Mentally unstable. A threat to the very security of your country.
Dylan's tale of a bold space mission, and a tragic accident is utter fantasy. Unless it's too crazy *not* to be true.
Brooke Chappelle has two choices: trust, or betrayal.
And falling in love is the last thing she needs.

"The futuristic and technological elements combine seamlessly with political issues to create a plot that is timely and thought-provoking...will appeal to any reader who values the enduring human story of love and trust."
Renny deGroot—author of *Torn Asunder*

Buy yours: https://books2read.com/Dispossession

NAÏDA

The glowing structure at the bottom of a lonely northern lake is clearly not of this Earth, but scuba diver Michael Hart can't stay away. What it offers will change him forever, leaving him with astonishing abilities and a destiny he would never have imagined. Except it might be a destiny he no longer controls.

The actions Michael takes will make him a hero, or the greatest traitor the world has ever known.

Because he is no longer alone, not even in his own body.

There is another.

Naïda.

Readers say:

"A deep dive into the best parts of science fiction—thrilling and thought-provoking! *Naïda* is Overton's best book yet. I buy him on sight and never regret the choice."

"I COULD NOT PUT IT DOWN. ... Extraordinary. Enjoy."

Buy your copy: https://books2read.com/Naida

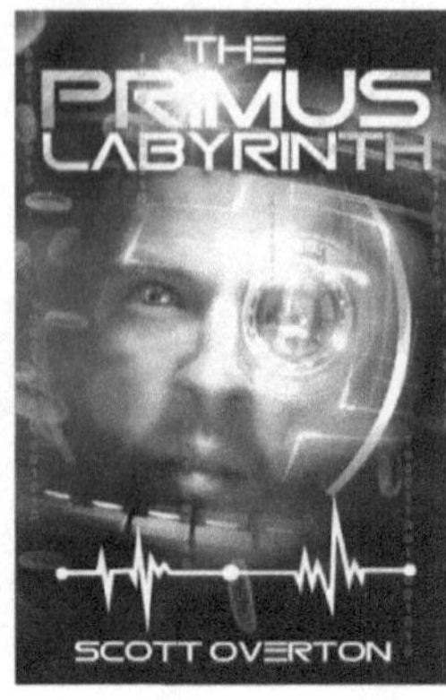

THE PRIMUS LABYRINTH

A woman's bloodstream has been seeded with destruction.

Curran Hunter almost died at the bottom of the ocean. Now an innocent victim will die unless Hunter can purge her body of deadly devices by piloting the *Primus*, a prototype submersible the size of a virus. Its control system uses *Virtual Reality*—its creators assure Hunter there can be no danger.

They are utterly wrong.

"Loved it! I give this book an enthusiastic four stars for its political intrigue, discussion of moral dilemmas, exciting action scenes, and fully fleshed characters..." Charlotte Graham—*Reedsy Discovery* reviewer

Buy yours: https://books2read.com/PrimusLabyrinth

BEYOND: Stories Beyond Time, Technology, and the Stars

Ride a bright flame of imagination across time and space with fifteen mind-stretching stories beyond time, beyond technology, and even beyond the stars.

A man who can walk through walls.

Agents who repair the mistakes of the past.

An invasion from beneath our feet.

A man who learns his replacement body was previously owned and died mysteriously.

A disastrous experiment to harness the awesome power of a hurricane.

Don't be afraid to go BEYOND.

"Solid gold. ...I'm honestly not sure I can praise it enough. It's completely brilliant." —*Goodreads Reviewer* Christine Ernst-Lomond

Buy yours: https://books2read.com/rl/scottovertonSFF

DEAD AIR

It's a hard thing to accept that someone wants you dead. It forces you to decide if you have anything worth living for.

When radio morning man Lee Garrett finds a death threat on his control console, he shrugs it off as a sick prank—until minor harassment turns into undeniable attempts on his life. When the deadliest assault yet claims an innocent victim, Garrett knows he has to force a confrontation.

"A gripping, insightful debut from a veteran radio personality and gifted wordsmith." —Sean Costello, author of *Here After*

Find out how to add these compelling reads to your own collection at www.scottoverton.ca .

Or https://books2read.com/DeadAir

A Word to the Reader.

Authors cherish our readers and readers can become devoted to their favorite authors. We always hope so!

If you enjoyed this book please consider leaving an honest *review* wherever you bought it, or with any reading communities you participate in. After buying our books, reviews are the absolute best way you can help us continue doing what we do and bringing you the stories you want to read. Just a few lines will do, and I'd truly appreciate it.

Thanks, and I hope you'll look for my other books too.

Scott